THE
HIDDEN
GIRL

BOOKS BY ROGER STELLJES

ROGER STELLJES

THE HIDDEN GIRL

bookouture

Published by Bookouture in 2021

An imprint of Storyfire Ltd.
Carmelite House
50 Victoria Embankment
London EC4Y 0DZ

www.bookouture.com

ISBN: 978-1-80019-956-9
eBook ISBN: 978-1-80019-955-2

The Hidden Girl is dedicated to my family: my wife, my son and daughter, my mom and dad, my mother-in-law, my brothers and sisters-in-law and nieces and nephews. They always provide the encouragement, excitement and interest that keeps me going. I thank you all.

CHAPTER ONE

"Out here, nobody can hear you"

"That was a fun game to watch," Heidi said to her husband as they drove along Highway 6. "I haven't seen you guys get into the game that much in a long, long time."

Dan Newman laughed. "Well, those young flat-belly boys thought they were all that and then some." He was referring to their softball opponents for the night, a collection of twenty-year-old students from Central Minnesota State University in Manchester Bay. "They thought coming over here was like playing intramurals. Us middle-aged guys have a trick or two left up our sleeves on a Friday night."

"What was funny was watching them get frustrated as you guys hit single after single while all they did was try to hit it over the fence."

"They succeeded a few times."

"Sure, that one guy hit two of them into the pine trees in left field, but there was nobody on base. Then you guys would get those little soft hits, the rollers between their players, and the little fly balls that dropped in—"

"They call those bloops, dear."

"Oh, right, bloops, those little bloop hits over their infielders' heads. They died the death of a thousand cuts, and they got so… pissed. Ha!"

"Yeah, they figured they'd handle us old guys. What they didn't realize is we've played thousands of games. We know a few things," Dan replied, stifling a burp. "Oof, that sausage and pepperoni pizza tonight." He patted his stomach. "I think I shook a hair too much cracked red pepper on it. It's kind of getting to me."

Heidi had already reached into her purse and handed over two antacid tablets.

"Thanks, honey."

He turned right onto the dirt road and headed into the woods. "It'll be a great night for sleeping. Nice and cool."

"What time is Cara coming home?"

"I told her one a.m."

"That's a late curfew."

"Her mom has been giving her that one, so I feel like I should too, so we're consistent."

The woods cleared on the right and the bright white rail fence that defined the front of their property appeared. Dan slowed, turned right and pulled up the driveway into the garage.

"Tomorrow we need to weed the flower beds in the front yard before you go off and play golf," Heidi said as they reached the back door.

"Again?"

"Yes. It shouldn't take long."

"I should hope not," he replied as he unlocked the door and pushed it open. "We did it just a few weeks ago."

"Hey, we have to keep up to keep it all looking sharp," she replied as she stepped into the kitchen. Dan quickly locked the door and followed.

He sensed sudden movement from his left.

Thump!

The blow hit him high in his back and sent him crashing face first into a kitchen cabinet, then down to the floor.

Heidi spun around to see a huge man swinging a crowbar. "Dan! Dan!"

Thump! Thump! Thump!

"Da—" She was slammed to the floor from behind. "No! No! Get off me!"

Someone pulled her arms behind her back. The large man dropped the crowbar and approached. He wore a ski mask and took something black out of a pocket.

"You got her?" he asked.

"Give me a hand."

"Stop! Stop!" she pleaded as the two men put something around her wrists and pulled it tight. She heard a ripping sound. "Stop! St—" The man on top of her stuck a piece of duct tape over her mouth.

Heidi kicked with her legs and tried to wriggle free as the man on top of her eased up, but it was only so he could turn around and hold her legs together. She felt the same type of restraint dig into the skin around her ankles.

She looked at her husband sprawled out on the floor, unconscious. Blood dripped from his mouth and forehead. She tried to scream his name, but her voice was muffled behind the tape.

The patting on his cheek was rhythmic at first, then harder, and then... *Slap!*

"Wake up, Dan! Dan, wake up sleepyhead..."

His eyes bolted open. In front of him was a behemoth of a man dressed in all black, wearing black leather gloves.

He tried to speak, but there was tape on his mouth.

The large man crouched to him. He didn't say anything, just turned his head to the left. Dan's eyes followed.

"Heidi! Heidi!" he tried to scream against the tape.

Heidi was face down on the couch, squirming, thrashing, fighting. A skinny man was on top of her, dressed in all black, including a ski mask. He too wore gloves. In his right hand was a long hunting knife, and he was slicing through the back of Heidi's tank top. Her panicked eyes locked on her husband's.

Dan thrashed, trying to break free. His arms were secured behind him and around the fireplace post. He tried kicking with his legs, but he saw that his ankles were bound with what looked to be nylon zip ties. A tall, athletic man, he nevertheless had no leverage, no ability to mass his strength.

"You can fight the restraints all you want, but you're never getting free. Your pretty little wife can scream and squirm and flail all she wants, but she isn't getting free."

Dan looked over to his wife as the other man started pulling down her pants.

No! No! No!

He closed his eyes, banging his head back against the pillar, again yanking at his restraints. He had to try. He had to try, even knowing it was futile.

"I bet you have no idea why we're out here, do you? Why we came after you? You're totally clueless, aren't you? You're thinking, what did I do to these guys?"

Dan shook his head feverishly.

"The question will be whether those responsible for putting you in this position do."

This time Dan looked back at him quizzically.

"You know what your truly fatal mistake was, Dan?" The hulk of a man in front of him pulled out a long bowie hunting knife. "It was living out here in the middle of nowhere." He took off his mask. "Out here, nobody can hear you. Nobody can save you. And tonight, we can do whatever we want. And we will."

Dan renewed his struggle against the restraints on his wrists and ankles.

"Fight all you want," the man said, knowing that eventually Dan would exhaust himself. Then resignation would set in, and finally the knowledge of how it all would have to end. "You ain't getting free of this. But you do have a front-row seat for the show."

*

A half-hour later, Slim rolled away from the woman. "It's been a while since I felt all that," he said to D as he zipped up his pants. He had already put the used condom in a plastic bag and stuffed it into a backpack they'd brought along.

D, who had been sitting in a chair watching Slim have his way with the woman, stood up and pulled out a black nylon rope from his back pocket, then went and stood in front of a sweaty, teary-eyed Dan Newman. He made a point of slowly wrapping the rope tightly around each hand and then pulling it taut.

Dan knew what was coming next. "No! No! Noooooo!" he screamed behind his gag as D turned around and approached Heidi. He quickly had the rope around her neck, dragging her up from the couch and turning her toward her husband.

"Heidi! Heidi!" Dan pleaded, pulling frantically against his restraints. His eyes never left those of his wife as D slowly and methodically tightened the rope around her throat, the black strands digging into her skin as she fought with what strength she had left. He held her off the floor, his forearms vibrating with the effort. He didn't kill her quickly, keeping his own eyes focused on those of her husband. Tears streaked down Dan's cheeks.

After a few minutes, Heidi's body fell limp, the fight gone. D undid the rope and let her drop to the floor. Then he nonchalantly walked over and stuffed the rope in the backpack.

"Let's get her to the bathroom."

Slim nodded and knelt. With one arm, D lifted Heidi's body over the other man's shoulder so he could carry her to the back of the house. He watched for a moment until Slim disappeared. Then he slowly turned around and looked a broken Dan Newman in the eye as he reached down into the backpack, pushed his pistol aside and made a show of pulling out a long, jagged knife from its sheath.

Slim was using the portable shower head to wash Heidi. He'd been standing barefoot, running the water over her for fifteen minutes now, wiping down her whole body.

D walked into the bathroom.

"What time is it?" Slim asked.

"One twenty. We need to get moving."

"Is he done?"

D nodded.

"You… went off out there. I mean… with the knife and all. Holy moly."

"You got what you needed, I got what I needed," D said. "You about ready to prop her up?"

Slim sat Heidi's body up against the tiled wall and adjusted the shower head so that the stream of water flowed down and between her legs. As they stepped out of the bathroom, they heard a thud and felt a vibration.

"What the…"

*

I'm so in trouble, Cara Newman thought as she tore down the long, narrow road that cut through the dense woods. She was late, extremely late, potentially getting-grounded late. Her curfew was generously 1:00 a.m., and it was now almost 1:30.

Why does Dad have to live out in the middle of nowhere like this?

It wasn't as if she'd lost track of time completely. She knew she was pushing it, but then Ashley had needed a ride home and, well, that threw everything off kilter. Of course, it didn't help that her dad and stepmom lived so far from Manchester Bay. She always underestimated how long it took to get over to Crosby.

She had no doubt they would be upset with her. She was surprised she hadn't heard from one of them, but she was certain there would be stern words. *Stay calm and just apologize.* There was an out-of-town soccer tournament next weekend, and she didn't want to miss that. Contrition was the strategy. Just say you're sorry, she told herself. Don't argue, don't fight, just admit you blew it, give them nowhere to go.

As she emerged from the tunnel-like road, the house was on the right, set back quite a way. The good news was it looked dark, with few lights on and no exterior lights.

Could it be she was catching a break? Maybe they weren't home yet. Maybe they'd stayed out late with friends. That was the hope, although just to be extra sure, once she turned onto the driveway up to the house, she turned off her headlights.

She pulled up in front of the garage and parked. As she got out of the car, she looked to the house. She'd figured there would be a light on in the back, but there wasn't. There was a light on somewhere deep inside the house, but certainly not in the kitchen. She'd expected that when she reached the back door, either her father or her stepmom would be pacing the room, ready to pounce when she entered.

If they were home, maybe they were already asleep. Maybe I can sneak in, she thought hopefully.

When she reached the back door, she found it locked.

They said they were going to leave the door open. Again, maybe a sign that they weren't home. She fumbled with her key ring and found the house key, then opened the door and stepped into the dark house. The only light was to the right. She flipped up the switch and set her purse, keys and phone on the center island. As she glanced around, she realized that the family room looked odd. Couch cushions were scattered on the floor. She took another step and to the left saw her father leaning oddly against the fireplace pillar, his head tilted to the side, and then the blood.

"Dad!"

She heard a noise to her right. A man, stepping out of her parents' bedroom. He was dressed all in black, wearing a ski mask.

"Oh my God! Oh my God! Who—"

He took a step toward her.

Cara turned and bolted out the back door, turning left and making for the driveway. As she came around the corner, a second man in a ski mask appeared from the front of the house. His angle cut off her path down the driveway to the road.

"No! No! No!" she screamed, frantically looking around for an escape. "You stay away from me!" she yelled, searching for anything to defend herself with. Turning, she saw the other man, who was much bigger, coming out the back door, lumbering toward her.

The two men were slowly closing in on her.

You're dead if they get you, she thought. She looked to her right.

The woods. It was her only chance.

The smaller man charged at her.

She took off, sprinting, vaulting over a downed tree and into the woods. *Run and hide*, was all she could think. *Run and hide. Run and hide.*

She leaped over another tree trunk, but then caught her foot on a branch and tripped, falling face first. As she pushed herself up, she looked back to see the men closing on her.

Go, go, go, she told herself, heading to her right, what she knew was northeast. It was so dark, she couldn't really see the obstacles in her path, and she stumbled again, landing hard.

Dazed for just a moment, she glanced back once more. The men were still coming, the smaller one out in front, closing rapidly.

He had her trapped.

She felt a long branch under her right hand. She quickly stood up and swung it at him. The man raised his right arm to deflect the blow.

"Aargh," he groaned, falling back.

She swung and hit him again, this time knocking him to the ground, then looked up. The other man, the big one, was closing in.

She threw the branch at him, spun away and ran again, deeper into the woods, hurdling obstacles as she saw them, ducking under branches, feeling thorns and sharp twigs slice through the skin of her legs, hands and face.

She snuck a look back. The men were both still coming, but she had managed to create a sizable gap now. As she ran, it seemed like she'd stumbled onto a narrow path. Pumping her arms, she sprinted on.

*

"Do you see her? Do you see her?" D growled urgently, constantly tripping over the uneven ground and downed branches. "Dammit!"

"Where's your gun?" Slim asked.

"Back at the house in the backpack," D replied angrily. "Do you see her?"

"I had her just a second ago," Slim said, ten feet ahead. "I think… I see her! I see her!"

"Just go."

Slim ran on as D trailed behind, panting.

*

As Cara followed the little zigzagging path, she saw the glint of moonlight off water ahead. The small lake at the edge of her dad's property, thick with reeds and cattails.

What now? Swim for it? Dive in and hold her breath? Could she hide in the reeds and cattails?

Down to her right, she saw a grouping of big rocks.

She didn't like the lake. If they got her into the water, the men would drown her. She picked up a rock and heaved it out into the reeds.

Kerplunk!

*

Kerplunk!

"Did you hear that?" Slim whispered to his left. "That sounded like water."

Kerplunk!

Kerplunk!

"Is she going into the lake?" D exclaimed. They carried on running; another couple of hundred feet and they reached the shoreline.

*

On all fours, Cara crept back inland, slithering as best she could along the ground. As she peeked up over the brush, she could see the silhouettes of the two men, fanning out left and right. She lost sight of the smaller man, but the big one was shuffling along the shoreline, moving in her direction but looking into the reeds, hunting her.

Ten feet in front of her were what looked like three downed trees, lying askew. She crawled towards them, careful and slow with each movement. Of the three, one was extremely old, rotten and partially hollowed out. She slid inside; though she couldn't go far, it at least provided a few feet of cover. She made like a ball, her back against the left side, her knees pulled tight to her chest, her mouth closed, breathing through her nose.

She could hear voices whispering in the distance, and then heavy footsteps coming in her direction.

Slow. Deliberate. Getting closer.

She froze. Ten feet away, she could see two feet. Then she heard more footsteps. Another set of feet were now just outside the tree.

They were right there.

She closed her eyes. *Go away. Please go away.*

*

"I've been searching, but the reeds are so thick," Slim whispered. "I don't think she went in. There's nobody in the water. She's still in the woods here somewhere. Has to be."

D took a moment to scan with his eyes, but there was no movement. She was hiding, or… "She could be doubling back. She could have looped around on us."

"The house. If she gets back there…"

"Or she's playing us," D said. His eyes had adjusted to the dark, and he peered around, hunting for movement, listening for any sound.

"Can we risk that?" Slim said anxiously. "We're sitting ducks out here."

"Go."

Slim led the way back down the path. "Who is she?"

"I'm guessing their daughter."

"She wasn't supposed to be here. She was supposed to be at her mom's."

They exited the woods and made their way back to the house. The girl's car was still there. Her purse, phone and keys were still in the kitchen. D knew it was at least a mile in any direction to get to another house.

"What do we do! What do we do!" Slim yelped, panicked, hyperventilating.

"Stay calm," D replied. "Keep your head. That's what screwed our boy in the first place, not thinking things through. What we do is grab that backpack and leave, right now, just as we planned."

"But the girl…"

"Saw two men dressed all in black and in ski masks. That's all she saw."

CHAPTER TWO

"Wonder Woman isn't a sidekick"

Tori stirred awake as a cool breeze flapped the curtains at the bedroom window. She took in a comfortable breath, feeling the long, muscular arm wrapped tenderly around her waist, her naked body warmly enveloped by Braddock's angular six-foot-four body. She could feel the light heaves of his chest against the soft skin of her bare back as he slept. It had been a relaxing night. They'd taken a long boat cruise on the lake, then had grilled chicken on the deck before watching documentaries about the Fyre Festival and the college admissions scandal on Netflix with a bottle of wine, capping it all off with an energetic first hour in bed. All in all, a wonderful night in a summer full of them. She let her eyes once again drift closed, nuzzling her body further back into his.

Ring! Ring! Ring!

She waited for him to move.

Ring! Ring! Ring!

"Braddock?"

"Yeah, I hear it," he said with a sigh as he reluctantly pulled his arm away and rolled over to his nightstand.

Tori checked her own phone: 4:50 a.m. A call at this time of the morning was never good. She listened as Braddock said, "Yeah? Whoa, hold on. Where? Okay then. On the way."

"You're off?" Tori said sleepily when he hung up.

"I think I need you to come along on this one," he replied. "We have a double murder over east of Crosslake. Gory scene, yet somehow the couple's seventeen-year-old daughter survived it. She's a witness."

"Survived it? How?"

"That's what we need to go and find out."

Fifteen minutes later, Braddock was driving rapidly northeast toward the small town of Crosby.

"Who is on scene right now?" Tori asked as they sped along Highway 210, east of Manchester Bay.

"Dewey with the Crosby PD, plus our guys."

"Dewey." Tori smiled. "That guy. I see that guy and just… laugh."

"He's humorous, that's for sure. As for our murder scene, it's a house out in the woods. Two bodies inside. Dan and Heidi Newman."

"Anything else?"

"I guess it's…"

"It's what?"

"Staged."

"Staged? How?"

"I don't know. We'll find out when we get there."

"Did you call Cal?"

"I wanted to see what we have before we got him out of bed."

"Why should Cal get special dispensation?"

"Because he's the boss and he employs me and now you on a more frequent basis."

"I'm going to need a raise."

"You FBI types, always making demands."

Twelve months ago, that was what she was: an FBI special agent, based in New York City. And not just your standard special agent. The elite of the elite, she was the bureau's go-to on missing children cases. At a moment's notice, she and her select team could be on a chopper or an airplane, a new disappearance to investigate. Tori thrived professionally, continually driven to find children and reunite them with their families.

Problem was, her motivation came from her own heartbreak. It had started with the disappearance of her identical twin sister, Jessie, twenty-one years ago, just before her senior year at Manchester Bay High School, and was followed a year and a half later by the death of her father, the legendary Shepard County sheriff Big Jim Hunter, while she was away at college in Boston. While the official cause of death was a heart attack, the real cause was the disappearance of his daughter on his watch and the broken heart it had left him with.

With no remaining family to bind her there, Tori had left Manchester Bay. Whether intentionally or otherwise, she'd cut off all contact with the place and after some years, never intended to return. But while the tragedy had been effective in motivating her professionally, the grief from it metastasized unchecked for nearly twenty years.

Then a year ago, she was lured back to Manchester Bay by the resurfacing of her sister's killer, who'd abducted another woman on the twentieth anniversary of Jessie's disappearance. Although coming close to death herself, Tori had finally solved her sister's murder, and the murders of many other women. While investigating the case, she'd met and fallen for Braddock. A New York transplant, and a man with his own history of loss, Braddock reached her, understood her, and started to care for her like no other before.

Solving her sister's case and her evolving feelings for Braddock had forced Tori to finally confront her past. She'd spent two months intensely working through it, and even now went for therapy sessions every so often to strengthen her gains.

These days, life was slower. While she consulted with the FBI on occasion from afar, the only airplane she had been on in the last year was for a week's vacation to Barbados in late March with Braddock, her most relaxing week in twenty years. She taught a couple of criminal justice classes at the university in town, and on a not infrequent basis helped Braddock and the Shepard County Sheriff's Department on cases of interest that ran the gamut from homicide and missing persons to robbery. In the last six months, she'd worked enough that Cal had accounted for her presence in his latest department budget. Given Tori's abilities, reputation and familial history in Manchester Bay, the budget item was lauded and swiftly approved by the county commissioners.

"We're coming up on Crosby," she noted now.

"And our turn."

Braddock turned left and motored north out of Crosby on Highway 6 until he veered right onto a gravel road that wound its way through dense woods until a small clearing emerged on the right. They could see the patrol unit parked near the house, and a department-issue Tahoe along the road. Jake Williams, simply known as Steak—Tori's childhood friend and Braddock's top detective—was awaiting their arrival, while his partner, Sheryl Eggleston, was stringing out yellow crime-scene tape.

"This is obviously the place," Tori said. "Hey, see the sign." The wooden sign, perhaps a foot tall and three feet wide, was mounted on the large white elm just to the left of the driveway. It was dark brown, with *The Newmans* carved into it. Two green pine trees were painted on the left and a grouping of flowers on the right. It was the kind of sign that many Minnesotans with cabins and lake houses displayed to mark their homes. "It looks like the one you have."

"It kind of does."

Braddock's personalized sign featured carved shamrocks on each side. He'd had it specially made a few years ago to fit in with the rest of his neighbors. These days he didn't tend to notice the kitschy signs as he drove by the local lake homes, but seeing this one struck him for some reason.

"Have you been inside?" he asked Steak once disembarking from the Tahoe.

"Not yet. We've been here like a minute."

As a group, they walked up the driveway. The house was a one-story ranch-style building set in the middle of a wide clearing surrounded by thick forest. To the left was a three-car garage. On the far side of the garage, parked on a cement slab, was a trailered and covered pontoon boat, and in front, a white VW Jetta and an ambulance. Inside the ambulance, two paramedics were treating a teenage girl sitting on a gurney.

"That must be the daughter," Braddock murmured.

Tori observed the blank, almost catatonic stare on the girl's face. She was paying no attention to the paramedics as they patched her scrapes and wounds.

At the house, Crosby patrol officer Dwayne Jones awaited their arrival.

"If it isn't the immortal Will Braddock, and his sidekicks Tori and Steak," he said in a low voice as she shook Braddock's hand.

"Sidekicks?" Tori asked with raised eyebrows and a sly smile. "I am not a sidekick, Dewey."

"You could definitely pass as Wonder Woman," Steak quipped.

"Wonder Woman isn't a sidekick. She has her own movie. Besides, I like the Avengers."

"Wicked Witch, then."

"Tori is Black Widow, if anything," Braddock said, earning himself an approving smile from his girlfriend.

"Figures you'd like all the leather—"

"Okay, enough," Braddock said, stopping Steak. To Jones he said, "What do we have?"

"The victims are Dan and Heidi Newman," Jones explained, gesturing with his thumb to the house.

"And the girl in the ambulance is their daughter?" Tori asked.

"Yes. Cara Newman."

"Has she said anything?"

"She was obviously traumatized when I got here. From what I could make out, she got home and went into the house, saw her father's… body in the living room, spotted a man inside the house, another when she ran outside, and managed to get away by running into the woods. She hid out there for at least two hours, she thought, so by the time she called us, the killers were long gone. She was all cut up, scratched, bitten and bleeding, so I called for the ambo."

Braddock looked to Tori. "Why don't you talk to her?"

"In a minute," Tori said. "Let's have a quick look inside first. See what she saw."

Jones led Braddock and Tori around to the back door of the house. Tori took a long look around. "It's really isolated out here," she remarked. "And quiet."

"Too quiet," Braddock murmured. "I like having neighbors."

"What did you see inside?" she asked Dewey.

He grimaced. "I think ya'll just better just go in and see for yourselves."

"That bad, huh?"

"Oh yeah."

"Is a BCA crime scene unit on the way?" Braddock asked.

"They've been called," Steak replied.

The three of them pulled on white rubber gloves. Steak handed Tori and Braddock slip covers for their shoes, then they stepped inside the house.

The kitchen had been recently remodeled given the stainless-steel appliances, white marble counter tops, light gray painted cabinets and dark wooden floor. The wooden floor extended into the wide hall and entryway that divided the house in half front to back. Ahead they could see a living room. To the right was a hallway leading to the bedrooms and bathrooms.

"I'll take the right," Steak said, turning on his flashlight.

Tori led Braddock into the living room.

"Oh my," Tori murmured. Dewey hadn't been exaggerating.

Dan Newman was lying against a white pillar supporting the mantelpiece, his throat gruesomely cut from ear to ear, his head drooping and tilted to the left. Blood had streamed down the front of his chest and gray softball jersey and there was a pool of it dried around him on the tiled fireplace threshold.

Deliberate in her approach, Tori crouched to the right side of him. Newman was tall, with long legs, and had short dark brown hair with isolated grayish strands at the temples. His arms were wrapped around the back of the pillar and his wrists were secured with zip tie handcuffs. His ankles were secured the same way, and a single strip of wide gray duct tape had been placed over his mouth. From her angle she could also see the deep slice across the throat.

"Jeez, his head has been damn near sliced off his body," Braddock noted, bent over observing from the other side. "That slice with the knife is… deep. And it's not smooth either. It's like the killer had to work the blade in deep. This man was butchered."

"The blood. The sheer volume of it is… staggering." Tori took out her own flashlight and directed the beam. "I can see extensive bruising on the back of his neck that goes down below his collar line."

"He's got a good bruise on his forehead too," Braddock said as he moved to the man's front. "I'd say our killer used his left hand to steady the head against the pillar and with his right hand sliced across the throat left to right from a standing position. Thus the head drops to the left."

"Why tie him up here, though?" Tori said. She stood up and turned to look at the long white living room sofa centered with the front picture window. The cushions were all askew. Throw pillows were scattered on the floor. The coffee table looked to have been kicked to a crooked angle. She stepped closer to the couch and saw what looked to be a pair of ripped woman's underwear jammed down between two cushions.

Braddock stepped to the right side of the couch. "Here's a pair of pants and… Aw, man." He was pointing down to a woman's black tank top and a black bra that were lying between the couch and the wall. They could both see the fraying at the middle of the bra as well as the jagged cutting of the tank top. "It's like they sliced them off her," he said in almost a whisper.

"The crime scene people better process this couch very carefully," Tori said. "I think before he was murdered, Mr. Newman was made to watch something truly awful being done to his wife."

"Speaking of his wife, come back and take a look," Steak called from the hallway.

He led them into the master bedroom and gestured to the bathroom. "In there."

Tori and Braddock stepped carefully inside. In the shower, propped up against the wall, was a fully naked, wet and dead Heidi Newman. She was a small woman with short dark hair. It appeared that the stream of water from the shower head had been directed between her legs, which were spread.

"They put her in here and the shower washes away any evidence," Braddock said.

The sliding door to the shower was partially open. He took a careful step closer and peered inside. There was noticeable bruising and ligature marks around Heidi's neck.

Tori leaned in behind him. "She was strangled."

"Ligature marks around her wrists and ankles too," Braddock said.

The three of them backed out of the bathroom and, careful to watch their steps, made their way to the back door and out onto the patio.

As they stepped outside, a forensic team came around the corner. Braddock looked to Steak, who walked over to the crew to bring them up to speed. To Tori, he said, "Quick thoughts?"

"We'll see what the medical examiner finds, but from what I saw, the husband was tied to the fireplace post and forced to watch his wife being raped on that couch then strangled to death. She was dragged back to the shower to wash away any evidence our killer might have left behind. Then to finish it all off, the killer sliced Mr. Newman's throat and let him bleed out."

"Sounds about right," Braddock said as he started walking around the house. "Let's go talk to the daughter."

Dewey was standing just short of the ambulance.

"So that's her mom and dad inside?" Tori asked.

"Dad and stepmom."

"Has someone called her mom?"

"Not yet," Dewey said. "I figured we better get a handle on things here first."

Braddock knew the paramedic who stepped out of the ambulance, and called him over. "How is she?"

"Bruised, battered, scraped to hell. The gash on her left hand requires stitches. Another cut on her head might. There are insect bite marks on her arms and legs. I checked for ticks, but someone at the hospital should do it too."

"Is she responsive?"

"Shocked, although she is talking a little. We should get her to the hospital in Manchester Bay, so don't take long."

"You take the lead with her," Braddock suggested to Tori.

Tori climbed up into the back of the ambulance and sat down next to the girl on the stretcher.

Cara Newman was thin, but one look at her muscular legs told Tori she was athletic. Her brown hair, just past shoulder length, fell around her soft face. A small piercing decorated the left side of her nose. She was wearing black shorts, a dark blue sweatshirt and soiled gray athletic shoes.

"Cara," Tori said softly, "I'm Tori Hunter. I'm an investigator with the sheriff's office. And that tall guy, he's Chief Detective Will Braddock."

Cara nodded.

"I'm so sorry about your dad and stepmom. We both are. We're going to try and find out what happened to them."

Cara sniffled and wiped away a tear with a tissue.

"Can you tell me what happened to you?" Tori asked. "Just so we can start trying to figure all this out. Does that sound okay?"

Cara nodded again. "I came home. I was late, really, really late," she said.

"What time is really late?"

"One thirty. I was supposed to be home at one." She explained that she was trying to sneak into the house. She came in the back door, walked through the kitchen and looked into the family room. "Then I saw my... my dad," and the tears came.

"It's okay, it's okay," Tori said softly and slipped her arm around the girl's back. "Can you tell me what you remember next?" she asked after a minute.

"I saw this big man in a ski mask look out the door of my parents' bedroom. And I knew it was... bad. I... I just ran."

"Which was the absolute right thing to do," Tori said. It was what her dad had always told her and Jessie when they were little girls: run like hell and scream like hell. She noted the familiar logo on the sweatshirt Cara was wearing, torn and soiled as it was. "You know, I played Manchester Bay soccer," she said. "Way, *way* back in the day; my twin sister and I both did. Do you play for the high school team or the club?"

"Both," Cara replied.

"What position do you play?"

"Attacking mid."

"That requires you to cover a lot of the field," Tori said. "So you're speedy, quick, agile. You used that to your advantage. You ran."

"I got outside the house and then another man came from around the front."

"Two men, then," Tori confirmed, glancing to see Braddock jotting down notes.

Cara explained that she'd run into the woods. "I figured my only chance was to outrun them. I got all the way to the shoreline." She explained about throwing the rocks and hoping the sound of splashing water would throw the men off. "And then I hid in this hollowed-out tree."

"Smart," Tori said. "Really smart. What did the men chasing you do?"

"They tried to find me for a little bit. They were standing just by the tree I was hiding in. They were whispering, so I couldn't really tell what they were saying. After a few minutes, it seemed like they went back toward the house. It got really quiet. But I stayed out there in case they were…"

"Trying to trap you?" Braddock asked calmly.

Cara nodded. "I wanted them to think I'd jumped into the lake, run to some other house or something. Not that there are any others out here that are close."

She had reacted awfully well under pressure, Tori thought. She struck her as mature for her age. "What made you finally risk it and come back to the house?"

"I was getting eaten alive in that tree. Bugs were crawling on me. I got out and listened and looked around for a long time, and nothing moved. It was just… quiet. I walked super slow back to the house, found my phone and called 911."

"Can you tell me anything about the men?"

Cara shrugged her shoulders. "They were dressed all in black, or at least really dark. One seemed smaller, thin. The other one was big, but didn't move as fast."

"Anything else about them? Did you see their faces at all?"

She shook her head. "No. They wore ski masks."

"What about how they got here? Was there another vehicle here? Maybe in the woods or something?"

"I didn't notice one."

"And you said you were late? Why were you late?" Braddock asked.

"I was out with my friends from school. We were…"

"Drinking?"

Cara nodded. "Just a little. I had two beers."

"Not at all our concern tonight," Tori said. "Why were you late, though?"

"I was waiting until the last minute to drive back here from Manchester Bay. And then when I went to leave, my friend Ashley needed a ride home. She lives on the lake just west of town. I dropped her off at one, which was when I was supposed to be home, so I knew I was going to be late."

"Did you try to call your parents?"

"No. I'm not supposed to talk on the phone when I'm driving."

"It's a good rule," Braddock said. He asked her for Ashley's number, and also got the names of the other friends she was with.

"Do you know what your parents were doing last night?"

"On Friday nights my dad plays softball in a league in Crosby with people he works with. I'm sure Heidi went with. They usually go to the bar after the game. I'm pretty sure that's what they were doing last night."

Tori looked down at the wound on the girl's hand. It was oozing. She needed to get it treated.

"I really need to talk to my mom. Can I have my phone?" Cara was starting to shiver.

Tori reached for another blanket and draped it around her shoulders. "We have to hold on to it as evidence. But we'll call her and let her know you're okay." She stood up.

"I wasn't even supposed to be here this weekend," Cara blurted.

"You weren't?" Tori asked, sitting back down.

"No, I was supposed to be at my mom and stepdad's house in Manchester Bay, but since they had to go out of town at the last minute for a funeral, she and Dad agreed to flip weekends."

Tori and Braddock shared a quick look.

"When was that arranged?" Tori asked.

"It was kind of a last-minute thing yesterday."

She nodded and the paramedic gave her the sign to wrap it up. "Cara, you'll see us again, okay? We'll probably have some more questions, and I'll be checking on you."

As she stepped down out of the ambulance, a paramedic climbed back inside. Tori watched as the blank stare returned to Cara's face.

"What do you think?" Braddock asked.

"I think we'll need to talk to her again, maybe a few times."

"You think she was holding anything back?"

"No," Tori said softly. "My sense is her recall was probably pretty good. I just know the look. I know… what she's feeling and thinking and how her mind is just… spinning. She's numb, stunned and shattered."

"I know you know," Braddock said with a nod. "It's why I thought you should come."

"As the days go by and she relives it over and over again, she'll remember some other details. I know I did." They both glanced back at the ambulance. "Seeing her father like that, my gosh."

Braddock called Eggleston over and handed her a page from his notebook. "We need to confirm that this Ashley was dropped off at one a.m. and that she was with Cara all night. And Cara says her father plays in a softball league on Friday nights with co-workers. We need to track that down."

"On it, boss."

"The sun's coming up. I'm going to get a canvass started, such as there can be around here. I'll be right back." Braddock headed toward a gathering group of deputies and local police.

Tori looked at the ambulance again. The paramedic was helping Cara lie down on the gurney and securing her for travel. She closed her eyes. It was like looking at a reflection of herself twenty-one years ago, all the way down to the soccer sweatshirt. The paramedic closed the rear door, and she watched as the ambulance backed down the driveway and then sped away with lights and siren, heading to Manchester Bay.

When it had disappeared from view, she spent a moment taking in the isolated surroundings. Even with the sun now peeking over the horizon, given the dense nature of the woods, she couldn't see any other houses.

The Newmans' house was set well back off the road, sitting on something of a high point on the property. The grass was lush and well manicured, cut in a neat uniform pattern, with small flower beds set about. Tori imagined the couple spending the summer months working to beautify their yard. The lot itself was a large rectangular cutout into the woods, although a mixture of tall pines and white birches were left scattered about the property to create shade, particularly around the back of the house. The isolated setting was not her cup of tea, but it had a certain picturesque quality to it.

Thinking back to what Cara had told them about the Newmans going to softball, she eyed the garage. "If they went out, they got home at some point," she mumbled to herself.

The three-car garage had a main double door and then a third single stall door to the left. The building sat deeper on the property than the house by perhaps twenty to thirty feet. The side door was locked. Tori walked over to the back door of the house, took a step inside and immediately saw the control pad for the main garage door. With her still-gloved left hand, she hit the button. The door started opening.

Standing five feet back from the open garage, she turned on her flashlight, crouched and directed the beam to the floor, focusing on the area around the two vehicles: a Honda CRV and a Chevy Silverado pickup. Satisfied, she stepped inside. In the back bed of the pickup truck was a softball bag with an aluminum bat still in the sleeve. She carefully slid the bat out but didn't see any blood. Neither did she see any either in or outside the vehicle. They weren't attacked in the garage.

She walked to the back of the house and examined the back door. There were no obvious signs of forced entry. The Newmans didn't have a security system. She couldn't understand why people didn't install them these days. Heck, even Braddock had one.

Slipping the covers back on her shoes, she stepped into the kitchen again. The decor was tasteful, and photos including a nice framed one of Dan, Heidi and Cara added a homey feel. Peering at the photo, Tori saw that the three of them were sitting on the couch out on the back patio, a fire burning in the fire pit in front of them. A happy family.

She could hear the conversation of the crime scene techs and the rapid clicking of the camera in the living room. Undoubtedly the same was occurring in the master bedroom. But that wasn't what drew her attention.

What interested her now was how the killers had subdued Dan and Heidi Newman. They must have been waiting inside and got them when they came into the house.

"Hmm," she murmured as she looked at the lower kitchen cabinet just to the left of the stove. The stainless-steel handle on the bottom drawer was slightly bent. She turned on her flashlight and found a dark smudge on the left side of the handle, a small red streak on the bottom of the drawer, and two deep scratches.

Braddock stuck his head into the room. "What are you up to?"

"Sleuthing." She stood up and pointed.

Braddock examined the drawer, then walked into the living room to inform the forensics team.

"Two people had to be subdued," Tori observed. "The first would have to be the husband. He wasn't an insubstantial guy, had some height to him, was in decent shape if he was playing softball. Restraining him required some force."

Braddock saw it. "One of our killers is hiding behind the center island. Dan Newman walks by and…"

"Wham!" Tori said. "Crowbar, bat, something heavy and solid, sends him down into that cabinet. That could be the bruising on the back of his neck we saw earlier. That blow knocks him out."

"And Mrs. Newman?"

"Maybe she's not in here yet. Maybe she's still outside. Or she sees it but the other killer subdues her too."

"And while she may well have screamed, nobody would have heard her, not out here," Braddock noted. "I've got a canvass started, but my deputies warned me there isn't another house within at least a mile in any direction."

"In other words, this is the perfect place to do something like this. The killers probably scouted the house and the Newmans' movements. They knew they were out last night and knew they could get into the house before they returned. The thing is…"

"What?"

"Does this strike you as amateur hour?"

"No, no it does not," Braddock replied with a quick headshake. "It strikes me as someone who thought the whole thing out carefully. It would appear that Cara's arrival surprised them, but even so, they managed to slip away without her being able to provide any description beyond one big guy, one small one."

"Indeed," Tori said, then furrowed her brow.

"What is it?" Braddock asked.

"I feel like I've… not seen this, but…"

"But what?"

"This set-up is ringing some bells. The shower, the tied-up husband, something about it all."

"Will?" Steak's voice called over the radio.

"Yeah?"

"Cal's here."

"Copy."

Tori followed Braddock out onto the patio just as Sheriff Cal Lund came walking briskly around the corner of the house, pulling on rubber gloves, a vacant stare on his face. "Do you have a pair of covers for my shoes?" he asked, his eyes on the house. Braddock pulled a pair out of his suit coat pocket. Cal slipped them on and stepped inside.

"He looks like a ghost," Braddock muttered, and brought up his radio. "Steak, what did you say to Cal?"

"He asked what happened. I told him about the scene and he started walking your way."

"Maybe you're not the only one this rings a bell for," Braddock said to Tori.

Tori took out her phone and spoke into it. "Search Minnesota. Murdered married couple. Woman found in the shower. Husband tied up."

She scrolled through the results. "Oh boy. Huh. That's why it's ringing a bell or two."

"What?"

"There was one at least a little like it back when I was, like, fourteen years old." She was scanning the screen in front of her.

"That's… twenty-four years ago," Braddock said.

"Yes, but it can't be."

"What? Can't be what?"

"The Hugh Barr case." Tori said as an ashen-faced Cal came out the back door and walked over to them.

"Who the heck is Hugh Barr?" Braddock said.

"The killer in the biggest murder investigation Tori's father and I ever had," Cal replied.

"That case?" Steak's eyes were wide and he exhaled a whistle. Everyone went silent for a moment.

"What do you remember about it, Cal?" Tori asked, breaking the silence.

"Only everything, Victoria," Cal said. "Only everything."

CHAPTER THREE

Twenty-four years ago

"How about we rattle the boy first"

The siren bellowed, pushing the occasional stray vehicle to the right side of the road as the Shepard County Sheriff's Department Ford Bronco zoomed east on County Road 2, approaching the small intersection for the minuscule township of Pine Center.

"Keep straight through the stop sign, Jim," Cal directed Sheriff Jim Hunter.

"Gotcha," Hunter answered. "This is a hell of a way to interrupt our breakfast."

"Good thing we were having it at the H-4 Joint. Otherwise this is quite some jaunt from town."

"But we were at the Joint, man, I was all set to order the Two by Four."

"Which is why they call you Big Jim," Cal replied, thinking of the two eggs, four pancakes, four pieces of bacon and four pieces of toast that made up the breakfast. "Neither of us really needs to eat all that. Lucy already had to take my pants out a few months ago."

"Hey, speak for yourself, pal. Jessie and Tori have become health and fitness freaks. They keep remarking about my belly, and push yogurt, fruit and oatmeal on me all the time. I haven't had a slice of bacon in two months."

"That sounds like a you problem, boss," Cal replied with a chuckle. "You're letting Jessica and Victoria run your house."

"As if Lucy and your kids don't run yours."

"Fair. I think our turn is just up around this curve… and there it is."

The sheriff slowed, turned hard and charged ahead on the dirt road as it meandered through the woods. Flashing lights came into view, belonging to a deputy who had just arrived on scene. As they pulled to a skidding stop, Cal was quickly out of the Bronco. He and the sheriff approached the deputy and a woman straining to hold on to the leash of her excited white Lab.

"In the house! In the house!" the woman yelped.

"Ma'am, what's in the house?" Sheriff Hunter asked in a gentle voice belying his sturdy frame, short haircut and tightly trimmed horseshoe mustache.

Cal crouched down to pet the dog. "What's his name?"

"Moo… Mooney," the woman replied.

"Oh, that's a great name," Cal said as he expertly scratched the animal behind its ears. "That's a good boy."

"Ma'am, I'm Sheriff Hunter. This is Chief Deputy Lund. What is your name?"

"Glenda. I live just down the road, a mile from the Baumans' here."

"And it was you who called 911?"

"Yes. I was walking my dog along the road, enjoying the sunrise, when all of a sudden, Mooney started barking. At first it was little woofs, then he just started barking like mad."

"And that's unusual?"

"Yes. He's a very well-trained hunting dog." She pointed back down the road. "We were right at the edge of the treeline when a red and white pickup truck came screaming out of the Baumans' driveway, turned left and raced away north."

"I see," the sheriff replied. "Anything else about the truck? Chevy? Ford? Dodge?"

"I think a Chevy. I saw the gold logo on the tailgate, although I was a ways away."

"What did you do then?"

"After the truck left, I walked up to the end of the driveway here. I could see the side door was just sitting open. That door leads to the kitchen."

"You've been in the house before?"

"Yes. I know Jerry and Julie well. I went to the door and called in, but nobody answered. I stepped inside and I saw…" Glenda's eyes began to water. "I… I… saw Jerry propped up on the floor against the steps. He'd been… shot in the head."

The sheriff looked to Cal, who waved for the deputy to follow him to the house.

"Did you see anything else?"

"No. I ran out of the house and back down the road to mine to call 911."

"Did you see Mrs. Bauman inside?"

"No. Julie works early. Should I go call her?"

"No, no, we'll do that. Please wait right here." Hunter walked towards the house. As he stepped inside, he froze, then exhaled a long breath through his nose.

Mr. Bauman was propped up with his back against the wide post at the bottom of the stairs. His arms were bound behind his back with yellow nylon rope. His ankles were also tied together with rope. He'd been shot in the forehead, very likely at close range.

The deputy stood a few feet to the right, looking at the body. Hunter took his police radio off the clip on his hip and called for additional assistance, the medical examiner and a forensic team.

As he bent over to examine Mr. Bauman, something glinting on the floor caught his attention. "Deputy?"

"Yes, Sheriff?"

"When those forensics folks arrive, tell them to be careful. There look to be links, like for a necklace of some kind, between Bauman and the bottom of that banister."

"I'll make sure to tell them."

"Where's Detective Lund?"

"Upstairs. He heard water running."

Careful to avoid disturbing the body, Hunter stepped lightly around Bauman and then took the steps up to the second floor.

"Cal?"

"In here, Jim."

Hunter turned left into the master bedroom and then stepped left again into the bathroom. In the shower was a naked woman, with noticeable bruising around her neck, propped up against the beige tile wall of the shower. Water was dripping from the shower head. Cal screwed off the cover from a jar holding Q-tips and placed it over the drain. He stood a full bottle of shampoo on top to hold it in place.

"The water was running?"

Cal nodded. "I'm trying to save any evidence we can. The stream from the shower head was directed between her legs. I'm sure it was intended to wash away evidence. We need to get the medical examiner and a crime scene team here right away."

"We've seen enough for now. Let's back out of here to let the crime scene folks do their thing."

Cal nodded and carefully stood up from the shower. "Let's talk more with the neighbor," he suggested. "She seems to be a fountain of knowledge."

Glenda was distraught upon being told that Julie Bauman had also been murdered. "Oh my God," she whispered.

"I'm very sorry, Glenda," Sheriff Hunter said. "Just so very sorry for the loss of your friend."

Tears welled in her eyes. "My…" She shook her head. "Is there anything I can do to help?"

"Yes," the sheriff said softly. "You can tell us what you know, what you remember seeing. All that could help us."

"For example, you said Julie worked early," Cal added. "Where? What did she do?"

"She was a surgical nurse at the Shepard County Medical Center in Manchester Bay. She was on early shifts."

The medical examiner arrived and was quickly out of his van. Sheriff Hunter stepped away and walked him toward the house. "Two bodies inside. One on the main level, shot in the head. The other, the woman, is upstairs in the shower, naked. She has bruising about the neck."

"Strangled?"

"That's for you to tell me," Hunter replied. "I need a time of death. We're trying to piece together some events the neighbor saw."

The medical examiner scurried off inside the house. Hunter stepped back over to listen in as Cal questioned Glenda.

"And just to confirm, we're looking for a red and white pickup truck. Maybe a Chevy?" he was asking.

"That's what I saw."

"Had you ever seen the truck before?"

"No."

"Can you describe it in a little more detail?"

"It was mostly white, but it had red trim around the wheel wells and along the bottom of the frame as well as the top of the cab."

"Did it have a topper?"

"Yes. It was white."

"How about the license plate?"

Glenda shook her head. "No. I'm sorry. I should have looked closer."

"Did you get a look at the driver at all?"

"No."

"Are you aware of any trouble the Baumans were having with anyone?"

"No. Not at all."

Five minutes later, the Sheriff and Cal stepped away from Glenda as more assistance arrived.

"Cal, get over to the hospital and talk to Julie Bauman's co-workers," Hunter ordered. "In the meantime, I'll call down to Morrison County and have someone get over to the husband's office in Little Falls to interview the people he worked with."

"And family?"

"I'm on it. But more urgently, we need to see if anyone recognizes a red and white Chevy pickup truck."

*

Cal had called ahead to the hospital and arranged to meet the human resources director and head of nursing at the main door. They had managed to quickly identify the best employees for him to speak with about Julie.

"Word is spreading quickly about what happened to her," the nursing director said.

"I need to know if there is anyone who didn't appear for their scheduled shift, or who suddenly looked to leave before the end of their normal workday."

"You think someone at the hospital did this?"

"I have no way of knowing yet, but if someone was not where they were supposed to be, I want to know."

The first nurse he spoke with had worked with Julie for less than a year.

"I can't think of anyone who would want to harm her. Everyone loved her. She was such a good nurse. She was a mentor to me, someone to really lean on."

"Did she have any issues at home?"

"With her husband?"

"Yes."

"Gosh no, not that I know of. I met Jerry a few times. He was a super-nice guy. Julie always seemed happy."

"How about anything odd happening around home or here at work? Anyone following her? Any odd occurrences? Anything like that."

"No, not that I can think of," the nurse answered, her eyes moist.

"Do you know anyone who owns a red and white pickup truck with a white topper?"

"No," the nurse replied. "My goodness... I just can't fathom what's happened."

He spoke to four other staff who provided the same general answers. Julie Bauman was a great nurse and a veteran to lean on. One nurse noted that she and Jerry had only been married for a few years. "I think she dated a lot before Jerry," the woman said. "Looking for Mr. Right, you know. She'd kind of give any guy within reason a chance. With Jerry she finally found the right guy. She seemed really happy."

The fourth nurse said, "The person you really need to speak with is Linda Gibb. She's in surgery right now. Linda and Julie were very close."

Cal checked with the director of nursing. "When would I be able to get some time with Linda Gibb?"

"She should be out of surgery in fifteen minutes."

*

Cal broke the news to Linda Gibb as she was getting out of her surgical scrubs.

"Murdered?"

"Looks that way."

"But… how?"

"Medical examiner will have to determine that, but it would appear she was strangled."

"And Jerry too?"

"He was shot."

"But why?"

"That's what we're trying to figure out. I understand you knew Julie quite well."

Gibb simply shook her head in shock before sitting down. They learned that Julie Bauman had mentioned no problems at home. There had been no weird occurrences. Julie had just gotten a nice raise and Jerry was doing well with his accounting practice. "I always thought it a little odd that they lived so far out in the countryside," Gibb said. "But they seemed happy out there with the space and the quiet."

"Do you know anyone who drives a red and white pickup truck with a white topper?"

"Why?"

"One was seen fleeing the scene this morning by a witness."

Gibb's eyes went wide. "Red and white with a topper? A white topper?"

"Yes."

"Was it a Chevy?"

Cal nodded. "The witness thought so."

"Hugh Barr. He works here in accounting," Gibb said. "He had a thing for Julie a few years ago, just before she took up with Jerry."

"He was interested in her romantically?"

Gibb nodded. "They went out on a few dates, but then Julie dated a lot of men before Jerry came along."

"And was there a break-up between them?"

"I don't think there were enough dates for that. Hugh did keep kind of showing up around the nursing area for a while, I think hoping to rekindle whatever there might have been, but by that time, Julie and Jerry were an item."

"What does Mr. Barr do here at the hospital?"

"He works in accounting."

Cal excused himself and found the human resources director in the hallway. "Is Hugh Barr in today?"

"Let me make a call," the director said as she picked up a wall phone. "I'm calling the CFO. He oversees that area."

Cal got on the phone with the CFO. "Barr is at work at the moment?"

"Yes."

"Was he on time?"

"Well, we don't have a set schedule…"

"Was he here at his normal time today?"

"No," the CFO replied. "He was later than usual."

"Did he give you any explanation as to why?"

"No, but then again, I didn't ask for one. Are you looking to come up here and speak with him?"

"Not just yet," Cal said. "But I would appreciate it if you'd put a security guard discreetly nearby to keep an eye on him."

He hung up and took out his radio. "Sheriff?"

"Go, Cal."

"I need you to get up to the hospital. And bring Glenda."

While Cal waited, he interviewed two more co-workers of Julie Bauman. Another nurse also immediately thought of Hugh Barr when he asked about the pickup. "I remember him having a thing for Julie, and I've seen him driving that truck."

Sheriff Hunter arrived a half-hour later with Glenda.

"Glenda, you said you recalled seeing a white and red pickup truck with a white topper leaving the Baumans' house this morning, right?" Cal asked.

"That's right."

"Come with me." He led her around the corner to the staff parking lot.

"Right there." She pointed.

"Right there what?" Sheriff Hunter asked.

"That pickup," she replied. The red and white truck was muddy, like it had been driving on wet dirt roads, such as those near the Bauman house. "That's the truck I saw."

"You're sure?"

"Absolutely."

Cal looked to the sheriff. "We need to go talk to this guy."

"What's the rush?" the sheriff said. "How about we rattle the boy first. See what we get."

"I know just who to call," Cal said.

He led them inside the building to an administrative desk and dialed an extension. "This is Detective Lund. I need you to spread word around the accounting department that we're on our way up…"

"Cal?" A deputy's voice sounded from the radio fifteen minutes later.

"Yeah?"

"I just watched him turn the corner. He's on his way out the door."

Cal and Sheriff Hunter leaned against the car parked next to Barr's truck. Barr was walking purposefully with his head down.

He didn't notice the two men until he was about thirty feet away, and when he did, the look on his face said it all.

"Oh, I think we got our guy," Hunter said brightly.

"Mr. Barr, are you going somewhere?" Cal asked. Two deputies were now walking up behind the suspect, and a Manchester Bay police squad car had moved into position. "We'd like to ask you some questions about the murders this morning of your co-worker Julie Bauman and her husband, Jerry."

"I got nothing to say," Barr answered. "Not until I talk to my lawyer."

"You're not under arrest yet."

"I ain't talking until I speak to a lawyer."

"Well, tell you what. We'll help you with that," the sheriff said mildly. "Deputy, please take Mr. Barr down to the government center and let him call up a lawyer."

"Yes, sir."

"I'll get a search warrant for his house and the truck," the sheriff said to Cal after the deputy had led Barr away. "In the meantime, you go check out his office."

"Do you have the search warrants yet?" Cal asked an hour later, as he carefully searched Barr's desk.

"In process," Sheriff Hunter said. "We'll have them soon. Are you finding anything?"

"One thing of interest maybe," Cal replied. He held up a photograph of Barr with three other people. "Look at his right wrist. What do you see?"

The sheriff took out his glasses, slipped them on and looked closely at the photograph. "A bracelet on his wrist."

"I think it's a diabetic bracelet," Cal said. "I found insulin and syringes in one of his desk drawers. That got me thinking about those little links you noticed on the floor near Jerry Bauman."

Hunter smiled. "When I put the handcuffs on him earlier, he wasn't wearing such a bracelet."

"No, he wasn't," Cal said. "I figured maybe he doesn't wear it anymore. But then I had a deputy go dig into surveillance footage." He took a photo out of a folder. "This is footage from yesterday when he left the office. It's from the camera at the door leading to the parking lot. Look at his right wrist."

"Bingo."

*

"You don't often get your killer that fast," Braddock said. "Heck of a thing, Cal."

"Did you ever find his bracelet?" Tori asked.

"No," Cal answered with a headshake. "But we think that's why he was at the house with his truck."

"Ah, he went back to retrieve the bracelet, right?" Braddock said.

"That was our theory, anyway." Cal nodded. "Time of death was around one a.m. Big Jim and I figured the bracelet broke at some point in the night when he was dealing with Jerry Bauman's body. He realized after he left, but had to go back because it's likely his name was engraved on the back of it. He got most of the bracelet, but he missed those few links."

"You never found it or anything else at his house?"

"No."

"And he never had an explanation for you?"

"Didn't say a word."

"That doesn't seem like enough for the case, though," Braddock said.

"Well, we got the clincher a few weeks later. The search of the pickup truck. Two hairs were found in the front seat, on the driver's side. They were a match to Julie Bauman. With that, Barr was charged with first-degree murder."

"But he never talked?" Braddock asked again.

"He didn't claim he was innocent?" Tori added. "Didn't try to point the finger at someone else?"

"No," Cal replied. "He never uttered a word to us, or, as far as I know, to his lawyer either. He sat through his trial and I don't think his lips ever moved, even when the jury announced the guilty verdict. He was just… stoic."

"Weird," Tori replied.

"He was silent because he was guilty. He figured his only chance was to say nothing and hope we couldn't prove it. We had a circumstantial case, but Pen Murphy was brilliant at trial."

"I remember Pen," Tori said.

"He was really good on that one. He had the jury's rapt attention, especially during the closing argument. The jury took a few days to deliberate, but they finally convicted Barr, first-degree murder."

"And where is he now?"

"The Minnesota Correctional Facility at Stillwater. He got life."

CHAPTER FOUR

"You were otherwise an oblivious fourteen-year-old"

Tori and Braddock stood on the back patio, drinking coffee, while the crime scene investigators and medical examiner completed their work. Cal had spent the better part of the last half-hour on call after call after call. Eventually he rejoined them.

"Cal, did you know the Newmans at all?" Tori asked.

"No, I don't think so."

"Is this an old case coming back or just a somewhat odd similarity? Because you seemed to react like it was the former and not the latter."

"This looks a little like the Barr scene, but he's in prison for life. He didn't do this."

"I don't know, Cal. Our crime scene seems a lot like what you've described to us. You sure seemed to react like it had something to do—"

"I'll admit, when Steak described the scene, I had a moment. To see something like that again, that was a shock. It took me back to the Bauman scene, no doubt. But it's been twenty-four years, *twenty-four*. Long forgotten by most people around here."

"Maybe not by everyone," Tori protested.

"Come on, Victoria," Cal cautioned. "What Hugh Barr did wasn't anything terribly original. Shooting a man, strangling a woman, putting her in water to wash away evidence that he'd raped her. And remember, it was extremely personal for him. He killed a woman who'd rejected him, and the man she'd rejected him for. He would have likely succeeded, but he screwed up one little thing and was sentenced to life in prison for it. End of story."

Was that the end of it? Tori wasn't sure what to make of Cal's reaction, or hers for that matter. She had gotten more comfortable in the last year with memories of her father and her childhood, their shared life on the lake as a family. She'd been able to free herself to remember the good times the three of them had had together. What she hadn't done was spend much time thinking of her father in his role as sheriff. Yes, she was reminded of it from time to time by people who'd known him. They would say how much they'd liked him and respected him, and in some cases, feared him. But she didn't often think about the cases he'd worked on. The reality was, she didn't really remember many of them. Now, however, with the mere mention of Hugh Barr, there were suddenly a hundred different memories flitting around her mind.

"Ow," she exclaimed, slapping at her left arm. "Damn mosquito."

With the sun peeking up, the mosquitoes were coming alive for the day, nagging everyone on the patio. Braddock fetched a bottle of bug spray from his Tahoe and handed it to Tori, who went into the grass of the backyard and sprayed it on her arms and then around her face. "You close your mouth, yet you still end up tasting it," she said as she spent a moment rubbing the spray around her face and ears. "God, I so love being back here," she added sarcastically.

"New York made you soft," Braddock needled as he sprayed down his body. Spotting the medical examiner exiting the back of the house, he stepped back onto the patio, rubbing in the spray to exposed areas of his skin.

The ME, Dr. Galen Renfrow, smiled. "Living in the woods is great," he observed. "Except, of course, for the skeeters at dawn and dusk."

"What do we have?" Braddock asked.

"Liver temp says they were murdered around midnight. Bruising around Mrs. Newman's neck says to me she was strangled. Cause of death for the husband is rather obvious. His death was painful. His last moments were… Well, I don't want to imagine what they were."

"Was his wife sexually assaulted?"

"I'll be able to tell you once I examine her. Given how she was left, and what was found around the couch, I'll be surprised if there's not some evidence of it."

"What's the likelihood of finding anything useful on her?"

"We'll have to see. Assuming they put her under the water not long after she was killed, she was there for a good three, maybe four hours. A lot of what you and I would like to find is probably gone. I'll hunt, you know that, but just be prepared."

Steak and Eggs came around the corner together.

"I spoke with Cara Newman's friend, Ashley," Steak reported. "She says Cara dropped her off at one a.m. Her mother confirms that, as she was up waiting for her, so that checks out."

Ann Jennison, from the BCA forensic team, approached. "We're nearly done with the bedroom and bathroom. We've finished processing the living room and kitchen areas, so you can go back in there if you need to."

"Anything you care to share?" Braddock asked.

"Hard to say for now. We were able to get a closer look at the woman's throat. Doc Renfrow will get them for us, but it looked like there were strands of black and maybe red fibers in the wounds around her neck. We'll process it all for DNA, and maybe we'll get lucky and pull something or identify the specific rope. We printed the house, so we'll see if anything pops there."

"The couch?" Tori asked.

"We're going to take it back to the lab. Bad things happened on that couch. If there is something there, we'll pull it." She looked to Cal. "We need to clear the driveway of some vehicles so we can get the van up to the house."

"Come on, Steak," Cal said. "Let's go do traffic control."

"How about the bathroom?" Tori asked Jennison.

"We got down into the drain, so we'll see if we find anything there. If what we think happened on the couch happened, and then she was moved to the shower, water had three to four hours to work. Constant water will likely wash anything away, but we'll see."

Jennison left them and stepped back inside the house.

"You know what's bothering me now?" Tori looked at Braddock. "How they got here?"

"Right. Because how I see this going down, they were in the house waiting for the Newmans, so they sure as heck didn't drive up here."

Braddock looked to his left and saw Steak and Cal talking in the driveway. "Steak! Cal!" He waved them over.

"What is it?" Cal asked.

"We think the killers came in the back door and were in the house before the Newmans arrived home. Question is, where did they come from? This place is surrounded by woods. You two are the expert hunters. How'd they get here?"

"Steak and I'll take the left, you two take the right," Cal said.

It took fifteen minutes. "Will?" Cal called. "Steak has something."

Over in the northeast corner of the property, they found Steak directing the beam of his flashlight into the woods. "I wouldn't call this a path per se, but…" he focused the beam on a footprint in an exposed area of soft dirt, "that one is coming in our direction." He twisted his wrist. "And that one is on the way out, and is different from the one coming our way. They're not super fresh, but they're not that old either."

"I'll grab Jennison," Tori said, and walked back to the house.

Braddock took out his phone and started tapping on the screen, then held it out to Steak. His current position was represented by a blinking blue dot. He pointed to the right. "Is that a road?"

"Uh… I don't think so," Steak replied, peering closely, tweezing out the satellite image to focus on a smaller area. "I think that's a right of way for a… power line."

"How far is it to that?"

"Less than a half-mile, I'd guesstimate."

Tori returned with Jennison and another forensic scientist. Steak explained what he had found along the property line, and the two investigators prepared to process the area.

"Let's go around to the other side," Braddock said to Steak and Tori.

"I'll wait here and see if I can see you guys," Cal said.

After a five-minute drive, Tori, Steak and Braddock found the power line right of way behind the local school bus garage.

"Lots of different tracks along here," Braddock observed.

"Some are truck tire tracks, and the thinner ones are for three- or four-wheelers and motorbikes," Steak said. "I could see them ripping through here."

"If they used this as the way in, they had to follow it for at least, what? A mile?"

Steak evaluated the map on his phone. "Yes, at least that."

They got back into the Tahoe. Braddock turned left and slowly followed the right of way, which was a twenty- to thirty-yard-wide gap cut through the woods so that a power line atop thirty-foot-tall poles could run through the forest. There was a rough track to the left of the poles, which ended at the start of an incline that was partially washed out. The washout had left deep ruts and exposed rock.

"If we had your new Ford and its clearance, I'd keep going," Braddock quipped.

Steak chuckled. "I don't think I'll ever let you use my truck for police business again." His old Ford had been shot up, not to mention sliced up by the rear rotor of a helicopter, back in February as they were fleeing some very bad people. "You could make it up the right-hand side."

"I'm wondering if our killers might have made the same assessment. They may have driven along that side," Tori noted.

Braddock looked to the dashboard screen. "We're not far. I say we hoof the rest of it."

He opened the rear compartment and grabbed some orange marking flags, and they started working their way ahead along the roughening trail, which was a mixture of tall grass, washed-out ruts and exposed rock. Tori kept her eyes to the left, trying to get a fix on the Newmans' house.

"I think I see Cal waving his arm," she said, peering through the trees. "This is the area."

"Steak?" Braddock gestured to what looked to be tire tracks in the grass on the far right side of the pathway.

"Width of a pickup truck, I'd say," Steak replied. "Tori might be right about them driving up this side."

"You can see how they turned around and set themselves up to drive out again." Braddock placed two small flags to mark the area, then crouched and examined the ground.

Steak stepped out wider to the right, his gait slow and careful, focusing on the edge of the trees, where there was an uneven strip of bare earth before the grasses started growing. "I think they came out right here."

"I think you're right," Tori said.

"Let's see." Braddock made his way over and found a fresh print in some soft dirt. It had rained two days ago. He looked up and could see the dense canopy of the trees overhead. The bare ground received very little direct sunlight so had yet to fully dry out. He handed Steak flags to mark the area and took out his radio. "Cal, tell Jennison that when she's done at the house, she needs to come out here."

Twenty minutes later, Jennison and the other investigator arrived with Cal. Tori led them to where Braddock and Steak were waiting.

"We have a few good prints over to the left marked by the orange flags. They drove in here and approached through the woods. Over on the other side, we think that's where they parked. I put flags in two spots where you might be able to get a tire tread. We have to work the woods back to the house, see if we get anything."

"We'll do that."

"I make two different shoe treads at the edge of the trees," Steak said as he approached. "What's interesting is I don't recall seeing any dirt like this in the house. Did they wear covers on their shoes inside?"

"I'm sure they did," Tori said. "I think these guys planned this all out pretty comprehensively."

Braddock looked to Cal. "This still look like the Hugh Barr case you mentioned earlier?"

"Perhaps a little. Is it related? I don't see how."

"Did he have a partner?"

"Never connected anyone to him," Cal replied, shaking his head. "We only had evidence on Barr. Only he was tried for the murders."

"But you suspected he had one?"

"I wouldn't go that far. It was more like a question we asked. Could one man have taken both the Baumans down? Barr used a gun on Jerry Bauman. From our perspective it was entirely possible he did it all on his own, and there was no physical evidence whatsoever to suggest that he had any help."

"And what's Barr's current status?"

"Well, knowing you two and how thorough you tend to be, I made some calls, figuring you'd probably look into it. He's still in prison, but here's the rub. He's in the hospice wing. Terminal cancer. He might have just days to live."

"Just days, huh?" Braddock said.

It was 10:00 a.m. when Braddock approached the tall table at the coffee shop carrying two mugs. Tori was staring out the window, her look distant. She hadn't said much for the last hour or so as things had started winding down at the Newman crime scene. He sat down and slid her latte in front of her.

"You're quiet," he said.

Tori shrugged. "Just thinking."

"Had to be a walk down memory lane hearing Cal go through that old Bauman case, talking about your dad. You think it's connected somehow?"

Tori wrinkled her nose. "Seems kind of far-fetched, doesn't it?"

"Yeah, but just the same, what do you remember about it?"

"Not what Cal does, of course. I remember there was a double murder that had everyone's attention, and my dad wasn't around the house much for a week or two because of it. I do vividly remember the night he came home months later ecstatic about the conviction. We had a celebration, but beyond that…"

"You were otherwise an oblivious fourteen-year-old."

"Right. I didn't pay close attention to the details. I had other things that were far more important to worry about," Tori cracked, making Braddock chuckle. "But I did know enough that for Dad and Cal, the Barr investigation was *the* case. It was a big deal for them."

Braddock took a sip of his coffee. "You can sit this one out, you know. Maybe you should."

"Yeah, right. I can handle it," Tori replied. "Cal, on the other hand…"

"That scene really got to him."

"Why?"

"If a scene like that doesn't get to you even a little, you best get out of this game."

"Yeah, but his whole reaction to it, and then our questions on that old Bauman case, was… odd. He was kind of all over the place."

"He was thrown for a loop, Tor. It was grisly as hell and brought back a terrible memory. Sure, they got the conviction, but I'm sorry, those scenes, the victims, they stick with you, especially when it's normal working folks murdered in their home where they built their life. I've had cases like that. Those images are seared in my memory. They'll never leave me. Just like some of the disappearances you investigated will never leave you."

Tori nodded in agreement and took a drink of coffee.

"You can bet something like the Bauman scene never left Cal's mind. I think we can cut him a little slack."

"What are you thinking about all this?"

Braddock shrugged. "I don't know enough yet."

"No sale. I know you better than that."

"This one gives me a very bad feeling. My hope is that it was personal to the Newmans in some way. That we'll find a motive and it will lead to our killers." Braddock took a long slug of coffee and shook his head wearily. "These guys were prepared. They brutally murdered a couple in their home. They very likely raped Heidi Newman but then had the forethought to put her in the shower to wash away the evidence of the rape. And they committed it all out in the countryside where nobody could hear a scream, a cry for help, anything. But for Cara's unexpected return, it would have been hours, maybe days, before they were missed." He exhaled a sigh. "I fear that this is the start of something very bad."

CHAPTER FIVE

"It's my job to know these things"

By mid-afternoon, work at the Newman house had finished. Braddock gathered the investigative group at the government center. He'd commandeered a conference room for them to use. The meeting included Tori, Steak and Eggleston as well as Cal.

"Where are we at?" he asked, starting with Steak. "What do we know about our victims?"

"Dan Newman was the IT director for the school district in Crosby. He'd worked there for nearly twenty years. Before that he actually worked for Shepard County in IT. Cal, do you remember him?"

Steak handed over a photo, and Cal studied it for a moment. "Not ringing any bells. How long ago was he here?"

"Twenty-three years."

He shook his head. "No wonder I don't remember him."

"So that's Dan's employment history. Heidi Newman was a fifth-grade teacher at the elementary school. She'd worked there for a long time. They'd been married for nearly four years; it was a second marriage for both of them. I've contacted each of their former spouses. Heidi's first husband lives in Omaha, Nebraska, and hasn't spoken to her in years. Dan's ex-wife, Elise, lives here in Manchester Bay, though she's been out of town for a funeral.

I spoke with her briefly and assured her Cara was safe and under guard at the hospital. I haven't had a chance to really question her as of yet. Not sure what she would be able to add anyway. She sounded devastated by the murders. I had the impression she and Dan got along okay for a divorced couple."

Braddock looked to Eggleston. "What were the Newmans doing last night?"

"So far I've been able to track down a half-dozen of their friends from the school in Crosby. Cara was right; the two of them were at the softball game in town last night. After the game, the team and their significant others went to Ed's Tap in Crosby. Several people remember seeing the Newmans leave around ten p.m."

"Anyone recall seeing anything unusual? Anyone odd hanging around the ballpark? Did the Newmans mention to anyone about anything weird happening?"

"No. I asked every which way I know. Nobody saw or heard anything unusual. It was a normal night like any other: they played ball and went to the bar. I get the sense the Newmans were well liked and had an active social life. I've got all kinds of names of good friends in and around Crosby that I need to talk to, but that's the update as of now."

"I just spoke with Ann Jennison," Cal said. "The BCA is done at the scene. They were able to extract tire and shoe impressions. They'll go to work and see about identifying them. One would assume a truck with some clearance was used to drive along that power-line area. It would certainly appear that that was the way they came in. Probably where they observed the Newmans from as well."

"Did they search where Cara said she ran?"

"Yes. They found the tree trunk she was hiding in. The area is heavily ground-cluttered, so they didn't find anything down there from an evidentiary standpoint."

"Any indication they camped out in those woods to look at the back of the house?"

"Specific evidence? No. Just seems to make sense," Cal said. "As for the bodies, Doc Renfrow is starting his autopsies. Cause of death is clear for both. Hopefully he might find some evidence on Heidi's body that could help us identify our killers."

"The canvass of the area around the Newman house came up with squadoosh," Braddock noted. "Of course, they didn't really have neighbors. Nearest house is one point two miles away to the south. I've got a couple of deputies out working the area, talking to the businesses that back up to that power line right of way to see if they recall seeing anyone driving back there. Nothing yet, and to be honest, I'm not optimistic."

"What you're saying is we don't have much yet," Steak said.

"There is the similarity to the Barr case," Tori suggested.

"Which is like ancient history," Eggs noted.

Cal chortled. "Just like me."

"Yet a couple were murdered out in the countryside and the wife was found in the shower, the husband tied up before he was killed," Tori pressed. "Don't we at least have to look at it to check the box?"

"Barr didn't kill the Newmans."

"But you said you had at least a suspicion that he had a partner," Tori said.

"Your father and I wondered about it at the time. It wasn't a suspicion."

"Tomato, tomahto."

"No, it isn't," Cal retorted. "There was no evidence of it, Victoria. None. Plus, Barr never said a word. Hell, he never said a word to us after he said he wanted a lawyer. You think he's going to talk to you now, after all this time? Why would he?"

"I can be very persuasive." Tori playfully batted her eyes, causing everyone to chuckle. "But in all seriousness, if he's dying, in the hospice unit, and he did have a partner…"

"The partner is what, coming out of retirement? After twenty-four long years?" Cal asked. "And he found someone to help him?"

Tori's shoulder sagged just a bit. "I don't… Yeah, I see your point."

"However unlikely it is that the two cases are related, in the absence of anything else popping here, we need to look at it, pursue every avenue," Braddock said.

"That I agree with." Cal nodded.

"Let's get whatever records we have of that investigation and arrange to run down to the prison and talk to this cat before he croaks," Braddock said. "The Newmans were two ordinary middle-class people. This could be random, although I have to say, it doesn't have that feel to it."

"It feels personal," Tori said. "Very personal, the way Dan Newman's head was damn near sliced off."

"Exactly. What's the motive for that? Steak, start digging on the Newmans. Financials, employment, the usual drill. Eggs, grab help if you need it, but keep after friends and family. Is there a reason for someone to have it in for these folks? Tori is right about it looking and feeling personal. There is motive somewhere. Find it."

"On it."

The meeting broke up. Tori looked to Braddock. "We do have one witness. We should go talk to her again."

Cara Newman had been released from the hospital by mid-afternoon and was at home with her mom. They lived north of Manchester Bay, on the east side of Northern Pine Lake, at the end of a long leafy road. A sheriff's deputy was on guard, parked on the road in front of the house.

Inside, Braddock introduced himself and Tori to Elise Peterson, a short, slight woman with long, straight blond hair pulled behind her ears. Her husband, Malcolm, was medium height but stocky and muscular. They congregated in the foyer. Before she would let them talk to Cara, Elise had some questions of her own.

"Have there been any developments?" she asked, her eyes red, tired, sad. "Any at all?"

"No, but it's early in the investigation," Braddock replied. "I have a good team working it. We'll pursue everything."

"There are no other witnesses? Nobody saw or heard anything?" she asked in exasperation.

"Right now, our only witness is Cara."

"I told Dan once when I dropped Cara off that I didn't think it was safe out there. They were so isolated. Nobody nearby. He said that was the point, but it always made me nervous for Cara, and for him and Heidi."

"Had you spoke to Mr. Newman recently?"

"On Thursday. Mal and I needed to go to Milwaukee for a funeral. Cara was supposed to be here this weekend and I needed to flip with Dan. He had her every other weekend."

"How was your relationship with him?"

"Very reasonable. We'd been divorced nine years. We worked together to raise Cara."

"And how did that work out?"

"Well. Whatever our differences were, when it came to Cara, we were aligned. We made a point of talking once a week about her: school, friends, concerns, issues. We had joint custody and he could have insisted Cara be out there in Crosby half the time, but he knew she needed to be closer to school and her friends here in Manchester Bay, so he sacrificed. He was a good father. And Heidi was a good stepmom too. I liked and trusted her. They were good people."

"I'll second that," Malcolm said, putting his arm around his wife, who was now teary-eyed.

"Did Dan mention anything to you that concerned him?" Tori asked. "Any weird occurrences at work, at home, with an old acquaintance, anything?"

Elise shook her head. "No, but to be honest, if he had an issue like that, I'd probably be the last person he'd talk about it with. But I don't get why anyone would have it in for him or Heidi. He was an IT guy, for a school district. And Heidi was an elementary school teacher. They liked to garden, enjoy the outdoors and take their pontoon out on the lake. What kind of enemies could they possibly have? Who could have this much… hate in them?" She shook her head.

"That's what we're trying to find out," Braddock said.

"How is Cara doing?" Tori asked.

Elise exhaled a breath. "She's a mentally strong and mature kid, but I don't think it's really sunk in yet. That may take a day or two."

"Can we talk with her?" Tori asked.

Elise nodded and waved for them to follow. "She's in the family room."

She led them through the house and they found a weary Cara, her long hair pulled up into a loose bun, sitting on a sectional couch, curled up in a ball with a blanket wrapped around her.

Tori smiled at her and sat down next to her. "Hi."

"Hi," Cara replied quietly, not making eye contact.

"Have you gotten some rest?" Tori asked, undeterred.

"A little."

"Well, we know you're tired, so we'll be as quick as we can, but we need to run through a few things again, okay?"

Cara sighed and nodded. Tori started to take her through the sequence of events from the moment she got home. She let Cara recite the whole event uninterrupted, and while doing so, the girl became more animated and engaged. After she had finished, Tori went back to some key points.

"I want to freeze you in the hallway when you saw the first man," she said, locking her eyes on Cara. "Is there anything you can tell me about him? I think you said he was dressed all in black. You also said he was bigger. What does that mean?"

"He was… burly. Not fat or anything, but thick."

"Tall?"

"Not like my dad. Not like Detective Braddock. But he had big arms and legs, a little like Mal. And his head seemed big. Like a football player."

"Is there anything else you remember about him?"

Cara shook her head.

"Anything about his eyes? His mouth? Facial hair?"

She shook her head again. "Sorry."

"That's okay," Tori said. "But as the days go by, you might remember some other details, and if you do, we want to know, okay?"

Cara nodded.

"Now, I want to freeze you in the driveway, when you said you stopped because the second man came around the front of the house. What do you remember about him? You said he was smaller."

Cara closed her eyes for a moment. "He was. He was all in black too, and he had a mask on. He was…" she paused, "thin, skinny, gangly, I think. I remember looking back and seeing him as I was running through the woods, and I hit him with a branch a couple of times. He was short."

"Short?"

"You know, I don't think he was much taller than me, and I'm five seven."

"Okay, now when you reached the lake and then crawled into that tree, did you get a good look at them then?"

Cara shook her head. "Not really. It was so dark down there. They were standing just by where I was hiding, but I didn't dare move."

"You did the right thing," Tori said, patting her on the hand. "Just whatever you can remember."

"The big one, I saw him a little when I peeked out of the trunk before he got really close, but he was just this shape moving along the edge of the lake. I did hear his voice, though."

"And?"

"It was kind of…"

"Kind of what?"

"I don't know… nasal. He was a big man. I would have thought his voice would be deep, like Mal's."

"Did you hear what they said?" Tori asked.

"No," Cara said. "I tried listening, but it was muffled, whispered. I just heard the high pitch of the big man's voice."

Braddock jotted that down. "That's good to know."

"Every little piece helps," Tori said. "Had your dad or stepmom said anything about any odd occurrences at the house?"

"Like what?"

"Unexplained footprints in the yard. A feeling that someone had been there. That someone had been following them or watching. Someone who maybe creeped Heidi out. Anything like that."

Cara shook her head. "No. Do you mean like someone watching the house?"

"Possibly."

"They never said anything, but if you were going to do that, you'd have to get really close to see anything."

"Those woods are really thick, aren't they?" Tori said conversationally, keeping Cara talking.

"And there aren't any windows on the sides of the house, so if someone *was* watching, it would have had to be in the backyard. If they were doing that, I think my dad and Heidi would have noticed, because when they were at home in the summer, they were always on that back patio. They grilled every night. They had bonfires all the time. My dad was talking about mounting a flat screen out there so he could watch sports. He talked incessantly about being able to sit out there and watch golf. That was like his next thing he was going to do. They were out there all the time."

Tori nodded along, thinking of her own recall of the Newman house.

"Anything else you can remember?" she asked.

"No, I'm sorry," Cara replied, and it was clear she was tiring.

Tori took out a business card and wrote her cell number on the back. "You can call me at any time."

"If I remember something?" Cara asked.

"Or if you just need someone to talk to," Tori said. "I'm here to help."

As they returned to the front of the house, Elise walked alongside Tori. "I don't mean to be indelicate, but you have some… experience with this, don't you? What it's like to be in Cara's shoes."

Tori nodded.

"Then you know what she's going through? Feeling?"

"I do." In Cara, she saw herself in the first hours and days after her sister disappeared, the mixture of emotions running through her mind, knowing but not yet truly understanding how life had so completely changed in that instant. "I think your perception is right; it hasn't sunk in yet, really sunk in. When it does, that'll be tough, and the aftermath will be as well. She'll need some help with that."

Elise nodded, wiping away a tear. "I just don't understand why anyone would go after Dan."

"He worked at the school district for a long time. He was with the county before that, as I understand it," Braddock said. "Do you have any recall why he left that job?"

Elise thought for a moment. "That was so long ago. Uh… as I recall, at the county he was a worker bee, and with the school district they wanted him to run their IT, modernize it and all, and of course, pay him a little more. At his age back then, it was a nice step up. I'm not sure that when he took the job it was his intention to remain with the district all those years, but he did."

Malcolm cleared his throat. "How long will the deputy be out front?"

"A few days," Braddock said.

"Do you really think they would come after her?" Elise asked. "From what I've heard her say, she can't identify those men."

Braddock looked to Tori. "Elise, she has provided us with some useful information. Clear identification? No. But some details, some pieces that could prove important down the road. The thing that has us concerned is we don't really know why the killers picked Dan and Heidi. Until we have an idea of what this is all about, it makes sense to have someone nearby, as your little neighborhood is kind of isolated. I'd like a clear presence out here at least for a few days."

"You have a security system, a good one," Tori said, gesturing to the security panel on the wall. "Use it at all times. And keep an eye out for anyone paying an unusual amount of attention to your home. If you think someone is watching, let us know."

"You think someone was watching Dan and Heidi?"

Tori took a moment. "I think it's a distinct possibility. So whatever you do, don't leave Cara home alone until we can get a better handle on things."

"We won't," Malcolm replied. "And my shotgun and pistol are loaded and ready. I served in the National Guard. I can handle them."

Tori handed Elise her card with her cell number. "Call anytime if Cara thinks of anything, or if you need to talk."

Once they were clear of the house, Tori looked at Braddock. "Let's go back to the Newmans' place."

Braddock glanced at his watch. It had been a long day. "Why?"

"Humor me."

"No, why?"

"Something Cara said has me intrigued."

They made the twenty-five-minute drive back to Crosby, inter-rupted only by a stop for bottles of water. After crossing the crime scene tape and walking around the back of the house, Braddock said, "Okay, we're here. What's on your mind?"

"This morning, we agreed that this wasn't amateur hour," Tori said as she stood on the patio.

"Everything about this says it was planned out. Everything but Cara. She wasn't supposed to be here."

"Right," Tori said. "How would they know that, unless…"

Braddock nodded. "They were watching, and for a long time. However," he went on after pausing for a moment, taking a long look around, "Cara is right, it would be difficult for someone to sit in the woods and watch. You'd have to get pretty close to actually be able to see anything with clarity. And it's mid-July. If Dan and Heidi were out on this patio each night all summer, they would have noticed somebody sitting in the woods watching them unless they were far away, and if they were far away," he nodded, "they couldn't see. Okay, you've got me thinking now. What else?"

"These guys came in and were inside the house and waiting for the Newmans, right?" Tori said as she went to the back door.

"Yes, or at least that seems to be what most likely happened," Braddock agreed as he dug out a key for the house.

They stepped inside.

"Our killers were in here waiting," Tori continued. "They left little trace evidence behind. I don't remember seeing any dirty footprints or tracks in the house, so these guys covered their shoes. And they must have known that the Newmans wouldn't be here. That on Friday night they would be at softball."

"Go on," he said, now seeing where she was going.

Tori stepped into the living room. "And no sign of forced entry."

"No," Braddock replied. "No security system. Given where they came in from, I'd say they picked the deadbolt on the back door. Hardly impossible."

"The Newmans were… hunted. We don't know why yet, but it seems clear they were. If you were going to do that, and you couldn't do it from the woods out back, how *would* you do it? If you were going to attack them at home, you had to be certain you could get in. You had to know that you would have what you needed inside the house, and that you could do what you were going to do without anyone seeing or hearing it. So you'd have probably come inside and gotten the layout of the interior."

"Perhaps, although the layout isn't that complicated," Braddock said. "One-story ranch. Picture window to the right of the front door says the living room is here, that and the fireplace stack on that side of the house. Two double windows and a single window to the left says the bedrooms are to the left and the kitchen and dining in the back."

"Sure. But they tied Dan to that post by the fireplace. How did they know that was there? How did they know where to hide in the kitchen? They knew all that in advance."

"They came in and checked it out."

"Maybe. Or… they watched the house," Tori was now looking out the picture window, "from the front. You can't see the living room from the back, but you can from the front."

Braddock joined her and looked out as well, now following her train of thought. "The question is, from where?" On his phone, he tapped the maps app, looking at the satellite map for the area. "Huh." He grinned. "Agent Hunter, I think you're getting the hang of this murder-detecting gig. Come on."

Back in the Tahoe, Braddock drove south for a half-mile before slowing and turning right onto a barely visible narrow dirt road carved into the woods.

"Where does this lead?"

"It cuts over to Highway 6, but that's not where we're going."

"Where *are* we going?"

"I think… there." He pointed to the right as he slowed and pulled over, careful not to tip into the sharp drop-off to the ditch. Just ahead was what looked to be an old driveway. There was a leaning post sticking out of the ground that might at one time have been for a mailbox. "I'm thinking we should get out and walk in."

He opened the tailgate and grabbed a backpack, rubber gloves and a pair of binoculars, and they set off along the narrow driveway angling north.

"How did you even know this was here?" Tori asked.

"Because of this right here," Braddock answered as they stepped into a small gap where the driveway was not covered by trees. "I saw the worn tire trails on the satellite view of the maps app. They had to come off the dirt road we parked on."

"How did you know that dirt road was there?"

"It's my job to know these things."

They walked ahead, staying tight to the trees on the right as the path made its way through the dense woods. "This looks like an abandoned driveway, yet these tire impressions are fairly fresh," Braddock noted. "Particularly in this muddy spot here." He took an orange flag from his backpack and marked the impressions.

They kept walking and started up a short hill. At the crest, they emerged into a clearing, although much of it was now overgrown with scrub bushes and tall grass.

"I think a house was here once," Braddock noted, crouching. "You can see the outlines of what might have been foundations."

"You think our killers were watching from here?" Tori asked looking east. The rise allowed them to look down to the Newman house, the front of which was bathed in early-evening sunlight.

"Possibly," Braddock replied as he took out his binoculars and handed them to her. With them she could look right into the house.

"And we might have more here."

She turned to see Braddock pointing to a faded blue milk crate in the tall grass under a tree. She crouched to examine it. "It's a pretty good view, but this crate is ancient. It could have been here for years. How do we know the killers were here?"

"Footprints." He indicated a dirt patch to his left. "Those impressions look a lot like the tread we found in the woods behind the house." He held up one of the crime scene photos. "And what do we have here?" he added, now ten feet away near the thicker treeline. "Someone has been chewing tobacco out here, and recently I'd say." He gestured to the ground, taking a photo with his camera phone of a small, perhaps one-inch dark colored shriveled pouch. "That's a discarded dipping tobacco pouch right there."

"Pouch?" Tori asked.

"Instead of tobacco out of a tin, you just put the little pouch between your teeth and gum instead. There's another one over there," he said. "Steak uses those."

"That is such a disgusting habit," Tori protested.

"Well, he doesn't like wine like you, I guess," Braddock replied mildly.

Tori had the binoculars up to her eyes. "It's what, two hundred yards to the house. You can see the whole property—heck, with the picture window curtains open, you can see right into the living room. Through the paned window of the front door, you can see all the way to the back door in the kitchen. These guys sat here, watched them, hunted them, and then decided to kill them."

"Jennison is going to love me," Braddock said, holding his phone to his ear. "Hey, Ann, it's Braddock. Guess what?"

Three hours later, darkness and the mosquitoes descending, Jennison and her forensic crew had finished processing the area. "We found four of those pouches, Will. The impressions of the tires and the treads from the shoes look to be a match for what we found at the back of the Newmans' property."

"Can you get DNA from the pouches?"

"We'll see. A couple of them might still be fresh or recent enough. Now," Jennison said, hands on her hips, "are you guys done, or is there some other spot you're going to find for us tonight?"

"We're done for today," Braddock said.

Jennison headed off.

"What's next?" Tori asked.

"Home."

They got back to Braddock's just after 10:00 p.m. It had been a long day and they needed to unwind.

"How about a drink on the deck? Turn on the fire?" Tori suggested.

"I like where your mind is at."

She opened a bottle of Chardonnay and poured herself a glass. Braddock opted for a bourbon. It was a mild night with a light breeze. Tori lifted the aluminum cover off the rectangular table in front of the couch and turned on the small fire. Then she sat down on the couch and Braddock wrapped his long right arm around her. They sat quietly, chit-chatting, drinking, unwinding, the propane-fueled fire throwing off just enough heat to keep them warm in the cooling night air.

"Tomorrow we go see Barr?" Tori asked.

"Yeah, I had Cal call down and set us up. We're meeting the warden at one p.m."

"Seems like that'll take the whole day, then."

"Steak and Eggs will be out talking to people who knew the Newmans. The BCA and Doc Renfrow need time to work. The Crosby police are working this too, so… we'll see." He turned to her and twisted a strand of her hair around his finger, then took a drink of bourbon. "Let's talk about other stuff. I'm done working today."

"I really liked the Newmans' patio," Tori said, moving closer to him, feeling the warmth of his body. "It feels wrong to notice something like that given what happened, but…"

"It was nice," Braddock agreed, and gestured to the lake. "I've thought about building an area down there. Not as involved as what they had; just a paver patio, built-in fire pit, space for a table with umbrella so you could eat down there comfortably. Tie it all in with the flagstone path from the deck leading down to the dock. That could work."

"That would be nice. I'd like that."

"Would you now?"

"Yes," she said, leaning up and kissing him. "You could put a couch down there. We could make out on that one too," she added before kissing him again, this one a moist, deep kiss.

"Hmm," he murmured, taking another sip of his bourbon. "Should we have one more?"

"Do we have an early start?" she asked, fiddling with his shirt collar.

"Not super early."

Tori gave him a little smile and then downed the rest of her Chardonnay. "I don't need another one."

Braddock took her glass, set it on the table and moved in. She turned her body into him, sliding her leg up, extending her arm around his neck, drawing him close, kissing him, a slow, deliberate, lingering kiss. With his left arm, he lifted her and sat back so she was straddling him. She wrapped both arms around his neck, leaning in. He returned her kisses eagerly, starting at her neck and moving down. He sat back and unbuttoned her blouse, and then, surprising her, opened her bra.

"Will…"

He kissed her neck again before moving his mouth further down. She started rocking on him.

"Hmm…" she moaned, then murmured, "we should go inside."

He didn't stop. She wrapped her arms around his neck again and rested her chin on the top of his head, eyes closed, relishing his desire, as he kissed her breasts. With his left hand, he pushed her blouse more open.

"We can't do this out here," she whispered as she leaned her forehead down against his.

"Says who," he replied, looking into her eyes.

"You can have me inside."

Braddock stood up and Tori wrapped her legs around him. As he carried her across the deck to the sliding door, she gently cupped his face in her right hand. When she reached back to open the door, he started kissing her neck again. She gave a little giggle, not wanting him to stop.

Inside, he carried her up the stairs to the bedroom and laid her down on the bed.

Tori undid his belt, pulled it out of the loops and tossed it away before unzipping his jeans and pushing them down, then lifting his shirt over his head. She ran her hands over his muscular chest, looking into his eyes. He was forty-three, five years older than her, but just as dedicated to his fitness as she was to hers.

She kissed him aggressively, savoring the taste of the bourbon on his lips, his tongue. He slipped her blouse from her shoulders, then tugged off her pants and tossed them away.

Lying beside her on the bed, he took in her toned, tanned body. "God, you're beautiful," he said in almost a whisper.

"I bet you say that to all the girls," Tori cooed before pulling him down to her, wrapping her arms around him, kissing him again, feeling him, needing him. It felt so good to have this in her life, the intimacy and closeness that came with it.

She arched her back when he moved from kissing her neck to her breasts again, his left hand wandering lower.

"Oh." She moaned at his touch. "Oh, that feels so good." He knew her so well now, how and where to touch her, arouse her. She moaned louder as her body started to shudder, breathing heavily, her heart racing, getting closer.

She rolled Braddock onto his back, slid her right leg over and climbed on top of his long body. She leaned down to kiss him as their bodies worked in rhythm, her mouth inches from his, her breaths steady as their hips moved together, their pace quickening. She was close, oh-so close.

Twenty minutes later, the pillows, sheets and comforter spread every which way, they lay naked on their backs, the sweat cooling on their bodies, the ceiling fan cycling above, the curtains fluttering at the window.

"That was… that was… that felt really good," Braddock said, still breathing heavily.

"Yeah," Tori replied, laughing lightly. "It sure did."

An hour later, she lay naked under the bedsheet, Braddock's arm wrapped around her, enveloping her body into his. She exhaled a long, satisfied breath and closed her eyes, safe, secure, happy, loved.

CHAPTER SIX

"It's the case where they made their bones"

Tori stirred awake and rolled over to find the other side of the bed empty. She felt a slight vibration below her as Braddock closed the sliding glass door, off for his morning swim in the lake. She lay still for a few minutes, slowly waking, breathing in the cool, fresh morning air drifting in through the window screens. Then she got out of bed, took a quick shower, and dressed in black ankle pants, a cream blouse and a light gray one-button blazer.

As she walked down the hallway, she stopped in on Quinn's room. Braddock's eleven-year-old son had left a week ago for his annual three-week summer trip to northern Michigan with his cousins and their grandparents. Tori smoothed a couple of wrinkles in his bedspread, then glanced at the photo of a very young Quinn and his mother and father on the shelf over his bed.

Braddock's late wife, Meghan Hayes, had been born and raised in Manchester Bay. She'd met Braddock when they were college students in New York City, and they'd dated for a few years before marrying and having Quinn. But when Quinn was five, Meghan had died of brain cancer. Braddock was working with the NYPD Joint Terrorism Task Force when she passed. He himself was an only child, and his parents had long been deceased, so he had no family to lean on.

A few months after Meghan died, her parents, Roger and Mary, went to New York City to visit him. They saw first-hand that he was struggling to raise Quinn and manage his job.

"How did they convince you to move?" Tori had asked Braddock a few months back, when they were on vacation in Barbados, sitting on the beach.

"It didn't take much, actually. Roger took me to a bar down the street from my townhouse. We talked for about a half-hour and then he said, you know you're moving to Minnesota, right?"

"Just like that?"

"Pretty much. I was still grieving. I wasn't eating or sleeping. I was not in a good place. Roger threw me a lifeline. My only worry was what I would do for a job. Once he knew he had me, Rog said, you let me worry about that. I figured he would put me to work at his company, which probably would have been fine. I have a college degree. I could figure out a nine-to-five desk job, although I knew I'd miss the action, the pulse of what I do. But a few days later, he told me to call Cal. We talked for a few hours and before I knew it, I'd been hired as his chief detective. Once I got here, he told me that my first task was to teach this young guy who could barely tie a tie how to be a detective."

"Steak."

"Yup. First friend I made here."

"That's a good start. Steak knows everybody."

"Tell me about it."

He had spent the next five years getting over the loss of Meghan and making a life for Quinn and himself.

"There must have been other women after Meghan," Tori asked another night while they were on vacation, lying in bed.

"Not really," Braddock had replied as he ran his fingers along her bare back.

"I find that hard to believe."

"I mean, sure, there were women who showed interest, I went on a few dates, but you have to understand what I had with Meghan. She was pretty, funny, smart and driven—man, was she driven. She came to New York City and in a short time built a small fashion line in that snake pit of a world. She was amazing. Any woman I met I kind of compared to that."

"I see," Tori had replied, suddenly self-conscious.

"So the reason there were not many women between Meghan and you is because I didn't meet anyone who was like that until you showed up. And at first when you arrived, you were kind of busting my chops."

"Yeah, I was."

"So it took me a little time to see that I was working with someone who, while being a pain, was also exceptionally smart, intense, driven, complicated, and a little wounded like me. And add to all that you were hot."

"I was hot?" she asked, now rolling on top of him, smiling, looking him in the eyes.

"Oh yeah, even when you were pushing me to the limit of my patience, I thought you were a total smoke show," he said with a light laugh.

"Oh, did you now."

"You were very attractive, and you knew you were too."

"Oh, I did not."

"Stop with the false modesty. You tried to hide it a little bit with your pantsuits, although I knew how expensive and impeccably tailored they all were. And sure, you had your hair pulled back or up, and you wore glasses sometimes, but they were stylish and expensive, so even when you were downplaying it, I could still see it. It was impossible not to notice. You remember the night you did yourself up, loosened the hair, a button on your blouse, and went inside the bar to run that game on Gunther Brule?"

"Yeah."

"That's when it hit me. I was following you in and I was like, wow, she's gorgeous."

Tori giggled and gave him a little kiss.

"But look, it wasn't your beauty that really opened my eyes. It was all the other things that made me realize you were who I wanted, what'd I'd been looking for."

"You mean the assertive neurotic control freak? You like that? That's what you were looking for?"

"I don't think you're neurotic," he said, smiling. "I do think you're extraordinary. You're challenging, and complicated, and at times completely infuriating. I do love all that."

She'd taken the comparison to Meghan as the compliment Braddock had intended it to be. She hadn't felt the least bit insecure about her place in his life since. It was why she smiled now at another framed picture on the shelf, one of her and Quinn after one of his hockey games, arm in arm, smiling. She had the same photo on her phone, and was proud to show it to all her friends.

Down in the kitchen, she poured herself a cup of coffee and grabbed her cell phone, then walked down to the dock. She relaxed in a chair and watched as Braddock, who was perhaps three hundred yards away, swam his way back.

Her mind drifted to the case as she took a sip of coffee.

They didn't yet have a motive for Dan and Heidi's murders. It wasn't random, but the Newmans just didn't seem to the kind of people with enemies who would want to come after them. Yet there had to be something there. The viciousness of the killings told her that. What was it? She couldn't help but think that what they were going to be doing today, running down to the prison, wouldn't advance the case in that way.

Ten minutes later, Braddock was climbing up the ladder to the dock.

"I'm surprised you had enough energy to swim after last night," she teased.

"Last night is exactly why I need to take a swim. I have to keep my conditioning up."

Tori laughed, stood up and kissed him. "Good morning."

"Good morning."

"Go up and get ready, I'll fix us a little breakfast."

Twenty minutes later, a fully dressed Braddock came into the kitchen. Tori had toasted bagels and cut up some fruit.

"Have you heard from Quinn?"

"Oh yeah. He reports that they surfed all day yesterday." Quinn's Michigan cousins had a new Malibu surf boat. Quinn and his Minnesota cousins who lived just down the road were ready to graduate from tubing to surfing.

"He's going to want you to get one of those, you know."

Braddock grinned while chewing. "He's already planting the seeds. He's going to have me at Manchester Bay Marine before you know it looking at new boats."

"You could buy used."

"That's what Quinn said. He sent me links to two that are currently for sale."

"You're doomed."

"Tell me about it."

Before driving to the Twin Cities and the state prison, Braddock and Tori stopped at the government center to check in.

"For the record, I think this is a fool's errand and your time could be better spent on other investigative matters," Cal said. "However, also for the record, if we don't go down and attempt to talk to Barr before he dies, we might wonder later on if we'd missed something. So, you go."

"Agreed," Braddock said.

"And I'm sending you armed. A digest of the Barr investigation from back in the day. It has photos, a case summary and a list of witnesses, on the off chance you get Barr to talk. Based on my experience twenty-four years ago, I'd say good luck with that. But who knows. Maybe he'll fess up and put any lingering questions to rest."

The drive south took nearly three hours. Braddock had calls with Steak, Eggleston and then Ann Jennison for the first hour of the drive. That gave Tori a good hour with the Barr file until they were south of St. Cloud.

"What's the update?" she asked after he finished the last of his calls.

"Steak has assembled the Newmans' documented history. Financials, taxes, employment and business records. He's digging through them, but so far he said not much stands out. They lived comfortably but not ostentatiously. No financial alarm bells. Eggleston and a few others are spanning out to question friends, co-workers, neighbors, but they haven't yet turned anything up that seems helpful."

"And Jennison?"

"She thinks they'll have something on the tire treads they found at the house and the surveillance perch later today. She said they're processing the couch as we speak, but not to hold our breath; it doesn't look promising. But she spoke with Doc Renfrow as well."

"And?"

"Heidi Newman *was* raped. The guy used a condom."

"Any trace left behind?"

"The shower appears to have done its job," Braddock answered. "One item of note was those black and red rope strands from the wounds on Heidi Newman's neck. Renfrow extracted them and Jennison is going to examine them. Her quick thought is they might be from a tow rope—water skiing, tubing, surfing, that kind of thing—but that was more a guess than certainty."

"How about those tobacco packets?"

"They'll be processed. They have to go to the state lab, and there is at least a one-month backlog, so that's a longer-term and probably long-shot play," he said. "What are you seeing?"

"Kind of what we saw last night."

"Kind of?"

"Yeah, but Cal is right, it's not exact. Jerry Bauman was shot, while Dan Newman damn near had his head cut off. They were both tied to a post, Bauman a stairway banister, Newman the fireplace post. Bauman was tied up with nylon rope; zip-tie hand-cuffs were used on Newman. You can see some similarity there."

"Was Bauman made to watch what happened to his wife?"

"That's another slight difference. Julie Bauman was tied up and raped and then strangled before she was placed in the shower. But that happened in the master bedroom upstairs. Jerry Bauman was tied up downstairs. What they didn't know was whether he was shot before or after the rape. Body temperatures were inconclusive, so he might have been shot earlier than she was strangled. If he was shot after the rape, he'd have probably heard it happening."

"Was any forensic evidence retrieved from her body?"

"No. They didn't find any hair, semen, anything like that. In part, that was because a condom was used, and then she was in the water a long time. Perhaps seven to eight hours based upon time of death and when Cal and my father finally arrived on the scene and turned the water off."

"There are certainly some commonalities, but it's not what I would call…"

"Identical," Tori agreed.

"Okay, fine, the connection is tenuous, but we've made this drive," Braddock said. "We've been granted an audience with Hugh Barr. According to Cal, he didn't talk twenty-four years ago. So how do we get a different outcome?"

"I have an idea."

"I figured you might."

"Are you willing to let the daughter of Big Jim Hunter take the lead? Big Jim never got a shot with him. I'd like to serve as my late father's proxy."

"What are you going to lead with?"

"My name, and then this." Tori showed him a photo.

Braddock immediately understood what she had in mind. "That should get his attention."

Until recently, Hugh Barr had been incarcerated at the Minnesota Correctional Facility—Stillwater, the maximum-security state prison. With his cancer now so far advanced, he'd been moved to the nearby transitional care unit at Oak Park Heights.

They were cleared through security and led to meet with Earl Sills, the warden for the Stillwater facility. After brief introductions, Sills handed over Barr's prison file. "I've been with the prison for twenty-seven years, the last fifteen as warden, so I've been around his entire run here."

"What can you tell us about it?"

"Uneventful. He complied with the rules. No trouble with the guards. He was quiet, kept to himself, read a lot of books and was largely left alone."

"Any friends inside?"

"Nobody close, at least as far as I know. Day after day, he'd just sit in his cell and read. He regularly frequented the library. And he worked on the prison newspaper."

"He was an accountant by trade," Tori noted. "I see a note here that on occasion, other inmates would consult with him on financial issues."

"I saw that too. I followed up on that this morning, figuring you'd ask."

"Any idea who those inmates were?"

"No. I could try and find out, but as you can imagine, inmates tend not to talk about other inmates unless there's something in it for them. A deal to be made."

"I'm not sure we have that kind of leverage right now," Braddock said. "Or really need to have it. We're kind of checking off a box here."

"What I do know is that the help wasn't a regular thing. Barr wasn't someone you walked up and talked to. You had to know him, and he had to know you, and if he did, he might—and I emphasize might—talk to you. If you just went to see him cold, it didn't really matter who you were; he wouldn't respond, he'd just stare at you."

"That fits," Braddock muttered.

"How about faith?" Tory asked. "Any conversions we should know about?"

Sills chuckled. "Negative. In all his time here, I'm not aware of him having sought any spiritual guidance. If you're looking for any late-in-life desire to get in God's good graces, to repent for his awful sins, to get a pass from St. Peter, I don't think Hugh Barr's your guy."

Tori flipped to a copy of Barr's visitor's log. "Is this right? He only had one visitor in twenty-four years?"

"Yes. His mother came twice in the first two years. She hasn't returned since."

Sills led them to the hospice wing, where they were greeted by Barr's doctor, who explained his terminal status.

"I'm a little surprised he's hung in this long. Most inmates I see who get to this point stop fighting. They welcome the end of life in prison."

"But not Barr," Tori suggested.

"He's fought it every step of the way. He's hanging in there."

"Is he lucid?" Braddock asked.

"Yes."

"How about talkative?"

"Not in my experience."

Barr was secured to his bed in a private room. However, one look told them he wasn't going anywhere even if he could. He was emaciated. His cheeks were hollowed and his arms and legs gaunt. He was receiving oxygen via a nasal cannula and his pain medication through a tube running to his left arm. However, his eyes were plenty alert and alive. He tracked them all the way into the room.

"You know the warden," the doctor stated. "These other two are the detectives I mentioned earlier. They want to ask you some questions. This is Shepard County Sheriff's Department Chief Detective Will Braddock. With him is Tori Hunter, a consultant with the county."

Barr's eyes flickered when Tori was introduced.

Braddock took a moment to size up Barr before he handed Tori the case file and nodded for her to lead.

"Mr. Barr, you might remember my father," she said casually as she flipped open the folder, pausing for a heartbeat before looking Barr in the eyes. "He was Sheriff Jim Hunter. They called him Big Jim. I think he was actually the one to arrest you."

Barr nodded, and spoke for the first time, in a weak and raspy voice. "Does consulting mean you work whenever you want?"

"Or whenever they want me," Tori answered, curious that he was responding. "I was a special agent with the FBI, specializing in child and teen abductions. I left the Bureau last year and moved back to Manchester Bay. Now I help the sheriff's department from time to time on interesting cases."

"So…" he coughed and then breathed heavily, "you're not even a homicide detective?" He sounded slightly disappointed.

"Oh, call me a fast learner, Mr. Barr," she replied with a smirk.

"I can attest to that," Braddock said, his arms folded, eyeing Barr.

Tori continued. "The reason we're here is that yesterday, there was a double murder of a husband and wife just north of Crosby. Their names were Dan and Heidi Newman." She paused and looked straight at Barr. "You wouldn't happen to know anything about that, would you?"

Barr raised his eyebrows, and snorted.

Tori stared him down for a moment, waiting to see if he would say anything more, but he just stared right back. He was engaged, she thought. Time to see how much.

"Let's take a walk down memory lane." She laid out pictures from the Bauman murders twenty-four years ago. "I'm sure these have the look of familiarity."

Barr eyed the photos. He reached for one and examined it closely. It was the one of Julie Bauman in the shower. He closed his eyes, as if soaking it in. After a moment, he opened them again and slowly set the photo down. He said nothing, but glanced back up to Tori. She got a hit of something off the look.

She glanced to Braddock, who was intently focused on Barr. He was picking up on something too. He nodded for her to continue.

"Here's what we investigated yesterday," Tori said, and placed two color photos in front of Barr: one of Dan Newman with his throat slashed, his shirt soaked in blood and his arms bound behind him; the other of a naked Heidi, the strangle marks visible at her neck, propped up against the tile wall of the shower. The photos were graphic. Their selection was purposeful.

"Now, the only difference from twenty-four years ago is that Dan Newman had his throat slashed, viciously so, rather than just being shot in the head like Jerry Bauman. Otherwise, the husband was found with his arms bound behind him, tied to a post, made to watch or listen to the rape of his wife. After that, she was strangled with a rope and then placed underneath a running shower."

With skeletal fingers, Barr reached for the Newman photos and examined them. Tori noticed how the corners of his mouth formed the briefest of approving smiles and he nodded just slightly. After another moment, he laid his head back against his pillow, the small smile forming again for just a moment.

That's interesting. She was starting to realize what it was she was seeing, and glanced at Braddock. He was getting the same hit.

"That's all you got?" Braddock asked, pushing a little. "Just a satisfied grin?"

Barr's grin increased a little more.

"What did the Baumans do to deserve something like that?" Tori asked, then, tying the cases together, "What did the Newmans do to make somebody want to kill them so viciously? You have any insight you care to share?"

Barr kept grinning, but then waved his hand dismissively.

"Why kill them? Innocent people, guilty of nothing," Tori pressed. "*Nothing.*"

"Whatever," he muttered quietly.

"Dan Newman was an IT director and his wife an elementary school teacher. They were decent, honest people. Why would someone kill them like you killed the Baumans? What possible motivation could they have?"

Barr grunted and shook his head.

"What did the Baumans, people just like the Newmans, do to you?" Tori asked. "To *you*?"

"Those people…" Barr blurted, suddenly flashing anger. It was his admission that he had killed them.

"Those people *what*? What *did* they do to you, Hugh?" She took out a photo of Julie Bauman in a summer dress, smiling, her hair down to her shoulders, pretty, tantalizing. "Or was it simply that this vibrant, intelligent woman, a surgical nurse, a saver of lives, rejected you for Jerry, and for that, for loving Jerry Bauman and not you, she had to die."

Barr was breathing heavily now, his chest heaving, and there was anger in his eyes. After a moment, he shook his head slightly, sighed and fell back against his pillow, waving his visitors away with his left hand.

It was Tori's turn to grunt a laugh as she packed up the photos and slid them into the folder. She took one last lingering look at Barr, who stared right back at her, then turned to walk out with everyone else. The interaction had been illuminating.

"Your father… he cheated," Barr rasped out, his eyes closed, his head lying back against the pillow.

"What?" Braddock said, turning around.

"Excuse me?" Tori stepped back to the bed. "Care to elaborate on that?"

"He cheated," he murmured again, the same sly crease of a grin forming at the corners of his mouth, this time with an added sickly-sounding snicker. He was getting the last word.

Tori backed away from the bed, Braddock lightly directing her out of the room.

"What was that all about?" Sills asked.

"I don't know," Tori replied. "But when a man who never speaks says something cryptic like that, it means… something."

"It doesn't seem like he told you much," Sills suggested.

"Oh," Braddock said with a grin, "I beg to differ."

"Cal, he was never going to tell us anything directly," Tori said as they made the drive back. "But he said enough."

"You're telling me he said— and I quote—'Those people'. What did he mean by that?"

"It was the way he said it. The anger in his eyes. It was as if they'd done something to him. Julie Bauman married Jerry. She didn't go for Barr. So he killed her."

"Fine. So he confirmed that he killed the Baumans. He verified his motive. I'm gratified by that. We prosecuted the right man, I always knew that. But I don't see where that gets us with the Newmans."

"He knew who the killers were last night, Cal," Braddock said. "He knew. I'm betting they were with him when he killed the Baumans."

"Did he say that?"

"Not with words. We showed him some photos. He responded with his eyes, his expression, a reaction of approval and acknowledgment. His self-satisfied grin and laugh. His anger. They all told the tale."

Cal guffawed loudly on the other end of the line. "Well hell, son, those are just the kind of solid concrete data points I like to see an investigation based on."

Tori didn't like his tone. "Something funny about this, Cal?"

"No, Victoria. There is nothing funny about any of this. But are you listening to yourselves? You two are putting an awful lot of faith in two words and how he smirked, chuckled and blinked his eyes at some pictures. I hope you'll pardon my skepticism."

"I'm telling you, he knows who killed the Newmans," Tori insisted. "It was like he was satisfied. He approved of it all. As if he'd ordered it and it had been done and he got to see it before he died."

"Well good luck finding them," Cal answered. "We scrubbed his life completely twenty-four years ago. We talked to people from his high school in Frontenac Falls and they said he was a loner. We talked to people from Southwest Minnesota State, where he went to college. Nobody really knew him or claimed to know him as anything more than an acquaintance. There were the people he worked with at the hospital, of course, but none of them really knew him on anything beyond a superficial level. Nobody socialized with him outside of work. I spent months digging into him before the trial and couldn't find anyone or anything pointing to any real friends, let alone a possible partner or partners. And I wasn't some amateur, either. If there was another killer he was hanging with, they were doing a good job of concealing themselves."

"How about family?"

"His mother. She wouldn't speak to us back then, just like her son."

"Not even to claim that he could never have done something like that?" Tori asked.

"No. We dug in on her too, but as best we could tell, she and Barr were not terribly close. She'd lived in Frontenac Falls, a couple of hours to the west, for most of her life, but at the time of the Bauman murders, she was living near him in Pequot Lakes, though even then there was little contact between them. She was not involved in any way in the murder— she was actually back visiting people in Frontenac Falls the night it happened—so we had no leverage whatsoever on her."

"Is she still alive?"

"I don't know, I can check. Did she ever visit him in prison?"

"Twice. The last time was twenty-two years ago," Tori answered. "And before you ask, Cal, he hasn't had another registered visitor since then."

"Not one?"

"Nada."

"No visitors in prison for twenty-two years, yet you two say he knows who killed the Newmans last night. If he did have a partner or partners, he left no trail for us to find them twenty-four years ago. How do you think you're going to track them down now?"

"Cal, I'm not saying we're putting everything in the Hugh Barr basket. We have all kinds of avenues we have to pursue here," Braddock stated. "I'm just telling you: I think he knew who killed the Newmans. *He knew.*"

The line went silent for several seconds.

"Cal?"

"I'm here," he finally sighed. "What's next?"

"We're on our way back."

"Cal?" Tori asked.

"Yes, Victoria."

"Barr said one other thing."

"What's that?"

"He referenced my father; said he cheated."

"He cheated?"

"Yeah," Tori said. "Why would he say that? What could he be alluding to?"

"I have no earthly idea. It sounds like you might have gotten to him a little bit with your questioning. I know what it's like to be on the end of that interrogation method. Maybe that was his way of getting back at you."

"Jerking my chain."

"Barr was guilty. That piece of shit killed Jerry and Julie Bauman. He as good as admitted that to you. He got what he had coming. *Cheated*, my damned ass." Cal spoke angrily. "When will you two be back?"

"A couple of hours," Braddock said. "In the meantime, the only other person around who knows the Bauman case is Pen Murphy. We need to talk to him."

Cal exhaled. "Okay. I'll see when he's available." He clicked off.

"He's really fighting us on this," Tori said. "I don't get it."

"I do. It was a big case. They put Barr in prison for life, he and your father. It's the case where they made their bones."

"So?"

"He doesn't want to tarnish it. He doesn't want to even acknowledge the possibility that perhaps they didn't catch all those responsible. That in a way they came up short. How would you feel if your sister's case came back to life again? If the killer had a partner still roaming around out there that we didn't catch, that we didn't even know existed?"

"Fair point."

"I get his reticence. But it's not going to stop us. There is something there on Barr to pursue. He knows something about all this. So until we can eliminate a connection to those old murders, until we fully exhaust that avenue, until we are proven wrong, that remains a part of what we're looking at."

"You know what worries me?"

"What?"

"Barr kept silent for twenty-four years. If he had a partner or partners at the Baumans', he took all the weight for them, and they in turn stayed dormant."

"Or at least we assume they did."

"However, now that the only person who could identify them is dying, they suddenly feel free to finally act."

"They got a get-out-of-jail-free card."

"And they intend to use it."

CHAPTER SEVEN

"Functionally dysfunctional"

Cal met Tori and Braddock at Pen Murphy's house. A widower for going on six years, Pen lived high up on a ridge towering over the west side of Northern Pine Lake. He greeted them all at the door.

"Hi, Pen!" Tori said as she walked in and gave him a quick hug.

He returned her embrace. "It's so nice to see you after all these years. My, my, my, you look fantastic, young lady."

"As do you," Tori said. "Very sharp," she observed. Pen was nattily dressed in cordovan loafers, pressed khakis and a light cotton button-down shirt.

He waved for them to follow him. "I have coffee and soda. We can sit on the deck under the awning."

They all took chairs on the deck and gazed out to the lake some eighty feet below.

"This view is magnificent, Pen," Braddock said. "Is it higher than yours, Cal?" Cal's house on Norway Lake sat on a ridge as well.

"Very similar elevation," Cal replied. "Pen, were you out with Pete last night, fishing the drop-off?"

"But of course. And they were biting too. You should have been with us."

"Pete?" Braddock asked.

"Pete is Pen's fishing buddy. He lives two houses down. If he ain't fishing out there with me, he's fishing with him."

Pen Murphy had served as the Shepard County Attorney for eight years. When Tori was a child, he was the first lawyer she ever remembered meeting. Even back then, he was a distinguished-looking fellow, with his gray-streaked black hair, his impeccably tailored three-piece suits and his smooth, soothing speaking cadence. He possessed the answer to every legal question and could deliver it in the most reassuring of manners. Her memory of him had set in her mind what a lawyer should look and act like. It was influential when she had at one time considered going to law school before instead deciding to pursue her career in the Bureau.

Pen had applied all his talents to the successful prosecution of Hugh Barr. After he won that case, his star rose rapidly. He was appointed as a Minnesota State District Court judge not long after achieving the conviction. A few years later, he was appointed to the Court of Appeals, and then ultimately the State Supreme Court, from which he'd recently retired mandatorily at the age of seventy.

"Cal tells me you have questions about the Hugh Barr case and its relationship to these murders from Friday night."

"If—and that's a big if—it is related," Cal cautioned. "We're not in wholesale agreement on that point. I'm the skeptic."

"Whereas after speaking with Barr yesterday, Will and I are not so skeptical," Tori said.

"He didn't tell you a damn thing, Victoria," Cal asserted.

"He actually spoke to you? I mean, in words?" Pen asked as he opened his Diet Coke. "Hell, twenty-four years ago, that boy wouldn't even confirm his name, let alone speak. What did ole Hugh have to say?"

"Well, to be fair, not a lot," Tori acknowledged, looking to Braddock, who sported a wry smile. "Most of it was kind of unspoken."

"Unspoken?"

Tori and Braddock ran through their interview of Hugh Barr.

"That's it, huh?" Pen said. "He said, 'Those people', with an angry look on his face, and that was all?"

"That was the spoken part."

"And with his eyes, or his expression, he told you he knew the men who killed the Newmans." He took a breath. "You seem to be putting an awful lot of faith in all that."

"My point exactly," Cal intoned.

"Tell me you two never interviewed a suspect and didn't draw conclusions from expressions, eye movements, how they fidgeted," Tori said.

"Everything tells you something," Braddock added, quoting one of his favorite aphorisms. "In its proper context."

"Oh, I agree with that." Pen nodded. "Shoot, you got more words out of him than we ever did. As you know, he wasn't exactly communicative with us."

"Yet you got yourself a conviction," Braddock said. "Tell us about it."

Pen took a slug of his Coke. "It started with me being convinced by Cal here, and Tori's father, that Barr was our killer."

*

Twenty-four years ago

"Good morning, Pen," Sheriff Hunter greeted with a handshake.

"Hello, Jim. And you too, Cal. Come on in."

The sheriff and Cal entered Pen's grand third-floor corner office in the government center. Inside the ornate entrance was a long cherry-wood conference table surrounded by tall burgundy leather chairs, where he typically held meetings or conferences. However, this morning, he eschewed the conference table and instead chose to have Big Jim and Cal sit in the soft leather guest chairs in front of his mahogany desk, angled in the corner so that he had a splendid view to the west of the crystal blue waters of

Northern Pine Lake. It was the most impressive office in town, and perhaps all of northern Minnesota.

He sat back in his brown leather chair and steepled his fingers. Today's topic was the Bauman case. "Gentlemen, this is a tough one. Pretty much everything is circumstantial. On Barr, what we have is him fleeing the scene. The neighbor, Glenda, identified his truck—she's solid on that?"

"Yes," Hunter said. "She was absolutely definite. She can't identify Barr as the driver, but she is sure of the vehicle."

"Plus, two of her hairs were in the driver's seat," Cal added.

"The problem is that she worked with him," Pen replied. He stood up and started pacing behind his desk, as he was often wont to do. "They had a history of being friendly. She had car trouble a month before the murder. He helped and gave her a ride to a service station. It could be how the hairs got in the truck."

"Except they weren't on the passenger seat," Hunter argued. "We think they were on his clothes and transferred onto the driver's seat that way."

"Very plausible," Pen agreed. "But we're before the jury, and reasonable doubt is the standard. Every little argument like that raises some doubt. For example, the hair could have got there because they were getting close, romantic."

"No evidence of that. None. Nobody at their work has said that."

"Yet they dated."

"Years ago, before she met her husband."

"And if that were the case, why race away from the house?" Cal said. "He went back there for a reason."

"Ah, the mysterious diabetic bracelet."

"Mysterious?" Cal replied. "He was wearing the damn thing the day before."

"We can't find it anywhere and he won't tell us where it is," Hunter added. "Hell, that boy won't tell us anything. He's gone mute, Pen."

"He has that right, you know."

"He effing did it, Pen!" Cal insisted. "He did it."

Hunter grinned. A canny operator in his own right, he understood exactly what Pen was up to. "County Attorney Murphy, explain why he would go back to the murder scene to begin with. Time of death was around midnight. No need to be there at six a.m., unless he hosed it up and left something behind. We have provided a plausible explanation for why he returned. To retrieve the bracelet."

"You can't find the bracelet."

Hunter nodded. "No, we can't. Nor can he produce it. Why? It was broken at the Baumans'. He realized it was broken, and that the links were still there. So he did what he had to do; he discarded it so that it *couldn't* be found. It's in a ditch, or a pond, or a lake or a creek somewhere between the Bauman house and Manchester Bay. But that bracelet is why he went back. Hugh Barr killed the Baumans."

Pen nodded. "Yes, he did. That's why we are prosecuting him for first-degree murder. If he wants something less than that, he'll need to talk to us. He'll need to deal."

"Jeez, you had me worried there for a second," Cal said.

"Nah, he was just having us testify," Sheriff Hunter observed. "Ain't that right, Pen?"

"Kind of. You know as well as I do that the case against Barr is far from airtight, but at this point, he sure seems willing to go down for it. The one thing that gives me some pause is whether he had help. Are you guys anywhere on that?"

"We're still looking at it," Hunter said. "But there is no evidence, physical or otherwise."

"You suspect, though?"

Hunter shook his head. "No. We only theorize that it would have been easier to pull off with two people. That doesn't mean we think there *were* two. Like I said, there is no evidence to say so.

Plus, he had a gun. He used it. You can accomplish a lot pointing a gun at someone."

"But do you think there was a partner?" Pen pressed.

"I don't think we can say that. There is no evidence that another man was there," Cal said, looking to Hunter, who shrugged indifferently.

"So he was able to tie up both the Baumans by himself?" Pen asked.

"Barr is in the house and gets the drop on them. He has a gun pointed at them," Hunter said. "He says to Julie, I'll shoot him if you don't tie him up, or he says to Jerry, I'll shoot her if you don't tie her up. What do they do? They comply thinking it may be their only chance to survive. But Pen, hypothetically, even if we thought there could have been another man there but can't find him, what does that matter relative to Barr? We have *him*."

"It's just about doubt. The defense may argue there is no way one man could pull this off; that we don't have the actual killer or killers. I'll do all I can to blunt that argument. The thing that gnaws at me a bit is how we don't have a good grasp on his social network. Who were his friends? Who did he hang out with? I mean, have we found any acquaintances worth talking to?"

Hunter looked to Cal, who shook his head. "We've taken his history back to elementary school. Not many school friends to speak of. Nobody he has been in contact with for years. At college, he lived by himself in the same apartment for four years, yet hardly anyone who lived in his building even recognized a photo of him, and the ones who did said they could never recall any sort of conversation with him beyond saying hello in the hallway or vestibule. His only social group at school was the accounting club. We talked to members of that. Not many of them remembered him. Those that did said he was quiet, shy, not unfriendly, but not easy to know. He would show up to the campus club meetings but generally not to the off-campus social events."

"What off-campus social events are there for accounting club?" Murphy asked.

"Happy hour. House parties, the usual. College kids are college kids. Two classmates, Randy Hoyer and Myles Edson, vaguely remember Barr coming to one or two events early on, but nothing after that. Not a big crowd guy, I guess."

"At the hospital, he knew lots of people, but only a couple socially," Hunter added. "They both worked in accounting and the social events were quick lunches, the occasional beer, but they alibi out the night of the Bauman murder, and they've got nothing to do with nothing."

"Here's the thing. If he had a partner…"

*

"I said that if Barr had a partner back then, Detective Braddock, it was probably a relationship that he kept discreet, hidden. For their protection and his," Murphy explained. "I'm not blowing smoke just because Cal is here, or you, Tori, but Cal and your father knew their stuff. If they couldn't find someone then, I don't know how you find them now, after all these years. And if there was a partner, it must have been another psychopath with no record to tie him to Barr."

"Or two psychopaths," Tori said. "The murder at the Newmans' involved two killers. His partner back then either found someone new, or Barr had two partners twenty-four years ago that you weren't able to find."

"Might help explain why he was so committed to not talking," Braddock said.

"Or it has nothing to do with Barr and it's just two killers who've decided to follow his playbook," Cal argued. "There is nothing original about the set-up of the murders. If it happened two counties over, you'd never give it a second thought."

"Have you talked to his mother?" Pen asked Braddock.

"She's on the list."

"I wish you luck with that. Cal and Big Jim tried back then, and she declined the opportunity. She wouldn't say three words to us other than *go to hell*," he added with a little chuckle.

"And she and Hugh weren't close?"

"It didn't seem like it," Pen replied. "She was living close to him in Pequot Lakes, but there was little evidence they spoke often. Only a handful of phone calls, as I recall. I know she moved back to Frontenac Falls after the trial."

"You think she was in Pequot Lakes trying to connect?"

"Could be, Tori, could be," he said with a shrug. "But that would be supposition on my part. She never talked to us about anything, just like her son. I always thought he didn't talk because he thought we couldn't prove the case unless he did. She didn't want to say anything that could make things worse for him. It was an odd dynamic. Functionally dysfunctional."

"That a mother is protective even when her son does something wrong is not unusual," Tori suggested. "Even when the son does something like this. You almost wonder if she felt some responsibility for what he did and…"

"She wasn't going to make things worse for him," Braddock finished.

"Yeah." Tori nodded. "Something like that. But does she still feel that way now? We'll have to find out. And we still need to keep digging on him. If these new murders are related to the old, then we have to find the connection to Barr."

"I still can't believe he said anything to you two," Pen said.

"Tori has a way of… prodding." Braddock smirked.

Pen chortled. "I bet you know just how to get under somebody's skin, don't you?"

"You have no idea," Cal muttered.

"Mock me all you want," Tori replied with a grin. "I got more than you two did, or my dad for that matter."

"True that," Pen said. "He just looked at me in derision. In the end, he didn't feel any remorse for what he'd done. Under the respectable facade of being an otherwise competent accountant, he was a total psychopath. But that's ancient history."

"Or not," Tori said. "He was twenty-seven when he committed the murders. If his partner or partners, if he had them, were of similar age, that would make them late forties or early fifties. Still plenty able to be active."

"So after all this time, they came back to kill," Pen said. "Why? Why now? Barr had motive for killing Julie Bauman. What's the motive for killing Dan and Heidi Newman?"

"We don't know—yet," Braddock said. "But two men went there to kill them with a distinct purpose."

"Are you aware of any relationship between the Newmans and the Baumans?" Tori asked.

Pen shook his head. "Not that I can think of, but then again, until their murders, I'd never heard of the Newmans. What about you, Cal?"

"Uh… no."

"One ugly theory for motive is that Barr is dying," Braddock said. "Assuming he had a partner or partners, now that the one person who could identify them will soon be dead, they're free to be active again."

"That's the worst-case scenario," Tori added.

Pen raised his eyebrows and looked to Cal. "It's a reasonable theory, I suppose. I just wish I could help. I've told you what I remember. If these are friends of Barr's—and I use the term loosely—we sure couldn't find them then and I don't have any new insight for you now. And honestly, given all the years since,

I'm not sure how you're going to find them through Barr now. I don't know who could point you in the right direction."

"There is one person out there who could tell us," Braddock said. "And that's his mother."

*

D poured Slim another whiskey and sat down at the table in the kitchen. The windows were open. The only sound was the crickets.

"So quiet out here."

"That's why I come here," D said. "I do my woodworking, and nobody bothers me. I can fish, I can shoot shit, and nobody bothers me."

They pored over a map and pictures in front of them.

"We launch here." D pointed to a spot on the map. "It's not busy there and certainly won't be when we put in."

"How many times have you been there already?" Slim asked, now standing, his hands on the table, peering down at the map.

"Three times. I've been able to sit out there at about one hundred fifty yards or so and see in pretty well."

"Security system?"

"Yes."

"How do we defeat that?"

"Can you pick the lock for the side door to the detached garage?"

"Ah, that's a familiar approach. I can do that. Probably just your standard deadbolt. Any chance we can get a dry run at it?"

D nodded and took a sip of whiskey. "I was thinking either tomorrow night or Tuesday. Those aren't busy nights for you?"

Slim nodded. "I can probably swing it. We'd be going out late, right?"

"Very. We'll take a practice run all the way around."

"That sounds like a plan," he replied before pouring another drink. His look was pensive as he absorbed all the details. Slim was always the one who focused on the risk, in everything, business or otherwise.

"What's on your mind?"

"Any chance they'll see us coming? Any chance this will be anticipated?"

D sighed and sat back in his chair. "There is always the possibility."

"I know, but we've started. This next move…"

"Will escalate things," D replied. "After this one, it will get harder, but… we have the advantage."

"What's that?"

"The police have no idea who we are. They didn't twenty-four years ago, and they sure don't now."

"But they'll be looking for us."

"Of course."

"And they'll probably go see Hugh."

"They already did, today."

"They did?" Slim yelped.

"You knew they would," D replied. He'd fully expected Slim's freak-out.

"Yes, at some point. I didn't think it would be already. I didn't think they would connect it so fast. Did you?"

"I'm not surprised. The crime scene similarity meant they would at least give it a look, and since he's dying, they went down sooner rather than later."

"Jeez."

D knew that Slim would require cajoling at times. "Listen, man. We won't move unless the conditions are favorable to us. If we see a trap, we walk away and wait for the time to strike. We have no timetable here."

"And you don't think they'll connect Hugh to us somehow?"

"Only if we screw up. So don't screw up."

"And what about the girl from the other night?" Slim asked. "She's still out there. She saw us. I know we had masks on and everything, but now the police know they're looking for two people."

"You let me worry about that."

*

With the sun setting, Tori stared out the back window. Their talk with Pen Murphy was cycling around in her mind. She was certain that she and Braddock were right, and what had happened to the Newmans had some tie back to the Bauman case and Hugh Barr. She remained certain that Barr knew who the killers were. There was only one person who could give them some insight to who his friends were at that time, and that was his mother, Rita. *So how do we approach her and get her to talk, especially now, especially when her son is so close to death? How do we do that?*

"Things are close out here," Braddock called.

"Oh, okay," she replied. She stirred the baked beans and reduced the burner, then took the tub of store-bought potato salad and a serving spoon and put them on the deck table. Back inside, she picked up the tray with the buns, pickles, lettuce and tomato slices and delivered that as well.

"Perfect," Braddock said as he took a long sip of his beer. "The burgers are done."

"They look fantastic," Tori said, ducking back inside to retrieve the saucepan of beans. "Oh, one more thing." She grabbed two fresh beers and popped the tops off the bottles.

With the weekend winding down, the bay was quiet now. About half of the cabins and houses were occupied by weekenders, and the other half by year-around or at least half-year summer residents. On Sunday nights, she and Braddock would often go out for a long boat ride with a bottle of wine. There was no chance of that tonight, but they were at least having a late barbecue.

"You are an excellent grill master," Tori said after her first bite of her cheeseburger.

"A mandatory skill here in Minnesota. You can't enjoy the summer without it."

Braddock's phone rang. "Excuse me. Braddock... Uh-huh... Uh-huh... When? He say anything before he went?... Okay, thanks for calling."

"Who was that?"

"Warden Sills. Hugh Barr is dead."

CHAPTER EIGHT

"It's a matter of will"

Twenty-nine years ago

D climbed the stairs to the third floor of Campus Apartments West in Marshall, Minnesota, and walked down the long, dingy, dimly lit hallway, voices, laughter and music seeping through the thin walls and battered doors of the building early on a Thursday night. He found Unit B-310 on the far end on the left and knocked.

"D, come on in," a grinning Slim greeted, shaking hands. He was wearing a gray sweatshirt with the university emblem on it, a beer in his left hand.

D stepped inside the studio apartment and took off his fall coat. "Nice place, Slim."

"It's a dump, but it works," Slim answered, then gestured to the small love seat. "D, meet a new friend of mine here at school."

"I'm Hugh." The man in a plain black T-shirt and blue jeans stood up to firmly shake hands.

"Good to meet you."

The three of them hung out drinking beers in the apartment. Right away, D hit it off with Hugh. After a few hours, a case of beer, and all of them feeling a little loose, Slim suggested, "We're all twenty-one, let's go down the street to the bar."

The Stang was a three-block walk from the apartment. Inside, the three of them found a quiet booth in the dark back corner, able to survey the entirety of the bar. A curvy waitress named Rinda took their order and continued to return to serve them throughout the night.

"Is she a student at the university?" D asked.

"No, just a local," Slim replied. "I asked once."

Slim and Hugh hungrily eyed her as she sashayed between the tables in their area, her hips and breasts swaying. Bemused, D observed as the two of them awkwardly tried to engage her in conversation, Slim in particular trying to flirt with her. It was clear that she was in profit mode, and was thus very nice, playing along and smiling and laughing, touching them on the shoulders or arms here and there as they ordered.

"You know, we should go out sometime," Hugh suggested as he ordered.

Rinda smiled. "That's sweet of you," but she didn't say yes.

He broached the topic again a half-hour later, trying to close the sale.

"Well, you know, I am seeing someone, so I'm sorry."

D detected that was probably not true. It was clear to him that her interest in either Slim or Hugh was less than zero. They realized it too, although she tried to be nice about it. But that rejection bothered both of them, particularly Hugh. The way he looked at her after he asked the second time darkened.

D viewed the problem as solvable but didn't think either of them had the stones to really act on it, to really do what needed to be done. Rinda's gentle rejection did not deter conversation about her. As the beers flowed, they spoke of her attractiveness and what they would do to her if they had the chance, until Hugh blurted out, "We should just take her."

"Yeah, right," D replied sarcastically.

Hugh turned and looked him straight in the eye. "What if we did it?"

He was serious.

D was impressed. Hugh had read what he was thinking and knew he was with someone with whom he could talk about actually doing it.

"If you were going to take her, how would you?" he asked matter-of-factly, leaning forward, clasping his hands on the table.

"Hmm," Hugh murmured, first locking eyes with D and then turning and gazing back to Rinda.

"Are you two serious?" Slim asked, his mouth agape.

"You want to get over on her, don't you?" D said. "It can be done. It's a matter of will."

"I'd show that condescending bitch a thing or two," Hugh murmured. He glanced at Slim. "Come on. You know you want to."

Slim turned to look at Rinda, now hungrily contemplating the possibility, slowly nodding his head, eager to be part of something.

"It's Thursday night," D said. "Let's make a plan."

He retrieved his pickup truck and the three of them followed Rinda home that night. The next morning, they drove around the areas well outside of town and found a spot fifteen miles south that would work. On Friday night, they followed her to work, then went inside the bar and had a few beers while she waited on their table, chatting her up a little before leaving. They watched as she left the bar and went home, parking her little Mazda four-door in the last garage to the right in the long row behind her apartment building. The garage had some width to it, which was interesting. Then she pulled the garage door closed and walked to the apartment.

"You notice that?" D asked Hugh.

"Yes, that's our spot."

"What spot?" Slim asked.

D and Hugh laughed. Slim was no hunter.

"She didn't either unlock or lock the garage door," Hugh said.

"Tomorrow night we go," D declared.

Slim was skittish. "I don't know, guys. This is… crazy."

"We dress in all black, wear masks," Hugh said, steamrolling Slim. "She'll never know who it is." He looked back to Slim. "And don't wet your pants and screw up."

"Slim, Hugh and I got this. If we can't take her clean, we don't," D said. "We walk away. If we get her, you get to go to town on her."

On Saturday night, they followed her to work at the bar, but this time took two vehicles, D's truck and Slim's car. At midnight, D and Hugh broke off and went to her apartment. Slim stayed at the bar and would follow her home when she left.

Carefully making their way from the area behind the garage, D and Hugh quickly lifted the garage door and went inside, then shut it and took positions on opposite sides. They leaned back into the corners, squeezing into the sixteen-inch gaps between the vertical wall studs, becoming part of the walls.

Two hours later, they heard a vehicle approach. "Here we go," Hugh whispered, and D could tell he was eager and ready.

The door flew up and the headlights filled the back wall with light. D was on the driver's side. Rinda pulled into the garage, parked and turned off the engine and lights. He watched as she took the keys out of the ignition, reached across the seat for her purse and slipped out of the car. Stepping out of the corner, he had his hand over her mouth immediately, before she could make a sound, then he turned her around and pushed her to the floor. Hugh burst from the other corner.

"Get her hands," D whispered, and Hugh wrapped the pre-tied rope around her wrists and ankles.

"Tape."

Hugh ripped off a strip of gray duct tape. D took the strip and slapped it over her mouth, only a little blurt of sound escaping. D and Hugh both looked outside quickly. Nobody seemed to have heard. No lights were coming on in the apartment building.

"The trunk."

Hugh reached inside the car and hit the trunk latch. D picked Rinda up, tossed her into the trunk and slammed it closed. Picking up her keys from where she'd dropped them, Hugh got into the car, backed it out and took off, while D closed the garage door and stepped out to find an extremely nervous Slim waiting for him. He looked back as they drove away. Nobody had noticed anything.

They drove Rinda to the abandoned farm fifteen miles outside of town. Hugh and Slim took turns on her for hours. D declined the opportunity, instead serving as lookout. After Slim had finished with her one last time, D deliberately slipped a yellow nylon rope out of his coat pocket and made a show of wrapping it in his leather-gloved hands as he slowly walked around her where she lay spent and broken on the dirt floor of the barn.

This was what he was really here for.

Rinda looked up at him with defeated, weary eyes. "Please, no. Please… no, no, no… I don't know who you are…"

D pulled up his ski mask to let her see him, and Hugh did the same.

"No… Please… Why? No…"

A few minutes later, D released the rope from around her neck and let her drop to the barn floor.

"You like the kill, don't you," Hugh said approvingly.

Slim was not so calm. "My God! You killed her! I… I… I didn't sign up for that."

"What? Seriously? You think we can do to her what we did for the last several hours and just let her walk away?" Hugh said, almost laughing.

"But…"

"Think, man. There was only one way this ends."

"But… but… but what do we do now?" Slim yelped.

"Simple. We dig," D said calmly. "And we get rid of her car."

They buried her body in a deep hole just outside the dilapidated barn. They drove her car to a nearby pond, opened the windows, pushed it in and watched it sink below the surface.

Rinda was reported missing two days later. The police and sheriff's department never found a trace of her.

Hugh and Slim finished their senior year of college together. D went back to Central Minnesota State and finished his. D and Slim resettled in Keller, while Hugh moved to Pequot Lakes and took an accounting job in Manchester Bay at the hospital. Six months after college graduation, Hugh showed up in Keller on a Thursday night, unannounced. He and D took his pickup truck and a case of beer and went driving along the country roads. After a couple of hours, they stopped off on a dirt road looking out over a small, isolated lake. As they drank and skipped rocks, Hugh said, "I'm getting the itch again."

D knew what he meant. "I figured you might. I didn't think that was a one-time thing for you."

"Or for you. Tell me you don't want to do it again."

D let his non-response serve as an answer.

"That's what I thought. Let's get Slim and go find us a woman."

"You have one in mind?" D asked.

"I do. It's a road trip up north to Warroad."

They spent a long weekend on the hunt, the plan. Another town, another woman. After D finished it off, Slim freaked out again.

"You get all antsy when it's over, yet you don't hold back when you get your turn," Hugh noted with amusement.

"We could get caught is all. I don't think I'd do so well in prison."

"Then don't screw up," Hugh replied coldly. "You screw up, you suffer the consequences. It's as simple as that."

*

The start of all they'd done together ran around in D's mind again as he sat at the small table, his empty breakfast plate pushed aside, fully cleaned. His coffee cup half full and the *Star Tribune* main section open in front of him.

The diner was quiet now, the morning breakfast rush for the locals having come and gone. Now, just a few farmers in their plaid short-sleeved shirts and their green and yellow John Deere caps lingered drinking coffee. They were all congregated at a table in the far back corner, talking crops, livestock reports and the ominous chance of severe weather later in the day. In D's experience, farmers understood weather patterns better than most meteorologists, so he suspected they were onto something there. There was indeed a thickening humidity in the air, the kind that when it spent the day percolating could brew up a nasty concoction of thunder, lightning and wind. For now, though, the sun was out and the air still.

He took a sip of coffee and returned to the story covering the murders of Dan and Heidi Newman. The reporter had done her homework, noting the similarities between this case and the long-ago murders of Jerry and Julie Bauman, for which Hugh Barr had been convicted and sentenced to life in prison. Without sensationalizing the connection, the story made a point of reporting that coincidentally, Barr had passed away on Saturday night.

Neither the Shepard County Sheriff, Cal Lund, nor the county's chief detective, Will Braddock, both of whom were pictured, had any comment on the similarities. The investigation was ongoing.

No comment, my ass, he thought. The police knew or certainly suspected the cases were connected. And if he had any doubt whatsoever about that, it was alleviated all of ten seconds later.

The bell for the diner's front door jingled. D looked up and froze for a second before catching himself. Will Braddock approached the cash register, sharply dressed in a dark blue suit and light blue dress shirt, with his sunglasses flipped up on top his head. His badge was attached to his belt, as was his service weapon. There was only one reason for him to be here, a little over two hours west of Manchester Bay.

A waitress strolled over to him. "Can I help you?"

"Two large to-go coffees and…" he perused the case to his right, "two of those delicious-looking apple muffins, please."

"Sure thing, hon."

The waitress grabbed two large Styrofoam cups from the counter behind her and filled them, while Braddock assembled a collection of half-and-half creamer cups and sugar packets.

Elevating the newspaper and then turning the page, D snuck a look past Braddock to the parking lot, and saw a black Tahoe that had the look and feel of a police vehicle. A woman with shoulder-length hair and wearing sunglasses was sitting in the front seat. She looked to be on her cell phone. A partner, perhaps?

He pulled the brim of his baseball cap down lower over his eyes and held the paper up just that bit more, but Braddock never looked in his direction, which was good. Although it had been a couple of years since he was a customer in D's store, had the detective spotted him, he might have recognized him. D's experience with the police was that good cops possessed steel-trap memories for faces, names and places. Seeing people out of their normal context made them ask *Why?*

Braddock collected his two coffees with a friendly smile and thank you, left a tip in the jar and was right back out the front door. In the Tahoe, he handed the drinks to the woman and backed out of the parking slot. A moment later, he turned left onto the main drag. D immediately knew where he was heading.

He glanced at his watch. He had time yet.

*

Braddock kept checking the dashboard screen for his turn.

"I'll tell you when to turn," Tori said. "Frontenac Falls isn't that big."

"You ever been here before?" Braddock asked as they motored down the main tree-lined street.

"I remember coming through here on a school bus on our way over to Fergus Falls to play soccer back in high school. It's not much more than a one- or two-stop-light town," Tori said. "Take the next left."

He turned and drove south for five blocks through a residential neighborhood, past well-maintained one- and two-story homes with bright green grass yards and mature trees out front. The cemetery was framed along the street by a white picket fence. At the main entrance, he drove through the aged black wrought-iron arch. Once inside, the gravel road made a short rectangular loop through a small, heavily treed area. To their left up a gentle slope was a large pile of excavated black dirt. Further up the rise, two men stood next to a backhoe loader, having done the first half of their day's work.

"I don't want to be too conspicuous," Braddock said as he backed under the canopy of a large elm tree so that they were facing the grave site fifty yards away. Despite the humidity and stillness, the shade allowed them to sit in comfort with the Tahoe's windows open. The morning was still, birds in the canopy of the tree above them chirping pleasantly at one another. They both sipped at their coffees and took in the peace of the cemetery. Tori glanced around the well-maintained grounds, a mixture of upright and flat gravestones, several of which were adorned with fresh flowers.

Braddock reached behind the seat and grabbed two sets of binoculars. "Let's see if anyone else is watching."

The two of them silently scanned the area for fifteen minutes. "Anything?"

"No," Tori replied as she dropped the binoculars from her eyes. "Who do you think would actually show up? Double murderers aren't apt to have a lot of people attend their funeral."

"I wouldn't mind if a few people did show up. Pen Murphy was right: nobody really knew the guy. It's like he was invisible to people," Braddock mused.

"Killers often are," Tori said.

"Here they come."

A black hearse was pulling into the cemetery entrance to their left. Behind it were only two other cars. "So much for finding new people to interview," Tori moaned.

As the employees of the funeral home maneuvered the casket toward the grave, a priest slowly walked up the hill with two women. Tori had a picture in her hand and was looking between it and the mourners. "The woman on the left is his mother, Rita Ellis. She changed her name either when she divorced, or later, when her son…"

"Became a convicted double murderer."

"Are you going to try and talk to her today?"

Braddock shook his head. "No. That would be pretty cold, even if she is the mother of a killer."

"So what?"

"She wasn't the killer."

"She raised him."

Braddock nodded lightly. "She's human. And if I approach her today of all days, the day she buries her only son, I'll kill any chance of getting her to open up."

"You're going soft," Tori said, needling him for fun.

"No," Braddock replied. "She is under zero obligation to talk to me. I have no leverage on her. She has committed no crime. If I go up to her after the priest finishes with the prayers, do you think she's going to talk to me? You think she'd ever talk to me if I did that?"

"No."

"You and I are going to come back out this way tomorrow and knock on her door and see if she'll answer some questions."

"I wonder if I'm a good option for that."

"Why not?"

"Hunter. Tori Hunter. Like in Sheriff Jim Hunter. If you want her to talk, maybe your odds are better without the daughter of one of the men who arrested her son and assisted in putting him in prison for life."

"Depends."

"On what?"

"If you figured out a way to relate to her on some level. You're pretty good at that sort of thing. You identify with the victim. Get her to see you that way, and who knows."

*

D parked at the playground and took a quick look around. The parking lot and the playground itself were empty. He stepped out of the truck and walked along the gravel path that formed the perimeter of the small city park.

On the far west side, he glanced quickly around before turning into the woods. Soon the green valley of the cemetery came into view through the trees and undergrowth. Sidestepping to his right, he carefully walked ten feet through the brush and stopped behind a large tree with a trunk split in three at the base. From there, he watched as the hearse arrived at the cemetery, followed by the short two-car procession.

Taking a set of mini binoculars out of his pocket, he focused on the grave site. "This is as close as I dare get, old buddy."

Hugh's mother was there. She had another woman there with her for support, and then there was the priest. Looking further to the west, he saw Braddock's Tahoe. The detective and the woman in the front seat also had sets of binoculars to their eyes, peering around, no doubt looking for people to talk to. Best stick close to the cover of the tree, he thought.

*

An hour later, D followed Braddock east out of Frontenac Falls at a comfortable distance. When they reached Keller, Braddock turned right onto Highway 10 and drove through town. D was certain he was headed back to Manchester Bay.

He let himself drift back, but continued driving east as well, following.

*

"That was an odd… service, funeral, whatever you want to call it," Tori said as they reached Manchester Bay. "I mean, nobody showed up."

"No real surprise to me," Braddock said.

"Nobody showing for Barr, sure," Tori said. "But what about his mother? Doesn't she have more friends than that to support her?"

"She might," Braddock said. "But her son was a killer. Who wants to be associated with that? That's one she has to handle on her own. It's not like she spent the last twenty-four years in contact with him. It was all perfunctory."

"I suppose, but it was still bizarre," she said as Braddock turned into the driveway for her rental house in town.

"We're stopping here again why?" he asked.

"I want to grab a few things," Tori said. "Some clothes I want to bring out."

"Which ones?" Braddock asked from the kitchen. He'd fetched a bottle of water out of the refrigerator and was perusing the opened mail on the kitchen counter.

"Just some running gear. I ordered some things," Tori replied.

"Ah, that shopping habit."

"Be nice," she replied from the hallway.

There was an invitation to a fiftieth birthday party for Tori's old FBI boss, Richard Graff, in New York City in a few weeks. Underneath that, he found an interesting document and started reading it as she returned to the kitchen with a small duffel bag over her shoulder.

"Being nosy, are we?"

"Only about this one," he replied, holding up the letter from the owner of the house about her lease being up.

"Oh, that."

Braddock gave her a look. "Well, your shopping habit tells me you like spending money, but does that include paying for a place you spend no time at?"

"Is that your way of asking me to move in with you?"

"I think it might be better to phrase it as finishing the moving-in process."

Tori's eyes went wide.

"But we don't have to talk about it right yet," Braddock said, recognizing her sudden trepidation.

*

D trailed Braddock and the woman from the small white house in Manchester Bay back to a larger house along a bay on the southwest end of Northern Pine Like. It was a nice, sharply maintained two-story A-frame on a lot that sloped slightly down to the lake. Next to it was an oversized detached two-car garage. From a perch a quarter-mile away down the road to the southeast, he was able to look between two other sizable cabins and see that Braddock and the woman were sitting out on their deck. The gas grill was smoking, and every few minutes, Braddock stood up and opened the grill top, turning over what looked to be steaks while he held a beer bottle in his other hand.

They stayed on the deck until they suddenly looked up at the sound of a boom in the distance. D looked up too and realized the sky had rapidly transformed into a forbidding dark gray. The severe thunderstorms the farmers had been talking about were gathering. But he'd seen what he needed.

D poured Slim a whiskey at the small kitchen table.

"That storm blew through here pretty good," Slim said, taking a drink. "Totally killed our night at the restaurant."

"I imagine it did."

"Hard to cook when you don't have power for two hours."

"Didn't do much for me either," D said. "Other than some folks hanging inside the store for shelter, waiting for the worst of it to pass. I guess there was a small tornado that touched down north of Verndale further out west."

"Any damage?"

"Downed trees, probably some damaged crops, but nothing too serious."

"So there wasn't much of a turnout at the funeral today, huh?" Slim said, switching topics.

"Nope," D said as he picked up his glass.

"You saw Rita, though?"

D nodded. "Her and one other woman. The priest laid on the prayers right quick. Whole thing took maybe fifteen minutes. I also saw the sheriff's detectives who are investigating the case."

"They were at the funeral?"

"Not a real surprise, which is why I kept myself quite secluded. I'm sure they were there looking for old friends."

"I suppose so."

"You know, after tonight, the forecast for the next week is clean as a whistle."

"Then what you're saying is…"

"It's time."

CHAPTER NINE

"It was like she possessed a sixth sense"

It was late on Wednesday morning when Braddock and Tori once again drove west toward Frontenac Falls.

"I always find this part of the state to be kind of unique," Tori said.

"How so?"

"We'll be driving along through these green farm fields, the shoulder-high corn or the soybeans or hay, and then boom, you'll hit a beautiful little tree-lined lake, and then two miles later, you're right back into the farm fields. You just don't see that anywhere else."

"Well, it is the Land of Ten Thousand Lakes," Braddock said.

Tori nodded. "It's just the mixture out here to the west when you get out of Manchester Bay, which is much more forests and lakes. Out here you could be on the lake and see a silo and grain elevator, you know?"

"What I like is the little towns on this highway. All those old businesses with the classic storefronts. It feels like you've stepped back in time."

"You just hope these small towns can survive. I've noticed that interspersed with all those businesses are a lot of vacancy signs too."

They entered the eastern end of Frontenac Falls and drove along the main drag. "You know, you're right," Braddock said. "About every third or fourth building has a vacancy or for-rent sign. It's not glaringly obvious, but if you look for it, you see it."

Following the GPS map on the dashboard, they eventually found the small white house with a cottage exterior set on a quiet corner. It was well tended, with cut grass, manicured bushes, and neatly trimmed flowers and plants both around the house and in standalone beds framing the four corners of the yard.

Steak had put together a bio on Rita Ellis, Hugh Barr's mother. She was now seventy years old. She still worked part-time as a cashier at the small grocery store they'd passed earlier. She'd given birth to Hugh Barr fifty-one years ago, married at the time to Lance Barr. When Hugh was thirteen, Rita divorced Lance. Four years later, Lance committed suicide in Dickinson, North Dakota.

"Maybe the suicide is why he didn't talk to his mother basically from the time he graduated college until he turned into a killer," Tori had speculated on their drive out. "She bailed on his dad and later he kills himself. Son blames mom, ignores her despite her attempts to reconcile."

"Could be," Braddock said. "What I know from having reviewed what we have on Barr is we don't know nearly enough about him—who he knew, spent time with, or what he did socially before he killed the Baumans. He was a loner, sure, but if he had partners, they're from somewhere in his life before then. We can't find anyone who seems to be able to fill in the gaps with any detail. Rita is probably it. There is nobody else."

"From what Cal and Pen said, as well as Steak's research, it appears that Barr hardly spoke to his mother in that time. Do you think she can really fill in those gaps?"

"Until she talks, we won't know. But I'm willing to venture a guess that she knows more than you think she might. Moms just do. My mom and dad were hands-off when I was growing up. They were older. I came and went as I wanted for the most part. Yet my mom knew who I was hanging around with and when

I'd been up to stuff I shouldn't have been up to. It was like she possessed a sixth sense. Wasn't your dad the same?"

"Yes," Tori said with a laugh. "He was the sheriff. Jessie and I knew he had spies everywhere. We generally toed the line, at least until we got into high school and could drive. Then we started… testing it."

"And he knew?"

"He knew we were going to go to parties, drink, do what other high school kids did. We had this kind of détente where he knew what we were doing and looked the other way as long as we didn't embarrass him. It wasn't said, it was just kind of understood. The only thing he ever said direct was to never hesitate to call him for a ride. No questions asked, but we were to call and he'd come. And there were a couple of times calls were made, he came and that was it."

"No questions?"

"No, not really. He would just always say, 'you girls be careful now'. As long as we played by those rules, we were good. Plus, Jessie usually had me around to make sure she didn't go too far, because of the two of us, she was the one to push the limits. I was more the rule follower. And it was fine until… she disappeared. Then the sheriff got awfully protective, but that was my reality."

Tori closed her eyes for a moment, thinking back to the time between Jessie's disappearance and when she finally left for college a little over a year later. In that year, her father became almost smothering in his concern every time she left the house, worried that she wouldn't come back. She understood it, but that didn't make things any easier.

"The real question we have is did Barr's mom know?" she said. "Did she know what he was up to? Did she know or sense what he was capable of doing?"

"Twenty-four years ago, she wouldn't say anything about him leading up to the trial. I would have thought she would at least have attempted to defend him."

"Unless she and Hugh had a pact of some kind. He made her promise not to talk."

"And if she did, she could be…"

"In some kind of danger," Tori finished. "As long as she didn't talk, she would be safe."

"Maybe."

"Do we have anything to use on her to force her hand?"

"Not that I see. Steak did the background to see if she had any legal issues we could leverage, but he didn't find anything," Braddock said. "We're just going to have to charm her."

"Then we're doomed."

They'd arrived at 11:00 a.m. and went to knock on the front door of the house, but there was no answer. They retired back to the Tahoe and watched the place for an hour. "Let's go to that diner we stopped at yesterday," Braddock said.

They ate an early lunch before driving back to the house. They tried the door again, but Rita still wasn't home. This time, though, they didn't have to wait long. At 1:20 p.m., a black Honda Civic pulled up the driveway and into the one-car garage.

Tori reached for the door handle.

"Let's give her a minute or two to get inside."

They both observed as a smallish woman with short salt-and-pepper hair, wearing khaki capri pants and a light blue blouse, walked from the garage to the house. They waited ten minutes before the two of them strolled up the sidewalk. Braddock rang the doorbell.

Rita Ellis answered the door. "Yes?"

"Ms. Ellis, I'm Will Braddock, Chief Detective of the Shepard County Sheriff's Department." He held up his badge and identification. "This is Tori Hunter. She works with me."

"I love your yard," Tori said, genuinely admiring how well maintained it was.

"What do you want?" Ellis asked tersely. She clearly knew exactly what they were there for.

The cold reception was not unexpected. Braddock immediately sensed that a softer approach was needed. "Ma'am, I sincerely apologize for this intrusion."

"Then why *are* you intruding?"

"We are investigating a recent murder in our county. A double murder."

"So? Why would you be asking me about that?"

"Well," Braddock said calmly, "I don't know if you've seen some of the newspaper articles and television reports…"

"I have."

"Then I suspect you might recognize some of the reported similarities between what we're investigating now and the murders from twenty-four years ago."

"Again, so?"

Tori stepped in. "I know this is not a topic you or any parent would want to talk about. But when Hugh killed Jerry and Julie Bauman twenty-four years ago, we think it's possible he didn't do it alone. Others may have been involved. We think your son protected them all these years. Our worry is that those people are killing again, and we need help identifying them or we fear more innocent people will die. We were hoping you could help us with that."

"My son is dead. I buried him yesterday," Ellis said angrily. "I buried him and now you people are here accusing me…"

"Ma'am, we're not accusing you of anything, and if it sounded as if we were, we sincerely apologize," Tori said, keeping her tone even and conversational, her body relaxed. "I didn't have anything to do with the investigation or prosecution of your son's case all those years ago. I was fourteen years old, growing up in Manchester Bay."

"Your last name is Hunter. I bet you were related to the sheriff back then."

"Yes. He was my father," she answered honestly.

"Ma'am, I'm not from Manchester Bay," Braddock said, step-ping in. "I was a freshman in college in New York City at the time that all happened."

"We're both sorry to be here asking these questions, given the timing. But Hugh's passing… unfortunately, we think the timing matters. We don't think Hugh acted alone. And I can tell by the anguished look on your face, Rita, that you know what he did back then."

"I don't know what he did or didn't do. He had a right to remain silent. He claimed that right."

Braddock sighed. She wouldn't deny her son was a killer, but she wouldn't acknowledge it either. "Ma'am, we're not here to re-try your son's case; we're just trying to figure out who the killers are now. We were hoping you'd be willing to help."

"No."

"Ma'am, please consider the victims we already have and the lives that could be saved."

"A seventeen-year-old girl came home to find her father slaughtered," Tori said with a little more urgency. "She saw the killers, two men. She had to run into the woods to escape them as they chased her. She's going to be scarred for life by that. She's lucky to be alive. Please help us prevent that from happening to anyone else."

Rita sighed and her shoulders slumped as she closed her eyes and looked away, shaking her head. "I don't know anything about anything. I was barely speaking to my son when… when it all happened. Our relationship was… I can't help you."

"You don't know that for certain," Tori suggested, stepping in front of Braddock. "I know from experience that witnesses, family, friends often know more than they think they do. It is possible you might remember someone from Hugh's past we should be talking to. We're just looking for names of acquaintances. People your son knew from back in the day. Nobody will know you gave us those names."

"People are getting murdered again, Ms. Ellis," Braddock pleaded. "More people might die if we can't find these killers."

"Sorry, I just… can't," Ellis said, waving them off.

"Can't or won't?" Braddock asked. "There's a difference."

"You can leave now, please…"

"Ma'am I know this is hard," Tori said. "But—"

"Are you arresting me?" Ellis asked, now flashing anger, stepping aggressively forward, her hands on her hips.

"No, Ms. Ellis," Braddock replied after a minute.

"Am I under any obligation to speak to you?"

"No, ma'am, no legal obligation other than that you could help—"

"Get off my steps then. Get off my property. *Now!*" she snapped, a little more loudly.

Tori glanced around and noticed that some neighbors had stopped in their yards and were watching. "Come on, Will," she said.

Braddock hesitated, staring at the woman in disappointment.

Rita Ellis stepped back inside her house and slammed the door.

"Let's go," Tori urged, tugging at his sleeve.

The two of them slowly turned to leave.

"Well, that went well," she cracked morosely.

"I think she knows more than she's saying, but just can't bring herself to talk about it."

"Give it some time. Let her think about it. I have a feeling we'll be back."

CHAPTER TEN

"We gotta get out of here—now!"

D scanned the lake. There were no other boats visible. It was a breezy Friday night and there was just enough of a chop on the water that people had decided to stay inside. He turned and looked to the house. It remained dark, just like the moonless sky. "Time?"

"Ten oh two," Slim reported, sitting up front in the bow, raising the binoculars to his eyes.

"Time to go."

They each slid on a ski mask. D pushed down the throttle and motored ahead through the heavier than expected rollers, careful not to rev the motor too high. You could hear a boat's revving engine from a long way away across the water.

The dock was wide, two boat lifts to the left, an octagonal seating area to the right, which was his target landing spot. He came in slow, easing back on the throttle as he neared the dock. Fifty feet out, he had the bow lined up. Twenty feet out, he killed the engine and coasted, letting the wind drift him slightly right. Slim, up in the bow, was able to easily grab the corner post and let them ease up to the dock's side. The boat tied to a post, they collected their gear, Slim carrying a backpack, D picking up his crowbar, and made their way up the long dock to the yard, where each took a knee and listened.

"It's eerie out here," Slim whispered, the wind rustling through the reeds and cattails behind them, the tree limbs high above swaying with the breeze.

"Go!"

They stayed in the grass alongside the flagstone path as they ran to the left of the house and the side door of the detached garage. Slim kneeled and worked the lock, picking it in thirty seconds, and the two of them slipped inside and took up position on opposite sides of the garage door.

Fifty minutes later, the glow of headlights slowly began to fill the garage as they heard a vehicle approach.

"Here they come," D said, pulling his mask down over his face.

Slim did the same and exhaled a nervous breath.

D tightened his grip on the end of the crowbar he'd wrapped with hockey tape. He pressed his back against the garage wall, a barrel containing gardening equipment and brooms set between him and the door. Slim had drifted back into the corner on the other side.

The garage door opener motor began to hum, and the chain started pulling the double door open. Light hit the far wall, the workbench and shelves as the Lincoln Navigator slowly pulled inside. D gripped the crowbar tighter, now up on the balls of his feet, waiting… waiting…

There was the click of the driver's side door opening. The driver's left leg emerged and he unfolded from the SUV, getting out and then turning his back, closing the door.

D burst from his position, raising his right arm and swinging.

Thud!

The man crumpled onto the floor of the garage.

Thud! Thud! Thud!

The woman shrieked. Slim jumped her from behind, while D pulled out a zip-tie handcuff and quickly secured the man's wrists behind his back, then slapped a piece of pre-ripped duct tape over his mouth.

He pushed himself up and ran around to the other side of the SUV. Slim had the wife on the ground, his hand over her mouth. D yanked out a second zip tie and bound her wrists, then gagged her with tape, silencing her screams. Finally he secured her ankles with another rope.

The husband was starting to groan and stir from his beating. D picked up the crowbar and swung it again, hitting him on the upper back just to the right of his neck.

Thud! Thud!

He stopped moving. D spun around and looked outside, scanning the swaying trees, peering down the gravel driveway as it arced away and disappeared back into the woods to his left, then turning to his right and gazing out toward the lake, noticing the reeds flowing with the breeze. Not a peep. He walked around to where Slim had propped the terrified woman up against the side of the Navigator.

"Let's get them inside."

Todd Strom's arms were secured behind him and wrapped round the decorative pillar that framed the main hallway entry into the family room. He was perfectly positioned to see the long sectional couch on the opposite side. Slim had the woman mostly naked now, mouth gagged, only her pants still on, though pulled down to where the zip ties had her ankles secured.

D waved a smelling salt under Strom's nose. It took a few moments, but he started to stir. D stepped back and observed as the man's eyes flickered open. Strom was groggy, and D could tell he was having difficulty focusing at first, but when he did, his eyes went wide at the sight of his wife, Slim on top of her.

"Jen! Jen!" His screams were muffled as he pulled at his restraints.

Slim reached down and turned her head so she was facing her husband. "See, he's watching, he's watching me," he hollered in glee.

D leaned down, getting in front of Strom. "I bet when you took that call all those years ago from Portage County, you never thought you'd end up here, did you, Todd?" He backhanded him across the face. "*Did you?*"

The man frowned, not understanding, then looked across at his wife, his eyes frantic again. "Jen! No, Jen!"

"Hugh. Hugh Barr," D said, grinning at Strom before shoving the man's head back against the pillar.

Strom's eyes went wider, then he started shaking his head rapidly.

"You remember the name now, don't you? You know what you did and what you didn't do." D spoke tauntingly. "Time to pay for your sins. Time for you and…" he looked over to the couch as Slim went to town, "her to pay."

Strom's expression changed from fear to anger. He tried to pull free, thrashing his body, but his arms were secured tightly around the pillar.

"It hurts, doesn't it? To know just how badly you've let her down. To know you're the one responsible for this. To know that when she said yes to you all those years ago, this is what you were leading her to. That it's all your fault. That she's going to die because of you."

Strom squirmed, yanking against the pillar, but there was no give, no loosening, no slack, no escape. Not from this.

"You ain't going anywhere, Todd. There is no getting away from this, not out here in this isolated place, no neighbors for a mile. I can't begin to tell you how much I love the seclusion out here."

Strom thrashed with his bound legs, kicking out.

"Ha! Ha! Ha! Ain't nothing you can do but watch," D hissed, then he wound up and backhanded Strom across the face again.

Slim used the portable shower head to wash the woman's body while he held the extension hose in his other hand and maneuvered his way around the shower in his bare feet. He'd been running the water over her for fifteen minutes now, wiping her down as he did so. When it was time to leave, he'd set the stream for the area between her legs.

D walked into the bathroom.

"What time is it?" Slim asked.

"Four thirty. We need to get moving. You took a lot of time with her. A lot."

"*I* took a lot of time?" Slim answered. "You should have seen yourself. You really went off on him down there. I mean… with that knife and all."

"He had it coming," D growled. "You about ready to go?"

"Yes."

As he stepped toward the shower, a flash of light caught his eye in the bathroom window. "What the…"

"What? What is it?"

"Someone's coming." D thought quickly. "Get out of there, but leave the light on."

D reached the bottom of the stairs and looked left. Through the windows of the front door he could see the headlights of a truck approaching the circular drive in front of the house. He scrambled through the kitchen to the side door and made sure it was unlocked. The only light on in here was the one underneath the microwave mounted high over the stove.

He dashed back into the living room, scooped up the backpack and crouched behind a chair. He took the pistol out of the backpack. Glancing right, he saw Slim at the bottom of the stairs. With his fisted left hand, he gestured for Slim to hold his position, then raised his gun. Slim nodded and leaned back against the wall between the stairs and the kitchen. D reached back into the backpack, extracted the silencer and began to screw it onto the barrel.

They both heard an intermittent buzzing sound. It was coming from Todd Strom, his pocket, his cell phone. His friend outside was calling him. After about thirty seconds, the buzzing ended.

The two of them waited. D felt his heart beating rapidly. He glanced to his right. Slim was fidgeting, nervous, breathing heavily. D caught his eye and whispered, "Easy."

He turned his focus back to the side door. "Come on. Come on," he muttered to himself.

The phone buzzed again. The visitor was sitting outside wondering if his friend was awake. At this hour, D figured he was probably here to go fishing. The sun would start coming up in forty-five minutes.

When the buzzing finally stopped, D looked to Slim. "Turn the upstairs hallway light on," he said quietly.

Slim reached around the corner and flipped on the light switch. A few seconds later, they heard a truck door slam outside. That was followed by slow footsteps on the wooden planks of the steps outside.

The door creaked open. "Todd?" the man whispered. He waited a second, then, more loudly, "Todd? Todd, you up, buddy?"

Take a step, take another step, D thought to himself, breathing slowly through his nose.

Hearing no response from his friend, the man stepped inside the house and let the door close lightly behind him. "Todd?" He took one more step. D exhaled through his nose and depressed the trigger.

Crack! Crack!

The man crumpled to the floor between the center island and the stove, groaning.

"Go!"

Slim stepped around the corner.

"Get on him! Hold him down!"

Slim jumped on top of the man. D grabbed a small pillow from the couch and moved into the kitchen. He'd shot the man square in the chest. His breathing was labored and short, his look one of shock, his eyes frantic.

D kneeled, placed the pillow over the agonized man's face, and shot him.

He looked to Slim. "Grab our stuff. We gotta get out of here—now!"

CHAPTER ELEVEN

Twenty-four years ago

"That's a painful thing to be these days"

"Nice ski run there, little girl. Good slalom cuts."

"Thanks, Dad," Tori said with a big smile as she dried herself off. "The water is so perfect right now, total glass."

"You think that was good, watch this," Jessie said as she tossed the water ski in, then plugged her nose and jumped off the back of the boat feet first into the lake.

"Do you girls compete over everything?"

"Uh… yeah," Tori said.

Jim Hunter smiled and took a drink of his beer, the speedboat floating in the calm water on the south side of the bay. The sun was descending in the sky to the west on this late August night. There weren't going to be too many beautiful evenings like this left. Summer was coming to a rapid close, with just a hint of fading green in the leaves and even some odd yellows emerging. Plus, school started in less than a week, and once that happened, the warm weather would leave the state with the migratory birds.

Once Jessie reached the end of the tow rope, he started the motor, which rumbled reliably to life.

"Busy day at work, Dad?" Tori asked as she shed her life jacket.

"Pretty normal."

"What's new on that big case?"

"We arrested our suspect. The murder charges were filed today," the sheriff replied as he took another drink.

"Will you get a… what do they call it…"

"Conviction?"

"Yeah."

"Well, that's Pen Murphy's job now. You remember Pen, right?"

"Yes."

"Well, we catch them, the county attorney prosecutes them. There are no guarantees, but we feel good about it. But that's nothing you should be worrying about."

"Hey, don't mind me back here," Jessie hollered mockingly, leaning back in the water, the tips of her skis in the air. "You can feel free to hit it any day now."

"Your sister is developing a sarcastic streak," Jim said as he put his beer in the cup holder below his seat.

"Tell me about it," Tori replied, smiling. "You better hit it, Dad."

"Alrighty then. Here we go."

The motor roared to life and Jessie popped right out of the water.

"You're right, Tori," Jim Hunter said as he reached back down for his beer, "the water is absolute glass…"

*

Tori breathed in the fresh morning air, the crystal blue waters of the lake visible out the bedroom door and through the large windows on the front of the house. It was going to be another beautiful summer day.

Braddock pulled her close. "You've been looking out at the water for a long time," he said as he kissed her gently on the neck. "What are you thinking?"

"Just about when I was a little girl. Living on this lake, in the summer. I loved the water growing up. I wanted to be on it all the time."

"Hmm."

"You never saw it, of course, but my condo in Manhattan had a little balcony off the front of it. One of the reasons I bought it was because when I looked down the street to the west, I could see the Hudson." She rolled onto her back to face him. "It wasn't the pristine blue waters of the lake here, but it was water, and I just liked being able to see it. I would run along the Battery Park City Esplanade, right along the river, just for the smell and feel of it."

"Reminded you of here?"

"For some reason I could look at that water, the ripples and waves, the dark kind of semi-bluish color on a clear day, and I didn't remember the bad things that happened here, only the good."

"Like what?"

She gave a little smile. "Oh, at night, after dinner, the sheriff loved nothing more on a summer night than to either take us out in the boat or relax around the fire pit with a beer or two, maybe a cigar, listening to the Twins game while Jessie and I roasted marshmallows or made s'mores. He loved that, just hanging with his girls, the relaxing peace of it all. And we'd sit there and listen to the game with him."

"I've always thought that for someone who was a competitive soccer player, you had a more than passing interest in baseball."

"Not a lot of girls our age knew that the radio voices of the Twins were Herb Carneal and John Gordon, but Jessie and I did. A couple of times when I was at Boston College, I went with some friends to Fenway Park to watch the Red Sox. I always found myself checking the out-of-town scoreboard for the Twins score."

"It was second nature."

"Yeah, a reflex. You ever do anything like that with your father?"

Braddock thought for a moment. "I loved my parents, they were really good to me, but they didn't have a lot of…"

"Energy."

"Yeah. They were both quiet working-class folks who put in a good day's work and then got home, ate dinner and recuperated."

"You grew up on Long Island. Didn't you ever go to the beach?"

He chuckled. "Honey, Long Island is only an island if you look at it on a map. I grew up in Uniondale, just south of Hofstra University and the Nassau Coliseum. The ocean was many miles away. My parents weren't big on the beach, the water, stuff like that. There were very few vacations that involved travel. We were city, neighborhood New Yorkers."

"So what did you do?"

"My dad wasn't unlike yours. He was a casual Mets fan, but his love was basketball. The Knicks were his thing."

"That's a painful thing to be these days."

"Tell me about it. In his day they were good, though, and he lived and died with them. He liked nothing more than to sit in his recliner, drink a beer and watch and talk basketball."

"Did he play?"

"High school. When I was young, he put a basketball hoop up on the garage for me, showed me how to shoot, got me interested in the game. He liked that I ended up being a pretty good player. He and I had that together, that was our thing. He and Mom got to see me play in some games at LIU before they passed. I know that made them proud."

"What do you think they'd think now?"

"I think they would be highly amused that I now live on a lake in a northern Minnesota vacation mecca working as a sheriff's detective with a hockey-playing son. They'd be thinking, how the heck did *that* happen?" He looked down at her. "They would also see that their city boy was happy living here."

"Yeah, he is." Tori leaned up and kissed him.

"Are you hungry?"

"Yeah, should we make breakfast or go into town?"

"Let's get dressed and go into town. We can go to the office for a bit. We need to figure out how to follow up with Rita. But it's going to be a warm afternoon. We should definitely get out on the lake, maybe go to dinner somewhere along the way. We haven't been to the Channel Stop all summer. We could go there."

"That sounds great."

Braddock got up, took a two-minute shower, dressed quickly and headed down to the kitchen.

Tori jumped into the shower right after him. She dressed casually and made her way downstairs. In the kitchen, she found Braddock staring at his phone. He looked up at her with a blank expression on his face.

"What is it?"

"There's been another murder. Just like the Newmans."

CHAPTER TWELVE

"Symbolism of something"

"We worried this would happen," Tori said with cold fury. "And now it has. I shudder to think what comes next."

"These guys are grinding our gears," Braddock said angrily as he powered down the tunnel-like driveway carved through dense forest.

"I can't see more than ten feet into the woods," Tori noted.

"If you look up, you can't even see the sky," Braddock added.

They emerged from the driveway into a tree-filled open lot to find a single isolated house set on the northwest corner of Upper Goodwin Lake.

"Once word gets out about this, it's going to be a circus," Braddock said as he skidded to a stop, Steak and Eggleston rolling in behind him. Cal was already on scene along with a deputy named Jeff Frewer.

As she stepped down from the Tahoe, Tori took a quick glance around. There was the newish two-story house set to her left and a wide detached garage to her right. Straight ahead was what seemed like a wall of cattails and reeds, although there was a narrow walkway with a dock carved through them and two boat canopies visible perhaps a hundred feet out. From where she stood, she couldn't see another house or cabin.

Braddock walked directly to Cal and Frewer. "What do we have?"

"I haven't gone in," Cal said.

"Why not?"

"I told him not to," Frewer answered. "He knows these folks."

"You do? Who are they?" Braddock asked.

"Todd and Jennifer Strom," Cal said softly. "Todd is a lawyer in Crosslake. Jennifer helped him run his office. They've contributed to my campaigns in the past. They were real good folks."

Frewer pointed toward the garage. "That woman over there, sitting in her car, is Joyce Troy. Her husband, Dennis, who owns the green pickup truck she's parked behind, is lying dead just inside the back door. She found him and... everything else inside."

"Which is what?" Braddock asked.

Frewer shook his head. "You just need to go inside and see for yourself. The husband is on the main level, the wife is upstairs in the shower. I turned off the water and got the heck out of there."

"Steak." Braddock tipped his head toward Joyce Troy.

"On it," Steak replied, gesturing to Eggleston. "Come on, partner."

Tori and Braddock pulled on rubber gloves as they walked to the door to the side of the house. Braddock peeked in the side kitchen window before he pushed the door with the outside of his left foot and let it slowly glide open.

A man was lying dead on the floor ten feet inside the door, wedged between the center island and the stove and refrigerator to the left. He'd been shot twice in the chest and once in the forehead. The body lay at a forty-five-degree angle, the man's left arm awkwardly jammed in the gap between the bottom of the lower kitchen cabinet and the floor, his right arm serving as an unintentional barrier to contain a pool of his own blood. A gray couch pillow lay on the floor, a bullet hole through it.

"Oh my," Tori murmured.

They both slipped covers on their shoes before stepping inside.

Tori immediately noted the security system touch panel by the door. "Why didn't this go off?"

"We'll have to check that," Braddock replied as he moved around the kitchen island. Tori followed him further inside the house.

"Jeez," Braddock sighed. "My… Whoa."

Todd Strom was leaning back against one of the two ornate white pillars that framed the grand entrance from the front of the house to the family room. His head was slumped to the right and his arms were wrapped around behind the pillar. His shirt had been torn open and his torso exposed. They could see the massive vertical gash starting just above his belt line, slicing up through his abdomen and chest.

"My God, they gutted him," Tori said.

"Did they use a knife or a frickin' Sawzall?" Braddock looked around the room. "It appears they took the knife with them but stopped to wipe it clean before they left," he noted, pointing to a green and blue checked kitchen rag lying next to a chair that had been turned toward Strom's body. "There are a few blood drops on the floor from when he walked over here to sit down."

"The killer just sat in that chair and cleaned his knife like it was no big thing while the victim bled out." Tori shook her head in horror.

Braddock tilted his head toward the stairs and followed Tori up, the two of them stepping carefully, even with the covers on their shoes, avoiding using the handrail.

At the landing for the second floor, they entered the spacious master bedroom. The bathroom was inside on the right, reached through a walk-through closet.

A naked Jennifer Strom was lying sideways along the tiled floor of the shower. Water still dripped intermittently from the shower head. Braddock pulled the glass door fully open, then leaned inside. It was clear that Jennifer Strom had been strangled much like Heidi Newman.

"They strangle the woman and place her in the shower," Tori murmured, "but vary it for the husband: shot, throat cut, gutted. Why? I don't get that. Why that variation?"

Braddock shrugged. "Symbolism of something. What do you make of the fact that she's not propped up, but lying on the floor? Seems careless on their part."

"Dennis Troy. I'm thinking they weren't finished when he got here."

"That's a possibility. Let's get out of here and leave this for the forensic team."

Back down on the main level, Braddock went to the kitchen, closed the side door and directed Cal, Steak and Eggleston to meet them on the deck along the front of the house.

"What do you have?" Tori asked Steak as she stepped outside.

"Dennis Troy and his wife have a summer cabin over on Daggett Lake near Crosslake. They've been friends with the Stroms for years. They had them over last night. The Stroms left their house around ten thirty, ten forty-five to come home."

"And how is it Dennis ended up here?"

"Mrs. Troy says they'd arranged to get together today as well. Todd and Dennis were going to go fishing early this morning, Joyce was coming at nine for brunch, and then the plan was to be out on the pontoon."

Tori turned and looked out to the dock carved through the reeds. She could make out the tops of two dark green boat lift canopy covers at the far end. "What time did Mrs. Troy say her husband left this morning?"

"She said it was like four a.m. Early. They were planning to be on the water before sun-up."

Tori and Braddock shared a look, the two of them suddenly envisioning what had happened inside the house and how Mr. Troy had been murdered.

"What's next, boss?" Steak asked as two SUVs from the BCA arrived and parked, the medical examiner pulling in behind them.

"Let's get Joyce Troy out of here and home."

"I'll see to that," Cal said.

"How about us?" Steak asked, nodding to Eggs.

"Let's work out how the killers got here. Get all the deputies to help."

"On it," Steak replied.

Tori and Braddock stepped back inside the house.

"What the hell is going on?" Ann Jennison said.

"We had the Newman autopsies, and now three more," Doc Renfrow moaned.

"Assume that what happened at the Newmans' is connected to this," Braddock instructed. "Operate on that basis."

Jennison and Renfrow nodded and went to work.

Tori examined the living room while Braddock peeked out through the curtains to check on the status of the search. He saw deputies and patrol officers spreading out, examining the property's edge. He looked back to Tori, her arms folded, deep in thought.

"What are you thinking?" Braddock had his own impressions.

"Dennis Troy gets here at four thirty a.m. The killers see his headlights approaching the house."

"They're not out yet, though, and now they can't get out," Braddock noted.

Tori nodded. "They had to improvise."

"So they lay in wait. The door is unlocked, the security system is off. Dennis Troy comes into the house, looking for Todd. He gets inside just far enough. I'd bet with the lights off, the shooter concealed himself behind that chair that's turned toward Todd Strom. As soon as he has a clear shot, boom, boom. It's only ten or fifteen feet."

"The first two shots to the chest put him down," Tori noted, having stepped back toward the kitchen. "The third one to the forehead is through the pillow and finishes him off execution-style." The crime scene investigator had placed a number tent next to the pillow.

Braddock took cover behind the chair for a moment, his gun out, playing out the shot. He turned and looked behind him at the large faux-brick fireplace.

"Do you have any ejected shells over there?" he asked Jennison.

She shook her head. "I was looking, since the pillow was used to cover his face. He might have grabbed them. You?"

"Negative," Braddock replied as he carefully peered around for a spent casing. It would have likely ejected out onto the light gray carpet and would have been easily visible. "They cleaned up the brass, but I bet they didn't stay much longer than it took to do that."

"They have a gun and use it on Dennis Troy. Why not use it on Strom? Why not use it on Newman?" Tori asked. "It must be that the plan is to kill with the knife. A knife is more…"

"Personal," Braddock said. "Up close and personal. It's more… gratifying to the killer."

"Whereas the gun is more distant, impersonal."

"Dennis Troy was just an inconvenience to coldly dispense with. Todd Strom was the target and he had to pay. He had to be gutted."

"Because our killers were gutted," Tori speculated. "Gutted by what? The loss of Hugh Barr?"

"Possibly," Braddock said. "But if it's all related, why wait twenty-four years? Other than…"

"That Barr was dying," Tori replied. "That's probably part of it, but…" She shook her head. "It feels like there's something more going on here."

"It could be they've been killing all along but not in this way," Braddock mused.

"Maybe."

"That's all supposition on our part. We need to deal with this right now and get back to that later."

Tori looked out the window by the front door, seeing the driveway, but also the woods surrounding the property. She stepped back out onto the patio and observed the property line. She could see Steak slowly walking along the edge, and Eggleston further in the distance. For the first time, she noticed that the Stroms had framed their plot with a five-foot-wide strip of pine straw containing plantings of a variety of shade bushes and plants. The straw went right to the thick treeline. The woods themselves were dense with tangled underbrush. She walked to the other end of the deck and observed the south side of the property. The strip of pine straw and plantings ran along that side as well. Taking a long look around, she realized the Stroms really must have wanted their privacy.

Braddock too was analyzing the surroundings. "The woods are more like prison walls."

"Yeah, except in this case it serves to keep people out," Tori replied. It had her thinking of something else, which was how the killers had surveilled the Stroms. They'd surveilled the Newmans. It seemed logical to assume they would have done the same here. But *how* would they have done it?

An hour later, the entire property had been thoroughly searched. "We got nothing," Steak said.

Jennison stepped out of the house along with Doc Renfrow.

"What do you have?" Braddock asked her.

"Right now, not much. No signs of forced entry. No discernible footprints anywhere in the house. We're dusting for fingerprints, but these guys were wearing gloves. Mr. Strom also has significant bruising on his upper back and shoulders. It appears he was hit several times from behind. I'm guessing it knocked him out, because underneath his body was a smelling salt packet."

"They had to wake him," Tori said.

"Yes."

"And Mrs. Strom?"

"The living room couch was used like the one at the Newman house. Which is why we're taking it away with us," Jennison said. "It's wrapped. We'll be removing it shortly."

"Mr. Troy's cause of death is obvious," Dr. Renfrow said. "If I find anything useful on him, I'll get it to Ann for analysis."

Braddock nodded. "Two multiple homicides in a week. You both know things are going to blow up. We need something to work with."

"I hear you, Will."

"Doc is ready to remove the bodies, but we still have some work to do," Jennison said. "We'll be here a while yet."

"Anything back from what you processed at the Newmans'?"

"The one outstanding matter is those chewing tobacco pouches found out in the woods. They've been sent for DNA testing, but as I mentioned, with the backlog it could be some time before we get results."

"Given what we're now faced with here, we might be able to jump the line," Braddock said, and made a mental note to discuss that with Cal. A call to the commandant of the BCA to make the test a top priority could be in order. He turned to Renfrow. "What about you, Doc?"

"Cause of death for Mrs. Strom was strangulation. There are threads still in the wounds around her throat. I will say that based on what I saw on Mrs. Newman and now Mrs. Strom, whoever is strangling the women is doing it with tremendous force."

"A big guy?"

"A really strong one, for sure."

"Time of death?"

"Between three and four a.m."

Braddock looked to Tori. "And Mrs. Troy said the Stroms left her place around ten thirty, right?"

"Yes."

"They get home at eleven p.m., give or take. These guys jump them, and for over three hours, they rape Mrs. Strom, making her husband watch, then they probably make him watch them strangle her. And once all that is done, they try to cut him vertically in half." He shook his head slowly in disgust. "These guys are goddam animals."

Jennison and Renfrow both nodded their understanding. "We'll do everything we can to find you something, Will," Renfrow said, and the two of them turned away.

"Just think, Mrs. Troy comes over here expecting brunch and a nice afternoon pontoon ride around the lake on a beautiful day, maybe followed by a cocktail or two," Braddock muttered. "Instead, she finds her husband and their two friends massacred."

Tori turned and gazed out across the reeds. "I can't really see the lake from here."

"It's out there. It's one of three on the chain. There's a channel to the south that hooks North Goodwin into Middle, and then further down, South Goodwin."

"Odd to put such a nice house back here."

Braddock shrugged. "This stretch of land was probably much less expensive."

Tori walked into the front yard and followed the flagstone path out to the start of the dock. The dock itself was over one hundred feet long, running through a tunnel carved into the thick reeds. The boat lifts she'd spotted earlier were set to the right, one for the pontoon and the other for a fishing boat. What she hadn't seen earlier was the octagonal seating area with four Adirondack chairs similar to those Braddock had on the end of his dock.

"Not many cabins up on this end of the lake," he said, gazing around.

"I'm still wondering how the killers got to the house," Tori said as she looked from the water to the house and then back out to the water.

"What are you thinking?" Braddock asked.

She stepped over to the left side of the dock, standing between the Adirondack chairs and the edge. From here, she could only see the second story and the peak of the roof. She examined the dock itself. Braddock's dock had post lights that he could turn on from the house. Here, she saw some reflectors but no lights of any kind.

She peered over the edge. A boat would sit low in the water here. In the dark, it wouldn't be visible at all from the house.

Braddock picked up on her train of thought. "You're thinking they came in a boat?"

"We've got no sign they came through the woods. But look around. The nearest cabin or house is a mile away at least, as best I can tell. You could park your boat here on the side of the dock. When the Stroms arrived home, there is no way they'd have seen it. And people wouldn't look twice at two men in a fishing boat out at night in the middle of summer."

Braddock nodded along in agreement.

"They probably scouted the lake enough to know that it would be unlikely anyone would be out fishing at four or four thirty in the morning when they left the house and snuck away."

"And there are public boat launches on both Middle and South Goodwin Lakes," Braddock added as he looked at his phone. "The one on South Goodwin is a big one. The one on Middle is smaller, at the end of a long road. I'd bet they used that one."

"Any chance there would be a surveillance camera there?"

Braddock shook his head. "We'll go look, but I'd be surprised if there was one at either of them. But if Dennis Troy got here at four thirty, that means they will have got back to the boat launch around five. Someone could have seen them pulling their boat out then. Long shot, but I'll make a note to have someone go around and ask some questions."

They both turned and looked back at the last of the bodies being stretchered out of the house.

"Next question," Braddock said. "They arrive by boat. How do they get in the house? How do they avoid the security system?"

"The Stroms left the Troys and drove back here. They get back, park in the… garage."

They made a beeline for the garage. The main door was closed. The small side door was locked, although it was a deadbolt that could be picked. Braddock went to the house and found the button for the garage door opener. Inside, they immediately saw the reddish-brown spots on the floor next to the parked Lincoln Navigator. "They wait in here for them to come home," he said. "When Todd gets out of the truck, they hit him."

"Tie them up in here, walk them to the house," Tori added. "Put a gun to one of their heads to turn off the security system."

Braddock went back to the house and told Jennison what they had found. The garage needed to be processed.

"Okay, we know what happened here. We know what happened at the Newmans'. The question still remains…"

"Why," Tori said.

"This isn't random. These people were killed for a reason, and there is some sort of connection to the Bauman case. It all ties back to that somehow."

"What do we do next?"

"Get back to the government center. We have work to do."

CHAPTER THIRTEEN

"I assume for the usual amount?"

"You can make the Finnish flag part of it?"

"You bet, no sweat," D replied with a nod. "It'll be painted and have a bit of carve in it." He gestured to a picture behind the counter. "It'll look a little like the Irish one, or the English one, or Swedish. You get the idea."

"I like that roughish look to it."

"Yeah, it gives it a little texture that makes for a look of quality."

"It sure does. I'll take one."

"Great. Let's get it written up."

He worked with the customer for another five minutes, finishing the order, running the credit card for payment, chit-chatting through the entire process.

"When will it be ready?"

"Three weeks," D replied, and then extended his hand. "Thank you for your business. I do appreciate it."

The order complete, he looked over to the convenience counter and saw his two clerks taking care of customers. Another employee was helping someone in the recreation section. His store manager, Ryan, approached with some papers to be signed. "This is for the soda delivery."

"Very good," D said. "Everything else okay around here?"

"Just a typical Saturday."

D trudged up the steps to his office, sat down behind his desk and yawned.

It had been a sleepy Saturday just like this nearly a year ago when Hugh's prison buddy had showed up at the service desk for the wooden signs. D had had his eye on the man because he'd been lingering around the store, occasionally looking in his direction but not coming over. After about fifteen minutes, he finally did.

"Are you D?"

"Yes."

The man took another quick look around before whispering, "I have a message from your friend down in Stillwater. You know the one I'm talking about?"

D froze for a moment and then made his own discreet scan of the store. "Follow me."

He led the man up a set of stairs to his second-floor office. He closed the door. "And you are?"

"A friend of your friend."

"I see. How long have you been out?"

"A couple of weeks."

"What were you in for?"

"Let's just say I did some thieving and fencing."

"I see. How is our mutual friend doing?"

"He has cancer."

D sighed and shook his head. "How bad?"

"Terminal."

"Is there anything they can do for him?"

"No. It's inoperable. It's killing him, but very slowly. He's still able to live in his cell and is getting some treatment for the pain, but eventually he'll end up at the hospital. He thinks he has maybe a year left. But listen, there is something you need to know."

Hugh's friend had a story to tell about something he'd learned while he was the subject of an investigation in Wisconsin. "Our mutual friend's lawyer never knew about it. If he had…"

"He could have been acquitted."

"That's right," the man said. "From what I understand, the case against him was circumstantial to begin with. With this information, who knows…"

"Did the police and prosecutor know about this evidence?"

The man nodded. "I had a friend of a friend check." He pulled out an envelope from his back pocket and handed it over. "It's all in there. And there's one more thing…"

The note was in Hugh's distinctive handwriting. It was short and to the point.

D, thanks for sending help over the years. I don't have much time left now. My friend has told you what he knows about my case. You owe me. You know what to do. H.

That was the moment that had set everything off. D thought about it now as he watched the steady rhythm of a warm Saturday afternoon purr along. There were sixteen gas pumps below. It would be rare on a Saturday that at least half of them weren't occupied at all times, such was his prime location and the flowing traffic on State Highway 10.

He evaluated the receipts from last evening and saw that everything balanced out. He watched like a hawk with cameras everywhere inside the store. He'd learned the need for that the hard way. Four years ago, the books were balancing but he had a suspicion they weren't quite right. The income was often lighter than it should have been given the volume of business. Something was off, but he couldn't find it. He'd finally called Slim in to review the books.

An accounting savant, Slim found the pattern after a couple of nights and some good whiskey. Someone was changing the prices and bar codes on certain items in the recreation section. Items like kneeboards, water skis, kayaks and paddleboards. Not so much that it would look odd when the product was rung up, but sufficient to make a difference if done often enough.

"But it's not on all the kayaks," Slim pointed out. "You see on this day. You sold two kayaks at the proper price. This third one is rung up at a different price. Same with this paddleboard. You sold four that day, three at the proper price and then this one. Now you want the kicker?"

"What's that?"

"I found twenty-two instances of this over about four months," Slim said. "And just two credit cards used for it. So I think you have an employee working with two others. He gives the sign to come in and make the purchase. They're reselling these items and pocketing the profit. And I bet these guys are running this scam other places. No way it's just you."

D figured out the next day which employee it was. However, the guy must have realized he'd been discovered. He didn't show for his next scheduled shift, and despite his efforts, D couldn't track him down.

D was not someone to ever forgive and forget. With the help of a government employee with access to certain data, he managed to track his former employee and his accomplices to northern Wisconsin, where they were running the same scam. There he put an end to it. The employee and his partners in crime would not be heard from again.

That contact would now come in handy once again. D reached for his Rolodex and flipped to a card that read *DMV*. From his office safe he took out a prepaid cell phone and placed the call.

"I need a favor."

"Yeah?"

"I need you to run a plate number."

"I assume for the usual amount?"

"Yes." D recited the number.

"Give me three hours."

That call complete, D's office phone rang. He had another customer inquiring about a carved sign. "I'll be right down."

Two hours later, the traffic in the store and at the pumps was waning, as it often did by mid-afternoon on a Saturday. D told an employee he would be back in an hour and left out the back of the store, where he got into his pickup truck.

Was anyone watching?

He started the truck and headed off. The drive east required one stop at the four-way intersection dissecting the town. As he slowed, he took note of the vehicles in his rear-view. He detected nothing of concern. He was largely on his own on the highway when he saw the towering sign on the south side for his destination: Ruthie's House.

The parking lot contained only a handful of cars at 3:30 p.m., at least half of which likely belonged to employees. Inside the restaurant, he went to his usual seat at the end of the lunch counter and reached for the menu.

He peered around at the now sparsely populated restaurant. It wouldn't have been that way an hour ago. Ruthie's was known far and wide. On a summer weekend, the restaurant always did a brisk late breakfast and early lunch business with the weekenders at their cabins. During the week, it was consistently full of locals. The food was that good.

D tended to stay away when it was crowded. And he liked eating in the middle of the afternoon, long after the lunch rush and before the dinner crowd.

Ruthie came out the kitchen door to his right. When she saw him, she nodded slightly and picked up the coffee pot.

"Hello."

"Ruthie."

She filled a cup while he perused the menu. "Are you going to the planning commission meeting next week?" she asked. "They're talking about frontage road improvements."

"Well, I am on the commission," D said pleasantly. "Have you a concern you wish to express?"

"I'd like to see the potholes and ruts addressed. I've had a few complaints from customers."

He'd had to avoid a couple of holes himself when he'd driven in today. "I've seen the problem first-hand. I'll make sure we get it on the agenda," he promised. "Is he still here?"

"Yes. I'll send him out in a bit. He didn't finish the books last night."

D was a large man. His eyes were small and appeared all pupil as they were set deep under his brow. His round pumpkin-sized head sat atop a sturdy six-foot-one body. He had unnaturally thick arms and strong legs, muscles he'd developed long ago as a heavyweight wrestler. While the years had added an extra pound or two, he remained a physically imposing presence. He made a point of trying to soften that appearance with an amiable personality, a helpful neighborly attitude, and by wearing stylish dark-rimmed glasses to go with his button-down shirts and tailored slacks. Some days he wore a tie, and some days he didn't, but he always dressed nicely and required his employees to wear store logo apparel with clean pants and shoes.

A server approached and took his order for bacon cheeseburger, fries and a chocolate malt. She topped off his coffee. As she poured, a man sat down next to D and asked, "Can I get a to-go coffee and one of the pre-made turkey and ham sandwiches."

"Sure can. Be right back."

The waitress scurried off to fill the order. With his left hand the man slid a piece of paper across to D, who slid it the rest of the way toward his plate before pulling an envelope out of his pant pocket and handing it to the man under the counter. The waitress returned with the coffee and sandwich already in a white bag. The man paid with cash and left.

With the restaurant quiet, D sipped his coffee and let his eyes drift up to the flat-screen television mounted high in the corner. It was tuned to the local station, which was televising a baseball game. After a few minutes, the game was interrupted by a news update.

The reporter stood in front of the Shepard County Government Center. Footage played of Sheriff Cal Lund providing an investigative briefing to the press. The remote was sitting on the counter, and D turned up the volume.

Slim pushed his way through the door from the kitchen area and glanced up at the screen, a look of concern on his face. The news break was quick, and then the baseball game resumed. D reduced the volume, then briefly scanned the restaurant, but nobody was near enough to hear them.

"You get the books done?" he asked before taking a drink of his coffee.

"Very funny," Slim answered. "I just hope we got away clean. The boat launch…"

"I'm on it," D replied, tapping at the slip of paper on the counter.

CHAPTER FOURTEEN

"Creative thinking"

Braddock had assumed Cal would call in reinforcements after what had happened at the Strom place. With two multiple homicides that were clearly connected, perhaps the investigative division of the BCA would be asked to assist. The group that assembled in the conference room, however, consisted only of Braddock, Tori, Steak, Eggs, Cal and two other department investigators.

"We're it?" Steak asked, eyebrows raised.

"Yes," Cal answered curtly. "This shit is happening in our county. We'll clean up our own mess, is that understood?"

"Cal—" Braddock started.

"Is that understood, Detective Braddock?" Cal turned angrily to his chief detective.

"Yes, sir."

"You are all investigators. Investigate. We have two multiple homicides that are clearly connected. I've been a skeptic, but maybe they do tie to the old Bauman case. Figure out who is doing it and get them in our cages before they kill again. We need to end this now."

"Cal, come on—"

"You're the FBI investigative hotshot, Victoria," the sheriff barked back. "We're paying you enough. Show me something. Anything."

Tori had never heard Cal speak to his troops this way. She looked at Braddock with a raised eyebrow, as if to say, what the hell?

Braddock plowed ahead. "You want quicker results, pressure the BCA to put any DNA testing Doc Renfrow or Jennison have to the front of the line. A hit there could fast-forward this thing."

"I'll do that. I'll start making calls now."

"We're going to need more boots on the ground, Cal. There's a lot of people we need to be talking to."

"Pull in any uniformed sheriff's deputy you need and put them in plain clothes. All overtime is approved. Don't even ask, just do it."

"And you're sure you don't want to think about getting investigative agents from the BCA to help?" Braddock asked, knowing they would be better qualified than deputies.

"Is there an echo in here? I thought I made myself clear, Chief Detective," Cal growled. "I don't need a bunch of extra people from another agency sticking their noses in. Keep this in house and get it done."

His phone started ringing; he read the display and left the room.

"What the hell was that all about?" Eggleston said. "I've never seen him do that to anyone."

Braddock had a wry smile on his face. "That was like a flashback. My lieu talked to me like that at least once a week when I was NYPD."

"Still…"

"Guys, Cal is stressed. And you heard the man, he now agrees that this is at least possibly connected back to the Bauman case. The question is how. Let's get to work."

Tori frowned. Braddock, ever loyal, was covering for his boss and shrugging it off, but she thought there was something else to the exchange beyond just stress.

She left the conference room and walked down the hallway to Cal's office. "Hey, what gives? That wasn't like you?"

"It is when I feel like we're not getting the job done," Cal retorted, leaning against his desk with his arms folded.

Cal was usually unflappable, a calm eye in the storm. Even when Tori was a kid, he was always cool and easy-going, which often offset her father's intensity. Not now. He looked anxious and twitchy. "Is there anything I need to know?" she asked.

"No."

"Barr said my dad cheated. Did he?"

"Hugh Barr killed the Baumans, Victoria. What I will say is I think you and Braddock could be right: there is some tie between what is happening now and what happened back then. So follow your instincts and pursue it. Now I have some calls to make, starting with the BCA on those tobacco pouches."

As Tori walked back into the conference room, Eggleston was saying, "It's not like this happened in Manchester Bay. Both multiples took place well out of town."

"Manchester Bay is synonymous with Shepard County," Braddock said. "The mayor, county board, business owners, bankers—the usual collection of bed-wetters—are demanding results. Murder isn't good for business in vacationland in summertime. They're all fretting the loss of dollars like the mayor in *Jaws*. We're on the spot here. And Cal senses what I feel."

"Which is?" Steak said.

"We're way behind. He's wondering what's coming next."

"Are we, though?" Tori asked.

"Are we what?"

"Behind. These cases are all connected. It also tells us that our killers are close. They must be to pull this off." She looked to Braddock. "I just had a little chat with Cal, and he's come around to our thinking that there may be a connection to Barr."

"We just have to figure out what that connection is," Braddock said. "And we don't have a moment to waste. Newmans, Stroms and Baumans. What's the link? We have to find it, because I get the sense these guys aren't done yet. They're going to keep going."

On the conference room table there were five boxes marked *Bauman*. To that they could add what they had from the two recent killings. Braddock looked to Eggleston and the other investigators. "I've already texted three deputies to come in. That'll make six of you. Two-person teams. We need to start talking to people connected with the Newmans and Stroms and see how they intersect. Go back on all the people we've already talked to and add the Stroms' friends, families, acquaintances to the list. Eggs, you know what to do. You're running that."

"On it, boss," Eggleston answered, and she and the other investigators left the conference room.

Braddock looked at Tori and Steak. "Let's get to work."

*

Cal closed the door to his office. Behind his desk he twisted the window blinds down before he sat in his chair and shut his eyes.

His phone rang. Seeing the incoming call number, he answered with no preamble. "I got a nervous feeling when I saw the Newman murder scene, but you said it wasn't connected."

"I didn't think it was."

"Well how about now?" he roared. He closed his eyes and pinched the bridge of his nose. "It's all coming back on us, what you, Jim and I did. I thought after all these years we'd ducked it, but… We shouldn't have done it. We shouldn't have…"

"And then what? Barr possibly walks? Did you want him to keep killing? If he walked, he was going to keep going. If not here, somewhere else. He was a killer."

Cal sighed. "I know, I know… I always dreaded what the fallout could be. But this? My God, it's beyond comprehension."

"We can still contain it. *You* can still contain it."

"Is there anyone else involved that I need to know about? I mean, shit, Pen. We should have had people watching Todd and Jennifer. Their blood is on our hands."

"We couldn't have seen this coming. If I'd had any idea it was a possibility…" Pen's voice trailed off. "What are you doing for now?"

"I'm keeping it in house."

"How long can you do that for?"

"It all depends."

"On what?"

"On what happens next," Cal said. "In the meantime, I'd load your shotgun. I know I've loaded mine."

*

Fortified by takeout Chinese and then, later, pizza, the three of them sifted through the material for the Bauman case, along with everything they knew thus far on the Newman and Strom killings.

"What do we see?" Braddock asked, standing at the whiteboard, black marker at the ready.

"Two killers," Tori said. "They plan meticulously, despite the appearance of Cara at the Newmans' and Dennis Troy at the Stroms'."

"They weren't ready when Cara came home, but they were sure ready for Troy," Steak said.

"They were," Tori agreed. "They knew which night they could get into the Newmans' house and lie in wait. Somehow they knew the Stroms would be out last night. They took them in the garage because the house had a security system. We also think they approached the Stroms' place by boat. We need to check the public boat launches."

"I can tell you there are no surveillance cameras at the launches," Steak said. He checked his watch. "It's nearly eleven. We should get someone to the launches in the morning. If someone was going out this morning around five, they might go tomorrow morning too. Fishermen are creatures of habit. They like to go to their favorite spots."

Braddock took out his phone and called Eggleston to arrange for someone from her team to go to the launches in the morning.

"We're assuming Strom and Newman are connected to Bauman, but what if killing with a knife as opposed to a gun is a way of saying Barr *didn't* kill the Baumans twenty-four years ago?" Steak posited.

"If he was innocent, he would have said he was innocent," Tori said. "Barr killed the Baumans."

"He was convicted of it," Steak clarified. "Doesn't mean he did it."

Tori wasn't having it. "He did it. And he knew who killed the Newmans and the Stroms."

"So you say, but you're basing that on what? Your intuition?"

"I saw him. I met the man. I spoke to him. And not only am I certain he knew the killers, I'm starting to think he unleashed them to go on a spree because he was about to die."

"I do get your point," Braddock said to Steak. "That's a twist I hadn't thought of, and we need to see this case from every possible angle. However, Barr definitely killed the Baumans, or at least he was certainly a big part of it. The links found at the scene and his missing bracelet, not to mention not saying a word for twenty-four years, make the sale on that for me. If he didn't do it, he'd have been proclaiming his innocence."

"That there were two other killers working with Barr?" Steak asked. "Where's the evidence for that?"

"What's happening now," Tori asserted. "These killers are like cicadas, except they hid for twenty-four years, not seventeen."

"I get the skepticism, keep it up," Braddock said to Steak. "We need to question everything. What makes me scratch my head as to Barr's silence is that the case against him was far from ironclad. It was totally circumstantial. I get not testifying at trial. But not to talk to your lawyer? Not to put up a defense? It's like he took the life sentence lying down."

"Maybe it's because he screwed up," Tori said. "He went back to the Baumans', was seen by the neighbor, and still ended up with two of Julie Bauman's hairs in his truck. It was his fault."

"Still, why take the hit for all of it?" Steak asked.

Braddock pulled out a file marked *Barr Employment*. "The only real insight I've seen in all the documentation in these boxes is his work record. His staff reviews reveal a high-performing employee. And seemingly honest. He uncovered someone who was skimming dollars off Medicare billings and turned them in, even after the person offered him a taste of the scam. He wouldn't go for it."

"I read that as well," Tori said. "There was also an instance where he made an accounting error that cost the hospital thousands of dollars. He could have tried passing the buck—others missed the error as well—but he owned it. He accepted accountability for it."

"You're saying Barr was… honest," Steak said, fulfilling his role as skeptic. "An honest killer? Really?"

"In a way, why not. Look, I get where you're going," Tori said. "Most killers, if they could throw someone else under the bus to lessen their time, they'd do it in a heartbeat. You solve cases on the backs of people like that. But what if Barr wasn't one of those people? He screwed up, but he wasn't taking anyone else down with him. He wasn't taking down his partners or friends."

"What friends, though?" Steak asked. "I can't find anyone outside of employees at the hospital and a couple of guys from college who even admitted to knowing him, let alone any actual friends."

"Doesn't mean they don't exist," Tori replied. "Perhaps the only person who could tell you who his friends were was him, and he didn't. If I were to profile a bit… Barr was an accountant. They are disciplined, organized, rules-based. There is no gray in accounting; it's numbers, black and white. And he lived it. He found someone skimming and he turned them in. He was honorable in a sense."

"Oh yeah, real principled."

"I'm just trying to get in his head a little. Barr was clearly someone who operated on some level with a set of rules. He was honest in his job. He demanded it of others. He walked the walk. For someone like him, why wouldn't his principles, his rules, still apply to what happened at the Baumans'? He screwed up with the bracelet. In his mind, it was his mistake; he owned it, he took the fall for it."

"He was going to prison for life if convicted, or he walks if Pen doesn't convince the jury of his guilt," Braddock said. "Why take anybody else with him?"

"Say you're right, where does that get us?" Steak said. "Understanding him doesn't tell us where to find these guys who are out there killing people."

"What it tells us is we have to find another way," Braddock said. He walked back to the whiteboard. "Assignments. Eggs is already running the tracking-down of family, friends, co-workers, witnesses on the Newman and Strom cases. Plus she'll get someone to the boat launches. That's covered. Steak, let's start the paper chase on the Stroms, add it to what we've started on the Newmans, merge in the Baumans. Financials, personal records, histories, the usual drill. Who are these people, what do they do, and is there any connection between them?"

"I got it. Venn diagram, where does everybody intersect. What are you two up to?"

"Creative thinking," Braddock replied.

"Creative thinking?" Tori asked.

"Yeah. I can't help but think that we're missing something here."

"Something that explains all this?" Steak asked.

"Yes. The Newmans and Stroms weren't random; they were hunted. Why? And what did they have to do with the Baumans? What ties it all together? That's what Tori and I are going to try and figure out."

CHAPTER FIFTEEN

"But I've learned that you can learn to live with it
without reliving it"

Wednesday morning. With the 5:45 alarm, Tori rolled out of bed and said, "I'm going for a run."

"Well," Braddock said, sitting up, rubbing his eyes, "I'm going for a swim."

"It's not a contest, you know."

"Like hell it ain't," he said with a laugh. "I can't let myself end up looking like a schlepp next to you."

"Ah, so I'm motivating you."

"Hell, yes, but only in a good way." He patted his flat stomach.

Ninety minutes later, Braddock handed Tori a coffee tumbler and they were out the back door and heading to the office.

"Will today be the day?" Tori said whimsically as Braddock drove down the road.

"Man, we need something to break, if only to get Cal off my back. He's been relentless."

"I'm telling you," Tori insisted, "something is up with him beyond just the stress of this thing. He's not right."

"Let me know when you figure out what it is."

It had now been an excruciating five days since the Stroms were murdered. Twelve days since the Newmans. The pressure was mounting.

While there wasn't much local media in Manchester Bay, just a small regional television station, the Minneapolis/St. Paul media was now interested in the story and was poking around, along with the *Star Tribune*, the state's biggest newspaper.

Cal was ever present, prodding and pushing and downright bearish, loudly lighting up Braddock for a lack of progress.

They'd worked feverishly the past four days, yet still no clear picture had emerged. They'd had an investigative team meeting last night, after Cal had ripped Braddock a new one loud enough for everyone to hear.

"Guys, do we have anything?" Braddock pleaded. "Or one of you is going to have to face Cal next time."

The BCA forensics unit had started drawing some conclusions. The truck tire molds from the Newmans' were from a tire commonly found on factory-issued Dodge Ram pickup trucks sold in the last three years. The problem was that Dodge Ram pickups were plentiful, particularly in out-state Minnesota. Ownership was in the several thousands.

"And that's assuming our killers' truck is registered in Minnesota," Steak said. "While likely, since we're smack-dab in the middle of the state, it's not guaranteed. And while Dodge may use those tires for their newer trucks, the model isn't so special or limited that someone else couldn't put them on their truck as well, so…"

"The kind of truck in and of itself isn't enough to get us there," Braddock said. "We need at least another variable, if not two or three."

One possible variable was boat ownership. Steak ran a search for Minnesota-registered newer Dodge pickups, and boat owners. "We're still in the many thousands," he said. "Pickup trucks and boats around here go together like beer and wings."

"Criminal records, then?" Tori had suggested.

"Still a big list," Steak said after he ran the search. "In Minnesota alone, I get over three thousand hits."

"How about within a hundred miles of Manchester Bay?"

"I'll try it," Steak said as she looked over his shoulder. "Close to two thousand."

It was still a very large list to work from.

Ballistics were not helpful. The slugs pulled from Dennis Troy did not provide a match to Jerry Bauman or any other shootings. "Small-caliber. Common for a nine-millimeter," Braddock muttered.

"Minnesota doesn't require gun registration, though," Tori said.

"But we do require a permit to carry," Braddock noted.

"Guaranteed I run *that* search, we're back into the many, many thousands," Steak sighed. "Pickup truck, fishing boat, gun. If you included Ford trucks, I'm on the list myself. It's like the official Minnesota outfit, as long as you add the flannel shirt and shitkickers."

"We do have a size thirteen hiking boot print and nine-and-a-half shoe print," Tori noted. They also had a brand they could possibly match up if they found something to match to.

The black and red strands found in the wounds around the necks of Heidi Newman and Jennifer Strom were from a nylon rope, most likely the type used for ski, surfing or tubing tow ropes. The BCA was trying to identify the specific manufacturer, but even if they could, ropes of that kind were sold at thousands of locations in Minnesota, from large retailers, recreational outfitters, boat and RV dealers down to small mom-and-pop gas stations and convenience stores.

The key item they were still awaiting results on was the tobacco pouches discovered at the site the killers had observed the Newmans from.

"There was no other DNA evidence collected from the Bauman killings beyond that for Hugh Barr, and Julie Bauman's hairs in Barr's truck," Braddock noted. "There's no match to anything else anywhere."

After business hours last night, Braddock had had everyone into his office with the door closed for a drink. It did not have the intended bonding and relaxing effect. They were all tired, and frustrated and sniping.

"This is all connected," Braddock said. "Why the time gap? Is it just because Barr is now dead? Or is there more to it?"

"There is one possibility," Tori suggested wearily. "Barr's partners were inactive because they were in prison too."

"I could buy that. It would be a logical explanation," Braddock agreed.

"Or maybe they were active elsewhere, in a different way," Eggleston posited.

"In other words, they only waited twenty-four years to kill *here* again?" Tori said as she ripped off a page of random scribbles from a legal pad. She balled it up and threw it angrily at the wastebasket. "I'm just spitballing and trying to make some sense of what we have. I'm not succeeding."

"A witness sure would help," Braddock moaned. The only witness was Cara Newman, who'd confirmed there were two killers and given general descriptions of them, but those descriptions had not yielded any investigative momentum.

"How about trying Rita Ellis again?" Steak asked.

"Maybe," Braddock said. "With the Stroms' murder that might be worth pursuing, although given her response, I think we need some sort of leverage to break through."

"Leverage?" Eggleston asked.

"Something to make her look at all this a little differently," Tori said. "When we went out there, she could only see it in the context of her and her son. We need something to break through that."

"Like what?" Steak asked.

"I don't know," she answered with a headshake.

Steak's Venn diagram project had not yielded anything illuminating either.

"I have found zero evidence that the Newmans and Stroms ever crossed paths in any meaningful way," he said. "The only minor connection I've seen is that Dan Newman and Todd Strom both worked for Shepard County way back when. Newman was in IT and Strom worked in the county attorney's office, but both tenures were over twenty years ago. Newman was with the county for a little under three years and Strom for a shade over two. They did briefly overlap, so I suppose it was possible they had some interactions back then, but I've seen no documented record of that. The IT department is buried down in the basement of the building and always has been, and the county attorney's office is up on the third floor."

"We only see IT when there's a problem," Eggleston said. "Otherwise, they're invisible."

"Correct," Steak said. "Other than that, I've got nothing. Dan Newman lived in Manchester Bay until about five years ago, when he and Heidi bought the house north of Crosby. Heidi taught in the Crosby school district her whole professional life.

"The Stroms lived mostly in Crosslake, other than when Todd was in law school down in the Twin Cities, when they lived in St. Paul, and during his first two years as a lawyer, when he worked here in Manchester Bay. I've seen no evidence that the two couples ever interacted socially, and there's no connection in their financial records. And before you ask, I've found no professional relationship between the Stroms, Newmans and Baumans, nada."

"And they have no friends in common either," Eggleston noted. "Nobody I spoke to about the Newmans knew the Stroms, and vice versa. Same with the Baumans."

"Why do they have to be connected?" Steak asked. "Maybe these guys just want to rape and kill, and they picked on two couples who lived in isolated homes and were easy targets. Why can't it be that simple?"

"Because it isn't," Braddock replied. "Because of Barr. Because of what he said, because this is all happening around the time of his death."

"They're connected," Tori insisted. "Somehow this all ties together."

"If there is a connection, I can't find it," Steak moaned in frustration. "I'm sorry, but I don't think it exists. We're whistling at the graveyard."

"It does exist," Tori retorted. "We're missing something or don't have something or haven't found something. The Newmans and the Stroms were hunted. There has to be a reason, a specific reason that the killers did this. Has to be."

"The Stroms and Newmans did something to draw this attention," Braddock agreed. "They may not even have known what it was themselves, but they did *something*."

"Well I'm damned if I can find it," Steak shot back.

"I'm not pointing fingers," Tori said, looking to her old friend. "I'm just saying we're…"

"Missing something. Yeah, I heard that the first time. And by the way, I thought you and Will were going to figure that out with all your creative thinking. How's that going?"

"We're still thinking."

"Yeah, well think harder!"

Nerves were frayed.

At home later, with Braddock especially ornery, Tori took it upon herself, despite her own frustrations, to cheer him up, distracting him with one of her rare attempts at solo cooking, making chicken penne with a home-made sauce. It turned out decently and she paired it with a nice bottle of white wine and a candle at the table, hoping the low-key atmosphere would calm both of them.

"That was delicious," he said after a second helping, the surprise evident in his voice. "I mean, really. Ah, sorry that came out wrong, didn't it?"

"Don't be so surprised," Tori teased. "Just because I don't cook very often doesn't mean I'm completely inept in the kitchen. It's just that living alone and being on the road for so long, I never had the time to do a lot of it. Now, how about we clear up and then we go upstairs and I rub your back…"

The night was a respite, albeit a very brief one. As Braddock parked the Tahoe at the government center early the next morning, Tori could already sense the tension returning. They found Steak in the conference room, hovering over a laptop computer.

"Have you guys heard about the explosion up in Remer?" Remer was a small town in Cass County, an hour to the north.

"Explosion?" Tori asked. "No. What happened?"

"I picked it up first from the radio when the call went out," Steak explained, holding up his walkie-talkie. He maneuvered the mouse on the website. "The TV station is already on scene. Apparently they were up there to report on some parade in the town later today. The house goes boom and the story becomes the fire."

"My goodness, it's fully engulfed," Tori said.

"It was worse ten minutes ago. They've actually started tamping the flames down now. I think they were making sure it didn't spread to nearby properties at first. There was no saving the house."

"I'm betting gas leak," Braddock said as he looked at his phone.

"Was anyone home?" Tori asked.

"I hope not," Steak replied. "I don't know how they'd survive that if they were."

"Did you guys hear about the explosion?" Eggleston said, coming into the office.

They all looked back at her from the computer.

"That would be a yes, I guess. At least not in our county, for once."

"Thank God for that," Tori said, before getting down to business. "Sheryl, I meant to ask last night, but did we ever get anything from the boat launches over on Middle or Lower Goodwin?"

"No," Eggleston answered as she poured a coffee. "I've had someone there every morning since Sunday, but no one recalls seeing anyone arriving back at the launches early that morning. One thing that did occur to me is that our killers, if they used a boat, may have played it cool."

"They actually went fishing, in other words, on Saturday morning," Steak suggested.

"Yes. Leave the Stroms', go fishing until eight a.m. and then pull the boat out, maybe with a couple of fish on the stringer. That way they look totally normal. Oh, and they also spend the time dumping the knife, the gun, bloody clothes and anything else that might tie back to the Strom house to the bottom of the lake."

Tori nodded. "That makes some sense."

Her phone started buzzing. She didn't recognize the number, other than the 218-area code. "Hello?"

As Tori arrived at the Peterson house, Elise Peterson slipped out the front door.

"Good morning," she said, shaking Tori's hand. "I meant to ask. How should I address you? Detective? Agent? Ms. Hunter?"

"Tori works just fine."

Elise had called because Cara was struggling. "She's worried about the fact that these killers are still out there, and she saw them, and they killed another couple. And worse, I think, she's blaming herself for what happened to her father."

"I see."

"I reread the newspaper article from last summer on that case that involved your sister's disappearance. I hate to impose, and if I'm out of line, please say so, but I know you went through something like this when you were Cara's age. You seem to have gotten through it all somehow."

If only you knew how poorly I handled it, Tori thought, but she understood where Elise Peterson was coming from.

"I was hoping you might be able to talk to her and give her some advice. She's not in a good place. I'm really worried about her."

"Has she talked to a professional yet?"

Elise shook her head. "Mal and I know she needs to, but we're still trying to find someone who can help with this. In the meantime, I was hoping you could, you know... provide a little light and hope."

"I can try, but I'm not a psychologist."

"I know, I know," a frazzled Elise replied.

"I do know a good one who might be able to help. She likes interesting cases, and Cara would provide one. I could certainly call and ask."

"That would be really good," Elise replied. She glanced up at a window on the second story of the house. "Still, could you talk to her now you're here? She's just kind of shut down right now, not leaving her room."

Tori nodded, thinking back on how she herself had felt in the days after Jessie's disappearance. She hadn't had anyone to talk to at the time who really understood what she was feeling and experiencing. If she had, perhaps she wouldn't have ended up burying everything the way she ultimately did. Maybe she could help Cara not do that. "Is there something she likes to drink?"

"My credit card statement tells me she likes those coffee coolers."

Elise led Tori upstairs and knocked on Cara's bedroom door. After they heard a "come in", Elise opened the door. "Cara, you have a visitor."

"Hi, Cara," Tori said.

"Hi," Cara replied quietly, but also with something approaching a smile.

"You know, I'm really in the mood for an iced coffee. You want to go get one with me?"

*

Cara was dressed casually in Lululemon running shorts, a navy-blue T-shirt and white sneakers. Tori observed that she sat a little balled up in the passenger seat, as if in a defensive, protective posture.

Tori didn't want to force anything, so she drove them in relative silence to a bustling coffee shop a block off the Central Minnesota State University campus. Even though it was summer, there were a lot of college students around, and nearby shops that created an upbeat vibe that Tori hoped would relax Cara. They bought their coffees and then Tori said, "It's nice out. Let's take a walk around the campus."

Her approach was to let Cara make the first verbal move. She led the girl across the street to the long grassy mall that dissected the campus west to east. After a few minutes, Cara finally broke the ice. "My mom called you, didn't she?"

"Yup," Tori said as she sipped her iced vanilla coffee. "She's worried about you, so I said I'd come over and see you."

Cara nodded. "I can't stop thinking about that night."

"I don't know how you wouldn't."

"I searched you on Google," Cara said. "I read about the case last summer. That man… the one who had you down in that room."

Tori nodded.

"Do you still think about that?"

"Yes," she replied with a nod. "I don't think of it as often as I did say seven or eight months ago, but it pops into my head from time to time. I've talked to someone about it. I still do."

"Mom says I'll need to do that."

"She's right," Tori replied. "Your mom also says that you're blaming yourself for what happened to your dad and stepmom."

"I keep thinking that if I'd gotten home sooner…"

"Don't do it to yourself," Tori said as she eyed up a bench in the distance. "It's not your fault."

"But if I'd have been there…"

"You'd be dead," Tori replied, stopping and locking eyes with Cara. "It's not your fault. It's the killer's fault."

Cara nodded, and they started walking again. "My mom said that you went through something like this when you were my age."

"I did." Tori veered left to the bench.

"With your sister?"

She nodded.

"I'm sorry, I shouldn't have…"

"No," Tori said, patting Cara's hand. "It's okay. I can talk about it now. I've learned how." She took a moment to collect her thoughts. "My sister's name was Jessie. We were twins." She paused. "We were inseparable from the day we were born. Our mom died when we were young, so we were raised by our dad. He was this big dude, and we were his little girls. We got our lack of height from our mom. She was a little pixie married to this big galoot. Dad was the sheriff around here for years. Everyone called him Big Jim."

"I didn't know that."

"Jessie and I did everything together. Soccer, school, friends, you name it."

"Clothes and stuff."

Tori smiled. "No, actually, that's the one thing we didn't share. It's funny, we were identical twins but very different people. Let me show you." She pulled out her phone and found a picture of her and Jessie from a month before she was killed. "See."

"Wow, you *were* identical. I see the differences, though. Clothes, hair, you wore glasses."

"We had very different personalities and tastes, and our differing styles meant people could tell us apart, but we were best friends. We were always together, and we looked out for each other. If someone on the soccer field fouled Jessie, what do you think happened if that player came my way?"

"You fouled her back."

"Darn right, and it would have been a much harder foul. You messed with one, you got the other, you know what I mean?"

"You had each other's backs?"

"Exactly," Tori said, but then let out a little sigh. "Except one night. Just one night. The night Jessie was murdered, I was off with my new boyfriend. She told me to go be with him. Heck, she practically set it up. But because of that, I wasn't there when trouble struck. For a long time, Cara, a very long time, I wondered *what if*. I still do."

"How did you get over it?"

"I haven't. I don't think you do."

"Oh," Cara replied.

"I just want to be honest, okay. How you're feeling isn't something that will just magically go away. But I've learned that you can learn to live with it without reliving it. Do you understand what I'm saying?"

"I think so." Cara nodded. "How did *you* learn to live with it?"

"For a long time, not very well," Tori said with a whimsical smile. "But here's where I can offer expert assistance. I can tell you all the things *not* to do."

"Like what?"

"For starters, don't run away from it. After my sister died, I went away to college in Boston because I couldn't handle being close to home. I just wanted to escape and be somewhere where nobody knew anything about what had happened. Then my dad died when I was a college freshman. For a long time, I blamed myself for that too, for being so selfish that I didn't think of him and what he was going through. After that, I was really messed up in a lot of ways. I needed help, but I didn't get it, or listen to those who suggested I should."

"What did you do?"

"For twenty years I ran from it. I didn't talk about it. I just tried to ignore it and bury it in the hopes it would go away. Like it was all a bad dream that I needed to wake up from."

"But it wasn't."

"No, it doesn't work that way," Tori said with a long headshake. "And even when I solved Jessie's murder a year ago, that didn't give me closure either, because I'd never dealt with the original guilt or the loss. Then one night maybe a month afterwards, I was alone in my condo in New York City. I had just solved a big case, taken all these congratulatory phone calls from some pretty important people. It should have been the high point of my FBI career, and I was alone and miserable. It was then that I had this moment of clarity where I realized I needed to change things. Life was passing me by and I was missing out on it. I finally got some real help. And then I started to get better."

"Who helped you?"

"First it was my old college roommate. She's a psychologist and she helped me work through it. Problem is, she's based in Boston, and I wanted to move back here."

"Why?"

"Detective Braddock."

"Oh, you and he are…"

"Yeah," Tori said with a smile. "He was another reason I wanted to get better. I decided I wanted to be with him, but I still needed to do some more work on myself. So now I have someone here that I talk to every so often. She's a psychology professor at the university. Her office is in that hall right over there." She pointed to the Brooks Social and Behavioral Sciences Building.

"My mom says I'll have to talk to a psychologist."

"The sooner you do, the better. It really does help. I could ask Professor Lane if she'd be willing to sit down with you."

"You like her?"

"Very much. We meet in her office every couple of weeks, have a cup of coffee and just talk about things."

"Like this?"

"Yeah, kind of, except she's a professional who is good at poking around in your attic and getting you to talk about things that need to be talked about."

"If you think she's good, I'll go see her."

"Good. And I want you to promise me something."

"What?"

"Don't blame yourself for any of this. Don't ever tell him I said this, but Detective Braddock is a very wise man. He told me once that what happened to my sister was tragic, but it wasn't my fault. What happened to your dad and stepmom is awful, but it's not your fault."

Cara nodded and took a long sip of her drink, her eyes moistening.

"You know, you remind me of my younger self," Tori said with a big smile on her face.

"I do?"

"Oh yeah. Soccer player, smart, analytical... cute. Do you have a boyfriend?"

"No. Not right now. I did have one."

"Now you're playing the field?" Tori said with raised eyebrows.

"Maybe."

She laughed. "That would make you like Jessie then. When does soccer practice start for the high school?"

"A few weeks. They're having captain's practices right now."

"Haven't you been going?"

"No."

"Do you like playing soccer?"

"I love it."

"Then go play," Tori urged. "It'll be good for you."

"Mom says that too."

"She's right. Did your dad enjoy watching you play?"

"Yeah, he was at most of my games."

"He'd want you to play, so play," Tori said.

Her phone started buzzing. It was Braddock.

"Hey, Cara and I are just finishing up."

"Good. I need you back here. We might have just caught a break," Braddock said. "We have a DNA match on those tobacco pouches."

"To what?"

"That's the rub. It's a match to another murder, twenty-five years ago."

CHAPTER SIXTEEN

"It's easy when you unilaterally decide what the evidence is"

"Wisconsin?" Tori said as she burst into the conference room. "Seriously?"

"Plover, Wisconsin, to be exact," Braddock said. "Twenty-five years ago. The DNA was found on a hair left at the murder scene of a Paul Harstad and Melanie Solmes."

"Where is Plover, Wisconsin?" Tori asked.

"I had to look it up myself." Braddock showed her the map on his phone. "It's in the middle of the state, basically a little southern suburb of Stevens Point."

"What do we know about this case?"

"That's just it," Braddock said. "We don't know a darn thing beyond the names. I have a call into the Portage County Sheriff's Department to get more information, get a copy of their case file, whatever there is. It'll be interesting to see what they have to say."

"Pen and I have a pretty good idea of what they're going to say."

Braddock and Tori turned to see Cal and Pen Murphy. Cal was closing the door to the conference room.

"Cal?" Tori said. "What gives?"

"And why is Pen here?" Braddock asked.

"Because of what the Portage County Sheriff's Department will tell you when they dig out the case file that ties to that DNA match."

"There are some things you all need to know," added Pen.

*

Twenty-four years ago

"The DNA that Portage County has doesn't match Barr," Sheriff Hunter said to Pen Murphy, once he'd closed his office door. "Despite that, and the fact that their murders occurred fourteen months ago, they called because of the similarity of their case to the Bauman murders."

"How similar are they?" Pen said.

"Enough that they got *my* attention, Counselor."

Pen closed his eyes for a moment. "Jim, did they send you anything?"

"They emailed me an investigative report and I discussed the case with them." Hunter sat down at his desk and flipped open a folder. "The woman was tied up with a yellow nylon rope, raped and then strangled. The man was tied up with the same rope and had his throat slashed. She was found dead in the bedroom, the man in the family room."

"Do they think he was made to watch?" Pen asked, folding his arms. "Or could he hear?"

"Watch?" Hunter shook his head. "They're not sure. Hear it? No question. The house is small. Where he was tied up was only twenty feet from the bedroom. The detective said the man would certainly have heard the rape taking place. There was evidence he struggled against the rope, but to no avail."

"One or two killers?"

"Again, they're not sure. The only evidence from the scene is the hairs on the woman, which are from a Caucasian male. Nothing that says one way or the other how many killers there were."

"Did they say what they think?" Pen pressed.

"They think at least two men."

"Tell me about the differences in the cases."

"The woman was left on the bed, not placed in the shower. The man had his throat cut instead of being shot. The Baumans lived out in the country on some acreage. The Plover house was on a two-acre lot abutting some woods on the edge of town. There are neighbors within the vicinity, but nobody heard anything. The couple were murdered early on a Sunday morning but weren't discovered until Monday."

"Time of death?"

"Estimated to be between one and three a.m. The victims had been at a bar in Plover that night with friends, then went back to the house, where the killer or killers awaited their return."

"Jim, is it at all possible Barr was there?" Pen asked, his eyes wide.

"It is... possible," Hunter said, grimacing. "Cal took a look at that."

"He knows about this?" Pen raised his eyebrows.

"He is the lead investigator, after all. From here, it's a five-and-a-half-hour drive to Plover. Barr had charges on his credit card on Saturday evening at a convenience store here. There is another credit card charge the next morning, also in Manchester Bay. There was a little over fourteen hours between the charges." The sheriff sighed and sat back in his chair. "You do the math. There is a window of time that he could have driven over, done the deed, and then driven back. It would be tight, not much margin for error. Plus, Cal checked and there is no credit card history of any kind for Barr over in Plover or Stevens Point or Wisconsin period."

"Tell me about the victims. Were they a married couple?"

"Not married," Hunter answered. "They were together, but not for very long. They weren't married or engaged or anything, not even living together. Paul Harstad was forty-two. He bought the house in Plover eighteen months ago. Melanie Solmes was younger, twenty-seven. One of the reasons Portage County called us is that until two years ago, Harstad lived in Minnesota—Wadena, and Keller before that—so they wondered if there could be some tie to the Bauman case, especially given the similarities."

Pen started pacing, pinching the bridge of his nose, his eyes closed. They were a month before trial. A month. And now this. What to do? "Jim, what records exist of your contact with Plover?"

"There are my own notes, this emailed report, and the log of the calls with Portage County. There's also the original call that came into your office, which your assistant took and then passed on to me. At this point, you, me, Cal, and your assistant know about this."

"Have you requested copies of any tests, evidence, reports, crime scene photos? Have you interviewed anyone here about the Plover case?"

"No," Hunter said. "Portage County called us and were just asking questions. They sent the report for our impressions and interest. They're just fishing right now, trying to solve their case. Cal and I were cooperative, helpful, but we didn't express any overt interest or belief in a connection."

"And it was Portage County that checked the DNA, not us."

"Yes. We put Barr's DNA in the system months ago. They checked. No match. But there were enough similarities that they called anyway."

Pen went to the coffee pot in the corner and poured two cups, handed one to Jim, and then walked slowly around the office, drinking his coffee, deep in thought. After a few minutes of ruminating, he looked at Hunter. "Be honest, Jim. What do you think? Is this real? Is this related?"

"I think Barr killed the Baumans."

"Dammit, Jim, that wasn't my question."

"I'm not going to answer your damn question," Hunter shot back, "until you answer mine. What could this do to the case against Barr?"

"It could kill it," Pen answered simply. "We're a month before trial. We've already provided our discovery responses."

"Do we have a duty to supplement?"

"If there is something relevant, yes," Pen replied tersely. "Our case against Barr is circumstantial. It can take a few hits at trial, but you put another similar unsolved murder in Wisconsin into the mix, especially if it doesn't look like Barr could have made it there and back…" He sighed and shook his head. "Well, that might be enough for the jury to say he's not our guy."

"You buy that?"

"Sure. Heck, as of now, defense counsel may not even put on a defense and may simply argue that we haven't proven Barr guilty beyond reasonable doubt. That approach could work if he successfully chips away at our case on cross-examination. This Plover case, the similarities to ours and the fact that the window for Barr to get over there and back is so tight, it could be enough to tube us completely if he starts cross-examining you and Cal on it. I don't know if he's seasoned enough to do it right, but all it would take is a juror or two to have doubts and Barr walks. *He walks.* And if Barr did commit this Wisconsin murder, plus ours, that means he's a killer. If he goes free now, he'll kill again."

"What do you want to do?"

Pen exhaled a long breath and walked over to the window. He stared out for several minutes, deep in thought, weighing the options they had, none of them good.

Hunter gave him a few minutes before he pushed himself out of his chair and walked over to stand next to him. "Pen?" he said quietly.

"Don't write another thing down, Jim. Don't type any reports, don't record any further calls and don't call them again. You and Cal never spoke to Portage County about this."

"We're not disclosing this? Are you sure?" Hunter asked, eyebrows raised.

"Barr's a killer."

"I agree, but—"

"He killed the Baumans, Jim," Pen asserted. "We retain no record of any contact with Portage County. If it comes up later, we'll just say it was a quick trivial inquiry. We took the call as a courtesy. We get lots of calls. It didn't get logged, administrative error, whatever. We can't find the report, the email must have been deleted."

"Are you sure it's worth the risk?"

"I'm making the call, unless you're telling me you're good with Barr walking."

"Huh." Hunter shook his head, irritated. "You're going to put it all on me like that?"

"This doesn't work unless we're both on the same page."

He exhaled a nervous breath. "Well, shit."

"Look, this is really my call, Jim. I just need you to not make a thing of it. Corral Cal and disappear any records in your system. I'll do the same in my department. If it comes to light, if there is a hit to take, I'll stand up and take it."

"This is an awfully big risk, Pen."

"Reward sometimes requires risk."

"Well, you could maybe try a plea with Barr again. Get us off the hook from this… shit."

"I'd do a plea in a heartbeat, Jim. His lawyer knows that. But a plea would require Barr to tell us what he knows, and he just won't do it. I don't know why, but he won't. Word is he won't say a word to his lawyer beyond *no deals*. We're going to have to try the case. The only way we get him is if we convict him. If we disclose this, I think the chances of a conviction become remote. We'll lose, he'll walk, and then for sure there won't be a damn thing we can do to him."

"Unless he kills again."

"That's right, unless he kills again."

*

"Oh my God," Tori murmured in shock. "You withheld evidence."

"And let me guess, Pen. The assistant county attorney was Todd Strom," Braddock added.

"Yes," Murphy replied. "And I didn't know it then, but I suspect that the IT employee who removed system evidence of the calls and email from Portage County was Dan Newman. Jim Hunter arranged that, and I never asked him who did it."

"Nor did I," Cal said.

"But look, at the time, I thought there were valid reasons not to disclose this," Pen argued. "I'll defend that decision to this day. There were enough differences in the murders for me to credibly argue that we fully disclosed what *we* investigated. We didn't investigate the Portage case. We took a few phone calls is all."

"You know where you make that argument, Pen? In court," Braddock asserted. "You disclose it and then you take all the persuasive ability you clearly possess and argue it's irrelevant and get the judge to rule it inadmissible at trial. You don't get to pick and choose which laws and rules you comply with and which ones you don't. You don't withhold evidence. You know why? Because eventually it gets out. And if this gets out, then every case Cal or Sheriff Hunter ever investigated, and every case, Pen, every single one you prosecuted or presided over as a judge, is open to scrutiny. Every case!"

"I think you're overreacting…"

"I'm overreacting? Are you kidding me, Pen! Five people are dead because of what you pulled twenty-four years ago. I'm not going to sit here and say you and Jim Hunter should have seen this coming all these years later, but you're both sure as hell responsible for it."

"Now hold on a minute," Tori said. "My father was a good man."

"I'm sure he was," Braddock said, then looked to Cal. "You knew about this?"

Cal nodded slowly.

"Cal wasn't part of the decision twenty-four years ago. That was Jim and me," Murphy said.

"But I knew. And I knew how risky it was," Cal said. "I could have done something, I could have challenged Jim, or gone around him, but I didn't."

"Fine, Cal, you knew. But it wasn't your call. It was ultimately my call. *My call*," Pen insisted. "I decided, but we had to tell you because you knew all about the case in Wisconsin."

"And Sheriff Hunter?" Braddock asked.

"Jim went along. He agreed."

"Could you have done it if he hadn't?"

"No. But he and I were not going to let Barr walk. The man was guilty. He was a killer. He killed Julie and Jerry Bauman. Besides, there were notable differences between the crime scenes. I legitimately viewed the Plover case as unrelated and prejudicial to our case if it were disclosed."

"Well, if that isn't just a bunch of lawyerly bullshit," Braddock snorted.

"You weren't there. And you aren't a prosecutor."

"You're right, but now I'm dealing with the ramifications of what you decided to do. I'm stuck with the mess you and Sheriff Hunter created."

"Obviously, in retrospect, maybe they were wrong," Cal said. "Maybe *we* were wrong."

"Cal, I'm not going to agree with that." Pen turned to the group. "You have to understand the circumstances. The murder of the Baumans sent shock waves through the community. An innocent couple, brutally murdered in their own home. And Barr did it. Jim and I were going to make sure it didn't happen again."

"Except it just happened twice more," Tori said angrily.

"I didn't connect the Newmans to this," Pen said. "Not when it happened. I never knew who Jim used to erase evidence of the contacts with Portage County."

"Well how about now!" Braddock railed, looking from Pen to Cal. "How about when the Stroms were murdered?"

"At that point... I didn't think..." Cal stuttered.

"Oh come on, Cal," Tori growled angrily. "I stood in your office the day the Stroms were killed. I asked you point blank if there was anything we should know."

Cal nodded. "And I said no."

"You lied."

He hung his head in shame.

"You lied to me," Tori repeated sadly. "Cal..."

"You were covering your ass," Braddock barked at Pen, before turning on Cal. "And *you* were chewing me out, while all the time you guys were trying to figure out if you could keep this little secret to yourselves and save your skins."

"Easy, boss," Steak warned, getting between Braddock and Cal. "Easy."

"Fuck easy," Braddock retorted. "This Plover case is the same killers we're dealing with now."

"We didn't know that at the time," Pen said. "I had good reason to—"

"Bullshit!"

"We know now, we didn't at the time. Twenty-four years ago, I wasn't going to let them use that case to create reasonable doubt. I wasn't going to give the defense that case to work with. He would never have tracked it down on his own. Why hand it to him?"

"Because the criminal procedure rules required it," Braddock answered. "You could have been disbarred for that, Pen. Maybe you should have been."

"Now hang on…" Cal started.

"Instead, you rode that case all the way to a seat on the state supreme court."

"I'm not going to dignify that."

"Dignity left the room twenty minutes ago, pal."

"Will…" Cal tried again.

"Do you realize the risk you took? That Jim Hunter allowed to be taken?" He looked to Cal and Pen. "And do you realize the position we're in now? Clearly the case was relevant. And now there are five more people dead and some of them shouldn't be and wouldn't be if you had fessed up two weeks ago. Cal, you sensed at the Newmans' that something was up. You were white as a ghost."

"I didn't make the connect—"

"Bullshit."

"How could you?" Tori asked. "How could you not come clean then? The Stroms might still be alive."

"I'm sorry," Cal muttered. "We should have…"

"I just didn't see that coming." Pen spoke over him. "I didn't know it was Newman that Jim used. He just told me it was handled. Maybe I should have asked him for details, but I didn't."

"You knew about this case in Plover and didn't tell us about it," Braddock railed at Cal. "I don't get it."

"Because I could have stopped it back then but I didn't. I'd hoped you might solve it without all that coming to light."

"Cal, it wasn't your call," Pen said.

"It wasn't my call, but I could have made it my call. I had my reservations at the time, I could have voiced them and voiced them strongly. I could have gone around Jim or gone to the judge on the case. And it's sure as heck my call now and I haven't made it, and because of that, some good people are dead. You and I are responsible for that, Pen."

"Barr was guilty," Pen insisted.

"Yes, he was, on that I will not waver," Cal replied. "But what does that make you, me, and Jim now? Will is right. Five people are dead."

"That may be," Pen argued. "But how many more might Barr and his cohorts have killed if we hadn't done what we did?"

"Isn't that a convenient argument to justify yourself," Braddock asserted.

"He cheated," Tori said in almost a whisper. She looked to Cal and Pen in disbelief. "That's what Barr said to me about my father. He cheated. This is what he was talking about, isn't it?"

"How would he have known?" Pen asked. "How would Barr have known that?"

"It doesn't matter how," Braddock replied in almost a whisper, shaking his head. "All that matters is that he did. That the men he killed with did."

"Then why didn't he use it? If he knew at the time, why didn't he use it?" Pen asserted.

"I don't know. Maybe he didn't know then. Maybe he only found out recently. But somehow, some way, he knew what you did," Braddock said. "Is there anyone else you haven't told us about? Anyone else that we should be putting protection on right this minute?"

"No," Cal said. "There is nobody else."

"No," Pen affirmed.

"Except you two. You two might be next, and right about now, I'm of a mind to let them come after you."

"Come on, boss," Steak said to Braddock. "Let's all cool down."

"Or maybe this is what they want," Pen asserted. "For you to do what you're thinking of doing."

"Which is?"

"Throwing me and Cal to the wolves. Having us exposed for this. Making us responsible for all these deaths because of what we did."

"Sounds awfully damn tempting," Braddock retorted, leaning against the wall, arms folded.

"Of course, you do that, you'll have punished us but still won't have caught the killers."

Braddock snorted his disgust. "Don't patronize me to absolve yourself. This is what happens when you don't play straight. When you play fast and loose with the rules. Cripes, we're supposed to be the good guys."

"My father *was* one of the good guys," Tori asserted, turning to Braddock. "He was a good man."

"Not on this one. He didn't play this one straight, and innocent people are dead as a result. Dan Newman did what your father asked him to do. He's dead because of it."

"How dare you," Tori charged. "Where do you get off—"

"Five dead bodies is where, Tori. Are you ready to explain this one to Cara Newman?"

"You… bastard!"

"I guess we didn't all go to the Will Braddock school of investigative ethics," Pen retorted.

"Pen, when it comes time to testify, I'll be the one with his hand on the Bible able to swear to tell the truth and the whole truth. I won't have to make shit up."

"Nobody is testifying to anything," Cal exclaimed.

"Everyone in this room is going to end up testifying," Braddock exclaimed. "We have five dead bodies because of this. And now there's a credible argument that Barr should never have been in prison. Fuck!"

"You don't for a minute think Barr was innocent," Tori replied.

"Hugh Barr killed the Baumans, or certainly he was there," Braddock replied. "But what I think doesn't matter. You look at the similarities between the Plover case and Bauman, and that tight window on those credit card charges, and a lot of people may think you got the wrong guy. That's what made that case relevant."

"We didn't get the wrong man."

"I don't think you did either. But you still have to prove the case."

"I did."

"It's easy when you unilaterally decide what the evidence is. I guess you decided to be a judge before you really were one."

Pen shook his head. "I don't need to take this."

"The hell you don't. This is a real problem. We now have a DNA match. I don't even know the facts of the Plover case, I haven't read a lick of that investigation yet, and I know it's relevant. I know it and so do you. You know it now, and you knew it then. I shudder to think what's in Portage County's investigative file about their contacts with this department back then. And if there is something, you don't think the county attorney's office isn't going to have some questions about this? You think it's uncomfortable in here now, just you wait."

"They'll play ball," Pen asserted.

"I'm not so sure," Braddock said. "County Attorney Backstrom and Assistant County Attorney Wilson, in my experience, are not the types to fall on a grenade like this and jack up their own careers. I got news for you. They don't have any skin in this game you've been playing. They weren't around when you and Sheriff Hunter decided to play God. Those two aren't going to care who you were."

"They won't want the mess. They'll make it go away."

"That's easy for you to say when you're sitting on the easy street of retirement."

"My conscience is clean."

Braddock laughed. "You make me want to vomit."

"Enough!" Cal barked, and then sighed a breath, trying to lower the temperature. "Now. Will is right about one thing. We have a mess." He looked to Braddock. "What do you propose?"

"You're off the case."

"I'm the sheriff. I can't just—"

"You do this, or I call Backstrom and the BCA and bring them in right now. It's probably what I should do. Do you want that?"

"No."

"Okay then. You take a seat on this one. I'll do all I can to protect you and Pen, but we can't make this worse." Braddock looked to Tori. "I hate to say it, but you have to step back too."

"Me? Why?"

"You're the daughter of Jim Hunter. The case is already dirty; having you continue only makes it look worse."

"*I* make it dirty?"

"You know what I mean."

"Do I?" Tori replied, her anger rising again. "It's interesting. I didn't hear you mention my father's name as one that needed protecting. You've spent the better part of the last hour obliterating his reputation. You looking to throw him and his memory under the bus on this?"

"Tori…"

"Tori, come on, that's not what he said," Steak asserted.

"I don't like the picture you're painting of my father, Will."

"I'll be careful to—"

"Because I can see how this is going to play out. I can see the wheels turning in your head. How do I clean up the mess with as little damage as possible? And yours, Cal—oh, and you too, Pen, especially you. I can see the escape plan forming in all your minds. Who better to blame than the sheriff who's been dead for twenty years? He can't be here to defend himself. Put all the blame on him, it was his call, let him take the hit while you two get free and clear."

"You think I'd do that to your father, Victoria?" Cal protested.

"Tor," Braddock said, stepping toward her. "Come on. You know I wouldn't—"

"He paid a huge price. My family... I... I don't have any family left. The only thing I have is memories. All that is left of my father is his good name. You take that..."

"I don't have an escape plan for anyone," Braddock said. "I don't think there is any escape from this. Everyone ends up tainted. As for your father, Pen couldn't have done this without him. He knew what the risk was, and he did it anyway, reluctant or not. I can't let what was pulled twenty-four years ago compromise getting these guys. Actions have consequences. Sometimes things have to play out the hard way."

"Yeah, I guess they do, don't they," Tori replied, and picked up her bag.

"Tori," Braddock pleaded, reaching for her arm. "Come on."

"Don't. Don't you dare," she said. She glared at him for another moment, then walked by him and out of the conference room, nearly bowling over Cal's assistant on his way in.

"I have the Portage County Sheriff on the phone."

Cal looked to Braddock. "Well, I guess that's a call you better take."

*

Tori opened the door to her house and pushed her way inside, wiping away one last tear. She tossed her shoulder bag onto the kitchen table and went to her small wine fridge, taking out a half-finished bottle of Cabernet and pouring herself a full glass.

Sheriff, what were you thinking? she said to herself as she took a slug of wine. "Damn you!" she yelled, and threw the glass against the kitchen cabinet.

As she stood looking at the broken glass on the floor, her phone buzzed. She glanced over. It was Braddock—again. She hit the decline button. It was the third time she had done so. There was a text or two from him as well, but she had zero interest in reading them. She was as angry with him as she was with her father.

Her phone was sitting next to her mail pile. On top of the pile was the invitation to Richard Graff's fiftieth birthday party in New York City tomorrow night. She picked up the invitation. The party was at McCall's, a bar and restaurant they'd often gone to for drinks after work. It was just down the street from the New York City FBI Field Office.

I'm getting out of here, she thought.

Fifteen minutes later, she had booked a flight to New York City for tomorrow morning.

CHAPTER SEVENTEEN

"You sound like you want your old job back"

Braddock arrived at the office early after his long morning swim. He had slept in a half-empty bed and didn't like the feeling of it. He liked even less that Tori wouldn't answer his calls and texts, other than to message saying she was going away for a few days.

Where? For how long? She didn't say. When would she be back? She didn't say that either. She'd left him completely in the dark.

At the office, his assistant had already printed and organized the emailed files from the Portage County Sheriff's Department related to the murders in Plover, Wisconsin, twenty-five years ago. Braddock had a call scheduled with an investigator from that office later in the morning.

The Plover murders had occurred fourteen months before the killing of the Baumans. The DNA from hairs found on Melanie Solmes's body matched the DNA extracted from the tobacco pouches recovered from the spy perch they'd found more recently, a quarter-mile west of the Newmans' house.

"So, we have a DNA match," Braddock muttered. "Now we have to figure out the tie between the Plover case and ours."

When Steak and Eggleston arrived at the office, Braddock brought them up to speed and handed them a small stack of documents. "These are backgrounds on Paul Harstad and Melanie

Solmes, murdered twenty-five years ago. Do they ever intersect with Hugh Barr? Do they intersect for any reason with the Baumans? Harstad lived in Keller and Wadena; did he have any issues out there that might be of interest here? Any enemies we should be talking to?"

After he'd given them their assignment, Steak hung back for a minute. "Did you talk to Tori?"

"No," Braddock said with a headshake. "She sent a text that she was going out of town."

"Where?"

"She didn't say, but if I had to guess, New York City. She has friends there."

"For how long?"

"She didn't say that either."

"You could try her again."

Braddock sighed wearily. "If she didn't respond to my numerous texts or answer my three phone calls, making another attempt is not going to do any good."

"Keep trying."

"You know her as well as I do. When she's running this hot, there's no talking to her."

"Don't let her do something dumb, buddy."

"At the moment, I have zero control over that. The ball is in her court. I'm ready to talk when she is."

Detective Len Pratt from Portage County called promptly at 11:30 a.m. The call bled into the afternoon.

"Detective Braddock, I'd vaguely heard of this case once or twice over my ten years here, but I'd never had cause to review it until your BCA contacted our office with that DNA match. I spent some of last night and this morning digging through it, as I'm sure you have."

"And I'm still reviewing," Braddock said. "What can you tell me?"

Pratt went through the history of the case. Paul Harstad and Melanie Solmes were murdered between 1:00 and 3:00 a.m. on a Sunday morning in June. Their bodies were not found until 5:00 p.m. the following day, by a friend of Mr. Harstad after he didn't show for work. The couple were last seen when they left a local bar together on Saturday night just past midnight.

"The detectives at the time concluded the killers were in the house, lying in wait," Pratt explained. He added that Mr. Harstad was struck from behind, as evidenced by two lines of bruising on his upper back and neck. "Given the bruise pattern, he was probably hit with a crowbar."

Melanie Solmes was raped, strangled and left on the bed in the master bedroom with the rope still wrapped around her neck, her ankles and wrists bound. "She had bruising around her face. She fought her attackers as best she could. The medical examiners thought one of the bruises was from a headbutt. She fought them."

Paul Harstad's injuries were more intriguing and brutal. "Harstad had his throat cut, but that was only after he was stabbed several times in the stomach."

"I noticed this morning that he was stabbed nine times," Braddock noted. "Was he… tortured?"

"That was the interpretation at the time," Pratt responded. "The M.E.'s report noted that the stab wounds would have inflicted tremendous pain but none of them individually was fatal. The finding was that the first wound was just below the sternum, and then they progressed down, each one just a little deeper."

Braddock shuffled through the photos. "Those stab wounds. Kind of signals this was very… personal, doesn't it?"

"Could have been. They certainly made him suffer. The M.E.'s report indicates that when it came time to slash his throat, the killer pressed Harstad's head against the post he was tied to and cut it left to right. Have any of your recent victims experienced that?"

"The repetitive stabbing, no. Our first victim was slashed ear to ear, damn near cut his head off. Our second male victim was gutted vertically. The amount of blood was staggering."

Pratt explained that the operating theory back at the time of the murder was that the killers had approached the house from the rear, through the woods, and worked the deadbolt for the back door. "It was the only way in."

"We have two killers now," Braddock noted. "We have a size thirteen footprint and a size nine and a half. Did you find anything like that?"

"No. Other than the two hairs found on the female victim, there were limited forensic findings. The only thing of any significance was a couple of fresh smudges on the floor just inside the back door of the house. The investigators thought they contained traces of axle grease and motor oil."

"Did they come from the victims?"

"No traces of those substances were found on any of the shoes belonging to either victim at Harstad's house or Solmes's apartment, or in the house's garage. Harstad and Solmes both worked in office environments."

"Unlike our victims here, it doesn't appear Harstad and Solmes had been together long."

"No," Pratt said. "Dating for three to four months from the looks of it. Harstad had moved to our neck of the woods from Minnesota. He lived in Wadena for a few years. Before that, he'd been in Keller for five years, and Fargo, North Dakota, before that. Never married."

"Notes suggest he was something of a ladies' man."

"I saw that too. He had a busy recent dating history prior to his untimely death. Names of old girlfriends we tracked down are in the file. Lots of interviews."

"Are any of the detectives who worked the case still around?"

"No, sadly. One died of cancer fifteen years ago. The other was the sheriff at the time. He's now in a memory care facility. He can't help you."

*

Twenty-four years ago

Tori followed Jessie into the house. As they stuffed their soccer bags into their cubbies, Jessie whispered, "Tommy Press is going to call me in a few minutes. Do you mind if I have the room to myself for a bit?"

Tori smiled. "I'll do my homework at the kitchen table."

"Thanks, sis. You're the best."

She watched as Jessie took her backpack and walked briskly through the kitchen, saying, "Hi, Sheriff." It was what they always called their father.

Tori rummaged through the refrigerator before pulling out the jug of orange juice and pouring herself a glass. Her dad was sitting at the kitchen table, a bottle of whiskey and a half-full glass in front of him.

She sat down opposite him and spread out her schoolbooks, yet her dad just stared blankly out the window, as if he hadn't even seen her.

"Sheriff? Sheriff, are you alright?"

"Uh…" He stammered, breaking from his trance. "Uh… fine, honey, everything's fine."

"You seem kind of distracted."

"Oh… well, it's just some work stuff I'm thinking of is all."

"Is it something on that big case?"

The sheriff smiled. "Nothing to worry your pretty little head about. How was soccer practice?"

"It was good. The coach is playing me at sweeper."

"And what position is that?" The sheriff loved watching his girls play, but he didn't know anything about the game. It was a mystery to him.

"I'm a defender still, but I get to roam around, play side to side."

"I assume that means more responsibility, right?"

Tori nodded and took a sip of her juice.

"Are you iced out of your room because your sister is on the phone with a boy?"

She shrugged.

"I'll take that as a yes," the sheriff said with a wry smile. "You know what I bought?"

"What?"

"Some apple…"

"Pie?"

"Want some?"

"Uh-huh."

"Good, give me a hand."

Tori got out two small plates and forks while the sheriff cut them each a piece of pie. He was still unusually quiet as they ate. If Tori sat at the table with him on a school night, it was usually twenty questions about everything, quizzes to make sure his daughters were paying attention at school.

"Sheriff, you're sure you're alright?"

"Fine, really, honey."

"Someone at school said that case you've been working on with Uncle Cal goes to trial soon."

"Next month."

"Are you worried about it?"

He smiled. "Honey, I'm always worried when a case goes to trial. I have to be a witness and tell the jury what we found in the investigation. And the attorney for the guy we charged with the crime gets to ask me questions too. It's not something you need to concern yourself about. The sheriff will be fine."

*

Tori stared out the window as the plane started its final descent into Newark, the skyscrapers of Manhattan visible to her left. As she thought about that conversation all those years ago, she couldn't help but wonder if that was the day the sheriff and Pen had made their fateful decision. She'd defended her father to Braddock yesterday, ripped Braddock for criticizing him, but if she was honest with herself, she knew he was right.

Jim Hunter had raised his girls to ask themselves one simple question when they were in a tough spot, when someone was asking them to do something questionable: *Is that the right thing to do?*

That was the way he'd put it to Tori when she was a sophomore in high school and was caught cheating on a social studies test with her friend, Lizzy. The teacher had called the sheriff, and he'd sat her down at the kitchen table and asked her: *Tori, was that the right thing to do?*

Her father was part of a conspiracy to withhold evidence. It meant a guilty man had gone to prison instead of possibly going free. It may also have led to five other people being killed.

Tori couldn't stop asking the question: *Sheriff, was that the right thing to do?*

*

After his call with Pratt, Braddock spent the afternoon sifting through interviews with family and friends from the Plover murders.

As victims, Harstad and Solmes were different from the others. They weren't married and had only dated for a few months. Solmes was fifteen years younger than Harstad. She had two long-term relationships in her past but an otherwise sporadic dating history. She worked at a local bank as a loan officer and had no criminal record.

Paul Harstad was forty-two and worked in medical supply sales. He'd moved to Plover two years prior to the murders. There was a long list of women he'd dated, and investigators had interviewed many of them. After Braddock had read through five interviews, he started putting together a rough timeline of Harstad's dating history going back eight years. There were not many gaps in the timeline, and several overlaps.

"You dog," he muttered, shaking his head.

He was struck by a comment that Harstad liked to pursue married women. One woman had told an investigator, "A few months after we stopped seeing each other, I ran into him at a bar. He was honest. He said he was more attracted to me when I was married." When asked why she thought that was, she replied, "When I look back on it, I think when I was married, I had to leave, I had to go home."

Another woman said, "I think he was a forever bachelor. He liked the chase, the pursuit, the capture, but then, after some time, he got bored and wanted to do it all over again."

There was a photo in the file. Harstad had dark flowing hair, a wide smile, a handsome face, the look of a salesman. "A real good-time Charlie," Braddock muttered.

It appeared that Solmes understood who Harstad was. One of her friends said that she had a healthy skepticism of how long her relationship with him would last. "He was a fun guy, and she was having fun with him, but she didn't get the sense he was angling to settle down."

Harstad had one semi-criminal record of note, several years before his move to Wisconsin: a bar fight in Wadena with the husband of a woman he'd been involved with. There was no record in the file of the name of the husband. Braddock rang Steak with the investigation file number for Wadena to follow up on.

As he flipped through the documents, he finally came to the section he was dreading: the sheet titled *Shepard County*. He sighed and turned the page.

*

Ah, New York City, Tori thought as she walked casually along the sidewalk, shopping bags in her hands, the streets bustling in the late afternoon, the Empire State Building glistening in the sun in the distance.

Her flight had arrived at Newark at 10:50 a.m. The trip to the hotel was eventful, with her driver, Sal, alternately barking at other drivers, weaving in and out of traffic, and carrying on an intense conversation with her about the Yankees and Twins. He went right to it the moment she got into the car with her Twins baseball hat on, calling her Minnesota, or Sota for short.

"Come on, Sota, you know the Yanks will crush the Twins in October, right? Twins have lost like eighteen or nineteen in a row in the post-season, and most of them to the Yanks."

"That means the Twins are due, Sal."

"No shot, no shot. Your boys get the Yanks, and it's sweeparoni time, babe."

They went back and forth on it for the half-hour of the drive. When she got out, Tori tipped him an extra twenty bucks. "I'm coming to take that back in October after the Twins win, Sal."

"That happens, you get a free ride, babe," he said, handing her a business card.

"Deal."

"See ya, Sota."

She checked into her hotel and immediately went shopping for a dress for the party, which then necessitated the appropriate accessories and shoes, the whole ensemble. She enjoyed visiting some of her favorite stores, getting a hot dog off a corner, picking up an iced tea as she wandered around, settling in with the familiar vibe of the city.

Now, back at her hotel in the late afternoon, she pulled back the curtains at the large picture window, gazing out at the panoramic view of the Hudson River to the west. Five stories below, she could see the outdoor bar and patio that also looked out to the river. As she craned her neck, she could even make out the edge of her old condo tower a few blocks south.

Her last shopping stop before returning to the hotel had been a liquor store. Now she poured herself a bourbon. It was 5:00. The party started at 7:00 p.m. and was at the bar across the street from the hotel.

She had intentionally ignored her phone since she got on the plane this morning. A quick check showed two missed calls, both from Cal. Nothing from Braddock since last night after she texted that she was leaving town for a few days. He'd simply replied: *Okay*.

Did she want him continuing to call her, wanting to talk, or did she want him to let her be for a few days? She decided not to think about it. Instead, she finished her drink, poured another, and decided it was time for a bath.

It was 7:25 when she took one last look in the mirror at her V-neck black sundress and heels and her little Coach purse. She knew she looked good.

When she entered McCall's, she saw the sign for the party pointing to the back, where she knew there was a private room with patio access. She made her way through the crowded bar and peeked inside the room, seeing a few familiar faces. Giving her hair one last flip, she walked into the party. It didn't take long.

"Oh my God!" Geno Harlow called out, a huge grin on his face. "As I live and breathe."

Harlow was standing with Graff, who turned around and smiled broadly, pleased at her surprise appearance. "You're late, Special Agent Hunter."

That call-out got everyone's attention.

"Happy birthday, sir. It's good to see you," Tori greeted, steeping in to give her old boss a warm hug.

"It's great to see you too," Graff said, a big grin on his face. "You look…"

"Fantastic!" Harlow exclaimed loudly. Clearly he'd already had a few. He stepped toward her. "Give me some."

"Geno!"

"Well I'll be damned," Tracy Sheets hollered, coming in from the patio out back having heard all the commotion. "You told me you couldn't make it."

"It was a last-minute thing. I decided to surprise everybody."

"You must have solved that big case you were working."

"No," Tori replied, then leaned in, "more like taking a forced break from it."

"Ah," Tracy replied with raised eyebrows. "And your guy, is he with you? Did you bring him?"

"No," Tori said again. "But enough about all that. Let's get a cocktail." She slipped her arm through Tracy's. "I want all the gossip."

*

Steak knocked on Braddock's door. "Staying late?"

Braddock nodded. "Yeah. What are you still doing here?"

"Finishing a few things up is all," Steak said. "You got any bourbon left in that bottle in your desk?"

"Grab a couple of coffee cups and then close the door." Braddock dug out his stash bottle and poured them each a whiskey.

"I can tell you that thus far, Sheryl and I can't find any connection between Melanie Solmes or Paul Harstad and the Baumans."

"What about the incident in Wadena?"

"The guy he got in the fight with is dead. Has been for years. I put a note in the file."

"Dead end then," Braddock muttered. "DNA match for two crime scenes, no name, no identification."

"The Plover case fits with everything else," Steak said.

"Sure does." Braddock nodded. "Did you see the bit where they stabbed Harstad multiple times?"

"Yes."

"It was personal. Someone really wanted him to hurt."

"He was a ladies' man who like married women or women already in relationships. Those are dangerous waters to fish in," Steak observed, and then changed topics. "What's in the file about contact with Pen Murphy or Sheriff Hunter?"

Braddock sighed. "Well, it could be worse."

"Yeah?"

"They note two phone calls with Jim Hunter and one call with Todd Strom in the county attorney's office. There's a note that a file was emailed to Sheriff Hunter, but there's no copy of the email. I presume the file was the main summary that you and I have both read, but there's no way of knowing for sure."

"So not much in there to say there were in-depth conversations and coordination of investigation between the two agencies that Pen, Hunter and Cal didn't disclose."

"No."

"Good."

"We know otherwise. They still shouldn't have done it."

Steak snorted. "Get off your high horse, would you."

"Excuse me?"

"What, you don't like it when your subordinate calls you on your shit?" Steak asked with bemusement. "The way you thundered away at Cal and Pen and even Tori last night? You were really kind of a dick about it."

Braddock shrugged.

"Not many people get away with being an ass to their boss. A really good boss, by the way."

"Are you speaking about present company or Cal?"

"You're a really good boss too. Maybe just not right now."

"I wasn't wrong. What Pen had them do could put every case—"

"Yeah, yeah, yeah." Steak waved dismissively. "There's like a one percent chance that would happen."

"You can say that now that we've seen the Portage investigative file. But what if—"

"I'm not saying you were per se wrong on the substance. I kind of agree with you there. You were just wrong on the tone."

"Tone?"

"You came off all holier-than-thou. As if you've never fractured a rule or regulation or operated in a gray area. You worked the Joint Terrorism Task Force. Are you telling me you didn't take a liberty or two over the years? Every case subject to review? Pfft, give me an effing break."

Braddock took a gulp of his bourbon.

Steak didn't stop; he was rolling, getting things off his chest. "And as to what they did twenty-four years ago, it's easy for you with the benefit of history to judge them now. You weren't there then."

"What if it turned out that Barr was innocent?"

"He wasn't."

"What if he was?"

"He wasn't," Steak replied. "And you know he wasn't, so stop. You also know they wouldn't have done it if they thought there was any chance he was innocent. You think Cal would do that? Or Pen? Or Tori's father?"

"Cal? No. Jim Hunter? I never knew the man, but I find it hard to believe given Tori. You don't raise someone to be that dedicated and principled without walking the walk yourself. Pen? I know people in these parts think highly of him, but I'm not so sure."

Steak shrugged. "He didn't look good yesterday. I actually didn't mind that you pounded away at him."

"He has blood on his hands. So does Jim Hunter, God rest his soul, and Cal." Braddock sipped his whiskey. "And mark my words, somehow, some way, this will all come to light. It's not a matter of if, it's only a matter of when."

"You were right to have Cal step back. That's probably a smart move."

"That was the bare minimum. And Tori? How about her?"

"She's Jim Hunter's daughter." Steak nodded before taking a long drink from his cup. "You know, boss, it wasn't that you took her off the case that has her pissed at you, although she didn't like that either. She's pissed because of the *way* you did it. You stomped on her father's grave."

Braddock was stunned. "I didn't stomp on his grave."

"Well you sure as hell stomped on the memory she has of him. To her, I'm not sure there's much difference," Steak said. "It really hit *me* when she said she had no family left, only the memories of them. She suffered a lot of loss before she was twenty, and she suffered it alone. She was alone for a long time."

"She's not alone anymore."

"Walking out of here last night, I think she felt very alone again."

Braddock sighed and shook his head in disgust with himself. "Yeah, I imagine she might have," he said, before downing the rest of the whiskey and pouring himself another. "Still, she didn't have to run off to New York…"

*

More and more people came up and greeted Tori. She made the rounds for a few hours, saying hello and catching up with old friends and colleagues. Eventually, as was always the case at parties, she and her closest friends congregated in a corner out on the patio.

Geno Harlow's wife, Britt, admired Tori's outfit. "I just love that dress," she said wistfully. "I can't afford anything like that, though."

"Kids in college," Geno said, throwing his arm around her shoulders. "Two of them. They'll both be off the payroll in a few years, and then, honey, I'll buy you that dress. From Tori. At a discount."

"Ha!" Britt cackled. "That sounds about right."

"What's the big case these days?" Tori asked. "You guys working anything interesting?"

"No, we're just grinding away like always," Tracy said, speaking for the group. "Only more so. There's a hiring freeze on right now."

"Yeah," Harlow moaned. "The stack of files is two feet tall at this point. Could use your help, Tor."

Tori laughed. "I miss you guys, I really do," she said with a big smile. She looked up and around, at the skyscrapers overhead. "I really miss New York too. The hum of the city. Living up in the woods, sometimes it's just so… quiet. Too quiet."

"You sound like you want your old job back," Graff said.

"I thought there was a hiring freeze."

"There is. You want your old job back?" he asked, this time with a hair of seriousness.

"Are you making me an offer?"

"Are you looking for one?"

"Well…"

"No, she is not looking for one," Tracy interjected, throwing her arm around Tori. "She's just fine where she is."

"I'll say. I mean, look at you," Ruby Gaines said. "The dress, the long, gorgeous hair, all toned up and looking so fine. Whatever it is you're doing in Minnesota, it sure suits you."

"Yeah," Tori said, doing a mock twirl.

Ruby spoke more seriously. "You look so… different. You got this ease about you now."

"I do?"

"Oh yeah."

Graff laughed. "Well, if you ever are interested in coming back, we could sure use you. The door is always open, just say the word."

"I'll keep that in mind, sir," Tori said, clinking glasses with him. Graff stepped back from the group, his wife pulling on his arm.

Tracy saw her husband holding up his wrist and pointing to his watch. It was time to go. "Give me a minute," she said, and drew Tori aside. "Listen, I have to go. The hubby and I have some things to take care of in the morning, some appointments. But listen, you're coming over tomorrow night for dinner."

"I am?"

"Yes," Tracy said, her tone serious. "We need to talk."

"About what?"

"Why you're really here."

CHAPTER EIGHTEEN

"The less you know the better"

Braddock woke early. As he swam in the cool water of the lake, he replayed the argument with Cal, Pen and Tori in his head. He floated on his back in front of his dock, looking up to the light blue sky, running it over in his mind again and again.

Steak was right.

He had been a self-righteous ass. Directing that righteousness at Pen, and to a lesser extent Cal, was, in his mind, justified, but he'd gone too far with Tori. Yeah, Big Jim had screwed up, but that didn't mean she had to take responsibility in his place.

He showered and dressed, taking in how quiet the house was. For a few minutes he stood in Quinn's room, missing his son, who was away for another week. He picked up the picture of himself, Quinn and Meghan. Quinn had been three at the time. He remembered the day they'd taken the photo, in Central Park at the playground. Meghan had just started having headaches, thought they were migraines and was talking about maybe going to the doctor.

They never could have imagined what was coming. Two years later, she was gone.

He looked up to another shelf, and there was the photo of Quinn and Tori at the hockey arena. That had been a good night.

Quinn had scored a big goal and she'd been there to see it. They'd come back to the house with pizza and the three of them had sat around the table talking for hours, like a family. One of the things that had made him happy was how much Quinn had grown to like Tori. The two of them had become very fond of one another. The house had been a very lively place the last several months. At least until now.

In the kitchen he brewed up coffee and felt the quiet of the house suffocating him. *I have to get out of here.*

He grabbed his truck keys and headed for the Wavy Café. For the next two hours, he sat at the diner counter, eating breakfast, chatting with some fellow hockey dads who had stopped in, reading the *Star Tribune* cover to cover, and then, after that, the *New York Times* on his phone. A native New Yorker, he liked to keep up with home. It had been a few years since he'd been back, and he was thinking it was time to get Quinn there now that he was old enough to appreciate the city. And there were old friends he would like to see. He suspected that was what Tori was up to.

He was staring at his phone, contemplating giving her a call, when a familiar face appeared on the screen.

"Sheriff Corbin Hansen, what can I do for you this fine morning?"

"It's what I can do for you, my friend," the Cass County sheriff replied. "I need you to meet me in Pine River."

"Pine River? Why?"

"I just got a call from a guy who I think you and I both need to talk to. I only spoke to him for a few minutes, but my gut says he knows something about two murders I'm looking into, and he might have seen something I hear you're looking for as well. When can you meet me?"

Braddock checked his watch. "How about an hour?"

*

Corbin Hansen was a wise old owl. Cryptic as his message had been, if Corb was of the mind that Braddock needed to give this his attention, he had to trust it was worth the drive. When he pulled into the parking lot for the local bank, he found Sheriff Hansen parked and waiting in his Explorer.

"You didn't give me much, Corb. Why is it you and I are interested in this guy?" he said.

"Did you hear about the explosion up in Remer earlier this week?" Hansen asked as they started walking toward the bank. "It was on the local news."

"Yeah. Gas leak or something, right? I saw the footage. Big ball of flame."

"That's it," Hansen said as he opened the door into the bank. "The gas line was leaking. The house was filled with fumes. The homeowners opened the door, flipped a light switch and *kaboom*. But it was no accident. It was homicide."

"Homicide? You're sure?"

"The gas line was intentionally tampered with. No doubt about it."

"Who were the victims?"

"Alan and Jan Sampson," Hansen said. "And that's where Leo Brooks, this guy we're going to speak with, comes in. He's the manager here and was a friend of the Sampsons. He may know something that interests both of us."

Brooks was in his mid-forties, with graying hair and a slight build. He led them to a conference room and pulled the blinds closed. When they were all seated, he related that he and Alan Sampson had met up to go fishing very early last Saturday morning on Middle Goodwin Lake. "I live here in Pine River and Alan up in Remer, so what we'd usually do when we were going fishing was meet in Emily and figure a lake to go to. Last Saturday, Alan decided on Middle Goodwin."

"What time?"

"We planned to go out at five a.m. We met in Emily at four forty-five, got coffees and donuts, then drove over to the launch."

"And which boat launch did you go to?"

"The smaller one on Middle Goodwin. Traffic is usually pretty light compared to the big one on Lower Goodwin. You can get in and out quick and there's space to park. The interesting thing was that when we got there, a truck was pulling a boat out of the water."

"It was early for that, wasn't it?"

"Yeah," Brooks said, nodding. "If someone was there launching, that's completely normal. But taking a boat out at that point seemed odd. Not unheard of to fish all night, but people who do that usually live on the lake. I didn't really think anything of it at the time, though. They took out the boat and were on their way and then we launched and went fishing. By the time we got out on the water and dropped our lines, the sun was starting to come up."

"Did you fish the next day?" Braddock asked.

"On Sunday? No."

"So how is it you came to call Sheriff Hansen?"

"First, a detective from the sheriff's office called me about their investigation of the explosion at Alan's house. He told me they were treating what happened to Alan and Jan as a possible homicide. The detective asked questions about why someone would want to kill them. I had nothing for him. Alan and Jan didn't have an enemy in the world."

"Yet here we are," Sheriff Hansen said.

"Right," Brooks replied, getting to it. "Last night I was talking to another fishing buddy who likes to move his boat around. He would fish with Alan too, and he said that last Sunday, when he was at the Middle Goodwin launch, sheriff's deputies were asking if anyone had been there Saturday and seen someone coming off the lake early that morning."

"The guys you saw coming off the lake. Describe the truck and boat," Braddock asked.

"The truck was a Dodge Ram, I remember that. It was black, just like the fishing boat."

"And the boat?"

"Like I said, black, fiberglass kind of body on it that would sit low in the water. A twenty-footer, I think. Big black outboard motor, so it had plenty of power. I didn't take the closest look at it. But seeing black truck, black boat in the dark kind of made it a little memorable."

"What brand of boat?"

"I wish I could remember, Detective. Like I said, I didn't look that closely, and while I like to fish, I don't keep track of all the boat models. I left that to Alan—he was really into that kind of stuff."

"But you remember it was a Dodge Ram truck?" Hansen said. "How come you remember that?"

"I saw it when we came down that narrow road to the launch area. They had the trailer backed in, taking the boat out of the water. The truck was nose out. Dodge Rams have those distinctive front grilles. That truck had that, a shiny chrome grill."

"License plate number?" Braddock asked, knowing the answer.

Brooks shook his head. "No. I didn't get that. Never even bothered to look."

"Was it one man or two taking the boat out?"

"Two," Brooks said. "Though I only saw them briefly. And really only the one guy. He was finishing cranking the boat onto the trailer and securing it."

"Describe him?"

"Uh…" Brooks thought for a moment. "I know I keep saying this, but it was dark, not much for light. He was Caucasian and seemed kind of skinny."

"How was he dressed?" Hansen asked.

"You know, that was another thing a little odd. He was dressed in all black. You'd think if you were out at night, you'd wear something reflective or light-colored to make yourself a little more visible."

"But this guy, he was in all black?" Braddock checked.

"At least in dark colors for sure," Brooks said. "I think Alan even said something joking to the effect that these guys were all stealth, sneaking up on the fish."

"Did you get a look at the other guy?"

He shook his head. "I just saw there was a driver. I couldn't tell you anything about him."

"Big guy? Little guy?"

"I'm not sure. I just know the one guy I did see was kind of skinny. But like I said, I only looked at him for all of ten or fifteen seconds from fifty feet away in the dark. I mean, I don't think I could pick him out of a lineup."

"Answer me this. Did they pull out normally or did they race away?"

Brooks paused, thinking. "You know, there is one thing I don't think I saw them do."

"Take out the plug?" Hansen asked. "Drain the water?"

Brooks nodded. "That and they didn't strap the back of the boat to the trailer either. Now maybe they drove down a little way and took care of those things, but usually you do it right there. Taking the plug out takes what, twenty seconds with a wrench? Strapping the boat up another minute at most. They did just race out of there."

Braddock jotted down some notes and thought about what Brooks was telling him. The man seemed on the level and had seen something that he'd belatedly realized was important.

"One last question," he asked. "Do you think that if I found the Dodge Ram and the boat on the trailer together, you could identify it?"

"If I could see it all hooked up?"

Braddock nodded.

"Possibly. I'd probably be able to tell you if the setup looked right. Were those guys the ones who killed Alan and Jan?"

Braddock shared a look with Hansen. It seemed probable that these were the guys who'd killed the Stroms. They were trying to slip away before daylight, and Sampson and Brooks had just happened to stumble upon them.

"It's possible," Braddock acknowledged. "It's also possible that those two men killed Todd and Jennifer Strom, who had a lake home on Upper Goodwin, and their friend Dennis Troy. They may have got the license number for Alan's truck and tracked him down."

"Should my wife and I be getting out of town?" Brooks asked. "I mean given what happened to Alan and Jan, with the explosion and all, I'm worried now."

Braddock looked to Hansen again. "What do you think?"

"Mr. Brooks, I won't lie to you," Hansen said. "If what happened to your friends is related to what Detective Braddock is investigating, and what I'm investigating, and you did have a place to go to for a week, I wouldn't discourage you from doing it as long as you stayed in touch with me."

"I'm with the sheriff on that," Braddock said. "I just need to be able to reach you if I find that truck and boat."

Fifteen minutes later, Braddock and Hansen said goodbye in the parking lot.

"Keep in contact with this guy, Corb."

"He saw your killers, didn't he?"

"Yeah," Braddock replied. "I just wish he'd seen them a little better."

As he drove back, Braddock replayed the conversation with Brooks. He called Cal.

"I'm surprised to hear from you," Cal said.

"Things got heated the other day."

"Yeah, well, that happens. You're right, it's a mess and I screwed up. What's up?"

"We have a new IT director for the county, don't we?"

"Yes. She's been there a couple of months. Her name's Kathryn Turner. Seems like a very smart lady."

"I haven't met her, but I think I need her to do something. Can you make an introductory phone call and then have her call me?"

"When?"

"Now."

"What do you have?"

"Something I need checked, and given her limited tenure with the county, she might be perfect for it."

"I'll make the call right now," Cal replied. "Have you heard from Tori?"

"Man, everybody keeps asking me that."

"Everybody?"

"You and Steak."

"That certainly qualifies as everybody," Cal quipped. "I left her a couple of messages, but no return call."

"I think she's in New York City visiting some friends."

"That was sudden."

"Yeah, well…"

"I know the feeling. I'll call Turner. Are you sure you don't want to tell me what it's about?"

"The less you know the better."

Turner called him fifteen minutes later. "Sheriff Lund said you wanted to talk about something urgent."

"It could be," Braddock said. "Can I steal fifteen minutes of your time right now?"

"Sure."

"Where do you live?"

*

Kathryn Turner lived on the eastern side of Northern Pine Lake, two miles from town. When he pulled up, Braddock recognized her husband from the hockey arena. Their son was a couple of years behind Quinn. They chatted sports for a few minutes before Kathryn led him around the back of the house. They took seats at a table under an umbrella on the patio.

"So how can I help you?"

"It's a sensitive matter… either that or I could be sending you on a wild goose chase."

She laughed. "Well, as long as the task is well defined."

"Let me see if I can do that for you. First question, if I gave you a license plate number, can you track down if any county employees might have accessed it say in the last month or two?"

Turner thought for a moment. "Yes, I should be able to figure that out."

"Can you do it or do you have to have someone do it for you?"

She smiled. "I'm the director, and often directors are management types, not technical types. But my philosophy is probably much like yours: you can't be a manager or a director unless you understand and know how to do your employees' jobs."

"I hear that," Braddock said. "Good, because here's the second task. This one is more difficult, and it requires real discretion on your part, because I'm going to tell you some things you maybe ought not to know and can't tell others about. That and you need to be careful that nobody else knows you're doing this."

Turner sat a little more upright, but she nodded. "I understand."

"You know the big investigation we're dealing with at the moment?"

"Those multiple murders everyone is talking about?"

"Yes," Braddock said. "Twenty-four years ago, the then sheriff for the county, Jim Hunter, had an IT employee named Dan Newman."

"One of the murder victims," Turner said, putting her hand to her mouth.

Braddock nodded in confirmation. "We're pretty sure that Sheriff Hunter had Newman remove evidence of some information from the county systems. The information related to phone calls between Hunter and the Portage County Sheriff's Department, as well as a phone call to Todd Strom, who worked in the county attorney's office, from the Portage County Attorney's Office."

"Isn't Todd Strom a victim too?"

"Yes. Sheriff Hunter also had Newman remove an email from Portage County that contained a report. Are you following so far?"

"Yes."

"We suspect that Newman was killed because of what he did for the sheriff. The only way someone could possibly have known about that was through our own systems, probably email and phone. They went hunting for the information, we think most likely recently, and found it somehow."

"Why would somebody do that?"

"That is the very question I want to ask them."

"And you think it's someone who works for the county?"

"I think it might be someone who works for *you*."

"You think the killer works for me?" Turner blurted anxiously. "My God."

"Well, I suppose there is a small possibility of that, although my gut tells me it's more likely someone was paid by the killer to find the information. Someone who knows the systems, knows where the holes are, how to get at data and information, and probably somebody who has an idea of how to cover their tracks."

"And our systems, such as they were twenty-four years ago, are the only place this information would have been?"

"Yes, I think so."

"Do you have any evidence that someone has done this?"

"Specific evidence? No. Supposition? Yes. There might be another way for someone to have learned that Todd Strom took a phone call twenty-four years ago. That's documented in a file with Portage County. But Dan Newman's involvement was known only by Sheriff Hunter, and he's been dead twenty years."

Turner stood and started pacing around the patio, tapping her lips with her left index finger, deep in thought. "You're sure about all this?"

"Sure? No. But I think it's very possible. I can't think of any other way the killers would know of Dan Newman's role in this."

"I can't either."

"If I'm right, do you think you can track down that person?"

"Only one way to find out, and that is to try. I assume the sooner the better?"

"Yes." Braddock ripped out a piece of paper from his notepad. "Here is the license plate to check. Now, I think if someone did look it up, it would have been from last Saturday morning forward. Or at least that's the time period I'm interested in."

"And this license plate. Who does it belong to?"

"Their house was blown up in Remer last week because of something one of them may have seen," Braddock said.

"I saw that in the news." Turner's eyes were wide.

"Kathryn, listen to me. Only Sheriff Lund and I know that I'm asking you to do something. The sheriff doesn't know I'm asking you to do *this*. If you are uncomfortable about it, just say, and I'll understand and figure out another way."

"I know how to cover *my* tracks," Turner said.

"Don't take any unnecessary chances here," Braddock commanded. "Promise me you won't do that."

"I won't."

"Okay. If you find something, you call me and nobody else. Understood?"

"Understood."

As Braddock walked away from Kathryn Turner's house, he felt a little better, at least about the case. For the first time in days, he had a feeling that something was working for him.

CHAPTER NINETEEN

*"I thought it was supposed to be different
with the ones you love"*

Dinner was a barbecue with steaks, salads and dessert, with the wine supplied by Tori. After dessert, Tracy's husband Sam said, "I've got the dishes. You two go catch up."

They stepped out onto the small back patio and sat down on lounge chairs. Tracy wasted no time. "What did you and Braddock fight about?"

"Who said anything about a fight?"

"Are we really going to do that dance?" Tracy said, looking Tori in the eye. "You were taken off the case. You hardly mentioned him either last night or tonight. I bring up his name and you stare daggers. What gives?"

Tori took a long drink of her wine.

"He must have pissed you off something fierce to get you to fly here and make semi-serious inquiries about coming back."

Tori's eyes started moistening and she wiped away tears with the back of her hand.

"What happened?"

"It's about my father, actually…"

Tori spent the next half-hour giving Tracy a run-down of the situation. The Newmans and their daughter, the Stroms, Barr, the Plover case that hadn't been disclosed, Braddock going off on Cal, Pen Murphy and her father, and then her removal from the case. She could tell her everything knowing Tracy could be trusted to keep it all in confidence.

"I mean, I see this seventeen-year-old girl, Cara, cute, athletic, plays soccer, and I see myself, Trace. I mean, I see myself when Jessie went missing. That blank stare on her face when she was sitting in that ambulance. The grief, the guilt, I could feel it, I could actually *feel* it. And then mix in my dad's… decision and whether that was right or wrong and does he have this poor girl's father's blood on his hands and… God."

"Well, that sure sounds like a big old fat mess."

"You think?"

"Braddock took you off the case. You know he probably had to, right?"

Tori nodded.

"So what's the problem?"

She sighed. "He just wasn't very… sensitive about it."

Tracy laughed out loud.

"What?"

"He wasn't very sensitive? You of all people wanted him to be sensitive?"

"Whose side are you on?"

"Yours, always yours, sister," Tracy replied, patting Tori on the arm. "But be honest, sensitivity has not always been one of your strong suits."

"What do you mean?"

"This is me you're talking to here, Tori." She gave a sly grin, then took a sip of her wine. She was having fun playing psychiatrist. "I've known you how long? Fifteen, sixteen years."

"Your point?"

"You are one of the brassiest agents I've ever seen, man or woman. No time for fools. No filter. No compunction about telling superiors what you think ought to be done."

"Now hold on…"

"You know I'm right," Tracy said. "And I love that about you. I wish I possessed the audacity to speak out like you do. I always play it safe. If I say something, I wonder how it will impact my career. You never seem to care about any of that."

"It probably isn't my most endearing quality."

"It endears you to me. But look, if you're direct, people will be the same with you. Even the ones you love, and you absolutely love that guy, which is also why you're so furious with him."

"I thought it was supposed to be different with the ones you love."

Tracy laughed again.

"Is that the way it is with you and Sam?"

"Attorney and FBI special agent, what do you think?" She chuckled whimsically, shaking her head. "We've had some doozies over the years, but that's marriage. There *will* be arguments."

"I'm not married."

"But Braddock's the first man you've ever been this far down the road with."

"It's the first time down this road period."

"Hence it got a little rough, so you panicked and ran away to New York City and your comfort zone."

"I didn't panic."

Tracy raised an eyebrow.

"Come on," Tori pleaded. "Cut me a little slack here."

"You came here for slack?"

"Well… yeah."

"No, no, no," Tracy replied, shaking her head. "I'm here to provide a cold dose of reality. This will not be your last quarrel, row, spat, argument, or squabble. Not with two alphas like you and Braddock. He's a New Yorker, Tori. He had his shield with the NYPD. You think he's going to back down, not tell it straight?"

"Well…"

"He might be little mellower than you, but he's definitely Type A too."

Tori nodded reluctantly. "That he is."

Tracy smiled broadly. "I'd assume he's under a lot of stress. He got fired up about work, about this pile of crap dumped on him, and said some things in the heat of the moment that he'd probably like to take back, but…"

"But what?"

"He's right. Your dad screwed up. The prosecutor screwed up worse, and this Cal you speak so warmly of, like he's your favorite uncle or something, he's kind of screwed the pooch too. Not so much back then, but certainly now. What they did was create a ticking time bomb that finally went off."

Tori nodded again. "No way my dad could have seen this coming, though."

"No, probably not. But he took a big risk, touched the hot stove, and now others are getting burned. That doesn't happen when you follow the rules."

It was Tori's turn to laugh.

"What?"

"That's what Braddock said." She closed her eyes and exhaled a sigh. "You know, he's probably as mad at me as I am at him."

"Probably."

"So, I'm here and he's there. Now what?"

"The real question I think you need to answer is what do you want?" Tracy said. "I heard you last night asking about the job, and I could tell you were putting out just the tiniest of feelers."

"I don't know about that."

"You were."

"And what if I was?"

"I'd say you should think long and hard about the wisdom of that. I haven't really seen you in a year, but I've talked to you often, and I can tell how… healthy you are. I can see it, mentally, physically. I mean you look absolutely fantastic, but then again, you always did."

"Stop it."

"Tori, you're attractive. Men gravitate to you, they always have. I saw it in action again last night, the looks you got in that dress, guys sidling up next to you for a hug or a quick conversation. The smiles, the lingering looks as you walked away."

"I didn't notice."

"Yeah, right," Tracy replied, not buying it. "The fascinating thing to me is that the first man that ever got you to stick around for more than a week or two was Braddock—a New York City transplant, mind you, but a sheriff's detective in your old hometown. I never in a million years saw that one coming. That tells me that beyond being one handsome dude, he must have a little something special himself."

"He does."

"The sex is good?"

"Oh my God, yes," Tori said with a big grin.

Tracy cackled. "So, girl, what's the issue?"

"Why couldn't he have been here?" Tori said with a sigh. "Tracy, why couldn't I have met him here and not back in Manchester Bay? I mean, this case…"

"Is just a case."

"Braddock is right about it, though. What my dad, Cal and Pen did, if it gets out, it could really alter how my father was remembered. I love it when people tell me how much they liked and respected him. Hearing that for the last year has been nice. I hold on to it. I feel like I've been able to have him back in my life a little, let the memories back in. But this case…"

"It'll pass."

"Last summer it was Jessie. Now it's my father. What's next? I mean, I talk to a shrink and she's great, and Braddock, he's always there."

"You love him?"

"Oh, I do," Tori said, nodding. "I know I do. I feel it, you know, deep down. It's real. But it's all so… I don't know, complicated there. It gets to me at times, it really does."

"That's life."

"But sometimes I wonder why I'm doing this. I could live anywhere. Why live there?"

"You know why."

"Is that enough?"

"That's something only you can answer," Tracy said. "I consider myself qualified to offer this opinion, but he's been really good for you, it's visible. And you love him, and I just love to hear you say that. Whatever is going through your mind, make sure you think on that, because it took you a long time to find someone who got to you like that."

Tori nodded and sat back in her chair, eyes closed. After a few minutes, she said, "You know, I wasn't lying last night. I do miss New York City."

"Fine, but don't come back because you're running from something. Come back because it's what you really, really deep down want."

She was quiet again for a while, sipping her wine.

"Have you talked to Braddock since your little blow-up?"

"No. I know you're laughing about my complaint of his lack of sensitivity, but the way he went after my father… I'm still just so furious with him. I don't care if he was right."

"Well, you can stay that way until you get back," Tracy said. "But then put it away. You each say you're sorry and have some hot make up sex."

"Oh, and that just makes it all better?"

"No, but it can't hurt. When's your flight?"

"Tomorrow night, eight fifteen."

They sat for a few minutes listening to the hum of the Brooklyn neighborhood.

"I'm thinking about the case you described to me," Tracy said.

"And?"

"Someone needs to get this Barr guy's mom to talk."

"Braddock and I tried."

"Try again. You empathize with victims better than anyone I've ever seen. Make her see you not as an investigator or an agent, but as a victim, Tori. Do that and I'm betting you'll get her to talk."

"I don't know. She seemed pretty hardened in her position."

"Then get creative."

"I'll take it under advisement."

*

"It's dark," Deputy Lewis argued with Cal. "It's after ten o'clock at night. At least let me go out there with you and Pen."

"Not necessary," Cal replied, holding his fishing rods and tackle box. "It's a beautiful night with a little moon up there. I'm not sitting inside when the fish are biting the way they are."

"But, boss…"

"We'll just be out in front of the cabin, a couple, maybe three hundred yards," Cal said. "And amongst our friends. It'll be fine."

"I don't know. Braddock will shit a brick if—"

"I'm armed, well armed. I'm going."

Lewis sighed and then slowly nodded. "I guess you're the boss."

It was a perfect night to fish, a light breeze to keep away the bugs, and gentle waves on the lake as they walked along the dock. They could see their group of boats a quarter-mile to the south. "The boys tell me the fish are really biting," Cal said.

"Then let's get our share," Pen replied.

Two hours later, they had a couple of fish on the stringer. Cal would let Pen clean them, and they'd have themselves a fish fry for lunch tomorrow.

"It might be just about time to head in," Pen said. The other boats in their group had pulled in their lines and made for shore as the time slipped past midnight. There was just one other boat out. It was perhaps a hundred yards to their south, and from what he could tell, they too looked to be packing up. He could hear the outboard motor rumbling.

"You're probably right. Let me reel… Oh boy, wait a second," Cal said excitedly, leaning back in his seat. "Pen, I got one. I got one. A big one, I think."

"Oh yeah, look at the rod bend," Pen said as he shuffled to the front of the boat with the net. "Keep the tension on her, pal."

"I got it," Cal grunted as he slowly turned the reel, fighting the fish, keeping the line taut as he pulled it to the surface.

Pen took out a small flashlight and directed the beam down on the water.

"There it is! I can kind of see it along the surface there," Cal bellowed. "I'm going to bring it back to you now."

With his right hand, Pen dropped the net into the water. Cal rotated right in his chair, cranked the reel again and felt the fish turn back.

"And… got her," Pen yelled as he lifted the net. "Oh, it's a big one. She's a beauty!"

"Sure is," Cal replied loudly, reaching into the net and hoisting the big walleye out just as the other boat was pulling by. He held the fish up. "Look at that, huh?"

The passing boat turned on a bright flashlight and shone it on Cal and the fish.

"Wow, that's a big one!" a high-pitched voice called. "Great catch."

"Uh, Cal…" Pen said, now squinting at the other boat.

"Huge, isn't it," Cal said as he started extracting the hook from the walleye's mouth.

"Yeah, that's a hell of a fish," another voice agreed.

"Cal?"

Cal looked up to see Pen's eyes suddenly bulge.

"Look ou—"

Pop! Pop! Pop!

Pen collapsed back into the boat.

Cal spun and looked to the other boat.

Pop! Pop! Pop! Pop!

*

"I got them," D exclaimed as Slim drove the boat fast across the lake, no navigation lights on as they sped north on Northern Pine.

"Make for the channel?"

"Yes."

Slim kept looking back for pursuers, but didn't see any. He flipped the navigation lights back on as they motored into the winding channel in the northwestern end of Northern Pine Lake. "With them gone, that's it, right? We're done?" he asked anxiously.

"We're done."

CHAPTER TWENTY

"You hear what I'm saying"

Braddock snapped awake in the big roadster chair in his family room. His left leg was draped over the arm, his half-finished beer still in his right hand. Three empties sat on the coffee table. The television was on. It was pitch black outside.

What had awoken him? It was some kind of sound. He heard it again and realized it was his cell phone, which had fallen to the floor under the coffee table. "Yeah?" Braddock said tiredly. "Wait… what? Shot? Where? Are you kidding me? On my way there."

Fifteen minutes later, he pulled to a stop at the hospital and raced inside to the emergency room area, where he found a distraught Lucy Lund. "How is he?"

"He's in surgery," she said. "He was shot four times in the chest."

"And Pen?"

"He… died, Will. He died."

"What were they doing, Lucy?"

"Oh, they just went fishing, those two old fools," she said exasperatedly. "Cal told the deputy sitting outside Pen's house that they'd be out front of the cabin fishing with some other boats. Frewer was at our place, and Cal told him to stay and guard me, that it would be fine. I know Frewer protested, but Cal wasn't having it. I went to bed. The next thing I know, Frewer is banging on the door…" She started tearing up, and he looked back to see one of Cal's sons and his wife rushing into the ER area.

Braddock stepped back to let Lucy be with her family and walked further down the hall to talk to Frewer. "And?"

Deputy Frewer sighed and shook his head, looking down the hallway to Deputy Lewis who was talking to Steak and Eggleston. "I told the boss no, but he wasn't hearing it. He said he was going. Lewis and I both volunteered to go out in the boat with them. He blew us off. Said they were going with friends, it would be fine, he was armed. Maybe *you* can tell him to go pound sand, but I can't. Lew can't."

"I hear ya," Braddock said. "What happened?"

"There was a big-ass walleye in the boat at Cal's feet. If I had to guess, they had the fish on the line, and while they were working together to get it in the boat, these guys cruised up in another boat and smoked them."

"Who found them?"

"They were fishing out on the drop-off just south of Pen's place. One of the guys in the group was walking up to his house after getting the boat in his lift when he thought he heard gunshots. He went back down to the dock and looked out and saw the boat sitting there, and it didn't look right to him. Thank God for Cal's sake he went back out to check. Pen was dead, one in the head. Cal was all shot up, but he had a pulse. The guy immediately called 911 and drove the boat in."

"How bad is Cal?"

"He had…" Frewer closed his eyes for a moment, trying to keep it together. "He was shot four times in the chest. I heard a paramedic say they lost him in the ambulance, but then got him back."

"Anyone see the other boat?"

"I don't think so. I mean they were out there in the dark. You've done it. I've done it. You can't see shit out there. One boat looks like the next. But somehow these guys blended in, and I'll guarantee you they knew which boat Pen and Cal were in."

Steak and Eggs came down the hall when they saw Braddock.

"Let's have patrols hit all the launches," he said.

"Will, there are what, ten boat launches on the Northern Pine lake chain," Steak protested.

"I know. It happened over two hours ago, and these guys are probably off the lake by now, but all the same, check it."

"I'll radio it in. What are we looking for?"

"Dark-colored truck, maybe a Dodge Ram, with a dark-colored boat. If we see that combination anywhere, pull it over."

Braddock snapped awake in his hospital chair to see a familiar face. "Hey, Doc."

"How have you healed up?" It was the surgeon who'd patched him up last summer.

"Good. I have a nice scar, but otherwise good. How's Cal?"

"Alive," the doctor answered. "They got him good, though."

"I'm not family, you don't need to hedge. Bottom line. Is he going to make it?"

The doctor sighed. "I think so. We got all the holes. Vitals are holding. We're watching closely, but I'm optimistic. Now, you should go home and get some sleep."

Braddock snorted a bitter laugh. "My work is only just starting. Again."

Late in the morning, Braddock reconvened with Steak and Eggleston as well as Lewis and Frewer in his office.

"We've been knocking on the doors along the entire stretch of the lake," Steak said. "A few people wondered if they'd heard shots just after midnight, but they didn't see anything."

"How about the fishermen in the group?"

"We've talked to them. There are five boats in the group that goes out a few nights a week. They said there are often other boats out as well. That drop-off is very popular this time of year. One guy said there might have been ten boats in the area last night. Another said eleven, and another thought there were eight. Reality is, they came and went. But look, it's dark out there. Other than little navigation lights, which just tell you a boat is there, nobody could see anything. When the only other boat left was Pen and Cal, the killers saw their chance and took it."

"By the time the guy from their group got back out there, the shooters were long gone. They could have been all the way across to the other side of Northern Pine, or gone north to the Long Channel and on to all kinds of places from there," Eggleston said. "There's just so much water to cover."

Braddock nodded. "And the launches?"

"We've got people out asking questions," Steak said. "Nothing so far. I'm not optimistic. What's the security situation on Cal?"

"It's a fortress over there," Braddock said. "Nobody is getting to him."

"Has anyone called Tori?"

Braddock closed his eyes. "I probably should." He checked his watch. It was just after 11:30 a.m. He reached for his cell phone and made the call.

*

"Thank you for setting up brunch," Tori said to Geno and Britt Harlow. "It was great."

"It was so good to see you," Britt said, hugging her again.

"Yeah," Geno agreed, throwing his arm around her waist. "Just like old times."

"Yeah, only our brunches then were stale Danish and coffee sludge from the buffet at some hotel with Express in its name," Tori joked.

"But the conversation was every bit as good," Geno said, pulling her close. "That's what matters, whether you're here or a thousand miles away. You hear what I'm saying."

"Yeah."

Geno smiled. "Don't be a stranger. Don't be afraid to drop me a line every so often, let me know how you're doing in the woods."

Tori laughed. "I will."

She waved goodbye and started making her way back to the hotel, stopping for an ice coffee before finding a bench in a small park and sitting down. She replayed her talk with Tracy, thinking about where she was at in her life, about Braddock, about Manchester Bay, and whether she could handle it all.

Her phone buzzed in her shoulder bag with perfect timing. Braddock.

It was time to at least talk.

"Hey," she greeted warmly. "I've been thinking of you."

"I've been thinking of you too. We have some things to talk about."

"Yeah, we do. Look—"

"It has to wait, though," he said abruptly.

"Uh… okay."

"You need to get back here right now."

"Why?"

"Pen is dead. Cal has been shot. Four times."

Tori closed her eyes. "Is he alive? Just tell me, is he alive?"

*

Tori's flight arrived at 10:30 p.m. It was 11:00 by the time she got out of the airport. The drive north to Manchester Bay took over two hours. She pushed her way inside the house and found Braddock sprawled in a chair in the family room, an empty glass and half-empty bottle of bourbon in front of him, along with his badge and gun.

His eyes popped open. "Hi there," he said sleepily, sitting up.

She walked over and sat down in his lap, pecking him on the lips before gently rubbing his scruffy beard. "You need a shave."

He nodded, his eyes weary, his expression melancholy. But his arms wrapped around her tightly and he buried his head in her shoulder.

Tori held him for several minutes, lightly caressing his head, not saying a word. Finally she sat back and held his face in both her hands before giving him another tender peck. "Come on," she said, standing up and reaching for his hand. "Let's get you to bed, little boy."

CHAPTER TWENTY-ONE

"People you care about disappoint you sometimes"

Tori woke just past 7:00 a.m. and was surprised to roll over and find Braddock still in bed, lying on his back, hands behind his head, staring at the ceiling fan as it whirred around. She laid her head on his chest.

"Cal is awake," he said after a few minutes. "I got a text from Lucy an hour ago. He's conscious, weak, but communicative."

"I'm going to go see him," Tori said.

"You're like a daughter to Cal," he said as he lightly ran his fingers over her back. "He needs to see you. He needs to know things are okay between the two of you."

She nodded, listening to the soothing rhythm of his heartbeat.

"I better get up and get going," he said after a few more quiet minutes. "Long day ahead."

"You shower. I'll go downstairs and get something going," Tori said, rolling out of bed and pulling on a robe.

In the kitchen, she brewed coffee, then fired up the stove and made some scrambled eggs and sausages while also setting the table. She had it all done by the time Braddock came down, freshly shaved and sporting a dark navy suit and light blue checked dress shirt.

She stood back and looked him over. He still looked dog-tired, his eyes baggy, but she said, "You really wear that suit."

"Yeah?" he asked with a slight smile, his eyes brightening just a touch.

"Oh yeah, very dapper."

She plated him some breakfast.

"Looks great," he said.

"I've learned a thing or two watching you," she said. She put a small plate of sliced fruit on the table as well, and brought over the coffee pot and orange juice bottle.

They ate breakfast and chatted, falling into their normal routine, although there was a definite air of distance between them. Cal's shooting had brought them back together, but Tori sensed there would need to be a clearing of the air when the time was right. For now, she was just worried about him. She'd not seen him so downbeat in all their time together.

"Is there anything I can do to help?" she asked.

He shook his head. "You know I'd rather have you working this, right?"

"I know."

"And you're just a phone call away if I need to pick your brain for some reason."

"Yes, I am," Tori replied, feeling the indirect sting of rebuke for not answering her phone, but letting it pass.

"There is one thought I had as I was showering this morning."

"Which is what?"

"This might be over now, in the sense that if it's about what your father, Cal and Pen did, they've now wiped everybody out."

"Not Cal. He's alive."

"Yeah, well, he's in bad shape. He's going to be out a long time. Who knows if he'll ever make it back to the job," Braddock said. "Four to the chest. At his age, with his health, why would he? There's nothing left for him to accomplish, plus I wonder if he could even survive the scrutiny that might be coming. He and I have been holding County Attorney Backstrom off, but now? I don't how much longer I can do that. By tomorrow, I'm guessing he'll be demanding an audience. With Pen's death and what happened to Cal, it's all going to come out."

"Then it comes out," she said. "I don't think my dad could ever have foreseen all this."

"Hey, I don't either. I know your dad was a good man, and I'm sorry if I made you think otherwise."

Tori nodded. "But you were right. He was a big boy, he knew the risks. He took them."

"He's not here to take the heat," Braddock said. "And I don't think it's fair that you should have to take it, from me or anyone else."

"I'm more worried about having to tell Cara Newman that her father was killed because of something *my* father asked him to do seven years before she was even born." She exhaled a long breath. "That… that will be hard."

Braddock looked to her and nodded. "I can help."

"Nah," she said. "You have enough on your plate. Besides, it's something I have to do. She needs to hear it from me. I'll just have to find the right time. We're not there yet, I don't think."

"Well in the meantime, why don't we both drive to the hospital and see Cal."

They arrived at the hospital a half-hour later. Lucy greeted them in the hallway. "He's pretty weak, so not too long, okay? But he is awake, he's conscious."

"Is he with it?" Tori asked.

"Yes. He's fully aware of what's going on. And grumpy."

"Well then he's obviously going to be fine," Braddock said with a little smile and a wink.

They all filed into the hospital room. Braddock and Tori each took a side of the bed. Cal was lying on his back, head slightly elevated. Tubes ran into his left arm, and he had a nasal cannula for breathing assistance. He was gaunt, pale and weak, but his eyes were plenty alive. He looked to Braddock. "Anything yet?" he asked in a raspy whisper.

Braddock shook his head, knowing that his boss would want to discuss the case before anything else. "What do you remember?"

"We were getting ready to go in when I hooked a big fish. I was reeling it in, Pen had the net and flashlight out. I got it into the net and was holding it up as another boat approached."

"Could you see who was in the boat?"

"No," Cal said. "Two men, low in the water. They were twenty, thirty feet out. They had a bright flashlight that they shone on us as I held up the fish, and then they... fired."

"It was like they were shinning a couple of deer."

"Exactly. I don't remember anything after that."

"Okay, boss, you rest, get better. I've got everything under control, okay?" Braddock squeezed Cal's hand. "I have to go, but I think Tori is going to stay a while."

Cal nodded and Braddock left.

"Do you want a break?" Tori said to Lucy. "Go get a cup of coffee or something. I can sit with him."

"Are you okay?" Lucy asked Cal.

"Never better," he croaked out.

"Funny. I'll be back in a few minutes."

Tori watched her leave, then looked down to Cal, her eyes moistening. "Cal..."

"No," he said, shaking his head. "Don't. This has to stop. They might have gotten Pen, nearly ended me, but these guys? They're killers."

"It's over, Cal. I think they're done with all this."

"No," he repeated. "No, they're going to keep killing. They might stop for a while, but... they'll start again."

"Cal..."

"I know Will took you off the case, Victoria. But we don't have a sniff of these guys. And now they're probably going to go into hiding."

"Will, Steak and Sheryl have pieces of the puzzle," Tori insisted. "They just need time. They just need one good break."

Cal shook his head again. "There's something that has to be done, and I think you're the only one who can do it."

"What?"

"Barr's mother. She's our only bridge from the present to the past. We need to know what she knows. I don't care what you have to do, just get her to talk."

"What about Will?"

"Is he the boss?"

"He and I already had one fight we're going to have to work through at some point. I don't want another one. And I don't want to argue with you, but you... you lied to me. You lied, Cal."

Cal closed his eyes and nodded. "People you care about disappoint you sometimes."

Tori nodded, and he reached out and gripped her hand.

"Go see her again. Get her to talk, and then you can be done."

CHAPTER TWENTY-TWO

"The Ruthie?"

Tori pulled her Audi into the Peterson driveway. Elise let her into the house. "Do you want to see Cara?"

"I do, but I want to talk to you first. I assume you heard about Pen Murphy and Sheriff Lund?"

"Yes. It's just awful."

"It's the same people who killed Dan and Heidi, as well as Todd and Jennifer Strom. It all relates to a double murder from twenty-four years ago." She gave Elise the details and case theory, minus anything about withheld evidence. "We need to find these guys and put an end to this. There is one person who might—I emphasize *might*—know something that can really help us. I need to get her to talk to me. And I think Cara might be able to help me do that."

"How?"

Tori quickly ran down what she was thinking and what it would entail.

Elise pursed her lips, nervous. "I don't know. Will Cara be safe?"

"She'll be with me, for one," Tori said, pulling open her dark blue blazer to reveal her gun on her hip. "I have another one in my bag in the car. I'm taking no chances. I'm also going to have backup in Frontenac Falls."

"The reason I ask," Elise said, "is because Cara is going to want to do this."

"I know, which is why I'm asking *you* for permission. You say no, I leave and that's the end of it. And I would completely understand if that's how you feel. You are under no obligation to say yes."

"You think it could help?"

"Yes."

"Come on, then."

Upstairs, Cara didn't wait for Tori to finish explaining. "I want to go. Mom, I want to go."

"You do what Tori says. Exactly what she says. No deviations."

"I will, I promise," Cara said, bobbing her head, her body suddenly alive and eager.

Tori spent the drive west explaining and re-explaining to Cara what she was hoping to do.

"In other words, I'm just a prop?" Cara asked.

"Yes," Tori said with a smile. "I'm hoping you'll be highly effective in the role."

She had called ahead, and when she reached Frontenac Falls, she drove immediately to the police station. The police chief himself said he would follow her. "And I got two other patrol units that are going to be cruising the area. We've got you covered."

Ten minutes later, Tori parked on the street outside Rita Ellis's house. It was a warm, sunny summer day, not a cloud in the sky, just a light haze of humidity about. Scanning the immediate vicinity, she didn't see any other neighbors out in their yards, or prying eyes peering out nearby windows. The police chief was parked just down the street to the south. In her rear-view mirror she saw another patrol unit cross through an intersection. They were criss-crossing the area, armed with a basic description of the two killers. Other than two young kids riding their bicycles toward the main street to the north, she saw no other traffic or activity. She turned her attention to the small white house.

Rita was working in the yard. She was wearing a tan sunhat and gardening gloves, and was on her knees tending to a flower bed. From the look of the debris in her bucket and the amount of dirt on her yard gloves, Tori suspected she had been at it for an hour or two. An oscillating sprinkler watered a discolored patch leading to the front door.

It was as good a time as any to give this a shot.

"Do your thing," she said to Cara.

"Got it."

Tori had gone for the federal agent look today. Her hair was pulled back in a thick ponytail, and she wore a perfectly tailored navy pantsuit, muted light blue blouse, heels, boyfriend Movado watch and black shoulder bag.

"Here goes nothing," she murmured as she walked across the street and up the sidewalk before veering left to the side of the house. "Your garden still looks beautiful," she called out.

Rita Ellis looked up, a small bunch of weeds in her hand. "Can I help you?"

"Yes, I think you could."

Ellis's gaze narrowed as she suddenly recognized Tori. "I told you I had nothing to say. Why can't you people just stop harassing me. My son is dead. Whatever he did, he did a long time ago. It has nothing to do with me now." She stood and picked up her bucket, walking away.

Tori followed. "Yes it does, Rita. You recognized my name last time I was here because of my father. But that's not the only reason you might recognize it."

"Oh yeah?" Rita said as she kept walking.

"There was a case last summer that got a lot of media attention over in Shepard County. Do you remember the arrest of the man who killed all those girls and buried them at his property?"

Rita stopped and turned. "Everybody heard about that."

"One of the girls he murdered was my twin sister, Jessie. She was actually his first victim, killed twenty-one years ago this month. She was seventeen at the time."

Rita's hard look softened just a bit. "I'm sorry for you, Ms. Hunter, but I still fail to see what that has to do with—"

"You see, I was actually face to face with that killer. The man who killed my sister."

"I imagine you were, being a cop and all."

"No," Tori replied. "My hands were tied behind my back, my ankles were tied as well. I was trapped down in the basement under a shed, looking at a killer holding a knife to me."

Rita's rigid posture eased a bit more, less confrontational as she set her garden bucket down. "I remember reading about a woman, a cop, who was abducted and then saved, but there weren't any more details…"

"We kept as much out of the news as we could," Tori replied. "But I was the one abducted. The killer had a knife to my chest, to my throat. He was going to first rape me, then kill me. Just like he did to my sister."

Rita's eyes went wide. Tori knew she had her listening now.

"I know what it feels like to be a victim," she continued. She closed her eyes, reliving it now. "I know what it's like to think you're going to die. I know what it's like to stare back at someone I thought was a friend. Someone I grew up with and trusted. He killed my sister. He was going to kill me."

"I'm sorry you had to go through that, but I just—"

"And two weeks ago," Tori's voice got a little quieter and lower now as she turned and pointed to Cara leaning against the car, her legs crossed, her hands folded at her waist, her head down slightly, acting shy and nervous, "*she* had to go through something similar. That beautiful, innocent seventeen-year-old girl walked into her home at one thirty in the morning to find her father's throat slashed ear to ear, blood everywhere. Then when she turned around, down the hallway were the men who'd killed him and her stepmom. She was face to face with them, two men dressed in all black, wearing ski masks. Killers. The odds of her surviving that? I can't even fathom it."

Rita's mouth was now agape. "She's so young."

"She ran for her life, hid in the woods, and somehow—*somehow*—got away," Tori continued angrily, her voice rising at the thought of what Cara had gone through. "Rita, I know your son is gone and you don't want to have to relive what he did. You just want to be left alone. I can understand that. But the only way to really end this is to talk to me about him, and talk to me now."

"Why?"

Tori stepped toward Rita, reaching for her arm. "Hugh was the only person tried and convicted for those murders, but he didn't act alone. Whoever he killed with then is killing again, going after innocent people who were involved in the prosecution of his case."

"But why?"

"I don't know," Tori replied, not altogether truthfully. "That's the question I want to ask the killers. As long as they keep killing, the police are going to keep coming here. As long as innocent people are being killed, as long as Cara has to live in fear that these men will come back for her because she saw them."

"They're still after her?"

"We have to assume they are."

"Oh God," Rita said, looking to Cara.

"I think you could help us stop these killings. The only way to know is for you to talk about Hugh. Please, Rita. Please."

Rita sighed and finally nodded. "Let's go inside. Let's *all* go inside."

*

Inside the house, Tori introduced Cara, who greeted Rita with a firm handshake. Rita led them back to the kitchen, where, after washing her hands, she poured them all glasses of lemonade.

"Cara," she said with a deep breath. "In that hallway in the closet, on the top shelf, is a brown cardboard box. Will you get it for me?"

Cara retrieved the box and set it on the kitchen table.

"This is all the stuff I have of Hugh's," Rita said, opening the top flaps. "There are some documents, I think mostly from high school and college, a few photos, mementos. I'm sure you won't be surprised to hear, Ms. Hunter, he wasn't really the sentimental type."

"Please, call me Tori," Tori said, as she started to thumb through some of the documents. "Would you mind if I take these with me?"

Rita thought for a moment. "I guess not. Will you be… decent about how you use them?"

"Of course."

While Tori sifted through the box, Rita started talking with Cara. It was a bit awkward, but Rita was very nice. It was as if finally relenting to Tori had released a weight she had been carrying. Eventually their talk turned to soccer, and Cara mentioned that Tori used to play before she went to college and became an FBI special agent.

"You used to work for the FBI?"

"Yes." Tori gave Rita a quick run-down of her career, her return and why she'd stayed. She showed her identification with the sheriff's department. "I help on cases from time to time."

"And the man you came with last week, he's your…"

"Boyfriend," Tori answered with a smile. "He doesn't know I'm here, though."

"He didn't send you?"

"No, someone else did. Sheriff Lund. He also investigated your son's case."

"I see."

"I want to tell you another reason why I'm here." While skirting around the fact that the county knew about the Portage case, Tori explained that they now knew for certain that there was a tie between the current cases and the Baumans'. "We know they're connected, Rita. And Hugh…"

"Might have killed someone else."

"I'm sorry," Tori said, "but yes. It happened about a year, give or take, before the Bauman murders."

"You know, I always worried about him," Rita said slowly, shaking her head. "Even as a child he had this… darkness and quiet rage about him. I guess he was like his father in that sense."

"Hugh's father, his name was Lance, right?"

"Yes."

"You divorced?"

"Yes."

"Why?"

"It's a long story, but Lance was an over-the-road trucker. He was gone a lot, and I got… lonely." This last word Rita said almost in a whisper.

"You met someone?"

"Yes. Here in town. Lance found out and left us. He never came back. And I suppose you know that he later…"

"Committed suicide?"

"Yes."

"Was Hugh bitter about all that?"

"Very."

Tori nodded, imagining the impact his father's death would have had on a young and volatile Hugh Barr.

"I've reviewed the county's investigation from twenty-four years ago. It didn't appear to the investigators that you and Hugh communicated with each other a lot. Even when you lived in Pequot Lakes."

"They weren't wrong," Rita replied with a headshake. "My son grew up alone, no brothers or sisters. He always seemed to function best that way. I think he just tended to make people a little uncomfortable."

"That darkness you mentioned?"

"Yes. It was always there. I don't know how to explain it. I'd try to, you know, tell him to lighten up, because he seemed so tightly wound, like he was going to…"

"Snap?"

She nodded in resignation. "It seemed like it, but I never saw him… do it."

"I'm sure when he was arrested, you were shocked," Tori said quietly. "But I sense you weren't completely surprised."

Rita sighed before lightly nodding her head.

"Did he ever have any trouble at school?"

"No. That's the thing that always kind of gave me hope. If anything, he was something of a rule follower. It angered him when others didn't follow the rules or honor their commitments. If I maybe did one thing well as a parent, it was to get him to behave himself. I don't know how I did it. For someone who seemed kind of angry at the world, he didn't misbehave. Until later obviously."

"Perhaps that's what drew him to accounting in college. Rules. The numbers had to reconcile. There were concrete answers."

"Maybe," Rita replied. She took a drink of her lemonade and then poured them all another glass.

Tori switched topics. "Rita, did he have any good friends growing up?"

Rita shook her head. "Not really. Nobody that I remember."

"How about in college?"

"No…" She stopped and thought for a moment. "Well, there was one friend, kind of a homely, scrawny-looking fellow to be honest, but Hugh brought him home from college a couple of times on weekends. I think they were both in the accounting program."

"Do you recall his name?"

"What *was* his name. What was it?" Rita pondered as she started flipping through the small stack of photos from the cardboard box. "Here's one of the accounting club... There!" She pointed to the second row. "He's standing next to Hugh. His name was..." Her finger followed the names along the bottom. "Here it is. Larry. Larry Derner."

She handed the photo to Tori, who examined it. All the club members wore white dress shirts and ties. There was Hugh, not smiling, and to his left, the slight Larry Derner, with a kind of sideways half-smile.

Tori showed the photo to Cara. "What do you think?"

"I don't know," she replied quietly. "One of the guys was skinny, but I don't know if it was him."

"That's okay, worth a look," Tori said; then, to Rita, "Do you know if Hugh and Larry remained friends after college?"

"I think so," Rita answered. "As you said earlier, even when I was living in Pequot Lakes, Hugh and I didn't communicate all that much. It was just kind of how we were. These days people would call it dysfunctional."

"I understand," Tori replied. "But you believe Larry and Hugh remained friends, right?"

"Yes."

"How do you know?"

"Once on a Saturday I drove over to Hugh's house unannounced. I'd done some shopping and decided to see if he was home. He was in the garage. The front of his truck was up on blocks and there was a man underneath—I saw his legs sticking out. Larry was there too. He remembered me and said hello."

"Do you recall when that was?"

"It might have been a year before, you know, all the bad stuff happened."

"And who was the man under the truck?"

"I don't remember his name," Rita answered, thinking for a moment. "He was a bigger fella, that I remember. He came out from underneath the truck and Hugh introduced me, but for the life of me I can't remember his name. It was something short, just his first name. I'd never seen him before, and I haven't seen him since."

"And you think that was around a year before the Bauman murders?"

"Yes," Rita replied.

"Can you be any more exact?"

"It was… June, I think. The only reason I remember was that Hugh gave me a credit card."

"A credit card?"

"Yes. I was scraping to get by. Hugh told me to take the card for a few months so that I could get a little more ahead."

"Had he ever done that before?"

"No," Rita said with a headshake. "And a few months later, he took the card back. I think the accountant in him didn't like the look of his bill."

Tori smiled. "Still, that was nice of him," she said, but at the same time her mind was feverishly recalling the timeline of the Plover murders and the tight window created by the credit card charges. Rita had had the card in that window of time. Any last shreds of doubt she had had about Barr's guilt were gone.

"You said the other man was a big guy. Big how?" she asked.

Rita frowned, trying to remember. "He was just big. Not heavyset or anything, but strong, big arms, broad shoulders, a big head. Beyond that, I can't recall."

Tori snuck a look at Cara, who was paying rapt attention to the description.

"Do you remember anything else—anything about his face or voice, perhaps?"

Rita shook her head. "Sorry, it was so long ago."

"That's okay," Tori said. "Do you know where I could find Larry Derner?"

"I don't," Rita answered. "Sorry."

"That's okay. We'll track him down."

Once they were back in the Audi, Tori drove up alongside the Frontenac Falls police chief. "Can you run a check on a name for me?"

"Sure."

She gave him Derner's name, physical description and age. Two minutes later, the chief said, "There is a Lawrence Derner listed in Keller. Age, height and weight seem to fit. I have a photo on my screen here."

Tori got out of the Audi and leaned inside the chief's truck to look at the DMV photo. It appeared to match the photo Rita had given her from the accounting club, taking into account the years that had passed.

"Do you know the police chief in Keller?"

"Sure do. That's Errol Thompson. Cal knows him too."

"Could you make a call for me?" Tori asked.

Ten minutes later, as they were speeding along the two-lane highway, passing seemingly endless corn and soybean fields on their way northeast to Keller, her phone rang. It was the Frontenac Falls chief. "I spoke with Errol. He said Larry Derner is a local businessman in Keller. He's pulling together information on him for you. You can stop by and pick it up."

After the chief hung up, Tori glanced at Cara. "When Rita described that bigger man, that rang familiar with you, didn't it?"

"Yes. It was like she was describing the man I saw. Big head, shoulders, arms."

"That's what I thought. Okay, your job is done here."

"Ah, come on."

"Nope." Tori made a second call, this one to Elise Peterson. She would meet them in Keller.

"What are *you* going to do?" Cara asked.

"My job," Tori said with a smile. "You did good, Cara. Your coming helped. Seeing you made Rita break down and talk I think."

"Will it help you find the people who killed my dad and Heidi?"

"It might. The only way to find out is to start digging on this guy and see what we find."

Cara nodded. "That Rita, she didn't seem like such a bad person."

"She isn't," Tori said. "She's an anguished mom not wanting to think about what a monster her son ended up being."

They arrived in Keller an hour later, and the first stop was the police station. Elise was waiting in the parking lot to take Cara home.

Inside the police station, Errol Thompson greeted Tori with a small file. "I've known Cal Lund since I don't know when. Probably because, like me, he's been around forever. How's he doing?"

"He's alive, Chief. He's going to make it," Tori said. "And he can have visitors, so if you want to go over and see him, I know he'd like that."

"I just might do that," Thompson replied. "Now, you're interested in Larry Derner?"

"Maybe," Tori said as she flipped through the file. "Do you know him?"

"Yes. He and his wife own Ruthie's House on the eastern edge of town."

"I've heard of that," Tori said, looking up. "People over in Manchester Bay rave about the food."

The chief nodded. "It's really good."

The drive to Ruthie's House took five minutes. The restaurant may have started off in a small house, but it had been expanded upon perhaps several times, given the geometric form of the various sections. It was clear that the couple were operating a thriving business.

Tori hadn't eaten since an early breakfast. She parked and made her way inside. There were areas of tables and booths tucked into every nook and cranny, with a lunch counter just past the host stand. It was mostly unoccupied, save for a man in a business suit sitting in the middle, eating a salad, and a man with a short haircut wearing a dress shirt and pants sitting on the far end, starting in on what looked to be a big cheeseburger and malt. Tori sat on the third seat and reached for a menu.

*

D took another bite of his cheeseburger, stuffed in a couple of French fries with it and glanced to his right, towards the woman who'd sat down at the counter, setting a folder, shoulder bag and phone in front of her.

Ruthie came out the kitchen door and saw the new arrival. "Well hi there. Can I get you something?"

"Do you have anything you can make really quick? I see the chef salad here on the menu. How about that? Is that quick?"

"I think we can do that. I will say, though, it's big."

"Oh."

"But we could prepare it in a to-go tray for you. You could eat a little now and take the rest with you. It'll keep fresh in the container."

"That sounds terrific. I'll take it."

"I'll get that going right away then," Ruthie said as she wrote down the order. "You know, I don't think I've ever seen you here before. I think I'd have remembered. I'm Ruthie."

"*The* Ruthie?"

"The one and only."

"I'm Tori. Tori Hunter."

"Good to meet you, Tori. Hopefully we'll do a nice job on the chef salad, and you'll come back and visit us again sometime," Ruthie said.

"I bet I will."

Tori Hunter.

D kept his head down, his eyes focused on his plate, every few seconds taking a quick glance to his right. Five minutes later, Ruthie brought out the salad in the to-go container.

"Oh my God, you weren't lying. This thing is ginormous, Ruthie."

"We aim to please. Enjoy."

Hunter flipped open the top of the container, mixed in some salad dressing and dug into the salad.

Hearing her name, D now recognized Hunter from media photos he'd seen last summer during the major investigation in Manchester Bay. It was striking to see her in person. He was surprised at how petite she was. And now, only ten feet away from her, he also realized she was the woman in the Tahoe with Braddock at the cemetery in Frontenac Falls. He suspected hers was the little white house in Manchester Bay that he had followed them to after Hugh's funeral.

Slim came through the door from the kitchen, went to the cash register and started tapping at the touch screen.

D slid his eyes to the right. Hunter was subtly eyeing Slim. She had flipped up the cover of the red folder in front of her, and he could see that inside was a headshot photo of Slim.

He wiped the corner of his mouth with the napkin, left a twenty-dollar bill and quickly walked past Hunter and out the front door.

What to do?

A few minutes later, in the rear-view mirror of his pickup, he saw Hunter exiting the restaurant with her salad box in hand. He let her get going and observed as she made an immediate right turn to drive east on Highway 10. He dropped the gear shift and followed her. She was easily visible in her shiny Audi SUV. He took out a burner phone and called Slim, who answered on the fourth ring.

"We have a problem."

*

"Hey," Tori greeted Braddock when she got him on the phone. "What's your day looking like?"

"Still long."

"Any new developments?"

"No. But still, I'll be at the office late. We have media inquiries up the wazoo and County Attorney Backstrom wants to meet tomorrow. He's bringing his assistant, Anne Wilson, so..."

"Sorry."

"Where are you?"

"I'm going to go to my place. Hang out there since, you know, I'm paying for it. What time do you think you'll be home tonight?"

"Not sure. Late, probably, nine or ten."

"Let me know when you're done, and I'll drive out and be waiting for you." Tori hung up and glanced into the back seat to the box and the folder sitting on top.

CHAPTER TWENTY-THREE

"Change of plans"

Tori's phone beeped.

I'll be home 9:45ish, read the text from Braddock.

"That gives me forty-five minutes," Tori murmured, as she briefly glanced out the screened sliding door to the back patio. There was just the slightest hint of sunlight in the distance. It would be fully dark in less than five minutes. She sat back in her chair and stretched her arms, trying to loosen her now tense shoulders. She'd lost track of time. Since her return from seeing Rita Ellis, she'd managed to finish her salad, and had then spent her evening digging into the box that Ellis had let her take.

Apart from a few photos, the box contained mostly high school and college documents. Grade transcripts showed Barr to be a reasonably good student, a high school GPA of 3.2 and a college GPA of 3.1. And upon review, he clearly had a gift for numbers, as his math and accounting grades were far higher than his other classes. He'd gone into the right field.

She found his college apartment leases, the same unit in the same building all four years. Dude, if you want to meet people at college, you have to live in the dorms when you're a freshman, she thought. All her good friends from college she'd met her freshman year in her dorm. Had she made other friends along the way? Yes.

But she'd met them through the friends from her freshman dorm. Living alone in an apartment, even in a building of other college students, wouldn't work. "That is, if he wanted to make friends," she muttered. Perhaps a dorm would have been too many people for him.

It was clear, even from what little there was in the box, that Hugh Barr was a loner. That was consistent with what they knew of him. Yet he had joined the accounting club, so it appeared there was at least some desire to meet like-minded people. That led to the question of the night.

How much like Hugh Barr was Larry Derner?

Was he just a name, a random friend, or was he more? Rita had seen Larry with the large man whose description had drawn Cara's attention. How much stock could she put in that, a vague description from a seventy-year-old woman from twenty-five years ago, and a seventeen-year-old who'd seen the man in the dark under extreme duress?

On the table was the file she'd managed to cobble together on Derner. It was a combination of what she'd collected at the police station in Keller, plus what she'd been able to print off from her laptop at home. There wasn't much to be found.

Larry Derner had been born and raised in Keller. He was an only child. His parents divorced when he was young. His father, Howard Derner, had legal issues, with arrests for drunk and disorderly, assault and battery and then domestic assault. He did small runs of jail time and then would repeat offend. Eventually he served three years in prison. Not surprisingly, he died in a bar fight.

It did not appear that Larry had followed in his father's footsteps. He had no criminal record; in fact, no infractions beyond a few moving motor vehicle violations. Instead, he attended college, where he met Hugh Barr. Like Barr, he graduated with an accounting degree, although it didn't appear he ever became a certified public accountant. Out of college, he took a job at a small accounting office in Keller, but three years later left it to open the restaurant with his wife, Ruth.

Ruthie's House had a website, and Tori read through the history. The restaurant was currently celebrating its twenty-second anniversary. It had started out of an old two-story house, and as she'd suspected, had been expanded numerous times over the years. It looked to be an extremely successful business, despite the fact that it was located just off a busy highway—not exactly a garden spot. The Derners had one child, a daughter, now twenty-three, who lived in St. Louis, Missouri.

Derner had never visited Barr at the prison. There was no record or evidence of him having contacted him there.

From what she'd seen at the restaurant, and photos she found online, Rita Ellis's description of him was on the mark. He was a very slight man. He didn't appear to be particularly strong or agile. His college photo hadn't garnered the same reaction from Cara as Rita's description of the other man she'd seen.

Tori sat back in her chair and folded her arms. Was this really a valuable connection to Hugh Barr?

A firecracker went off in the distance, not an uncommon occurrence in the neighborhood in the summer, or out at Braddock's place, for that matter. Another one followed. *Crack! Crack! Crack!*

She looked back to her laptop and the documents spread out on the table.

What do you make of Derner, Tori? Is he a Hugh Barr accomplice? Or is he just some schleppy-looking friend who was one of his few social acquaintances? "What are you, Larry?" she muttered.

Another firecracker went off. Then another. Close enough for her to look up.

Pop!

The shot whizzed by her head, exploding into the wall behind her.

Tori dove right, sweeping her shoulder bag with her to the floor, away from the sliding door.

Pop! Pop! Pop!

As the door glass shattered, she scrambled across the floor into the kitchen, dragging the bag with her, and pulled out her gun. Then she reached up for the light switch.

Pop! Pop!

*

He saw her hand reach up to the wall. He fired again.

Pop! Pop!

The lights went out in Hunter's house.

Had he got her?

He took a step back, and then another. Exterior backyard lights started turning on. He turned and ran.

Bang! Bang! Bang!

Shots hit the ground around his feet as he fled.

*

Tori saw the silhouette of someone running. She pushed herself up, grabbed her cell phone off the table and exited the house through the side door that led to the detached garage. She turned right and sprinted through her backyard.

One of her neighbors had her rear exterior lights on now and had opened her door. She saw Tori running through the yard.

"Were those firecrackers, or was someone shooting?"

"Call 911. *Now!*" Tori hollered as she ran by. "Someone just tried to shoot me. Use my name."

She ran between the houses, staying close to the one on the left. At the front corner, she peeked around in both directions, but saw no movement. More houses were lighting up. She jogged across the street, her gun up now, as she made for the wide gap between two more houses.

The shooter appeared from behind a house ahead.

Pop! Pop! Pop!

He was using a suppressor, Tori realized. She dove left, scraping herself on landscaping rocks as she landed on her left shoulder behind a window well. "Ah, crap," she moaned, having felt her skin tear. She peeked around the edge of the well's steel casing, but didn't see anyone. The shooter had to be running to somewhere. A vehicle.

She pushed herself up and edged carefully forward, crouched, staying tight to the side of the house until she reached the corner.

Ka-thunk!

A door slam, to her right.

She sprinted through the backyard, veering out around a swing set and slowing as she approached the gap between the detached garage and the one-story house.

*

"*Go! Go! Go!*" D exclaimed.

Slim hit the gas and ripped ahead, blowing through the stop sign and speeding down the street, checking his rear-view mirror.

*

She heard the engine roar to life as she sprinted round the corner into the front yard, her gun up. The pickup truck was already a block north.

It was too far, too dark, too dangerous.

"Dammit!"

She pulled her phone from her back pocket and called Braddock. "You need to get over to my house."

"Why? I was just getting ready to drive home. I thought you were going to meet me out there."

"Change of plans."

CHAPTER TWENTY-FOUR

"You don't go looking for trouble, but damned if it doesn't know how to find you"

With flashing grille lights and siren, Braddock turned hard left and accelerated ahead toward the flashing police lights. He arrived to find two squad cars at Tori's house. Inside, two uniformed officers were talking with Tori while she cleaned a scrape on the back of her left arm.

"Let me look at that," he said to Tori, and took the rag from her. "Keep talking. I'll listen."

"How many shots were fired?" one of the patrol officers asked.

"At least five or six into the house," Tori replied. She pointed to the wall. "First shot is there. I was sitting at the table at my computer. Second volley was when I was scrambling for cover into the kitchen. A few more when I killed the lights."

"Then what?"

"After I slapped off the lights, I saw someone running out the back."

"Man? Woman?"

"Man, a bigger guy."

"You fired?"

"Three times."

"Do you think you hit him?"

"I don't know. Didn't seem to slow him down if I did, but a careful search is needed to see if I winged him and there's some blood. If there is, it'll be in the yard between the two houses out the back."

"Then you gave chase?"

"Yes." Tori described the sequence of events. "By the time I came around the corner, the pickup truck was a block away."

"Can you describe the vehicle?"

"It was dark-colored. It raced north on Blue Heron Street. Turned left a few blocks further north, and that was the last I saw of it."

"Did you see a plate?" Braddock asked as he applied some ointment to the scrapes on her arm.

"No. Too far away."

"How about make and model?"

She shook her head.

"Okay, we'll be back," the patrol officer said as he walked outside, speaking into his shoulder radio. "Black or dark pickup truck, last seen racing through the neighborhoods north of town two blocks west of the location of the call. We need officers sweeping that area."

Steak and Eggs pushed inside the house. "What the hell, Tori?" Steak exclaimed.

"I'm fine." She turned to look at the back of her arm as Braddock applied two large butterfly bandages.

"This long scratch is a little deeper. You don't need stitches, but the ointment should help it start healing properly."

Tori inspected his work. "Stings."

"I applied *a lot*," Braddock murmured with disapproval, telegraphing what was next. "Now, the question they didn't ask."

"Why?" Tori replied as she turned around and faced everyone. "Why is someone taking a shot at me? Especially since I was taken off the investigation."

"What have you been up to?" Braddock asked, his eyes raised. "Because it ain't nothing. I see a table full of documents and pictures, a half-empty box, plus your laptop. Fess up?"

"Cal asked me to do something, and I'm pretty sure now that I succeeded."

"At what?"

"I talked to Rita Ellis."

"Hugh Barr's mom?"

"Yes. A lot of this stuff here is from her."

"Barr's mother talked?"

"Yes," Tori replied. "She talked to me and Cara."

"You took seventeen-year-old Cara Newman with you?" Braddock asked, eyebrows raised.

"I got to Rita by playing on the fact that I was a victim, which I was, and I told her what Cara had been through. She took one look at Cara—who played innocent teenager to a T, by the way—and caved. Now, do you want to know what I found out or rip me for my methods?"

"And what did she tell you?" Braddock asked.

"Let's sit down." Tori led them into the living room, and while she drank a bottle of water, she ran through her day.

"So she gives you the name of this Larry Derner," Braddock said, holding up a copy of the DMV photo, "and you stop at the restaurant in Keller. Did you see him?"

"Yes," Tori said.

"Did you talk to him?"

"No."

"Then why stop?"

"I just wanted to make a visual assessment. I did meet his wife, Ruthie. She was super friendly, said she hadn't seen me in there before."

"And you introduced yourself?"

Tori closed her eyes before sighing out a little laugh. Was that it? Was that what had triggered all this? "Yes. But it wasn't Ruthie who shot at me. It wasn't Larry Derner either."

"How do you know?"

"Derner is thin, twerpy and walks just a little hunched over. I didn't get a good look at who was shooting at me, but it wasn't some little scraggy guy, I'll tell you that."

"That's hardly definitive…" Steak started.

"Look at his DMV photo. Five-nine, and I can tell you that's probably a little generous. One hundred fifty-five pounds. He's not a big guy at all," Tori argued. "Plus, he and his wife own SUVs, not pickups."

"Who were you chasing then?"

"I'm betting it was the big guy Cara described, and that maybe Rita Ellis described too. I didn't get any sort of real look at him, but I saw his outline. He was bigger, thicker."

"I get it." Braddock turned and headed for the door. "I want to go out and take a look around." He looked back to Tori and crooked his finger. "Come on."

"Sorry about this," she said as they stepped outside.

"You don't go looking for trouble, but damned if it doesn't know how to find you."

*

D kept a constant eye on the side-view mirror as Slim drove north for a mile out of town. "Turn right, let's get over to the H-4."

"You missed her? She's still alive?" Slim yelped as he drove along. "Oh boy, oh boy. We have to stop, D. This is getting out of control. We have to stop now and hope they don't find anything."

When they reached the H-4, Slim turned right, and they looped back to the south end of Manchester Bay.

"It's gone too far. They're never going to stop searching for us now. Never. We have to stop this, D. We have to stop. Go quiet and stop."

"Keep your head, Slim," D replied. "Get us to the fairgrounds."

Five minutes later, they exited Highway 210. Derner drove around to the back of the Shepard County Fairgrounds, where his Honda Pilot was parked behind the grandstand bleachers.

He quickly got out of the pickup. D reached into his right pocket before stepping down from the passenger seat.

"We need to hustle back," Slim said at the rear of the truck. "Just in case anyone comes looking."

"They'll be coming, Slim. For you." D pulled his hand out of his pocket and darted forward. In an instant, he had the rope around Slim's throat.

Slim grunted, wriggling his body frantically, trying to dig his fingers beneath the rope.

"The police are onto you, Slim," D hissed. "They have your photo. Tori Hunter was at your restaurant today. They'll get your DNA. It'll match to Wisconsin. I can't have you talking about that. You'd never hold up. You're too weak for that."

He pulled the rope tighter, and Slim's legs buckled beneath him. D dug his right knee into the small of his back. Slim clawed at D's head, gasping for air.

His arms shaking from the force, D felt Slim's resistance weakening. He lifted him and threw him down on his stomach between the truck and the Pilot, jamming his knee into Slim's spine and pulling the ends of the rope. Slim grunted. D knew it wouldn't be long now. He had the size and the leverage, and was able to pull the rope tighter.

Slim's body went still beneath him. He held the rope for another fifteen seconds, then rolled him over and checked for a pulse. Next, he quickly searched his pockets, extracting Slim's wallet and the burner phone he'd given him.

He glanced around the barren parking lot. The only sounds were vehicles racing along the highway in the distance. There was nobody else about. He quickly picked up Slim's body and shoved it into the back of the Pilot, then closed the tailgate.

He checked his watch. It was 10:15 p.m.

He got into his truck and calculated how quickly he could get back to Keller.

*

Braddock, Tori, Steak, and the two patrol officers searched the area behind Tori's house with flashlights. Tori had a sense of where the shots had come from. She found shell casings behind a side hedge for the house behind and to the right of hers. From there, the shooter would have had a good angle through the sliding glass door.

"I was sitting on the right side. I can see the hole in the wall from here."

"Oh boy," Braddock murmured, slack-jawed.

A suddenly pale Tori simply nodded.

"Two inches to the left and it would have been lights out," Steak remarked.

Tori and Braddock gave him a stern look.

"Dude, seriously?" Braddock said in exasperation.

"Oh… uh… Maybe I should go get someone to mark this area."

"Hey, good idea," Braddock said, still glaring.

"Okay then," Steak started walking quickly back to the house.

"Sometimes the filter just malfunctions with him."

"It's okay. His natural inclination is to make a joke, lighten the mood," Tori said. "Even when that might not be the best thing to say."

"One question I do have," Braddock said. "You didn't hear him coming?"

Tori shook her head. "Just before he started shooting, there were firecrackers going off in the neighborhood. Not constant, but enough that I noticed them. It was loud and they weren't far away. Who knows, maybe he was setting them off to cover his approach, or he hoped nobody would notice when he started firing."

"Okay, where to next?"

"I saw him running, and that's when I fired."

She led him slowly between the houses, both sweeping their flashlights, scanning for any sign that she had hit the shooter.

"I don't see anything," Braddock murmured. "We'll let the crime scene techs work it."

"I dove for cover behind that window well when he fired at me again."

"You were coming right into the kill box here."

"Couldn't see a damn thing. But neither could he really."

Braddock walked straight ahead, his flashlight sweeping the area, and caught a glint of brass in the grass near an air conditioning unit. He marked it with some small landscaping rocks.

Tori led him around the front of the house. "I came out over here to the right, and that's when I saw the rear of the truck racing away on Blue Heron."

A block ahead, they saw a Manchester Bay police officer speaking with a man and woman who were gesturing to the north. Tori and Braddock walked quickly toward them.

"Will, these folks are the Nelsons," the officer said. "Tell Detective Braddock and Ms. Hunter what you just told me."

It was Mrs. Nelson who spoke. "We had just got home from a ball game. We were emptying out our lawn chairs and cooler when we saw this pickup truck flying by."

"What kind of truck?"

"Dodge Ram," Mr. Nelson said. "It turned the corner there at 5th Street."

"Did you see a license plate?" Braddock asked. "Or the driver?"

"No," Mr. Nelson replied. "You?" he asked his wife.

"No. I'm sorry. I know the truck was a Dodge Ram, though, because our good friends have one like it. I recognized the shape."

"How about the color?"

"Dark," Mr. Nelson said. "I'd say black or dark blue."

"Did you see how many people were in the truck?" Tori asked.

Mrs. Nelson looked to her husband, who thought for a moment before shaking his head. "I couldn't tell you that. Like I said, it was going fast."

"Me neither," Mrs. Nelson added.

"Thanks," Braddock said, and he and Tori started walking back toward her house. "Dodge Ram pickup."

"Earlier on, I couldn't decide if Larry Derner was even worth looking into."

"How about now?"

"Will, you have to go out to Keller," she said. "You should go now."

"Come on then."

"Me too?"

"For now, yes."

CHAPTER TWENTY-FIVE

"It's a theory"

Tori and Braddock made the drive west to Keller with flashing lights. It cleared the left lane for them on the forty-five-minute journey. For the first half-hour, they were quiet, not a word exchanged. Finally Tori couldn't take it any longer.

"Say something."

"What is there to say?"

"Right."

"You could have told me what Cal asked you to do."

"Like you would have said yes after your sanctimonious soliloquy on investigative and evidentiary ethics the other night. You'd have shot me down. You wouldn't have said yes to what I wanted to do, so I went rogue and just did it. If Rita Ellis didn't talk, that was the end of it, but I was able to get her to open up."

"By using a seventeen-year-old girl."

"I did what I had to do. I had her mother's permission. I had police backup when I got out there. And you know what? I got the job done. In case you haven't noticed, I get Larry Derner's name and all hell breaks loose. It's a break, let's go."

"Fine."

"You're pissed."

"You're damn right. And not just about this."

Braddock fell silent again for a few minutes.

"I was a jackass the other night," he said, shaking his head. "I've replayed that whole thing in my head about twenty times. I think I was right about a lot of things, but I *was* an ass." He glanced over to her. "I am truly sorry about that."

It was Tori's turn to take a moment. "I am so angry at Pen, Cal and my father. Cal lied to me, right to my face. And I wish Big Jim were alive so I could wring his frickin' neck."

"As you know, I'm kind of right there with you," Braddock said. "At the same time, I've reviewed that Plover case now. Hugh Barr *was* a killer. And I'm more certain than ever that these guys probably have more bodies on them that we don't know about."

"You think there are others?"

"Yes, and I think Pen, Cal and your father suspected that was the case too. I think their motivation was altruistic. I think they thought they were saving lives and they took the risk on that basis."

"How has that worked out?"

"Not well," Braddock conceded. "I think what they did, how they did it, was the wrong play. But they were in a difficult position and made a tough decision. We're going to have to deal with the fallout of that now. Pen's dead. Cal is in intensive care. Someone tried to kill you tonight. Like you said, all hell has broken loose. There is no burying this now."

"I suppose there isn't."

Braddock shook his head and let out a long sigh. "God, Tori, where you were sitting at the house… how you're alive… Man."

"I'm fine, Will, I'm fine," Tori said, reaching for his arm. "You know what I want now?"

"To finish this."

"Hell yeah."

"In a few minutes, we'll start doing that. We're going hard on Derner, right now."

"I like the idea of catching him off guard," Tori said. "He knows something. He has to."

"Unless this was just these guys going after someone named Hunter tonight," Braddock cautioned. "They got Murphy and nearly got Cal. They can't get your dad, so why not go for you. You're investigating the case after all."

"I don't buy that. Do you?"

"No. What you did today stirred something up," Braddock said. "However, you said you didn't think Derner was the one shooting at you, correct? If it wasn't him, who was it?"

"The third man. We think there are two killers now, plus Barr back in the day. It's the one that's *not* Derner."

"So Derner, or his wife Ruthie maybe, sees you at the restaurant, knows you're involved in the investigation, or that you were in Frontenac Falls talking to Rita Ellis…"

"And I had a folder with me that had Derner's picture in it. I don't know how he could have possibly known that. I opened it for just a second when he came out from the back. There is no way he saw it. No way."

Braddock scratched his chin for a moment. "Surveillance camera?"

"We'd have to check," Tori said. "I didn't look for that when I was there."

Keller chief Errol Thompson called at 11:30 p.m., when they were ten minutes east of town.

"I was just at the restaurant. There were a couple of servers sitting inside at the little bar, having a post-shift drink, but it's otherwise all closed for the night. They told me Ruthie left a half-hour ago or so."

"How about Larry?" Tori asked.

"One of the servers said he wasn't around this evening. I think the best thing to do is to have you meet me at the Derner house. I'll be parked just down the street waiting for you in my Explorer."

Ten minutes later, Braddock pulled up behind Thompson, who emerged from his truck dressed in plain clothes: khakis, sport coat and golf shirt. He had a portable police radio in his hand, his badge and weapon attached to his belt. He greeted Tori, who then introduced Braddock.

"You're sure these two are involved in the murders over your way?" Thompson asked skeptically. "Shoot, Larry's a coat rack. He couldn't pull a dandelion out of the ground without great exertion."

"Do you know him well?" Braddock asked as they walked up the sidewalk.

The chief shook his head. "No, not well. I only know him to say hello to as a businessman in my town. He's the behind-the-scenes guy at the restaurant. Ruthie, on the other hand, everyone knows her."

"She was very personable when I met her today," Tori said.

"Yeah," Thompson agreed. "I'm not quite sure how she and her husband ended up together. If I were to be honest, I've always found him just a little off-putting. Ruthie's chatty, personable, bubbly, a really nice lady, although let there be no doubt, she's the one in charge, and you toe the line or feel her wrath."

"Tough boss?"

"But fair. Lots of long-term employees."

"They must be good businesspeople."

Thompson agreed. "I think Larry is a good numbers guy and Ruthie is the gourmet foodie and face. The restaurant is a nice little draw for the town. I'd really hate for either of them to somehow be mixed up in what you're dealing with. Frankly, I can't fathom that it's possible."

The Derners' house was a white two-story with black shutters at the windows and a covered front porch. It was completely dark. Chief Thompson rang the doorbell, but there was no response. He gave it a few seconds and rang again, pressing it three times before peering in the window to the left of the door. The house was quiet and still.

"Odd," he muttered.

Braddock stepped back off the porch with Tori, taking out his flashlight and resting his other hand on the butt of his gun. They followed the sidewalk around the house to the back. Braddock climbed a couple of steps up from a patio to the back door and directed the bright beam of his flashlight into the kitchen, searching for movement or signs that someone was home.

"Anything?" Tori asked.

"Negative," he replied, trying the door.

Tori turned and took the sidewalk up a slight incline to the detached two-car garage set just off a back alley. The garage door was closed. She stood on her tippy-toes and peeked through the small side window.

"Psst."

Braddock turned.

Tori nodded to the garage.

Braddock jogged down to join her, Thompson right behind.

"There's an SUV parked inside," she whispered. "The dome light is on."

She took out a rubber glove and turned the doorknob. It was unlocked. She looked back questioningly. Braddock and Thompson both had their guns out now and nodded to her. She pushed the door open, then stepped back to let Braddock carefully peer inside, sweeping with his flashlight. No movement. He reached down to his left and flipped the switch for the overhead light.

Tori walked around the SUV to the driver's side, and her shoulders slumped. Ruthie was lying on her back on the floor. "Dammit," Tori exclaimed as she rushed to her and checked her neck for a pulse. "No, no, no."

Braddock crouched and touched Ruthie's arm. "She's still warm. It hasn't been long." He glanced at her neck. "Strangled."

Tori looked inside the SUV and saw a purse and keys. "The house. He could be inside."

"It's been an eventful night. Let's be careful here," Chief Thompson cautioned. He radioed for immediate backup.

Two patrol units arrived within minutes. Tori sifted through Ruthie's keys and found what she thought was the house key. She opened the back door and stepped back. The patrol officers, followed by Braddock and Thompson, moved inside, turning on lights. The officers cleared the second floor while Braddock and Tori swept the main level and Chief Thompson the basement.

There was no sign of Larry Derner.

"Where is her husband?" Tori asked. "No second SUV here."

"We have to get an alert out for him and his vehicle," Braddock said.

"I have to make some calls." Thompson stuffed his gun back into his holster.

"Me too," Braddock replied. He took out his phone and tapped his screen for a number. "Steak, you're not going to believe this."

*

D pulled the side door of Slim's garage softly closed. He took a step and then heard the murmur of voices around the front of the house. Leaning to his left, he saw a small grouping of people on the sidewalk along the street. He quickly darted around the back of the garage, across the alley and through the gap between two houses to the next block over and his truck. From inside the cab, he looked to his right through the houses and down to the backyard of Slim's house. He saw a flashlight now sweeping that area.

That was fast.

From where he was parked, he could see the small side window of the garage. When he saw the inside lights for the garage come on, he started his truck but left the headlights turned off. Pulling away, he made several turns through the neighborhood, quickly putting distance between himself and the house. Soon he came into the southern end of Keller and the main four-way stop. He turned left and his store and service station up to the right were still lit up, ten minutes from closing. He looped through the side streets and made his way to his house, which backed up to the service station's rear parking lot.

Inside the house, he quickly changed his clothes and then crossed the backyard to the back door of the store.

His business building was two stories. The expansive first story held a convenience store, a recreation sales area and the repair garage and car wash. The second story was his office and product storage. He entered through the rear door to the service garage and walked over to the checkout counter, where two employees were going through the day's receipts.

"Did we have a busy night?" he asked.

"Uh, yeah," his employee, Ryan, replied, a stack of paper in front of him. "I was just finishing up."

"Good. I thought I'd come over and check on some things before closing."

"I thought you were going fishing tonight?" said Tony, the other employee.

"No, not tonight. I've been over at the house, finishing a book." D spun the paperback rack in the corner and grabbed a new one. He held it up. "I'll log it. How does the register look? Everything balancing out?"

"All good per usual," Ryan replied.

D walked over to the wall and turned off the main lights for the canopy over the gas pumps. The pumps remained on for anyone who came through to pay with a credit card, but the store was now closed. "You know what, you two get out of here. Since I'm here, I'll finish up."

"Yeah, okay," Tony said, and looked to Ryan. "You want to go get a quick beer?"

"Sure."

D locked the door behind his employees as they left. He turned off the last of the lights, set the alarm and then walked back across the rear parking lot to the house.

Collecting up everything he'd worn earlier, he stuffed it into a garbage bag, which he tossed into the truck. Then he drove north out of town on a county road, weaving his way through farm fields and forested areas.

Twenty minutes later, he reached the left turn for a gravel road that wound its way back to a pond. Only the cadenced sounds of crickets punctured the night's silence. He tripled up the garbage bag, then added the gun, gloves, rope and boots he'd used, plus a bunch of rocks from a small pile at the end of the road. At the end of a small grassy point, he swung the bag back and forth before heaving it with a loud grunt. It sailed through the air, landing thirty feet out and quickly disappearing beneath the surface of the water.

Next, he drove east, zigzagging his way for nearly forty minutes until he reached the small cabin with the detached garage. He backed his truck inside the garage and closed the door. Stacked in the corner were four semi-worn tires that had perhaps ten thousand miles of wear left in them.

He changed all four tires on his truck, tossing the ones he took off into the truck bed.

It was an hour's drive west to the town of Wadena, where he circled around the back of the salvage yard and tossed the four old tires over the tall chain-link fence into a pile of other discards.

It was 3:00 a.m. when he made it back to Keller. He pulled his truck into the service station, activated the car wash and had it run over the vehicle twice so that it was gleaming when he was finished. It was 3:30 by the time he returned to the house, took his bottle of whiskey and sat down at the table.

He had to think things through.

*

Just after 2:00 a.m., detectives from the Morrison County Sheriff's Department arrived on scene at the Derner house and immediately agreed to coordinate with Shepard County. An alert was issued for Larry Derner and his Honda Pilot.

Chief Thompson knew a long-time server at the restaurant and reached out to her for Derner's cell phone number. He tried calling it every five minutes for an hour. "No answer."

"I'd say he's running," Tori posited. "His SUV isn't here. He's not answering his phone. What do you think?" she asked Braddock.

"It's a theory."

"You don't sound convinced."

"We don't know enough. He isn't here, so it's natural to suspect him, especially given all that's happened today, but… he's not the man who shot at you."

"Well, fine, he wasn't the shooter, but where the hell is he then?"

When the chief left them to coordinate with his own detectives, Tori and Braddock slipped outside to get some space. "Does Larry Derner have a boat registered to him?" Braddock asked.

"No."

Braddock's phone buzzed. It was Steak. He put it on speaker. "Yeah, buddy."

"I'm standing next to a silver Honda Pilot behind the grandstand at the Shepard County Fairgrounds. The vehicle is registered to one Lawrence Derner."

"Any sign of Larry Derner with it?"

"If you consider him being stuffed inside it dead a sign, then yeah."

Braddock looked to Tori. "What the hell is going on?"

*

Halfway back to Manchester Bay on a mostly empty Highway 10, the passenger window open, the fresh country air still warm and humid, Tori turned to Braddock. "Are you and I alright?"

"We have some things to talk about," he replied. "I mean, running to New York?"

"Yeah." Tori shook her head. "I shouldn't have bailed out of here. I was just… upset."

"For now, let's focus on the case. We'll have a long talk about all that when this is over."

She reached over and lightly grabbed his right arm. "I'm really sorry."

As they came into Manchester Bay, Tori muttered, "Why do I have a feeling this is not the last time we're going to be making this drive?"

"My head is spinning," Braddock agreed. "This is the craziest night I've ever seen, and I worked New Year's Eve and Halloween when I was NYPD."

A Manchester Bay patrol car, its light bar flashing, was visible in the distance, parked at the main entrance to the county fairgrounds. Braddock slowed for the turn. The graveled parking area ahead of the fairgrounds was surrounded by thick patches of scraggly woods and wetlands.

"This place always kind of gave me the creeps," Tori said. "It's old, dilapidated and dark. I mean, have they ever thought about adding a light or two?"

"It's boggy, low-lying land," Braddock said. "The fairgrounds is about the only decent use for it. And no, it would not appear the county is investing heavily in infrastructure for this place."

The patrol officer looked them over, recognized Braddock and waved them forward. "Behind the grandstand, Will," he said.

Braddock pulled ahead into the parking lot strewn with empty bottles and cans.

"It looks like a garbage dump around here."

"There was a rodeo last weekend. I don't think the cleaning crew exactly gave it their all."

"It smells."

"Bog, swamp and that line of Porta-Potties along the fence probably take care of that."

The parking area swung to the left, following the curvature of the faded white fencing surrounding the rodeo grounds until they reached the long wooden bleachers of the massive grandstand. To the right stood several police vehicles with lights flashing, and the medical examiner's van. Portable lights illuminated the scene.

Steak waved them over, and they ducked under the crime scene tape. Inside the wide perimeter, forensic investigators were hovering around a silver Honda Pilot. The tailgate was open.

"How was this found?" Braddock asked.

"Patrol officer was making a routine sweep through here," Steak explained. "Sometimes high school kids will sneak in here to drink and do whatever. He'd heard the BOLO for the Pilot, and the plate matched up. He looked inside, saw the body in the back, and called it in."

At the SUV, Doc Renfrow was conducting his examination.

"You guys are keeping me awfully busy this month."

"I'm as ready for things to die down as you are, Doc," Braddock said. "No pun intended."

"How long has he been dead?" Tori asked.

"Given body temp, I'd peg time of death around ten p.m., maybe ten thirty, so not long," Doc Renfrow answered. "As for cause, looks like he was strangled. Look at the bruising around the neck."

Tori leaned inside to get a look and immediately noticed how soiled Derner's clothes were. He was dressed in all black—jeans, shoes and long-sleeved shirt. "His clothes are filthy," she observed. "Look at his knees. They're caked in dirt." There were streaks of dirt on the front of his shirt and the elbows as well, and even smudges on his forehead.

Braddock took a step back from the SUV. In the dirt on the left side of the Pilot there were four impressions, more like deep divots.

"He was killed right here. See these." He pointed to the marks. "Given time of death, they came here after shooting at you, Tori. Derner trusts the other guy, but when he turns his back…"

"The rope is around his neck like that," Tori said, snapping her fingers.

"Our killer gets on top of him, pushes him down to the ground on his knees and elbows and keeps pulling the rope until he goes."

Tori picked up on it. "And these dual tracks are Derner's feet as the killer was dragging him to the rear of the SUV so that he could stuff him in the back." She looked to Braddock. "This is all just so weird."

Braddock was silent for a moment. "Think about it. You show up, Derner hears you and Ruthie talking. He calls our other guy and says, hey we have a problem."

"All I had was a name, maybe a little suspicion. All I was doing was taking a quick look before I came back to tell you about it."

"Derner and the killer don't know that, though," Braddock says. "Our other killer first tries to cauterize the wound by taking you out."

"But he fails…"

"And now decides he has to cut off any link back to him."

"Which means Derner… and his wife?"

"She knew the killer too."

"Or at least she knew where her husband was going to be tonight, and if he didn't come home, she would know who to call and ask," Tori said. "That holds together as an explanation for tonight."

"So now what?" Steak asked.

"All kinds of stuff," Braddock said, and then yawned. "We'll let the doc finish up and the forensic techs do their thing. It's three forty a.m. Get some rest. We'll pick this up in the morning."

CHAPTER TWENTY-SIX

"Sunlight is the best disinfectant"

Tori stirred awake at the sound of a cabinet closing downstairs. She looked at the clock on the nightstand. 9:30 a.m. A little over four hours of sleep.

Downstairs, Braddock was rummaging around the kitchen. She got up, put on her robe, and made her way down, lured by the aroma of freshly brewed coffee. He had a cup waiting for her. She took a sip before yawning and shaking her head to wake herself up. "Four hours," she said before taking another sip. "It's going to be a long day."

"A lot of caffeine will be needed."

"The action is in Keller."

"I agree," Braddock said. "Problem is, I have to go in and meet with County Attorney Backstrom and Assistant County Attorney Wilson first."

"You can't put that off?"

"After last night? *Riiiiiiight.* You should come along. I could use the help. And…"

"And what?"

"I'd like to keep Steak and Sheryl out of this as much as I can. Whereas…"

"I don't have as much at stake, at least professionally."

"Something like that."

"Okay." Tori quickly changed topics. "What's up with Quinn? Is he having a good trip?"

"Yeah, he's good, having a great time," Braddock answered. "The thing I like about that trip is it's just fun. No sports, just time on the lake, in the boat, on the beach, hanging and enjoying himself. It's good for him."

"He *was* playing a lot of hockey. He was at the rink a lot."

"Yeah. He's getting good and he loves it, and the high school coaches are zeroing in on him a little bit. It's far too early for that if you ask me, but he likes the attention, and it makes him want to be at the rink more, to get noticed more, to get that wink and nod from the older kids and the coaches. This break is good for him, and his cousins, 'cause they're all getting sucked in to."

"When is he back?"

"This coming Sunday, which is good. I'm really starting to miss him."

"Me too."

"Yeah?"

"I find him and his cousins highly entertaining," Tori said. "They're good kids and they're funny, the things they say and do. And fair warning, you're going to have issues."

"Why is that?"

"They're getting interested in things other than hockey."

"Girls," Braddock chuckled. "Yeah, I saw the boys checking on the older girls a few weeks ago when we were anchored up on the sandbar. They're still pretty young, but…"

"It's coming," Tori said. "Quinn is going to be a good-looking kid. There will be lots of girls hanging around. They kind of already are."

"You're probably right." He let out a sigh. "We should go and get this over with. But first, I need a shower."

Tori gave him a moment to go upstairs before making her way up after him. She stopped briefly in the bedroom before stepping into the bathroom and sliding open the shower door. As Braddock turned around, she made a point of deliberately slipping off her robe and letting it fall slowly to the floor. She stood in front of him, naked as could be, giving him her best come-hither look.

"I was wondering if you were still *really* mad at me…"

As they drove to the government center, Tori giggled just loudly enough for Braddock to hear.

"What?"

"Just something Tracy said to me over the weekend when I was talking about our argument."

"What's that?"

"Something about hot make up sex after a fight."

Braddock smiled. "It was really fervent, I'll say that. But that doesn't mean you and I don't have some things still to discuss."

"I know."

George Backstrom and his chief assistant, Anne Wilson, were awaiting their arrival. There was no idle warm-up chit-chat. "What in the hell is going on?" Backstrom asked without preamble. "I have to know."

"It's a big old mess, George," Braddock said.

"I think you better tell us why."

Braddock and Tori walked Backstrom and Wilson step by step through the case. The murders of the Newmans and the Stroms and the tie to the old Bauman case. They described how Pen, Sheriff Hunter, and to a lesser extent Cal had withheld disclosure of the Plover murders to Barr's lawyer. Braddock then covered the removal of Cal and Tori from the case, Cal and Pen's shootings, and Tori's move to get Rita Ellis to talk, leading to the crucial identification of Larry Derner and the shooting at Tori's.

When they were done, Backstrom looked over to Wilson. "Well… damn." He was a politician, and worried about perception. "Not disclosing evidence? There's no good way to spin that."

"In a case twenty-four years ago where the guy they prosecuted was guilty," Braddock argued. "I'll die on that hill. He was no innocent man who went to prison. Barr was a killer."

"I'm as angry at my father and Cal as you probably are at Pen," Tori added. "And I can't believe Cal and Pen didn't say something sooner. I'm still just… stunned by that."

"They were covering their asses is what they were doing," Backstrom said. He looked to Wilson. "Thoughts?"

If Backstrom was all politician, Wilson was all prosecutor. It was about the case and the facts with her. "Pen, Cal and Sheriff Hunter were right about who Barr was and who his friends were," she said. "How it all plays out now in light of everything that has happened? Hard to say. If I were faced with this issue today, would I have made the call they made? I don't think so. Too much risk of it coming to light and blowing up in your face at trial, given how readily available information like that is today. But back then? Who's to say? They made a call and took a risk. The good news is they weren't wrong about who they were prosecuting. I agree with Will, we don't have an innocent man who spent his life in prison. We have a now dead guilty one who can't argue the technicality."

"Do the ends justify the means, though?" Backstrom asked. "And look at the potential fallout."

Wilson shrugged. "Who could have foreseen this? I'm with Tori. Had Cal and Pen come forward sooner, maybe after the Newmans, then the Stroms might still be alive. That, to me, is where there will be… vulnerability here. Unfortunately for Cal, he's the only one who can really answer for that."

"Anne, bottom line, did they have to disclose it?" Tori asked. "Pen tried arguing he didn't."

"Yeah, probably. Was it prejudicial not to? Maybe. If Barr were alive today, might he have a case for appeal? Possibly. But here is one thing about this. All the players except Cal are gone. From what you're telling us, the hierarchy of decision-making on this thing was Pen, your father, and then Cal, right?"

"Yes," Tori said.

"So the people who decided, who really decided, are dead. They can't explain or answer for themselves. Barr is dead. Derner, who might have been there, is dead. Who is really impacted by this?"

"We can't just sweep it under the rug," Backstrom said. "We try that, and it won't hold up."

"I'm not saying that you do," Wilson replied flatly. "What you do is very quietly have someone independent come in and investigate and issue a report. Someone with no tie to the department who has an impeccable reputation. Sunlight is the best disinfectant. My point is, however, that nobody who was key to that decision is around anymore. Cal will be hit by it, sure, especially for not coming forward sooner, but you do what is right now, ride it out, and see what comes."

Braddock looked to Tori with a look that said: not awful.

"Has to be done," she said.

"Okay, George. You do all that, but in the meantime, the case is hot. I need to be out in Keller. I can't be dealing with you and that at the same time."

"Get after it," Backstrom said. "But… and I'm really sorry, but not with Tori."

"Come on," Tori pleaded. "Don't ice me out now."

"Tori, what's your last name?"

She sighed. "Hunter."

"Yeah. You can't officially be involved in the investigation now that we know all this. Your name can't show up anymore, especially after last night."

"So, I'm out—again."

"If I heard George right, the operative word is *officially*," Braddock said with a sly smile.

"I did say that, didn't I?" Backstrom nodded. "Seems to me you have one killer left to find, and Tori, Braddock needs your help. But do it from the sidelines."

"Everyone works from home these days anyway," Wilson said with a smile. "Computers and all."

"Okay, fine," Tori said.

"Now find this guy," Backstrom said.

*

Less than an hour later, Braddock was at the restaurant in Keller. Chief Thompson was waiting. "Anything at the house?" Braddock asked.

"Nothing that looks promising," Thompson answered. "Larry and Ruthie were sleeping in separate beds, using separate bathrooms, so his comb, brush, toothbrush, all that is bagged and tagged and being sent to the BCA. I wonder how long until you can run DNA from Larry and what you have and see if there's a match?"

"It's going to the head of the line. We'll know quickly."

"We found his cell phone in his desk," Thompson reported. "For what that's worth."

"It would have prevented anyone from using it to track him," Braddock said. "That tells us something. Is there any sort of surveillance system here?"

Thompson found an assistant manager amongst the employees congregated in the restaurant. She led them into Larry Derner's office.

"It doesn't really show much of anything," she said. "One camera is set on the front area, the bakery and diner counter. The other is set at the bar. Larry and Ruthie wanted to keep their eyes on the cash registers. Those are the two places that transactions are run."

Braddock gave her the time range he wanted to look at. The manager pulled up the black and white footage. After fast-forwarding through five minutes, Tori came in and sat down at the diner counter.

"Stop it," Braddock said, and observed the freeze frame for a moment. "Pretty grainy."

"The system isn't modern," the manager said. "I think they just liked the idea that people knew there was surveillance. I'm not sure they actually ever used it."

Braddock sat down at the desk. The camera was centered on the till. The diner counter was to the right, but you could see the full length of it. Tori was sitting on the left-hand side near the till. There was a man sitting a couple of seats to her immediate left, and then another man two more seats down at the opposite end.

They fast-forwarded to the point where Ruthie greeted Tori, and then again to the point where she returned with the salad. After she had delivered the order, Braddock ran the tape on to when Larry Derner came out from the kitchen. He saw Tori lift the cover of her file folder, glance down at the photo, then discreetly look at Derner before dropping the cover of the folder down. Tori was a pro, discreet in what she was doing, but if you looked for it, you could tell she was eyeing him up. A minute later, Derner left the screen. Five minutes after that, Tori boxed up the rest of her salad and left.

"Not much to see," Thompson said.

"Doesn't seem like it."

Braddock reached down for the mouse. "I want to watch Larry again."

He ran the footage back and restarted it.

"What?"

"He doesn't ever look in Tori's direction," Braddock said. "He came out a few minutes after she told Ruthie her name. I was thinking he came out to get a look at her, but he never even glances in her direction."

"Maybe he did before he came on camera."

"Possible, I suppose."

"Let's start talking to people. I think we have everyone here we're going to have." Thompson explained that he'd corralled all the restaurant employees, giving them the news of what had happened and of the need for investigators to speak with them. "They've been waiting, and I've wanted you here for the interviews."

"Tell me about the staff."

"There are about forty of them."

"Forty?" Braddock said warily. "We better get going then."

*

The good part about not being in Keller was that Tori could sit outside on the deck at Braddock's while she worked. She made a pitcher of iced tea and settled herself at the long table under the umbrella, working through Braddock's full and up-to-date case file.

She found the notes of his interview with Leo Brooks interesting. She could tell that he thought the guy was on the level and that he'd seen a boat coming off the lake at about the right time. If they found the truck or boat, he could be a helpful witness.

The next file on the stack was for Cal and Pen's shooting. She dug in on that.

*

It was a tale of two people when it came to Ruthie and Larry Derner. The employees all knew Ruthie well and spoke to her frequently, and while she could be a volatile boss on occasion, she also took good care of her employees. A server named Angela told Braddock, "Ruthie demanded a lot. When you worked here, you worked, you know."

"No slacking off."

"Never. No standing around, ever. 'I don't pay you to stand around,' she'd yell. 'Grab a rag and clean something.' But if you delivered for her, she delivered for you."

"Give me an example."

"My mom died suddenly seven years ago. Just dropped dead of a heart attack. It was…" Angela's eyes watered, "it was a real shock. We ordered food from the restaurant for the luncheon at the church after the funeral. Ruthie delivered it personally, and wouldn't let us pay a nickel. She stayed, she served, she worked the tables, raved about my mom, and talked about how proud she was that I worked for her. And around here, if Ruthie was doing that for you, people looked at you like you were something, you know." She dabbed a tissue at her eyes. "That was just Ruthie. If you worked for her for a long time, she really viewed you as family."

Larry, on the other hand, was a mystery man. Another server, Judy, said, "I've been here for eighteen years, and I don't feel like I ever really knew him."

"How is that possible?"

She shrugged. "He was quiet and spent most of his time in the office crunching numbers."

"Was he nice, friendly, mean?"

"Not mean. Nice? Kind of, in a klutzy way. He didn't have the gift of the gab that Ruthie did. She was a natural. He would try and make a joke, but it would usually land like a lead balloon, you know. Wrong joke, wrong time, wrong people present."

"He lacked the ability to read the room?"

"Exactly. They both would come out and talk to people in the restaurant. Everyone lit up when they saw Ruthie. With Larry, they were…"

"Polite?"

"Yes," Judy said. "He and Ruthie seemed like such an odd match, if you ask me. Maybe that was why she yelled at him worse than she yelled at us. She could really just get on him and it could be… uncomfortable."

"Why do you think that was?"

"It's Ruthie's House. She was the show, the draw. She owned him and liked to make sure he and everyone else knew it."

Like everyone else they'd talked to thus far, Judy didn't know of any friends or acquaintances Larry might have had. "I mean, he and Ruthie knew everybody in town because everybody in town came here," she said. "As for friends outside of the restaurant, I have no idea. They both always seemed to be here, so I guess this place was their social life."

A little after 3:30, a pack of local businessmen came to the restaurant looking for information.

"Chief, what is going on? We were all just down at Ted's place talking, and he said he heard something had happened to Ruthie and Larry, that they were killed," local bank president, Joe Fern, said.

"We're trying to figure that out, Joe," Thompson said. "You aware of anything Ruthie and Larry have been up to that we should know about?"

"Gosh, no," Fern replied. "How about you guys?"

"I spoke with Ruthie just the other day, and she was as ebullient as ever about the business," said Gene Barnes, a tall, thinnish man wearing a white dress shirt, with four pens and a notepad in his chest pocket. He owned the hardware store. "I talked to Larry too; he seemed fine, said every trip to see Joe was a good one."

"I can attest it was," Fern replied. "They were flush. Anyone else? Ted, how about you? You've known Larry a long time, all the way back to high school."

"Uh… I think things have been good," replied a thickset, bespectacled man dressed in button-down shirt and tan slacks. "I saw him the other day when I came in for lunch and he seemed fine. Ruthie was Ruthie, you know. She was giving me her opinion on some planning commission issues just the other day. I certainly didn't sense she was anything other than her normal self."

"The other day?" Braddock asked. "What day was that?"

"Sunday."

"What happened to them, Chief?" Fern asked. "We're hearing murder. Is that right?"

"I'm afraid so."

Fern was gobsmacked. "I mean, who would want to kill them?"

"That's what we're trying to figure out. Anything you or anyone else in town might have to tell us would be greatly appreciated."

"We'll all spread the word," Fern said. "You can count on that."

Braddock watched them intently as they filed into their SUVs and drove away. Then he went back to Derner's office and replayed the video of Tori's visit.

"What is it you're looking for?" Thompson asked.

"This," Braddock said, sitting back in the desk chair. He pointed to the computer screen. "The guy at the end of the counter. He looks like one of the guys who just left…"

"That's Ted Rand. He owns Big D's Sports and Service on the west end of town."

"I know that place. I bought a wooden sign there."

"Then you bought it from Ted. You didn't recognize him?"

"Not out there, but now that you mention it, I think it was him I ordered from."

"So he was here for lunch. Not a shock. We all are from time to time."

"It's interesting. He said he came in on Sunday. Why not say he was in yesterday?"

"Maybe he confused the days," Thompson said before stepping out of the office.

Braddock replayed the video segment again.

*

Around 1:30, Tori was starting to fade from her work reviewing the investigation files. Needing a break, she went for a run, her first exercise in several days given her trip to New York City. It amazed her how quickly she felt it these days if she took some time off. It seemed to take just a little longer for her muscles to warm and loosen. *Forty is only a few years away.* It was not a thought she particularly relished.

When she got back, she showered and changed and went back outside, this time with a cold beer. If she was relegated to working from here, she might as well be relaxed and hydrated while doing it.

The one file she hadn't reviewed yet was the old Plover file. That was intentional. She was just so exasperated with her father, Pen and Cal, she wasn't sure she wanted to read about what they'd all done.

As she dug into the case, the parallels to the Bauman killings, and the Newmans and Stroms as well, were apparent. The one oddity was that the only intended male victim who was shot was Jerry Bauman. Paul Harstad, Dan Newman and Todd Strom were all killed with a knife. She set out the four photographs.

"A gun is almost impersonal when compared to a knife, which is so up close and personal. With a knife you plunge it in, you slice, you… feel the kill," she murmured, studying the photographs.

All four female victims were raped and then strangled. The strangling method used on Melanie Solmes and Julie Bauman looked similar to that on Heidi Newman and Jennifer Strom. A yellow nylon rope had been used for the first two; the black rope with red accents for the others. She set four photos of the woman below the four photos of the men.

She sensed that she was seeing something as she surveyed the photos together.

What was it?

Derner wasn't the strangler. He was short and just didn't possess the strength. Barr had only been there for the first two, yet the strangling looked virtually the same for all four women, so she concluded it wasn't him either.

It was the third man, the big one, the one who'd tried to kill her last night. He was the strangler. He kills the women, she thought.

Was he the one killing the men too? Did he kill Paul Harstad? Did he kill Jerry Bauman? Why kill Bauman with a gun and Harstad with a knife? Why kill Dan Newman and Todd Strom with a knife even when Dennis Troy's death told them the murderers carried a gun with them?

The gun was for… just in case.

A gun is almost impersonal when compared to a knife, which is so up close and personal.

Newman and Strom were killed with a knife because they'd had some role in Barr being found guilty of murder. Pen and Cal had been shot because they had not disclosed evidence that could have served to free Barr from prison. That killing was personal too, even though the knife wasn't used.

What had made Harstad personal?

She dug through the files. Harstad was a womanizer. They didn't use the term back then, but now he might be considered a player. It was well documented that he'd left a trail of pissed husbands and boyfriends. He was a hound. He'd got into a fight with a husband in Wadena, but the guy was now long dead, according to Steak's note.

Tori took a long sip of her beer as she examined all the photos again, thinking about the specific uses of the knife on the male victims. She felt like she'd learned something, seen a picture of something emerging. But she still didn't have a name.

*

It was after five, and Braddock was fatigued, the days taking their toll. The interviews at the restaurant were all providing the same information, and he was ready to tap out for the day. Thompson said he and his men would keep going and finish them up. He'd call Braddock if anything popped and would send summaries of everything.

Braddock got into his Tahoe. But rather than turning right onto the highway, he took a left, driving through Keller and pulling in at the large sign that read *Big D's Sports and Service.*

After filling his gas tank, he walked into the store and perused the aisles for a few minutes, taking in the mix of sports and recreational equipment and supplies, with an emphasis on water sports, fishing, sailing and boating. He stopped to look in particular at packages of ropes for tying up a boat and for tubing, eventually grabbing dock ropes and then a tubing rope as well.

As he stood up and looked to his left, he saw Rand at a service counter for the carved wooden signs.

"Mr. Rand, hello," he greeted with a wave.

"Oh, hello… it's Detective Braddock, right?"

"Yes. I thought you might have remembered me earlier. I bought one of those custom signs in here a few years ago."

"You did? I'm sorry, I don't recall you. We sell a lot of them. Wait now… it's coming to me… Maybe I do remember this. Did you have green shamrocks on each side?"

"That's right."

"Has it worked out for you?"

"You bet. I get lots of compliments on it."

"Great to hear. What do you have there?"

"Oh, just some ropes. I like the color of these, black with the red flecks in them. They match the color scheme of my boat."

"Ah," Rand replied. "I see. Want me to ring them up?"

"Sure. I feel like I've seen one of these somewhere else recently," Braddock said. "Can't quite picture where it was."

"They're a pretty popular type," Rand replied. "Lots of places sell them."

"I suppose so. Do you use them on your boat?"

Rand looked at him for a moment, expression blank. "How do you know I have a boat?"

"I don't know, you own a store with big recreation section. I just figured, you know."

"I do have a fishing boat."

"Do you have a lake place, or do you move it around?"

"It's on a trailer and I move it around, fish the lakes, you know."

"You don't have a lake place?"

"Nope. I live right behind the store here. That'll be $44.95."

Braddock handed him his credit card. "Oh, wait, let me grab a bottle of water." He was back ten seconds later. Rand ran the card, handed it back to him and placed the ropes in a plastic bag. "There you go."

"Thanks." Braddock turned to walk away. "Oh, one thing I was curious about."

"Yes?"

"You said you were at the restaurant over the weekend. Sunday, right?"

"Yeah, that's right. Talked to Larry."

"Hmm," Braddock said. "Are you sure it wasn't yesterday?"

"Uh… I don't know. I go there a lot. Maybe I thought Monday was Sunday or something."

"Oh, okay." Braddock nodded. "Thanks for the help."

"Come back again."

Braddock made the drive back to Manchester Bay and arrived home to find Tori sitting out on the deck, drinking a beer. He grabbed one and joined her. It was a pleasant night, the bay calm and quiet.

"How was your day?"

"Long," he said.

"You find anything?"

"A couple of things to think on. How about you?"

"I sat out here and went through everything up to today."

"Any insights you want to share?"

"I have a few, but…" she looked down toward the lake, "nothing that will lead to any kind of breakthrough for now. And to be honest, I'm kind of sick of the whole thing at this point."

"I hear that."

"You know, I'm not really in the mood to cook either, are you?"

Braddock chortled. "No. Not in the least."

"Is there anything you have to do tonight?"

"Nothing other than keep my phone close. Thompson is handling things in Keller. Steak and Eggleston are working the Derner murder scene at the fairgrounds, and we're awaiting forensic results there."

"No lead on who Derner's partner might have been?"

"No, I don't think so. Nothing actionable tonight."

"So you have the night off?" Tori asked leadingly.

Braddock smiled. "What do you have in mind?"

"I say we take our beers, get in the boat and cruise up to the Channel Stop. If something comes up, we can be back here in ten minutes. But barring anything like that, I call a moratorium on talking about the case tonight. We can talk about anything but that."

"Deal."

It had been a milder, more comfortable day, the temperature only reaching the low eighties. Now the night was cool and less humid, with just a few clouds in the sky, a gentle breeze creating a ripple along the otherwise quiet lake on a Tuesday night. The gentle hum of the boat's inboard engine and the cold beer in her hand, combined with the light rock emanating from the boat's speakers, allowed the investigation to slowly drift to the back of Tori's mind. Braddock, in sunglasses, loose shirt, shorts and canvas deck shoes, seemed equally relaxed as he sat back in the captain's chair.

"Could you grab me another beer?" he asked, his bottle empty.

Tori fished him out another cold one from the cooler. It didn't have a twist-off cap. "Do you have an opener?" she asked.

"Yeah," he said, taking the bottle. "Keep the wheel steady for me."

Attached to the boat keys was a yellow-encased Swiss army knife. He pulled out the bottle opener from one of the many slots, popped the top off the beer, then retook the wheel.

They cruised at a leisurely speed up to the northwest corner of the lake, hewing close to the tree-lined and ever steeper shoreline, the two of them admiring the upgraded cabins and expansive homes perched high upon the ridge looking down to the lake. They agreed that the views from above must be spectacular, but "I couldn't imagine hoofing it up and down all those steps," Braddock said. "Some of those stairways have to be over a hundred steps long and, they're really steep."

"You wouldn't have to swim every day," Tori said. "You could just do ten flights of stairs instead. Think of the good sweat you'd have."

Braddock chuckled. "I'd much rather swim."

He maneuvered the boat into what the locals called the Long Channel, which led from Northern Pine up to the rest of the lakes on the chain. The channel was narrow, with cabins and their docks protruding from both sides. Further ahead was the area called the Y Junction. The left arm of the Y took you into Norway Lake, where Cal's place was. The right arm led into Red Pine Lake, from which another narrow channel accessed a series of other lakes connected by similar short channels.

They weren't going quite as far as the Y Junction tonight, although it was visible to their left as they pulled up to the Channel Stop bar. Braddock turned right into a vacant boat slip and Tori tied up. Wanting to listen to the live music on the patio, they sat down at an open table under an umbrella, ordered burger baskets and beers and relaxed. A few local acquaintances stopped by to say hello, but for the most part they enjoyed a night to themselves, with Braddock only occasionally checking his phone and taking quick update phone calls from Eggleston and Chief Thompson out in Keller.

As the sun started to set, they headed home at a leisurely speed on the calm waters of the lake, drinking a last beer, music again playing quietly on the boat's stereo system.

"Any update on Cal?" Braddock asked.

"I talked to Lucy around four this afternoon. She said he was sleeping but was doing as well as could be expected. His sons are still here, so lots of family around. She asked me to stop by tomorrow."

"Good, I think you should," he said as they entered the bay, Braddock's place visible on the western side.

He pulled the boat into the lift, raised it, and they slowly walked up to the cabin.

"That was a good idea tonight," he said, throwing his arm around her shoulders. "We needed the break. We'll be fresher in the morning."

"I know you said we had to talk at some point," Tori said, as she slipped her arm around his waist.

"Yeah, we do, but not tonight, huh," he said, kissing her on the head. "Tonight, I just want to go upstairs, maybe put on a movie and relax. Back rubs might be nice."

"They would indeed."

CHAPTER TWENTY-SEVEN

"And you received what for this accommodation?"

Braddock was up early, going for his usual swim. From the deck, Tori was able to catch glimpses of his long freestyle strokes to the southeast. He usually swam down to his in-laws' house a quarter-mile away, and then back again. The past few weeks he would stop when he reached their dock, and get out and check on the house, since Roger and Mary were in Michigan with Quinn and his two cousins on the summer trip.

As he emerged from the water, Tori went back inside to pour herself a coffee.

"You look a little more refreshed," she said when he joined her.

He nodded, but then glanced at her stack of papers on the table. "What was your insight from yesterday?" he asked as he continued to dry his hair.

She brought him a cup of coffee. "I don't know how helpful it'll be," she said as she laid out the photos and explained her theory on the personal nature of the killings.

"Take Harstad: you see how he was stabbed multiple times before they slit his throat. He was made to suffer, really suffer. It looks very personal to the killer, and I think the killer was neither Barr nor Derner. I think the killer of the women *and* the men is our mysterious third man. The big guy who tried to shoot me. I mean, I look at Harstad and I see a vengeful killing. Just like the killings of Newman and Strom. The way both men were butchered was… ruthless, merciless, pick your adjective. Jerry Bauman's death isn't as personal. He was shot. But Bauman was personal to who?"

"Barr."

"Right. Bauman's death was just a job the killer had to do. But I think the rest of the killings were personal to our third man. The big guy."

"Newman and Strom were personal because of their roles in what Pen and your dad did. I get your interpretation that Harstad's murder looks personal. But we're still stuck with the question: to whom?"

"That's just it. There was one decent prospect. A bar altercation in…"

"Wadena. Yeah, I had Steak look that up."

"Yeah, the man's name was Dowd Rand," Tori said. "He's been dead ten years."

"Uh… wait a second, did you say Rand?" Braddock asked, suddenly slack-jawed.

"Yes." Tori nodded, seeing his reaction. "Why? What is it?"

"I have to show you something. Let's go up to the office."

Upstairs, Braddock fired up his computer, opened his email and clicked on a video file. "This is the surveillance video from when you went to Ruthie's Place on Monday." He pointed to the right side of the screen. "See this guy sitting to your left?"

Tori nodded.

"His name is Ted Rand."

He started the video again, fast-forwarding to the point when Ruthie came out and she and Tori introduced themselves. "See that?"

"Run it again," Tori said.

He rewound and pressed play.

"I see it now," Tori said. "Rand, his head snaps right when I say my name. Interesting."

Braddock fast-forwarded to the moment when Larry Derner came out to the cash register. Even with the grainy quality of the video, they could tell that Rand was peering in Tori's direction as she lifted the cover of the folder to check the photo. He was discreet, but he was looking.

Braddock let the video run after Derner left the cash register. Tori continued to eat her salad. Rand abruptly stood up, tossed cash on the counter and walked out of view, half a hamburger, a plate full of fries and two thirds of a shake left.

"What's the description Cara gave us of our third man?" Braddock said. "Big guy, big shoulders, looks like a football player."

"With a nasal voice," Tori added.

"That's right. I talked to him twice yesterday, and his voice is kind of high-pitched."

"Twice?"

"He came to the restaurant with some other businesspeople to ask about the Derners, and I thought I recognized him from this video. He said he'd seen Derner on Sunday at the restaurant, but not Monday, when you were there. Before I came home last night, I drove to Big D's Sports and Service, his business. In fact, hang on a second..."

Braddock ran downstairs and out to his truck. When he came back upstairs, he was carrying some ropes. "I was walking the aisles at the store after I filled up for gas, and I bought these."

Tori grinned. "Black with red flecks in them. We need to get these to Jennison."

"Right. I spoke to him there as well. And I really don't buy his excuse that he was confused about the day he was last at the restaurant. If you went somewhere yesterday, you'd remember."

Tori sat back. "This guy is setting off my Spidey senses like he's setting off yours. Let's say he is our killer—we don't have nearly enough to prosecute him. This is mostly gut feeling, beyond the tie to Dowd Rand and Harstad, which is certainly probative."

"It's enough to start focusing on him and start asking some questions about his whereabouts at certain points in time."

"Such as the Newman and Strom murders?"

"And Saturday night for Cal and Pen."

Braddock's phone rang. It was a government center exchange, although he didn't immediately recognize the number. "Will Braddock."

"Detective Braddock, this is Kathryn Turner. I need to see you. Can you come to my house?"

On the drive back to Manchester Bay, Braddock filled Tori in on Turner's role as the IT director for Shepard County, and what he'd asked her to do.

"I kept going over the argument we had in Cal's office asking how anyone would know about Dan Newman and what your father had him do, erasing any links of contacts with Portage County over in Wisconsin. Todd Strom's name was in the file from Portage County as having been contacted. But there was no mention of Newman in our investigative file or in the Portage County one. And then Corbin Hansen calls me to meet him in Pine River and talk to Leo Brooks about Alan and Jan Sampson, killed in that explosion in Remer. Turns out Alan Sampson and Brooks were at the boat launch when our killers took their boat out after killing the Stroms. They must have taken down Sampson's license plate, but again, how would a civilian identify someone just from a license plate? You have to access that information somehow. I started thinking that they had to have had some help. So who had access to Sampson's license plate and could dig into old electronic files and somehow track down Dan Newman's involvement?"

"Brilliant," Tori said. "You get a Scooby Snack for this one."

*

Kathryn Turner led Tori and Braddock to her home office, where she had three screens up on her desk. "I'll spare you the technical jargon," she said. "I started with whether anyone checked the license plate for Alan Sampson. His record was accessed the day after the murders at the Stroms', by a former employee named Sarah Jones."

"Former?"

"Yes. She left the sheriff's department three weeks ago. The search was done using her old credentials."

"How about the Bauman case."

"Those were accessed seven months ago by Scott Johnson. He too is a former employee, who left a year ago."

"What computer were the searches made from?"

"A laptop from the IT department that has a general username and department password, so you wouldn't necessarily know who signed in. It's one of our spares."

"Someone was covering their tracks."

"Yes. And I think it's an employee named Ron Berg," Turner said.

"Why do you think it's him?" Braddock asked.

"One, his pass card was used on that Saturday to get into the government center and our department. Two, he was responsible for removing the credentials for both Scott Johnson and Sarah Jones from the system. As you suspected, he has worked in IT for years and knows where all the little holes to exploit are. According to the system, Scott Johnson has accessed information on four separate occasions since he departed the county."

"Is there any way to prove Berg was the one who actually accessed the files?" Tori asked.

"Absolutely prove? No. But there are two other things I can tell you. Around the time Scott Johnson was supposedly accessing old emails and data on the Bauman case, Ron Berg was carrying out

work on the computers down in the case file storage area. He did
the work after normal work hours, which is common protocol;
the IT department often update computers then so as to limit
service disruption to the public. He may have been down there
unsupervised. He could have accessed the old paper files as well.
You'd have to check."

"What was the other thing?"

"Motive." Turner handed over a folder. "That's Berg's payroll
file. He's subject to two child support garnishments. He has
himself a couple of baby mamas who are taking a big bite out of
his paycheck."

"He did it for the money," Tori said. "He told the killers who
Alan Sampson was. That way, they could get rid of their witness."

"For the money. A story as old as man himself," Braddock
muttered as he quickly flipped through Berg's file. "Okay, Kathryn,
here is what we're going to do…"

A half-hour later, Braddock and Tori were back at the government
center. There was a knock on the door of Braddock's office, and in
came a slight, blond-haired and mustached man casually dressed
in blue jeans, brown lace-up shoes and a black button-down
shirt. "I'm Ron Berg from IT. I understand you're having some
computer issues?"

"Yes, come in Ron," Braddock said, and stood up from his desk.

Berg came around the desk, sat down in Braddock's chair and
shook the mouse to wake up the screen. As he did so, his eyes
went wide.

At the same time, Turner stepped into the office.

"Why?" Braddock asked. "Why did you access that information on Alan Sampson using the credentials of an ex-employee,
Sarah Jones?"

"I… I didn't."

"Oh wait, so you didn't also use Scott Johnson's credentials to access information on the Bauman case?" Braddock watched as an expression of horror crept across the man's face. "Oh Ron, I think you did."

"Oh, oh," Tori chirped. "Not good there, Ronnie boy. Not good."

"I know you did it, Ron," Turner asserted. "I traced it." She held up a folder. "I've got it all right here."

"Why?" Braddock pressed, sitting on the desk, sliding close to Berg, staring down at him.

Berg closed his eyes. He knew he was caught. "I needed the money." He put his face into his hands. "How much trouble am I in here?"

"I think the technical term would be a shit ton," Tori quipped. "You need to start thinking about what you can do to help yourself. People are dead because of you."

Berg looked at her through his fingers, stunned.

"Who paid you for this information?"

"I… I don't know. This guy."

"This guy?" Braddock asked incredulously.

"Do you have a name, Ron?" Tori pressed.

"No. I assumed he was some sort of insurance investigator. He called me a few times over the years for a license plate number check or two. That was the thing he called for a couple of weeks ago."

"And you received what for this accommodation?"

"A thousand dollars in cash. It had to be cash."

"Was that your standard fee?"

Berg nodded. "Like I said, I needed the money."

"And why did this man want this information?"

"I don't know."

"You sure about that?" Braddock asked.

"I don't know why he wanted it and I didn't ask. I figured the less I knew the better. But again, I figured it was for insurance purposes."

"What about all this stuff on the Bauman case?" Tori asked. "Why did he want that?"

Berg shrugged. "He offered me five grand cash for it, so…" he sighed, "I did it. I mean, what he wanted to know about was so old. Who cares?"

"What did you access besides the electronic file?"

Berg's eyes closed. "I went and pulled the old file boxes and made copies."

"How did he get your name?" Tori asked. "Is it possible you've done this for some other folks too?"

Berg sighed and nodded his head. "Like I said, I needed…"

"The money. Yeah, yeah," Tori finished. "Have you met the man in person?"

"Yes."

"Where?"

"Usually at Ruthie's House in Keller." Tori and Braddock shared a quick look. "I'd slide him the information and I'd get an envelope."

"You don't have a name," Tori said. "So describe him."

"Bigger guy, pretty solidly built, big head, usually wearing business clothes. Like I said, I thought he was some sort of insurance investigator looking to get information."

"Is he this guy?" Tori showed him a picture of Derner.

"No."

"How about this one?" She handed him a picture of Rand.

"That's him."

"And you last saw him when?"

"A week ago, Saturday. He called me around noon, gave me a license plate number and asked me to run it. I drove out to Ruthie's House, gave him the information and collected the cash."

"Okay, you're going to write all this down," Braddock said, and called in a uniformed officer to stand watch. In the hallway, he was thanking Turner when Steak walked up.

"And?" Braddock asked.

"Ted Rand owns a black Dodge Ram pickup truck and a twenty-foot black fishing boat."

"Now we have something tangible," Tori said. "Ted Rand is our other killer."

"Okay, I have to get back out to Keller," Braddock said.

"And let me guess. I have to go home and miss all the fun," Tori lamented.

"Hey, you broke this case from home without knowing it," Braddock said, pulling her in and surprising her with a quick public kiss, stunning her. "You're on a roll. Keep working it."

CHAPTER TWENTY-EIGHT

"You should have learned from how well that went"

Braddock collected Steak and Eggs for the drive to Keller and called Thompson. "I'm on my way out right now. Does the name Dowd Rand ring a bell?"

"Oh sure. Dowd owned Big D's, started the business way back when. You met his son, Ted, yesterday. He took the business over when Dowd passed. Why?"

"Chief, I need to tell you a story." Braddock related the details of the Harstad murder from twenty-four years ago. "Paul Harstad was the man murdered in Plover, Wisconsin. He and his girlfriend at the time, Melanie Solmes. A few years before Harstad moved to Plover, he lived in Wadena and got into a bar confrontation with Dowd Rand."

"Oh boy."

"The altercation had something to do with Harstad having an affair with Rand's wife."

Thompson sighed. "I was on patrol back then, and I had to go to the Rand house a few times to settle things down between Dowd and Eileen. Dowd was a good-looking guy, but he was volatile and had a dark, moody side to him. Eileen was, I think, restless. She ran out on Dowd with another man, I remember that. A few years later, she committed suicide, and after that, well, Dowd just slowly drank himself into the grave."

"Harstad had himself quite a reputation as a ladies' man," Braddock said. "Eileen wasn't the only married woman he shacked up with. However, his only criminal record entry is that altercation with Dowd Rand. You say Ted is a prominent guy in Keller. Has he always been that way?"

"Hmm…" Thompson paused for a moment.

"Chief?"

"Well, when he was a younger fella, he got himself into some trouble. He wasn't afraid of a fight, I'll tell you that. He could handle himself and had a vengeful streak if he felt he'd been wronged. He had an overnight stay or two in our jail way back in the day. I walked him in once after a fist fight outside a local watering hole. The other fella ended up in the hospital."

"I don't doubt it when you look at the size of him."

"And… Jeez, it's amazing what you remember once a little something triggers the memory."

"What, Chief?"

"He was a suspect in something else one time, albeit briefly."

"What was that?" Steak asked.

"Ted was married once, years ago. It didn't last long."

"Why?"

"I don't know," Thompson replied. "But soon after it ended, she remarried."

Eggs caught it. "Like so soon that it started before…"

"Uh-huh. Not long after that, Ted left town for several years and went south somewhere to work—I want to say maybe Texas. Around the time he left, his ex-wife died in a one-car accident."

"*Was* it an accident?" Braddock asked.

"My recall is there was some question about it," Thompson replied. "It happened north of here by Park Rapids. I have a lake place up that way and knew the sheriff in Hubbard County. He called me to ask about Ted. I didn't know anything, but if memory serves, there was some thought her car might have been tampered with. Ted worked at Big D's for his dad, knew his way around a vehicle and was, I believe, a certified mechanic. So there was at least a reason to question him, but nothing ever came of it."

"How long was he in Texas?"

"A few years. I remember he came back when his dad took a turn for the worse and could barely keep the station open. That was maybe ten, twelve years ago."

"Did he come back a new man?"

"Seemed to," Thompson said, nodding. "He's rebuilt Big D's into a thriving entity. He's prominent in our Chamber of Commerce, sponsors a bunch of youth sports teams and serves on the planning commission. He's viewed as a community leader, but then again, so was Larry Derner."

"But is he a new man? Or has he just gotten better at hiding who he really is?"

Thompson sighed. "I just don't know now. You've painted a pretty grim picture."

"You said he was a mechanic chief?" Steak asked.

"Yes."

Steak looked to over to Braddock. "Portage County found smudges of axel grease at Harstad's house. You know where you find axel grease?"

"Repair garage."

"You have what Tori figured out, you have what Berg gave you, the connection between Dowd Rand, Ted Rand and Harstad," Eggs said. "He's digging into old Bauman case material. Heck, there's even the suspicion he killed his ex-wife. Man, there's a lot of death floating around this guy."

"Sure is," Braddock said as he looked to Steak and then back to Eggs as a small grin emerged. They both smiled and nodded back to him. They had their man. Steak fist-bumped Eggs.

"We have one more thing to confirm," Braddock said quietly to the two of them, then to Thompson he said, "Chief, we think Rand is our guy. However, before we bring him in for a talk, I need you to meet me at the restaurant again."

*

When she got back to Braddock's house, Tori immediately called Rita Ellis. "Rita, I need to text you a picture. Tell me if you recognize this guy." She sent the text. "Let me know when you get it."

"Okay, hang on."

She paced around the desk in Braddock's home office, waiting expectantly.

"Oh my God, Tori? Tori?" Rita said excitedly. "Are you there?"

"Yes, I'm here." Tori noted the sudden high pitch of Rita's voice.

"That's him, Tori," she replied confidently. "No doubt, that's him."

"That's who, Rita?"

"The man I saw at Hugh's house that time with Larry Derner," she said. "He was the guy working on the truck."

"You're sure?"

"Yes. Who is he?"

"His name is Ted Rand. Does that sound right? He owns Big D's in Keller."

"Ted doesn't sound right."

"Oh."

"But Big D's does. I couldn't remember his name, but I remember it now. They called him D."

"You're sure?"

"Yes."

"Okay, Rita, I have to sign off…"

"Tori, hold on a second. I just opened my mail, and I got something really good, but also… odd."

"What's that?"

"A check from the prison. It was the money in Hugh's inmate account."

"For how much?"

"Over seven thousand dollars."

"Hey, good for you," Tori said, then stopped. "Did you ever send him any money?"

"No."

*

Chief Thompson met Braddock and Steak at Ruthie's House and they went immediately to the surveillance system in Larry Derner's office. Braddock sat down at the desk and maneuvered the mouse, clicking back to two Saturdays ago.

"There's Rand coming in and sitting down."

He fast-forwarded the footage ahead twenty minutes until a man came and sat next to him.

"That's Ron Berg," Braddock said with a thin smile, scratching his chin, recognizing the slight build, blond hair and mustache.

Berg gave an order to a waitress. After she walked away, they watched as he took out a folded piece of paper from his chest pocket and slid it along the counter to Rand. They then saw him reach under the diner counter and stuff something into his pant pocket. When the waitress returned with a white bag and a cup of coffee to go, Berg departed.

Braddock hit fast forward again to see if anyone else spoke to Rand. He stopped the footage. "I'll be damned."

"Larry Derner," Steak said. "What are they looking at? The surveillance camera?"

"No," Thompson said. "There's a television mounted in that corner. I think they're looking at that."

They watched as the two men conversed, then Rand lightly tapped the piece of folded paper on the counter with his right index finger.

Braddock let out a small self-satisfied laugh. "You see that?"

Eggs nodded. "He's tapping it as if to say looky what I got."

"He's telling Derner about Alan Sampson. Rand now knows who witnessed them at the boat launch," Steak said.

Braddock looked over to Thompson. "Ted Rand is our killer."

"Sure as heck looks like it. Damn. You're killing my economy here, Will."

Braddock's cell phone buzzed. Tori.

"What's up?" Braddock asked, and put her on speaker.

"Rita Ellis identified Rand as someone she saw with her son and Larry Derner not long before the killings in Plover. She said they called him D. Do people call him that?"

"Some do," Thompson answered. "D for Big D's."

Braddock relayed what Thompson had told them about Rand, his parents' difficulties and his mother's suicide.

"That's how Barr and Rand connected," Tori said.

"Derner is the cog in the wheel," Braddock said.

"Exactly. He's from Keller, where Rand is from. He went to college with Barr. He brings them together, but it's Rand and Barr who truly bond, over their parents' infidelities and suicides. And somehow that triggers the need to… kill. For Rand it was Paul Harstad, the man who broke up his parents' marriage. For Barr it was Julie Bauman, the woman who rejected him for another man. That's the connection."

"What was Derner?" Thompson asked.

"The little buddy," Tori said. "The guy who tagged along. He was the helper Rand needed, but when I showed up and he became a liability, Rand disposed of him like he was nothing. It's Hugh Barr that Rand really cares about. Barr went to prison for life and never said a word. He carried all that weight for all those years, and he carried it for Rand. But then somehow Rand found out what Pen, my father and Cal did, and he's been out for payback."

"Chief, we've got enough for search warrants," Braddock asserted. "It's time."

Thompson agreed. "Let's get to work."

Backstrom and Wilson, now up to speed, got on a call along with the county attorney for Morrison County. A judge signed off not long after, and Thompson assembled a team to serve the warrants and bring Rand in.

"Ted is almost always at Big D's or at his house right behind the store," he said. "Let's go."

The plan was to have Thompson and his man, followed by Braddock, Steak and Eggleston, go to the service station. Four officers would go to the house, with two more hanging back in reserve in case there was trouble. They headed west in a line of vehicles.

The massive red Big D's sign was visible high in the sky like a beacon a half-mile ahead. There were two tall red canopies in front of the store. The first, closest to the highway, covered the diesel pumps for large trucks. The second and lower canopy, closer to the store, covered the lanes for cars and trucks. The two-story white brick building itself was large and clearly had been added onto and attractively remodeled over the years.

"It's quite the place," Steak noted.

"It's even bigger than it looks," Braddock said. "There is a lot of stuff inside."

Thompson and his man led Braddock and Steak to the service station. The chief went in the front door holding up the warrant. A store manager approached. "Where's the boss?" Thompson asked.

"Last I saw him he was up in his office."

Thompson led them all up the stairs and knocked on a closed door at the top. "Ted, it's Chief Thompson, open up." No response. He tried the handle, but it was locked. The suddenly terrified store manager nervously handed Braddock a key. Braddock held his gun in his right hand and slid the key into the lock with his left, rolling the lock over. He pushed the door open, and he and Thompson carefully looked inside.

Rand wasn't there.

"Search the store," Braddock said.

They spread out down the aisles, but he was nowhere to be found on the premises.

Thompson reached for his police radio and called to his man at Rand's house. "Is he there?"

"I don't think so, Chief," the officer replied. "No answer to our door knocks."

Thompson looked at the store manager. "Do you have a key for the house?"

The manager nodded and handed over a key ring.

"We're on our way over," Thompson reported.

They went out the back door of the store and ran across the parking lot, through a gap in a hedge and around to the front of Rand's one-story house. Thompson approached the front door, Braddock, Steak and Eggs stacking up behind him.

He opened the door and everyone surged inside, searching the house.

Rand wasn't there either. However, the black Dodge Ram pickup was parked in the garage.

"Well where the hell is he?" Braddock exclaimed.

"We don't know where he is," Braddock said to Tori thirty minutes later. "He was at the store in the morning. According to the manager, he made a run to the bank, then went up to his office, and that's the last anyone has seen of him."

"What happens next?"

"We're watching the store and his house in case he shows. Thompson has men out looking for him in Keller. A statewide bulletin has been issued for him." Braddock sighed. "I'm thinking I must have spooked him."

"At the store last night?"

"Yeah. I bought the ropes, talked boats, and from that…"

"He figured you were onto him."

"Could be. I was going to take a closer look at him today, and then you found the Rand name in the Plover case. I should have called Thompson right then and there…"

"Don't do it," Tori counseled. "We solved it. It's Rand. Just figure out where he's going. If he went to the bank…"

"He was getting money," Braddock finished. "We're on it. What are you doing?"

"It's getting late in the day now. Rand is going to be all over the news in the next twelve to twenty-four hours, if not sooner. I'm thinking of going to talk to Cara tonight. I want her to hear what happened to her father and stepmom from me before she hears it from anyone else. I owe her that, I think."

"I assume you want to tell her everything?" Braddock asked warily.

"I do, though I need you to be okay with that. Are you?"

Braddock thought for a moment. "If you're up to doing it, you should be the one to tell her. Maybe talk to her mom first, see if she thinks Cara can handle hearing it, but if she gives the green light, go ahead."

"You want me to pull my punches?"

"No, I trust your judgment. Tell her what you think she needs to hear."

"Thanks."

*

As she drove into Manchester Bay, Rand's trip to the bank got Tori thinking of her call with Rita Ellis. She parked in the parking lot for the athletic fields for Manchester Bay High School. In the distance, she saw the girls' soccer team having an evening captain's practice. Cara Newman was playing.

She searched the contacts on her phone and found the number she was looking for. Warden Sills from the Stillwater correctional facility had been kind enough to provide both his direct line and cell phone in case she and Braddock needed anything. He picked up his cell phone on the third ring.

"Warden Sills, this is Tori Hunter. I'm sorry to call you so long after the workday like this."

"That's okay, Tori. What can I do for you?"

"I had a conversation with Rita Ellis earlier today—she's Hugh Barr's mother. She received a check for over seven thousand dollars from the correctional facility, her son's inmate account balance. She inherited it, I guess."

"Sure," Sills affirmed. "That's normal procedure."

"That seemed like a lot of money for an inmate, though."

"It's maybe a little high, but far from unheard of."

"You said when we were down there to interview him that he worked at the prison. Would that have been his earnings?"

"Not that much, no, although prisoners can also receive money orders from friends and family on the outside. Most do."

"Did Barr receive any of those?"

"I'd assume so, but I'd have to check." Sills paused for a moment. "Tori, why are you asking all this? What's concerning you?"

"His mother never sent him any money. He didn't have a visitor for his last twenty-two years in prison," Tori said. "How was it he had all this money? If someone was sending it, who was it? Was it Ted Rand, the guy we think is our killer? It would be good to know the answer to that. It would be another piece of the puzzle."

"Hmm," Sills murmured, and thought for a moment. "Tell you what, I'll look into it as soon as I get back to my house. My wife and I are driving for a workout at our fitness place. Maybe I'll have an answer later tonight."

"I'd really appreciate it," Tori said, and Sills clicked off. She had hoped for a quicker answer, but then again, it was well after work hours, and it would only possibly confirm what they already knew.

She got out of the Audi and made her way inside the stadium, climbing about two thirds of the way up the large home-side grandstand and grabbing a seat.

Cara was playing as a midfielder. She was a solid player, one of the best on the field, and fast. Tori watched her chase down several players, take possession and then make a proper play with the ball. It made her wonder when she'd last watched high school girls play soccer. In fact, when was the last time she'd played herself? It must have been years.

A half-hour later, the girls finished up the practice and slowly dispersed. Cara spotted Tori, waved and came up into the stands. "My mom said you might stop by."

"You looked good out there," Tori observed. "Speedy. Have you thought about playing in college? I bet you could."

Cara shrugged. "I've had a few emails from Division II and III coaches here in Minnesota."

"Any thoughts on where you're going to college?"

Cara took a drink from her water bottle. "I've looked at Gustavus Adolphus and Minnesota State Mankato. I heard from the coaches at both of those schools. I haven't decided if I want to play or just go to school."

Tori nodded.

"What do you think?"

She considered the question for a moment. "You have to *want* to play. It's a time commitment. You have to balance schoolwork with it and then having some fun too. But it's a chance to play four more years of some meaningful games and it'll keep you in great shape. You're probably not thinking this far ahead yet, but I know corporate America likes graduates with good grades who also had extracurricular activities. And," she added, "if you do decide to play, one thing being on a team does at college is give you a social network. Instant teammates and friends. It makes it an easier transition, I think."

"Did you play in college?"

Tori shook her head. "I wouldn't have been good enough at Boston College—that's Division I. I played some club soccer, though. Come to think of it, that's probably the last time I kicked a soccer ball."

Cara nodded. "I'll think about it. So why did you want to talk to me?"

Tori sighed and took a moment to collect her thoughts. "Cara, we think we know what happened now. It will all probably come out in the news in the coming days, and I wanted you to hear what happened from me, okay?"

"Okay."

She explained the case. "We know that this Derner man was one of the two who killed your father and stepmom and chased after you into the woods. I'm certain he was the one you hit with that log. The other man, Ted Rand, he was the big one that night." She showed Cara pictures of both men.

"And you're still trying to find him?"

"Yes. Chief Detective Braddock is working on it right now."

Cara stared intently at the photos for a minute, deliberately taking in the faces of both men. When she finally spoke, her voice was lower, and firm. "Why did they kill my father? What did he do to these guys?"

"He just did his job. This all goes back to when your dad worked for Shepard County, and my father, when he was the sheriff, asked him to do something. There was no way either of them could have ever imagined that it would lead to all this."

"What was it?"

"There was this case a long time ago. I was fourteen when it happened, younger than you are now, that's how long ago it was…" Tori explained the Bauman case, the arrest and prosecution of Hugh Barr, and the involvement of her father, Cal and Pen Murphy, as well as the small roles that Todd Strom and Cara's father had played when it came to the Plover murders. "At the time, I think my father, Pen Murphy and Sheriff Lund thought there might have been others involved in the killings but there was no evidence to support that. And Barr never said a word, not a one."

"And this other case, in Wisconsin?"

"At the time, it was hard to know if it was connected or not. Now we know for sure that it was. My father and Pen Murphy knew about the other case, but…" Tori closed her eyes and exhaled a breath, "they didn't disclose it to Barr's attorney."

"Should they have?"

"Well, that all depends on who you ask," Tori said, looking Cara in the eye. "I'll spare you the technicalities. What it comes down to is that they decided it was too risky to disclose it because it could have let Hugh Barr go free. Barr was a killer. Along with Derner and Rand, he killed Jerry and Julie Bauman, and we now know that they killed those people in Wisconsin too. They killed your dad and stepmom, the Stroms and their friend, and Pen Murphy, and they almost killed Sheriff Lund. Rand killed Larry Derner and his wife when we got onto him. These guys would have killed you. They took a shot at me the other night."

"I heard about that. Mom tried to tell me it was nothing, but…"

"It wasn't nothing," Tori replied with a headshake. She held her thumb and index finger an inch apart. "That's how close it was."

Cara's eyes bulged.

"Twenty-four years ago, whether my father and Pen Murphy and Cal Lund made the right call or the wrong one, they were guided by taking a man they were certain was a killer off the street so he couldn't kill again. Your father was asked by my father to do some technical things to help with that after the fact."

"He made something disappear, didn't he? Removed something from the system?" Cara asked.

Tori nodded. "Unfortunately, the killers found that out all these years later and killed him and your stepmom for it. Todd Strom played a similarly minor role and that's why he and his wife were killed. Pen Murphy played the key role, and he's dead. Sheriff Lund and I should probably be dead too." She looked down and exhaled a breath. "Here's the bottom line, Cara. This is why I'm here. Your dad was murdered because of a decision my dad made a long, long time ago. I thought you should hear that from me. I'm sorry. I'm… so, so, sorry."

Cara's eyes teared up. "It's not your fault. You didn't do it."

Tori nodded as she stared out to the field. "Still…"

Cara slid across the bench and leaned into her. Tori wrapped her arm around her.

"I'm so sorry. I'm so, so sorry."

A half-hour later, both of them all cried out, they slowly walked back to Tori's Audi in silence as the sun was descending in the sky. Elise Peterson was waiting for them.

"Can I still call you?" Cara asked when they reached her mother's car.

"Anytime you want."

As she watched them drive away, Tori's phone rang. It was Braddock.

"Anything?"

"No. When we really questioned the employees, they all realized it had been some hours since Rand had actually been seen. Chief Thompson got a warrant and went over to the bank in town to look at his accounts. Turns out he'd cleaned them out a couple of months ago, wiring the money down to some banks in Panama."

"He's running," Tori said. "Can we trace the money?"

"We're going to need help with that. If I had to guess, it isn't there anymore either. He's been planning this for some time. He was ready to run if he needed to."

"Maybe even all the way down to another identity," Tori replied. "Dammit!"

"And his truck is still here, so he slipped away with something or someone else," Braddock said. "The one thing that is bothering me now is his wooden sign business."

"*That's* what's worrying you?" Tori asked, confused, not following his train of thought.

"The signs are home-made, Tor. Where was he making them? The equipment isn't at Big D's. It's not at his house. He has no other property listed in his name. And where is his boat? So far we haven't found where he's storing it."

"He could be keeping it at some farmer's place who has space in the barn or something. Paying him cash."

"Maybe," Braddock acknowledged. "But where is he making the signs?"

"Did he rent space?"

"No evidence or documentation of that."

"Did you ask all the employees?"

"Yes. They don't know. They said he'd bring the signs in when they were ready, but they didn't know from where."

"What's your plan?"

"To keep searching. We're going through everything at the office and house. What have you been up to?"

"I talked with Cara."

"How did that go?"

"I felt so… She asked if she could still call me."

"That's a good sign," Braddock said. "Are you going to be at the house?"

"Yes. How much longer will you be out there?"

"Not long. I'm just waiting for Thompson to call me back on something and then I think we'll head back. Rand is on the run, so if he's caught tonight or tomorrow, I have a feeling it'll be a long way from here."

*

"What did you and Tori talk about?" Elise asked as she drove north out of Manchester Bay along East Lake Drive, leaving the town behind them. She turned on her headlights, as the sun was rapidly setting.

"Dad and why he was killed." Cara gave her mom a quick recap. "She thought she should be the one to tell me about it."

"That was good of her," Elise said as she turned left onto the long tunnel-like road leading to the lake and their house. "You like Tori, don't you?"

Cara nodded. "She seems really cool. I think she tells me the truth."

"She's going to be someone to lean on, honey. She's been there and she made some mistakes dealing with something like this. If she's willing, you should talk to her."

"She told me I could call her anytime."

"Have they caught the last man…" Elise began, but then looked up into her rear-view mirror. "What the…"

Cara glanced back. "Mom…"

A silver pickup truck had pulled up close behind and was now swinging out left, accelerating.

"Mom! Go!"

Elise tried to hit the gas, but fumbled the pedal. The truck was alongside them now, the engine roaring.

It rammed into them.

Elise fought the wheel, but the truck's nose was in front of the car. It turned into them again, pushing the car hard to the right.

"Look out!" Elise screamed, putting her arms up as the car careened off the road and into the trees.

Cara popped awake at the snap of the fingers. She instantly realized that her wrists and ankles were bound. She looked down to see the small zip-tie cuffs around her ankles, two of them, doubled up. Her arms were pulled around behind her and she could feel a metal post rubbing against the skin of her neck. And her mouth was taped.

Standing in front of her was a large man, burly, with big forearms. He was wearing dark-rimmed glasses and had tightly cut hair.

"Hi, Cara," the nasal voice greeted. He held up her cell phone. "Smile."

CHAPTER TWENTY-NINE

"We were perfect together"

"We're leaving now," Braddock reported. "It's getting dark. Time to call it a day."

"Anything new?"

"No. Thompson still has his guys out scouring the town, talking to people, but as of now, Rand is in the wind. I'll be home in maybe forty-five-minutes. I'll have to drop Steak and Eggs off first."

After Braddock hung up, Tori was contemplating opening a bottle of wine when her phone rang. It was Elise Peterson. She probably wanted to talk about what she'd told Cara.

"Hi, Eli—"

"Tori! He took her! *He took her!*"

"Hold on, who took her? What are you talking about?"

"Cara and I were driving home from the high school. When I turned onto the road to get to our house, this silver pickup came up behind us and ran us off the road into the ditch and a tree. It knocked me out. I didn't wake until Mal found me. Cara was gone."

"How long were you out?"

"I don't know for sure. It's fully dark now. Maybe twenty minutes, maybe more."

"Have you called 911?"

"Yes, but they're not here yet, although I hear sirens now. Tori, is it the man you're after? Did he take Cara?"

"I'm sure it is," Tori replied, her mind racing. "Elise, I'm going to start making calls now. I'm on this."

"You have to find her, Tori! *You have to find her!*"

"Keep your phone with you," Tori said.

She called Braddock.

"Hey…"

"Haul ass back here now! Rand took Cara Newman."

"Wha… What? How? Where?"

Tori quickly explained what she knew.

"Could Elise describe the truck?" Braddock asked.

"Silver pickup is all. She couldn't tell me any more than that."

"How long?"

"It's hard to say for sure. She thought she might have been knocked out twenty minutes or longer. Her husband found her. Police are on the way, but—"

"Okay, we're coming. We'll be with you in fifteen, twenty minutes."

"Will, if—"

"We're getting her back. Gear up. He's around there somewhere. We're going to find him. I'm putting roadblocks up everywhere."

Tori rang off. Why take Cara? she asked herself. Why do that, unless…

She suddenly felt as though there was a sickening pit in her stomach.

In the basement, she retrieved her Kevlar vest and strapped it on. From the gun safe she extracted an extra magazine for her gun. She also pulled out Braddock's Ka-Bar knife and sheath and shoved it into the side pocket of her vest. Then she ran back upstairs. In the kitchen, her phone rang again. It was Warden Sills.

"Warden, things have gone haywire. Rand has taken a young girl now."

"Oh my God. I'll be quick then. Tori, I'm sorry, but Ted Rand isn't the one who was depositing the money orders. They came infrequently, maybe once a year, perhaps every eighteen months, and were made by a Darwyn N. Dent." He spelled out the name for her.

"Do you have an address?"

"No. I'm sorry, I don't. I can probably get you one in the morning. We'll have to work through the third-party provider who handles those deposits."

"Do that. Thanks."

Sills signed off, and Tori wrote down *Darwyn N. Dent* on a notepad and examined it. The spelling was a little unusual she thought as she underlined the y. Her phone beeped.

It was a text.

From Cara.

She clicked on it and her heart sank even further. It was a picture of Cara, tape over her mouth, resting against a metal post of some kind. She exhaled a breath and steeled herself. She knew what was coming next.

Her phone rang. It was Cara's number.

"Hello?"

"Whether she lives or dies is entirely up to you," the nasal voice greeted.

"Rand, is that you?"

"Leave your phone. Leave your gun. Bring the boat keys and come down to your dock. Do it right now!"

The call clicked off.

She grabbed the boat keys from the hook. Her cell phone was on the center island. She quickly changed the setting for auto-lock to 'never' and then left her cell phone on the center island, with the text with the photo of Cara open. On the notepad next to it, she drew an arrow and wrote *lake*. Then she wrote the word *find* next to *Darwyn N. Dent*.

He's out there waiting.

She slipped out the back door and went to the right, her gun up. At the corner, she peeked down the slope to the yard before making her way slowly down. At the front of the house, she stopped again. The massive deck twelve feet above ran the entire length of the front of the house, with two rows of pillars to support it. She could use them for cover. She stepped under the deck and moved stealthily along the front of the house, crouched, scanning her field of fire.

"That's far enough."

The voice came from her back left. Rand was behind the massive oak tree halfway down to the lake.

"Hands up right now or I end it."

She was completely exposed. There was no cover beyond one of the support posts. How long until Braddock arrived? Could she buy enough time? She slowly put her hands up.

"Step out from under the deck."

She did as he'd ordered, her hands still up.

"Drop the gun and kick it away. Really kick it away. Don't test me."

She kicked it hard down into the yard.

Rand stepped out from behind the tree. She couldn't see his face clearly, but she could tell he was holding a gun with an elongated barrel. There was probably a silencer screwed on.

"You don't get to keep the vest. Take it off and toss it into the yard."

Tori thought of trying for the knife, but quickly decided the odds of success were remote. Instead, she slowly dropped her hands, pulled at the Velcro straps on each side, lifted the vest over her head and tossed it out into the yard to the left of her gun.

"Open your hands."

She complied.

"Empty your jeans pockets."

"The boat keys are in my left pocket."

"Hold them in your hands but let me see the pockets full out, and then turn around."

As she grabbed hold of the keys, she felt something on the key ring she hadn't thought about. She pulled her pockets out, then slowly turned around so he could see the back ones were empty too.

Where are you, Braddock? She listened for the sound of sirens in the distance, but the night was still quiet.

"Walk to the dock. Lower the speedboat. I'm sure you have the lift remote on the key ring."

Tori looked at the key ring and clicked the remote. The boat lift whirred, and the speedboat slowly descended into the water.

"Your boat. You're driving," Rand said, standing twenty feet back on the dock. "Get in."

Tori stepped off the dock, ducked under the lift's canopy and quickly inserted the key into the ignition. To the right of the key was the yellow-encased Swiss army knife. She quickly looked out to the lake. She didn't see any other boats about. It was a calm night, just light waves lapping the boat lift. The ride that was coming would not be rough.

With her back to Rand, she fumbled with the boat key, giving it just a short turn, stopping before the engine could catch.

Rer... rer... rer...

"Dammit," she moaned for Rand's benefit. "I don't start it often," she complained as she slid the small end ring for the knife into the slot on the larger ring.

Rer... rer... rer...

She was able to slide the knife's loop almost all the way around the larger ring while fiddling with starting the boat. "I have to prime it quick here, I think." She jammed the key in to prime the gas, and just as she did, the knife slid off the main loop. She turned the key all the way over and the boat started. She quickly slid the Swiss army knife into the small cubbyhole to the right of the throttle where Braddock stored his sunglasses. The boat rumbled to life, gurgling in the water.

"Hands up."

She slowly raised her hands but didn't turn around. She did peek back, though.

Keeping the gun aimed at her, Rand carefully stepped into the boat and sat down on the bench seat. "Okay, let's go."

Tori was still standing as she brought the throttle back with her right hand and backed the boat out of the lift slowly, letting it clear the corner of the dock.

"Where am I going?" she asked as she clicked on the boat's night navigation lights.

"The Long Channel. Ten to twelve miles per hour. Safety first, of course."

"Can I sit on the throw cushion?" All boats had to have a square throwable cushion with straps in case someone fell overboard. Most people used them to sit on while they drove the boat, so that they could see better over the windshield.

Rand nodded and Tori put the cushion on the seat. Sitting down, she pushed down the throttle and turned the speedboat northeast. She looked back to see Rand sitting eight feet away, eyeing her intently, his hand held low, the gun with a silencer attached pointed at her.

"Don't be stupid. I can end this at any time."

She knew he wouldn't. He needed to get her back to Cara so he could do to her what he'd done to Paul Harstad, Jerry Bauman, Todd Strom and Dan Newman. He wanted to make her watch as he took Cara's life before he took hers. It would be his final act.

She turned and looked ahead, angling for the center of the wide exit from the bay into Northern Pine Lake. She sneaked a look back at Rand, and then beyond him. Still nothing at Braddock's.

She glanced down to her right to the Swiss army knife. *Think, Tori! Think.*

*

Braddock raced down the gravel road, then turned hard left into his driveway. He immediately noticed that the back door was open. He ran into the house, Steak and Eggs right behind him. "Tori! Tori! Where are…"

He immediately noticed the cell phone sitting on the white marble center island, next to the word *lake* scrawled on a notepad. On the screen was a picture of Cara, tape over her mouth, bound to a pole.

"Dammit! Dammit!" he growled. He ran to the front and looked down to the dock. "The boat is gone."

Eggs was scrolling through the phone. "Will, there was a call from Cara's cell phone about a minute after the text."

"That was Rand," Steak said. "Has to be."

"What do you make of this? *Find Darwyn N. Dent*," Eggs said, looking at the notepad now.

"Don't know," Braddock said as he grabbed binoculars and ran out onto the deck, Steak right behind him. He shouted back to Eggs, "Call Elise Peterson. See if she has the tracking app for her daughter's phone."

"On it."

"Will, down there." Steak ran off the deck, down into the yard. "It's Tori's vest. And her gun. I think he got the drop on her." He looked up to Braddock.

Eggs came out on the deck. "Elise has the tracking app. She says the phone is… here."

"Have her call it."

Ten second later, Steak saw it. The phone lit up by the large tree in the yard halfway down to the lake. "It's here. Rand used it to lure Tori out and then left it."

"Damn," Braddock said, the binoculars to his eyes.

"Can you see anything? Navigation lights? Look for the lights." Steak had picked up Tori's gun and run back up to the deck.

"No… no… Wait, way out there, through the gap into the main body of the lake." Braddock handed Steak the glasses.

"Maybe. It's a Wednesday night. Not usually many boats out after dark that have…"

"A bright white tower light on the overhead rack. I can see the little red port light a lot lower," Braddock said. He glanced to his right, along the shoreline. "Let's go."

"Where?"

"To Roger and Mary's house," he replied, grabbing a set of keys from the hooks by the back door.

"They just have a pontoon," Steak said, following Braddock out with Eggs behind him. "Will…"

"They also have a WaveRunner. That thing hauls ass," Braddock answered. "Let's go! Let's go!"

He backed the Tahoe out of the driveway and roared down the road. "My Bluetooth is in the center console. Get it out."

A minute later, Braddock turned into his in-laws' driveway and drove right up to the back door. He was out in an instant, unlocking the door and pushing inside the house. He grabbed a set of keys off the key rack and ran down to the lake, Steak right behind him. Braddock jumped onto the WaveRunner and pushed it off the drive-up platform, wrapping the key lanyard around his right wrist.

"Hold on! Hold on!" Eggs screamed as she ran down from the house carrying a life jacket. "For crying out loud, you're going out on the lake in the dark with no headlight. At least put this on."

Braddock pulled on the extra-large black jacket. He immediately called Steak and slipped his Bluetooth in to test it. "Check? Check?"

"We're good."

"Stay on the line." He hit the start button and raced away from the dock, going full speed.

"Come on!" Steak yelled to Eggs. "Let's go."

"Where?"

"Tori's going north. We need to go north too." They got into Braddock's Tahoe and backed out.

"Dispatch," Eggleston called. "I need a search done on the name Darwyn N. Dent. That's D-A-R-W-Y-N…"

*

There was only the slightest crescent moon shedding light through a partly cloudy sky. As Tori looked about the dark lake, she saw a handful of other boat lights to her left, boats fishing the drop-off.

"So that's where you shot Pen and Cal, isn't it?"

"Yes. Pulled right up to them, within thirty feet or so. Your sheriff, he had quite the walleye on his line. Too bad it looks like he's going to make it."

"Yeah, that's just too bad," Tori muttered as she turned and looked ahead. She was well north now and could see the glow from the Channel Stop's neon sign over the treetops.

"Make for the Long Channel," Rand ordered. "And don't try to signal anyone, Tori. I have no problem doing you here."

She shook her head and focused as she turned the boat into the channel, easing back on the throttle and preparing for the first right turn.

"So why Cara?" she asked.

"You. It's about you, Tori. And I suppose your father in a way. I needed Cara because I knew if I had her, you'd try and save your new little friend who you've clearly bonded with. It's almost poetic if you think about it."

"Oh yes, totally poetic," Tori sniped sarcastically.

"It is. Your father got her father killed, and now you, the daughter of the great Big Jim Hunter, is trying to make things right."

"So that's what this is all about? You making things right?"

"For what your father, Pen and Sheriff Lund did, yes."

"And the Newmans and Stroms?"

"I had to get Murphy and Lund's attention somehow."

"And what did I do to you? Am I paying for my father's sins now?"

"I wasn't originally even thinking of involving you. You had nothing to do with what they did to Hugh."

"You mean put a guilty man in prison where he belonged?"

"But see, then you inserted yourself into this. You were at the cemetery in Frontenac Falls. You were investigating the case. And then you showed up at Ruthie's Place, eyeing up Slim. You forced my hand."

"Slim, that's Larry Derner?"

Rand nodded.

Tori started the slow left turn and then centered the boat to pass through the narrow opening under the channel bridge.

"Now don't go looking at all the people up on the patio at the Channel Stop. I'm watching."

As she emerged from under the bridge, she did slide her eyes to the right. The boat slips were about one third full, there was nobody down on the docks, and she could see only a few people still on the patio. It appeared most were inside at this point in the evening.

Once she was past the Channel Stop, she turned gently to the left and approached the Y Junction. "Am I going left, or right?"

"Right," Rand said. "Go right."

She eased the wheel to the right, slowing the pace, sneaking a peak down to the storage cubby. The knife was still visible.

"Why kill Derner?" she asked as she puttered ahead, the glow of light from the Channel Stop dissipating behind them.

"Because you had that photo of him. You were clearly interested in him. How did that come about?"

"Good detective work."

"You probably went and saw Hugh's mother."

Tori didn't respond.

"I always worried about Rita, but that was a risk I was willing to take. I wasn't going to kill her."

"Because you and Hugh were what? Soulmates?"

"I don't like your tone."

Tori snickered a laugh. "What was Hugh Barr to you?"

"You don't find someone like Hugh every day. A partner like him. He liked the women."

"But you didn't, did you?" Tori asked.

"No."

"You're the planner, the killer."

Rand nodded. "We were perfect together."

"And Derner?"

"Hired help. He was Ruthie's bitch. He did this to get over on women."

"At least until we got onto him."

"Slim wouldn't have held up five minutes under interrogation from people like you and Braddock. He'd have wilted like that." Rand snapped his fingers. "When I missed you in Manchester Bay, he had to go."

"And Ruthie too?"

"Well, she knew Slim was probably with me, so… yeah."

Tori nodded and looked ahead as they emerged into Red Pine Lake. "Where to now?"

"The northeast corner. We have one more channel to traverse."

*

"Can you see them?" Steak asked.

"No, I thought I spotted them in the distance, but then I lost them. I'm betting they went into the Long Channel," Braddock replied, throttle all the way down as he zoomed north across the lake. He couldn't see the speedometer in the dark, but he figured he was going forty to forty-five miles per hour. He saw the bright glow of the Channel Stop sign straight ahead and knew to angle left for the channel entrance, scanning for the red and green buoy markers and flashing lights atop them. He eased back just a little as he entered the channel and made the first right turn, banking hard, his right pant leg getting drenched as it dipped into the water. He sped ahead, turned left, raced under the bridge and past the Channel Stop and reached the Y Junction, easing to a stop.

"Steak, I'm at the Y Junction. I can't see navigation lights either direction. What do you think?"

"Left goes to Norway Lake, but that's a dead end. That lake is fully developed; hard to pull anything over there without someone hearing or noticing something."

"I'm going right," Braddock said. "Where are you?"

"We're approaching the bridge now. You need to direct us."

"You'll know when I know."

*

Eggleston had the notepad in front of her still, examining the name Darwyn N. Dent, still waiting for a response from dispatch. "It would be odd to spell Darwyn with a y instead of an i wouldn't it?"

"Yeah. Why?" Steak said.

"Tori underlined the y when she wrote this out is all. What's Rand's legal name?"

"Rand?" Steak asked. "It's not Theodore, I remember that. I think it's just Ted Rand."

"Middle name?"

"It was… related to his mother's maiden name, right?"

"Yeah, it was something with a W," Eggs said. "Oh, what was it? Wilson… Winter…"

"Wynn! It was Wynn. She was Eileen Wynn."

"Ted Wynn Rand."

Eggs wrote the name under Darwyn N. Dent, crossing off letters between the two names. "Well, I'll be…"

"What?"

"Darwyn N. Dent is an anagram of Ted Wynn Rand." Eggs reached for the radio. "Dispatch, I need that check on Darwyn N. Dent. I need it now. It's an alias for Ted Rand."

"Copy. Stand by."

*

Tori had driven ahead in silence as she approached the channel that led from Red Pine Lake. Rand had said one more channel. Their destination was coming close. She glanced back. He still had the gun directed on her. It hadn't moved an inch.

They approached a small resort on a point to the left just inside the channel. It had a gas dock with a bright light high on a post. As she passed underneath, she glanced back again, evaluating the six to eight feet between her and Rand. He was fifty years old, and while not the least bit overweight, he was a large and powerful man. He was big, strong, but she suspected slightly slow in his reactions, if she remembered Cara's description of when he and Derner had chased her. The one thing Tori had to her advantage was speed.

The channel snaked to the right and she turned the wheel.

*

Braddock exited the channel and looked ahead. There was a bright white tower light up to his right on the northeast corner of Red Pine. Then it was gone again.

He knew this stretch of lake well and hit the throttle, racing ahead at full speed, making the run a good hundred yards out from the east shoreline, following the direction of the light up the channel to Elm Lake. As he came around the corner into the bay, he saw the tower light deep in the channel, visible between the gaps of some tall trees, but then lost it again as the trees thickened, cutting off his view.

"They're in the channel between Red Pine and Elm. I'm easing back now. I'll try and direct you."

*

Tori continued ahead.

"Turn left," Rand said.

"Left?" she asked, looking back, surprised. There was no left turn.

"You heard me. You'll make it."

She carefully turned the boat left and drove into a thin area of wispy reeds.

"You might want to trim up the motor a bit. It's shallow, but very passable through here."

She trimmed the prop up as they traversed through the reeds and emerged into the lake known as Little Elm. In all her younger years boating on the chain of lakes, she couldn't ever remember driving in here. It was considered too shallow and mucky, with no good recreation or swimming opportunities. She wasn't even aware of any cabins being back here.

"Keep straight ahead."

*

Braddock drove into the channel and stood up, scanning for the tower light. "I've lost it," he said.

"You've lost it?" Steak said. "You're in the Elm Channel?"

"Yeah," he said as he raced forward through the twisting channel cut into the reeds, emerging into the short, stubby lake, only maybe five to six hundred yards long and half that wide. "I don't see them. I don't see the light."

"Did they make the channel on the south end that goes to Cypress?"

"Must have." He hit the throttle, zooming south.

*

The police radio burped in the Tahoe. "Detective, we have an address for a Darwyn N. Dent. It's on North Little Elm Road."

Steak and Eggs looked to the GPS map on the dashboard. "Here," Steak said, pointing. "Will. Stop!"

*

Braddock took his thumb off the throttle just short of the next channel to Cypress. "What is it?"

"Rand has a place on Little Elm. Northeast corner."

Braddock whipped the WaveRunner around and headed back north. He charged back into the snaking channel.

"Is there even a turn in here for Little Elm?" he asked.

"I think you just have to look for a spot to cut through," Steak said.

Braddock eased back and looked to his right. He spotted a thinning of the reeds and turned hard right. "Here goes nothing."

*

Two hundred yards ahead, Tori saw a single solitary light in a house set on a hill in the thick woods up from the lake. There was a short, rickety-looking dock straight ahead and what looked to be a black fishing boat tied up to the left side.

"What is this place?" she asked.

"Where I get away from it all and make the signs I sold," Rand replied. "There is no record of Ted Rand owning it. I inherited it from my grandmother on my mother's side. I sold it, but then bought it back in a different name."

"I presume that's the ID you plan to run with?"

He laughed. "Got it all figured out, don't you?"

"Too little too late," Tori replied as she shifted her eyes down to the knife in the cubby.

*

Braddock emerged from the reeds and saw the tower light several hundred yards ahead. In the distance, up a hill, he thought he saw a dim light.

"Where are you?" he called to Steak.

"On our way. We have to work our way around the closed road east of the Channel Stop. I'm trying to get us through."

Braddock zoomed ahead, trying to get a better look, then slowed maybe five hundred yards out, getting his bearings, scouring the shoreline.

*

Tori slowed and eased toward the dock, pulling back on the throttle to let the boat drift in. She was standing now to see where she was going.

She felt Rand stand up behind her. The dock was twenty feet away. She let her hand slide down the throttle to the cubby and pulled out the knife, using her thumbnail to snap out the knife blade.

Beating him straight up with the knife wasn't possible, but if she could do some damage, she might have a chance.

"Ease up now."

She slammed the throttle, ramming the bow into the dock. At the same time, she turned and threw the cushion she'd been sitting on at his head. He was off balance, and she charged him, using her left arm to push up his gun hand while knocking him back down into the bench seat and stabbing him in the left arm with the knife.

"Aargh!" he grunted.

She raised her hand and plunged the knife down into his thigh.

"Ah… fuck! Fuck!"

She felt him bringing the gun around, and raised her left arm to deflect.

Crack!

The blast was just by her left ear. He tried to push up and raise the gun again. She batted his arm away before throwing a right cross and hitting him square in the jaw, the knife blade slicing his cheek. But when she made the contact, the knife flew out of her hand.

He was stunned, but he still had the gun.

Tori turned, ran two steps, stepped onto the front seat and leapt from the bow over five feet of open water to the dock.

Crack!

Another shot whizzed by to her left as she sprinted away.

Crack! Crack!

More shots hit the dock.

She ran into the yard and up the hill to the house, taking a quick look back to see Rand trying to stand up in the boat.

*

Crack!… Crack! Crack!

"Shots fired! Shots fired!" Braddock yelled, and hit the throttle.

*

At the top of the hill, Tori found a small one-story cabin with a walk-out basement. She ran to the sliding door under the deck. It was locked. She glanced down to the lake and saw Rand now reaching for the dock.

There was a sturdy metal chair lying sideways on the cement patio slab. She picked it up, whipped it around, then threw it at the door. It crashed through the glass and she ran inside. She found herself in a basement area that was under construction, with some sheet rock hung but little else.

"Cara! Cara!"

She heard a thumping sound to her right. She burst through another door and turned on the light to see Cara leaning against a post, her arms and legs bound with zip-tie cuffs. She looked around frantically, but there was nothing in the room to cut them with. Racing back out into the main area, she found a toolbox. She dumped the box over and the tools spilled onto the floor. She found a pair of tin snips. She glanced back down and saw Rand on the dock now, lumbering his way up.

She raced back to Cara and snipped at the zip ties, trying to cut through. "Come on, come on." She severed the wrist restraints, then started cutting the ankle ties, finally getting them loose.

"Come on! Run!" She grabbed Cara's hand.

As they came out into the main room, Rand was nearly to the patio slab. Tori looked right. "Up the steps!" Cara turned right, Tori behind her. "Go! Go! Go!"

Crack! Crack! Crack!

One shot clipped Tori on the outside of her left arm. "Ah!" She reached for the wound.

"Tori?"

"Keep going! Keep going!"

Crack! Crack!

*

Braddock raced the WaveRunner past his boat and into the shoreline, running it right up to the mixture of sand and reeds.

Crack! Crack! Crack!

He jumped off and raised his gun. Where were the shots coming from? He dropped down into the ankle-deep water and ran up onto the shore.

Crack! Crack!

Those sounded like they were inside the house, but then he thought he saw movement to the right, toward the side of the structure. He made his way up the hill, his gun drawn, trying to get his bearings.

*

Tori and Cara burst out the front door of the cabin. Tori's first reaction was to run down the driveway to the road, but then she saw movement in that direction.

Rand. He'd anticipated her move.

"Other way! Other way!" she exclaimed, instantly changing tack and pushing Cara back to the left. They ran by a parked silver pickup truck with a topper and past a garage on their left. Cara's legs were working now, and she kicked it down, running for the woods, Tori right behind her.

Crack! Crack!

*

Braddock reached the house and peered inside.

Crack! Crack!

Those shots were out front. He ran right, to what looked to be the less steep way up to the front of the house. He ran up the side, stopped at the corner and peered around.

Crack! Crack!

*

Bark shards from the trees sprayed them in the face as they ran into the woods. Tori snuck a look back, and even in the dark she could see that Rand was still coming for them.

"Tori! We're running to some sort of pond here," Cara yelped. "Dead end."

"Not for you," Tori said. "Keep running. Go around it." She picked up a sturdy branch from the ground. "Go! Go!"

*

D lumbered into the woods, wiping away the blood from his face, limping, the gashes in his leg and arm aching and oozing.

Where are they? Where are they?

He didn't sense them running ahead now, didn't see the flashes of movement he was seeing before, even in the darkness.

It was suddenly calm. Quiet.

*

Tori stood still behind the tree, breathing through her nose. She could hear him approaching, the crunch of the ground beneath his feet as he stepped carefully but unevenly through the woods. She tightened her grip on the long branch. Down at her feet she saw heavy yet throwable rocks.

She heard another crunch. He was close. She reached down to grip the branch with her other hand as well.

He took another step. She caught a glimpse of him.

*

D took a step and saw a good-size tree to the left. There was no movement. He took another quick step forward and looked left. Nothing.

He felt movement from the right.

*

Tori burst around the tree and swung the branch. He saw her, pivoting and firing the gun.

Crack!

The shot missed as she hit him in the side of the neck. It stunned him but didn't knock him down. She swung again, but he deflected the branch with his left arm. She tried again, but he was ready, batting it away, knocking it out of her hands.

Tori dove left and scrambled back to the tree. When she looked back, she saw Rand turning the gun toward her. She threw the first rock, hitting him in the left shoulder. The second one struck him on the left cheek, but he kept coming. She was on her back, out of time, the gun barrel boring in on her.

A flash of movement came from the right. Cara, swinging a branch of her own, hit him in the back as the gun fired.

Tori scrabbled on the ground and grabbed the branch again.

*

Braddock heard the struggle down to his left and ran toward the woods, trying to catch a glimpse of something, anything.

Crack!

He saw the flash of light from the gun barrel to his left. Running in and leaping over a log, he saw the silhouettes of two people fighting, one big, the other small.

Crack!

And there was another person. Tori and Cara were both fighting him off.

Braddock set his feet, aiming high, at the bigger body.

Boom! Boom! Boom!

*

D felt the shots whizz by. He pivoted to his right.

Crack! Crack! Crack!… Click!

He was out.

Boom! Boom! Boom!

"Oof." He was hit in the right shoulder.

Boom! Boom!

He heard a siren in the distance.

*

That was friendly fire. Tori grabbed Cara and drove her to the ground deeper into the trees, seeking cover.

Click!

"Aargh!" Rand grunted, and then she heard footsteps moving away.

"Are you okay?" she asked Cara.

"Yeah."

"Tori! Tori! You out there? Tori!" Braddock called, his gun still up, scanning the woods.

"Yeah," she said, pushing herself up against a tree, Cara to her right.

"Where did he go?"

"He ran back toward the lake, I think," Cara said, pointing. "Away from you."

"Come on! Come on!" Braddock bellowed, pulling Tori up. "Back to the cabin. I'll cover you."

As they emerged from the woods, Steak and Eggleston were screeching to a stop in the driveway, both out quickly, guns drawn. More flashing police lights were visible in the distance as they reached the driveway. Steak handed Tori a gun. "It's yours. I found it in the yard."

"How did you get here?" Tori asked, noting that Braddock was wearing a life jacket.

"Roger and Mary's WaveRunner."

They all heard a boat engine start up, and ran around to the lake side of the house to see Rand turning his fishing boat and racing away. They fired, but he just kept going.

"Ah shit!" Braddock growled.

"Let's go!" Tori exclaimed, running down the hill. "Your boat is down there."

"Watch her," Braddock said to Steak and Eggs, pointing to the shivering Cara. "And call in the sheriff's department boats."

"They're already on the way."

"Send me updates."

At the dock, the boat was floating ten feet away from shore. Braddock ran into the knee-high water and pulled it toward him. Tori jumped in and started it up, while Braddock pulled himself in. She backed it out of the shallower water and turned it around, dropping the throttle and charging ahead.

"You should drive," she said. "You're better at it than me."

"I haven't done a lot of high-speed chasing, though," Braddock said with a sly smile. "Steak, are you still with me?" His Bluetooth was still in his ear.

"I'm with you, boss. A sheriff's patrol boat is making its way up here. They're halfway up Northern Pine but going full throttle. Another boat is leaving Manchester Bay now. Do you have eyes on him?"

"I think I see a boat out there. He doesn't have his navigation lights on, though."

Braddock had the throttle all the way down. He looked to Tori. "Put on a life jacket."

"Seriously?"

"I'm wearing one. This could get crazy."

Tori lifted a seat compartment and found her usual one, pulling it on and strapping it up.

"There's a spotlight in the glovebox," Braddock said.

She extracted the light and turned it on, aiming the powerful beam ahead.

"Is that him? Did I get a glint of reflection?"

"Yeah, I can see the ripples in the water from his path. He went into the reeds to get to the channel."

Braddock zoomed into the light reed patch and turned hard right into the channel, the back end of the boat swerving, sending a big wake of water into the reeds on the left. "Hard left coming," he warned, honking the boat's horn as they flew past the gas dock for the resort on the right.

"I don't see him now," Tori yelled.

"He's out there around the point, I bet," Braddock said as he swung left around the point and into the main body of Red Pine Lake.

"Steak, we're on Red Pine now. Heading southwest to the channel."

As they raced ahead, Tori scanned with the spotlight. She caught a glimpse of Rand's boat. "There he is, two o'clock to the right, I got him now."

*

D raced across the lake, his left arm and leg throbbing. He could feel the blood oozing from both, and from his face as well. He'd been winged in the back of his right shoulder.

He looked ahead. With the throttle all the way down, the boat could go a little over forty miles per hour. If he could just get through the big channel and out onto Northern Pine, he could lose them in the wide-open water of the lake and get to where he'd parked his truck in the woods just north of Braddock's house.

Taking another look back, he could see they were still coming. They had a searchlight on him.

Just get to the truck. Just get to the truck.

He turned and looked ahead, trying to find the little flashing lights on the top of the buoys marking the channel entrance. "Dammit!" They were to the left. He'd missed the mark. He yanked the steering wheel hard left, groaning at the pain in his arm.

*

"He overshot it! He overshot it!" Braddock yelled. They were on the straight line for the channel, cutting down the distance. They had a good eye and angle on him now and were closing the gap.

*

"Dammit!" D growled as he pushed the throttle back down, trying to regain the speed he needed, the speedboat closing in on him. He made the tight turn left around the little peninsula at the beginning of the channel, but the other boat wasn't far behind now, only fifty or sixty yards back.

*

They could see him now.

"Will, the sheriff's boat is through the channel bridge. They're heading your way!" Steak said.

"We're coming right at them, Steak. Tell them heads up."

*

D turned and looked ahead.

A sheriff's boat with flashing lights was coming straight at him.

He yanked the wheel to the right, swerving to avoid it. He almost took out a dock on his right, but he still had control. He approached the Y Junction and started turning left, re-accelerating.

*

Braddock veered smoothly slightly to the right and passed the sheriff's deputies. Tori glanced back to see the sheriff's boat make a U-turn to join the chase.

"Tori, he's going to turn hard left. I'm going to set you up," Braddock yelled. He started his turn as well, but shallower, cutting between a warning buoy and the shoreline. "Wait... wait..."

Tori steadied herself, her gun up. Rand started turning.

"Now! *Now!*"

Pop! Pop! Pop! Pop! Pop!

She strafed the back of the boat. A small flame started flickering on the outboard motor, but Rand kept going.

*

The speedboat was faster and more agile, and now, as D looked back, he realized he was on fire.

He turned around.

He was heading right at the dock for the Channel Stop.

He jerked the wheel hard right, feeling the boat groan as it dug into the water, pushing off a big wake. The stern careened into the end of the dock and jerked him right. The throttle was still all the way down. He was heading straight for the bridge.

He fought the speed, struggling desperately to steer. His arms were aching, not responding.

Gotta turn left! Gotta turn left!

*

"*Whoa!*" Braddock yelled.

Rand's stern rammed off the Channel Stop dock, shooting off a big wall of water. The collision didn't slow him down. Instead, it sent him shooting right at the bridge.

"He's going too fast. He's not going to make it!"

"The bridge! The bridge!" Tori yelled.

Rand's boat rammed into the bridge's concrete pillar.

The fireball was instant.

Braddock eased back on the throttle and started coasting slowly. The burning wreckage of Rand's boat was a hundred feet ahead now.

The sheriff's boat pulled up alongside them and the deputies looked over. "Everyone okay? Ma'am, you're bleeding."

Braddock snapped around and saw the blood running down Tori's left arm.

"Rand winged me at some point," she said, looking at the gash. The deputies let their boat drift alongside and handed over a first aid kit.

"You're going to need stitches for sure," Braddock said as he gave the wound a look, applying pressure with gauze. "Could be worse, though."

"I'll be fine," Tori said.

Patrons at the Channel Stop were running from the patio to the road and onto the bridge, phones on, lighting up the water. Three sheriff's department patrol units had arrived and were beaming light down into the water too.

"He hit the bridge," a deputy in the boat called into the radio. "We need the fire department out here at the bridge right by the Channel Stop. And the county's search and rescue crew."

"Any survivors?" the dispatcher asked.

The deputy looked to Braddock, who looked to Tori. She simply shook her head.

"Negative. There are no survivors."

CHAPTER THIRTY

"Everyone has their limit"

Twenty-four years ago

"Hey, girls! I'm home!"

"Sheriff!" Tori greeted, running over and giving her father a big hug, Jessie right behind her.

"What's in the bag?" Jessie asked excitedly. "It smells delicious."

"Ribs from Leo's," the sheriff said.

"Really?" Leo's was a big treat in the Hunter house. "What's the occasion?"

"The trial?" Tori asked, her eyes lighting up.

"That's right. We got a guilty verdict," the sheriff replied cheerily as he set the bag down on the counter. "The man who killed that married couple is going to prison."

"For how long?" Tori asked.

"Life," the sheriff answered. "It doesn't get any longer than that, girls."

"He never gets out?"

"Nope. It's a great day. We're going to celebrate. Let's get out some plates and silverware. I went big-time, got the full meal deal."

They sat out at the picnic table on the deck, looking west out to the lake. After the saucy ribs, corn on the cob, cornbread, baked beans and then ice cream was all consumed and the mess cleaned up, the big bear of a father and his twin daughters started a fire in the bonfire pit down by the lake. The sheriff had a beer in his left hand, a thick cigar in the fingers of his right and the Twins game on the radio while his girls made s'mores.

"Sheriff, you seem really happy," Tori said as Jessie handed him his sandwich made from gram cracker, marshmallow and chocolate.

"It was a really good day," he replied as he took a bite. "A really good day."

"Does this mean you'll get re-elected?" Jessie asked.

He laughed. "What you really mean is will you have to come with me in the fall and hammer in the lawn signs that say *Re-Elect Big Jim*."

"Yeah."

"I certainly think it does. Which is good. My job lets me take care of my little girls."

*

Tori snapped awake from her nap on the couch on the deck. She checked the bandage on her left arm, covering the stitches from the wound from two nights ago. If she squinted hard enough, she could see the far eastern side of the lake, where her childhood home still sat, albeit heavily remodeled and added onto.

My job lets me take care of my little girls.

She always remembered him saying that. The sheriff took pride in his job, but he thought of it first and foremost as allowing him to provide for his family. That was why Jessie's disappearance three years later would so break his heart. Jessie's disappearance was part of his legacy, but the Barr case was too, a big part of his history of good works in his years on the job.

She couldn't help but wonder what the fallout would be from all this. In some ways, it was a relief he wasn't around to deal with it.

After all that had happened two nights ago, today Braddock was meeting again with Backstrom and Wilson. There would be a press conference. The recent investigation would be addressed, and the independent inquiry would be announced to review the Bauman case. Backstrom had informed Braddock that a former United States attorney would conduct the review.

Tori's presence was not required at the press conference or the meeting with Backstrom, and she was fine with that. Instead, she had spent the last two days on her own form of cleanup, including a meeting with the owner of her rental house and his contractor regarding the damage from the shooting. The homeowner's insurer was being difficult, because insurance companies welcomed your premiums but hated to pay your claims. However, repairs needed to be made, and all that was really needed was some sheetrock repair and a new sliding glass door. "We'll work it all out," the owner said. He did inform her, however, that she wouldn't be getting her damage deposit back. It was hard to argue the point.

"That being said," he offered, "if you wanted to renew for another year, we could talk. Have you decided what you're going to do?"

She had checked in with Cara and her mother. Cara had made an appointment with Professor Lane to start talking about all that had happened. Tori was thinking that she herself might want to sit down with the professor as well. Her mind was full of conflicting thoughts that she needed to sort out. Things had been settled for several months, but now she felt a little like she was on tilt again.

She went inside, opened a seltzer and then went down to sit in one of the Adirondack chairs on the dock. As she watched scattered boats zoom or cruise by, she slipped in her ear pods, selected Braddock's easy listening playlist, put on her sunglasses and sipped her drink.

After some time, she felt the dock start to vibrate from footsteps and glanced to her right to see Braddock arriving. He was dressed in athletic shorts and a blue Knicks T-shirt, and had a beer in one hand and a seltzer refresh for her in the other. "You want the short or long version?"

"Short," Tori answered. "Very short."

"Well, thankfully Backstrom and Wilson handled most of the press conference, although I did get dragged in. We all tried to steer clear of talking about the Bauman case in any detail, but that was difficult once Backstrom announced the independent investigation."

"Which led to a million follow-ups as to why."

Braddock nodded. "This is not the last of it."

"What do you know of the attorney they're bringing in to investigate?"

"Well regarded and doesn't mess around. My guess is he's going to have a lot of questions for Cal."

"You think he'll survive it?"

Braddock shrugged. "I don't know. It might depend on whether he wants to or not. If I were him, I'd be looking for the exit. What's he need this for anymore? And I'll probably have to deal with this guy as well."

"You? Why?"

"It wasn't enough for me to have Cal step away from the investigation. Backstrom says I should have brought him and Wilson in at that point. In his view, as he's thought about it more—and no doubt about the impact it could have on him—we should have recused the whole department and brought the BCA in to take over the case instead of keeping it in house."

"He would have gladly washed his hands of the mess and made it someone else's problem."

Braddock nodded. "I suggested something along those lines, that he wasn't willing to put his hands into the muck and get them dirty. Backstrom countered that one could argue that I took steps to try to cover things up and what happened is the result of that."

Tori snorted a laugh. "He's really Monday-morning-quarter-backing this thing. His tune is a little different to the other day."

"Yeah, though I'm not that surprised by that." Braddock sighed. "I don't mind the guy, but he's such a politician. Sometimes you have to do difficult things and live with the results." He took a long drink of beer. "But I knew keeping the case in house had risks, and now I'll have to deal with it."

"So where does that leave things?"

"I don't know. I think there will be repercussions. How bad? Hard to say."

"Are you worried?"

"A little." He took another sip of beer. "I do like having a job."

"Do you think you're really at risk?"

"Cal created this job for me. There wasn't necessarily a chief detective position before I arrived. Who knows what happens if he goes? Who will take over? What will they want out of me; will they even want me to stay?"

"I'm sorry."

"Not your fault. It's something I'm going to worry about down the road." He paused. "We need to talk."

"About?"

"You and me," he said.

"Oh." She'd known this was coming, but the way he'd said it instantly had her on guard.

"Quinn comes home in the next few days, so we need to talk before that."

"Okay."

"I see him getting more and more attached to you. He really likes you being around. But," he sighed, "he's eleven, Tori. He's already lost his mom. I have to protect him."

"My trip to New York City," Tori said, closing her eyes.

"Yeah, that. It wasn't a trip; it was running away."

"I'm really sorry. I shouldn't have done that."

"You and I have been together a year now," he continued. "We've had a lot of good times. We've said we love each other, and we meant it."

"I know I did."

Braddock turned to her. "And that's the thing. I love you. I don't know that Quinn is there yet, but he's getting attached, and…"

"And what?"

"You have a lease up that you won't talk to me about. We have an argument, albeit a pretty big one, and your reaction is to flee to New York City. I call and text you and you ignore me for four days."

"You took me off the case."

"But that didn't mean I didn't still need you here. And then the first thing you do when you get back is go behind my back out to Frontenac Falls, speaking to Rita, interviewing on the case I just took you off."

"I did that for—"

"Cal, I know. But still, that's not what two people who rely on and trust each other do. And New York City… boy, that just didn't sit right with me. I mean, at the first bit of trouble between us, your reaction was to run, to escape. What do you think that says to me?"

"This relationship is the first one…"

"I know, you haven't been down this road before, but that is no longer true. It isn't new anymore. It's real. It's happening."

Tori closed her eyes and nodded.

"I have been where this could be heading. And for it to work, I know what it takes."

"What are you saying?" Tori asked.

"In this thing we have, your problems are my problems. My problems are your problems. I had this case and I had to remove you from it and you just left. As if only that mattered and not us. As if I didn't need you."

"I'm sorry…"

"I'm forty-three and I was alone for five years after Meghan died because nobody ever got to me like Meghan, nobody even came close… until you came along. I mean, you have your hooks in me good. *That's* what I realized when you went to New York.

How much I missed you and worried about where we suddenly were at and whether you were as invested in this as I am."

Tori nodded.

"This whole thing crystalized some things for me. While you were gone, I realized I can't think just about myself. Quinn has to be my priority. I can't go all in on this, invest him in it too, if we can only rely on you to be there in the good times and not the bad. And there *will* be more bad times. There always are, and when they come… you have to be there. That's what this thing we could have is all about. Being there."

"I know."

"Do you?"

"What are you asking for?"

"Total commitment."

"I am committed."

"Are you?" he asked skeptically. "I mean, are you really?"

"You want me to move in?"

"This is about way more than that, Tor. Way more." He shook his head in exasperation. "You already live here, in part, because you said months ago that you wanted more of this."

"I did. I do. Isn't what we have what you want?"

"I need more now. I want you to commit to it with everything you have, Tori. Everything."

"I have."

"Have you? Or are you still straddling the line."

"Will, come on," Tori pleaded. She hadn't been expecting him to press her like this. She was reeling and not ready for it.

"I mean, let's hit the big issue head-on here," he said. "You have a lot of history here to deal with. Jessie, solving her case last summer, the lingering fallout of that. Now all this, your father, Cal and what happened to him. And while you should feel zero guilt for what happened to Cara Newman's father and stepmom,

I know you bear the weight of it anyway, because that's just who you are and how you're wired."

"It's…" Her voice drifted away, and she shook her head. "It's so hard sometimes."

"I bet it is. It's a lot, Tori. It is a lot for anyone to handle, no matter how resilient they are, and there are few tougher than you. I know all this. I know how hard it must be for you to be here at times. I've kicked myself repeatedly over that damn argument, because I know it, and I blew it in that moment. I just blew it."

"I did too."

"I want to be the one you lean on. I want to be the one to help you through all that."

"And you have," she said, dreading where Braddock was going and knowing he wasn't going to leave her a choice.

"But here's the thing, and there is no getting around this. In the back of your mind, how could you not be thinking that maybe this is all too much? It's messy and complicated and stressful and haunting. You could move back to New York City, where none of this history exists. The FBI would take you back in a minute. You could say to yourself, I tried it back there, but I just couldn't do it. Who could argue with that given all that has happened? Everyone has their limit. Maybe you've reached it."

As usual, he was spot on with reading her mind, what she was thinking, what she had thought.

"Will…" Her eyes started tearing up. "I know you're saying I can't have those thoughts."

"I'm saying more than that. I'm saying we've reached a point where you have to make a decision." He locked his eyes on hers. "And it's a big one. It's a big one for you, for me and for Quinn."

"Will, please…"

"I need to know, Tori. Are you really, truly all in?"

A NOTE FROM ROGER

Thank you so much for reading *The Hidden Girl.* The exhilarating thing about building a story is that I get to escape from reality and create and shape a captivating, exciting yet perilous world for my characters. The great challenge is to write it with just the right amount of vivid detail so that you can visualize the settings and scenes every bit as much as I do when I'm sitting at my computer and crafting it. I truly hope you enjoyed reading the story just as much as enjoyed creating it.

If you did enjoy it and want to keep up to date with all my latest releases, just sign up at the following link. Your email address will never be shared, and you can unsubscribe at any time.

www.bookouture.com/roger-stelljes

One of the best parts of writing comes from seeing the reaction from readers. Did the book excite you, put you on edge, make you think, occasionally make you laugh or cry, and always make you want to read just one more page, one more chapter because you just couldn't put it down? That is my goal every time out and I like to know if you think I achieved it. If you enjoyed the book, I would greatly appreciate it if you could leave a short review. Receiving feedback from readers is important to me in developing and writing my stories, but is also vital in helping to persuade others to pick up one of my books for the first time.

If you enjoyed *The Hidden Girl*, Tori and Braddock and their growing collection of friends can also be found in *Silenced Girls* and *The Winter Girls* and in more stories to come.

All the best,
Roger

 @rogerstelljesbooks

 @RogerStelljes

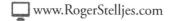 www.RogerStelljes.com

93451946R00215